LIES BEHI

HELEN MATTHEWS

Hashtag PRESS

Published in Great Britain by Hashtag Press 2019

Text copyright © Helen Matthews 2019
Copyright Cover illustration © Helen Braid 2019

The moral right of the author has been asserted

A CIP catalogue for this book is available from the British Library.

ISBN 978-1-9993006-1-6

Typeset in Garamond Classic 11.25/14 by Blaze Typesetting
Printed in Great Britain by Clays Ltd, Elcograf S.p.A.

Hashtag PRESS

HASHTAG PRESS BOOKS
Hashtag Press Ltd
Kent, England, United Kingdom
Email: info@hashtagpress.co.uk
Website: www.hashtagpress.co.uk
Twitter: @hashtag_press

For Alan, whose skill and imagination turned our 'ruin' in France into a home.

ACKNOWLEDGEMENTS

So many people have supported my writing and helped me shape this book. Grateful thanks to Helen Lewis and Abiola Bello at Hashtag Press for your advice and for making me feel a valued member of the Hashtag family. I'm indebted to my editor, Tiffany Schmidt for spotting the many glitches and plot holes and for advice that was motivational and encouraging. Thanks to Chloe Murphy for some interesting ideas and suggestions, and to artist, Helen Braid, for the beautiful cover design. I'm grateful to the publicity and marketing team at LiterallyPR for spreading the word about my novel.

Thank you to Karl Drinkwater and Yvonne Lyon for insightful manuscript appraisals that sent me back to the drawing board to revise and replot my story, and to Linda Firth for valuable feedback.

The themes in this book are a blend of things I know and many things I was ignorant of before doing my research. Generous friends—and even some, who were previously strangers—have answered my questions and helped me with fact checking. Massive thanks are due to Natalie and Tony Hubbard for advice on the minutiae of moving to France and putting me in touch with contacts; to Mark Watkins for details of running a bar; to Vincent Charneau for explaining police structure and procedures in France. Tony Bones answered my queries on commercial property development and construction and Roselyne Bizot checked my usage of French words and phrases. All remaining errors are mine.

When I first visited the Limousin, I had no idea it would become the setting for a novel but Limoges made a strong impression and kept drawing me back. Thank you, Anne and John Clark for coming with us on that first visit. Over decades of visiting France, I have met many fascinating people and characters, but one whose memory stands out was Nick Shotter, probably the best Mr Fixit of all time. Nick, we miss you.

I've had unstinting support from my writer friends in Oxford Narrative Group—Annie Murray, Benedicta Norell, Helen Newdick, Rachel Norman, Rose Stevens, Alison Knight, Kit de Waal, Claire Spriggs, John Vickers, Becky Watkins, Patrick Whitehouse and Paul Walton—thanks to you all. With the exception of Jane Sleight and Jennifer Riddalls, my friends in Rushmoor Writers were largely spared from critiquing this manuscript but they have always given encouragement and sound advice. I've been inspired by Melanie Whipman's expertise and her writing workshops, where I've been lucky to meet new writer friends Katrina Dennison, Jenny Rivarola, Di Stafford and Sue Stephenson.

Above all, to my family—my long-suffering husband Alan, my son Alex, daughter Bronwen and their partners, and to my sister, Fran—thanks for believing in me and giving me space to write.

PROLOGUE

The December sky is inky, starless. My fist throbs from hammering on the locked door. I wait. Silence. . .

The torch in my phone flickers like a guttering candle as I tramp across the uneven ground to the rear of the building. A sliver of light seeps through a gap between two shutters but dissipates without illuminating the ground.

Sliding one foot in front of the other, I inch across the pitch-black yard, churning up loose grit with each step, until I reach grass and mud. My eyes adjust. A shadowy bulk takes shape, black against the patina of the sky—the hired digger, its metal bucket suspended at a rakish angle. Close beside it, mounds of soil, banks of sand and gravel, and three freshly-dug rectangular pits.

I tread warily, remembering one is deeper than a grown man's height. My phone emits a feeble beep as the battery signals its death throes. Heart pounding, I snatch a breath and train my flickering beam down into the trench. . .

CHAPTER 1

EMMA

August 2015

From a distance, it reminds me of a Neolithic burial site with collapsed walls, overgrown and reclaimed by nature. As we draw closer there's evidence of a long, low building with one gable end, in the crumbling stone and smashed clay tiles.

We stamp along a track, trampling knee-high grass under our flimsy sandals. Monsieur Renaud, the estate agent, leads the way, gripping his tablet computer in one hand and brushing seed heads from his cream slacks with the other.

My husband, Paul, strolls alongside him, oblivious to the vegetation scratching his legs. At six-foot-two, he towers above the dapper estate agent and fires off rounds of questions about the property.

"How long has it been derelict? How much land is there? Where's the boundary?"

The agent responds in fluent English and seems to take this inquisition in his stride.

The path is fringed with nettles, so I scoop my four-year-old daughter, Mollie, up into my arms. Her blonde curls are plastered to her forehead in the heavy, humid air.

"Here you go." I hand her a bottle of water and glance around for my son, who is trailing behind as usual.

At ten years old, Owen sometimes acts as if he's semi-detached from our family. He's tall for his age and people often assume he's older—twelve, or even thirteen. I tell myself he's striving for independence, but secretly worry we embarrass him because Paul, Mollie and I are fair-skinned, while Owen is the son of my ex-husband, Zak, and rightly proud of the Nigerian side of his heritage.

The property is called Les Quatre Vents and is on the market at a rock bottom price. When Paul picked up the estate agent's particulars in Limoges, he tried to convince me it would be simple to convert it into a holiday home. I've agreed to this viewing to cheer him up, because he's been having a tough time at work.

Now we're closer, I see walls coated with ivy, a sagging roof that's open to the elements, and a limp vine clinging to one end. The rotting front door has been lifted off its hinges and propped up against the wall, giving us a glimpse of an earth floor inside.

"Surely this was never a cottage," I say as we come to a halt. It looks more like a cowshed. "You said someone used to live here?"

"*Oui*. Until ten years." Monsieur Renaud consults the property details on his tablet. "Madame Durand, aunt of the family."

Mollie wriggles in my arms.

"Let me take her," offers Paul.

Glancing to my left, I figure out where the photographer must have stood to take a soft focus shot through cherry blossoms.

"When was this picture taken?" I ask.

Monsieur Renaud looks sorrowful. "It was taken in spring." He consults his screen. "Spring of 2009."

"Well, we're here now. Let's look inside," says Paul, bending his head to duck under the low lintel.

The height of the doorway isn't a problem for me; I step inside, inhaling damp air. Paul sets Mollie down and she clings to my leg,

"It's creepy, Mummy."

"We won't stay long. Daddy just wants to look around."

In one corner is an old stove, the wall above stained black from decades of smoke. Close by, a stone sink bristles with dried-up corpses of flies and beetles. It's hard to imagine an elderly lady living alone in this place with no modern facilities or comforts. I try to turn on the brass tap, but it won't budge.

"Let me," Paul clamps his hand on the tap and twists; a few specks of rust drop into the sink but no water. "Bathroom?" he asks the agent.

"Outside."

We step back from the dank gloom into the August heat and Monsieur Renaud guides us to the rear of the building where he pushes an outhouse door to reveal a soil closet with two footplates, poised either side of a hole in the ground.

"Mummy—what's that?" Mollie asks.

"An olden days' toilet."

"Ugh!"

She pinches her nose between thumb and forefinger. But any unpleasant stench has long ago been swallowed by the earth and now it smells of damp and leaf mould.

"*Fosse septique* is over here."

The agent points out a bank of soil, edged with red clay roof

4

tiles—a flower bed in a former life—now carpeted with weeds. He grasps a clump of dried grass, coils it around his hand and tugs it out by the roots. With his tan loafers he pushes earth aside to expose buried concrete.

Paul peers into the hole. "Septic tank," he translates, though I'm the one who studied French at university, until I got pregnant with Owen and had to drop out because I couldn't spend a year abroad.

"It will need pumping out." Monsieur Renaud scrapes his shoe on a tile to remove the earth. "Perhaps it need replacing. We 'ave new regulations now in force."

This is a waste of everyone's time. I turn to Paul to suggest we should be on our way, but he's stomping across the field, towards the boundary, where the summer foliage of three majestic oaks coalesces: a green cloud against sapphire sky, so beautiful it takes my breath away.

Owen is poking his finger into crevices in a low wall. "Look Mum, a lizard."

The gecko sneaks out of its lair and scuttles across the yard.

"Where?" Mollie turns, but she's too late.

Paul strolls back up the field, holding his mobile phone out in front of him and talking to himself.

I hear him say, "Two hectares of land. Mature plum and walnut trees, oaks to boundary," and realise he's filming and recording a voiceover.

"Do you know it would be easy to renovate this place and make us a family holiday home," Paul says as he holds out his phone, inviting me to view the video clip on his minuscule screen.

I squint at the phone, as a cloud drifts in front of the sun and I rub my bare arms to ward off a shiver.

"All this land!" Paul makes a sweeping gesture with his arm. "If we could get planning permission to turn the outbuildings into *gîtes* to rent out we might even make some money."

"You're joking, right?"

He pretends not to hear me. Looking at properties for sale and dreaming of a different life is a game we play when we're on holiday but, until today, we've restricted our viewings to photos in estate agents' windows.

"Paul, it may be cheap, but it's a wreck. And what about the renovation costs?"

"A ruin, Emma—that's the French term for a project like this."

Monsieur Renaud is standing a discreet distance away, but he's been listening to our conversation and his estate agent antennae must register a call to action because he sidles closer, clearing his throat.

"Why's it so cheap?" Paul asks.

"The family of Madame Durand are waiting already ten years for their money."

Uneasily, I chip in, "But I don't understand. There must be local families needing homes?"

"They prefer new. And nearer to Limoges for work."

"How easy would it be to get planning permission for, say, a fifty per cent increase over the original footprint?" asks Paul.

The agent straightens his spine. "Footprint?"

Paul glances at me but decides my translating skills won't run to building terms. "Size, dimensions. . ."

"*Oui*. No problem. There is a local plan that allows construction in this area but you will need to apply for a *permis de construire*."

"Come on, Paul." I move into the space between him and

the agent. "Let's go. We've wasted enough of Monsieur Renaud's time."

A flock of gulls wheels overhead forming a diamond pattern with frayed edges. The leading bird swoops down, as if to land on the sagging roof of Les Quatre Vents, but thinks again and scrambles skywards, borne aloft on the wind, and disappears from view.

CHAPTER 2

EMMA

August 2015

As I chop red peppers for our lunchtime salad, I wonder, do other families spend their summer holidays trekking around tumbledown ruins they've no intention of buying?

It's two days since we visited Les Quatre Vents and Paul's mood flits between excited and morose, as repercussions of a fatal accident at the company, where he's a director, clamour for his attention.

I chose this rural location in the Limousin so we could relax but, since we arrived at the chilly, echoing *gîte*, we've been trapped in a land that time forgot.

The bedroom walls are mottled with black mildew and the swimming pool is closed for maintenance. The village of Sainte Violette, half an hour's walk away, has one hotel, a bar that opens according to the owner's whim and a *boulangerie*.

Every morning a bread van tours the outlying hamlets; it arrives at the end of our drive at seven-thirty, emits three blasts on its horn and drives off as I stick my feet into Crocs and chase after it.

Our *gîte* has satellite TV and Owen has brought his Xbox

but he and Mollie argue all day; she wants to watch the Disney channel, he wants to play games.

Paul spends his days indoors fending off a deluge of work emails. He can't sleep at night and his face is pale with exhaustion and, ironically, a lack of sun. His dark hair needs cutting and his ten-day growth of beard scratches my face when I kiss him.

To give him some breathing space, I drag the children out on trips or shopping at the local market, giving them each five euros to spend on tatty souvenirs.

The rest of the time I stretch out on a lounger, scowling at the scummy surface of the out-of-order swimming pool and immerse myself in a novel. The sun beats down and I ram a floppy-brimmed hat over my auburn hair, applying the highest factor sun cream but my pale skin is pink and freckled. I've abandoned contact lenses for brown-tinted glasses that block the sun's rays.

"Lunch!" I call.

Paul and Mollie take their places at the table but there's no sign of Owen. Paul notices Owen's absence and half-rises from his chair.

"Leave him," I say, passing round the salad bowl.

Mollie pushes aside the morsel of ham I've sneaked onto her plate and nibbles a piece of cheese.

"This is ridiculous!" Paul puts down his knife, strides out into the hall and bellows, "Owen!"

We all hear Owen's reply, "Don't tell me what to do. You're not my dad."

The verbal assault comes out of nowhere. A sliver of argument inflated into words that can't now be unsaid.

Mollie glances at me, bursts into tears and runs upstairs

to join her brother. I dig my fingernails into my palms as Paul returns to the table and stares at the sunflower pattern on the cloth.

"I'm sorry. I don't know what got into him."

Paul shrugs. "He's right, though, Emma. I'm not his dad."

He pushes his plate away and I'm furious with my son for causing more stress.

I remember how Owen used to worship Paul but at that time, he rarely saw his dad. Zak was working on contracts abroad.

Owen had just started school when I applied for a part-time job at the company where Paul worked and he was on the interview panel. I didn't get the job—who would employ someone like me with no degree and a stunted CV? When Paul rang to break the bad news, he talked me into meeting him for a drink and I abandoned my usual caution and accepted.

Gradually, Paul slotted into our lives. He and Owen spent hours in rough and tumble play, giggling at super-hero movies or kicking a ball around the park. Soon, the treats became more extravagant. Paul organised visits to theme parks and zoos; aquariums and museums—sometimes two in a single weekend. When Paul suggested a skiing holiday, I called a halt.

"Owen doesn't have a passport," I told him.

I could have added that we were happy with our lives and didn't need more treats, but I had something more pressing to tell him. "I'm pregnant."

Paul and Owen were thrilled and, before Mollie arrived, we left our old life and the unheated flat, which triggered Owen's asthma every winter, and moved into Paul's house in Wimbledon.

Paul reaches round to a shelf and hauls his laptop onto the table, sweeping crumbs away with his hand. As it powers up, I hear emails pinging into his inbox.

"Any news?" I ask.

Paul sighs. "Where d' you want me to start?"

When the accident first happened, the story was splashed across the news and played on a continuous loop.

A workman called Dorek had fallen from the thirteenth floor of an office block Paul's company was redeveloping. As operations director of Manifold Developments, Paul was called to the scene and thrust into the spotlight with microphones shoved in his face.

The media was on a mission, searching for a scandal. Some newspapers reported that the worker wasn't wearing a proper harness and that health and safety at Manifold was lax. A rumour circulated that Dorek had personal problems and his death was deliberate—suicide. Having stoked the fire, the media lost interest and withdrew, leaving Paul badly burned.

The list of emails waiting in his inbox are all marked with 'Confidential' and 'Urgent' in the subject line. His face is grim.

"Questions and more questions. They're looking for a scapegoat."

"But how can it be your fault if he decided to jump?"

I feel my face burning where I caught the sun yesterday.

"He didn't jump, Emma. That story was just press sensationalism."

"So that means. . . ?"

He nods. "I'm ops director. It's my responsibility."

I take a sip of my coffee; lukewarm, bitter.

Paul turns back to his laptop. A fly is buzzing against the window pane. I open the window and set it free. Suddenly,

I can't face another afternoon imprisoned in this dreary house.

"Come on, we're going out."

"Fine. There's a document I need to sign and send back to Manifold by express mail. Let's head into Limoges."

I stride into the hall and shout, "Owen, Mollie, come down now."

Sheepishly, they pad down the stairs and hover just outside the kitchen door.

"Owen, get in here and apologise to Paul."

My son makes a face and turns sullen eyes on me. "But I only said—"

"I know what you said. Now say sorry."

He shuffles a few paces into the kitchen, stops a metre away from Paul and keeps his eyes fixed on the ground.

"Sorry."

"Okay, let's forget it," says Paul. "Your mother wants us to go out."

I nod. "We're going into Limoges. Get your stuff, then wait in the car. Ten minutes."

I gather up bottled water and the guidebook. We all clamber into the car and drive to the city in silence.

We dawdle along narrow streets and stroll up Rue Raspail where the frontages of some ancient buildings are barely wider than the span of a man's arms. Close to the cathedral, green and white bunting zig-zags between half-timbered buildings across narrow, cobbled streets.

"Why don't you take the kids into the cathedral while I go to the post office?" Paul suggests. "I'll meet you back here." He points out a café with broad sun parasols.

Owen, Mollie and I enter the cool darkness of St Etienne

cathedral, where Owen breaks away to settle himself on a seat close to the main door and stretches his long legs out in front of him. I leave him to sulk while Mollie and I meander along a side aisle.

Stained glass windows filter light to cool blue and a vast urn of white lilies scents the air. In the silence, I hear a tapping sound: a guide is escorting three partially-sighted visitors with long white canes. I move closer, testing my French as I eavesdrop on her description of flamboyant Gothic style. She's explaining to her group that, in the Middle Ages, only bishops and clerics could view the full celebration of mass, but in the eighteenth century the sanctuary was rearranged and the altar moved, so the congregation could finally see what was going on. The blind group moves away, their canes echoing on the flagstones.

Mollie wants to light a candle for her grandma and grandpa so I give her a one-euro coin to put in the box and we murmur a quick prayer for Paul's parents, who both died before I met him. I hold her hand steady while she lights a new candle from an old one, then take it from her and add it to the bonsai candle forest of flickering flames and melting wax.

"Can we blow it out now?" she asks excitedly.

"No, darling. It burns down on its own."

The simple candle ritual, the majestic ancient building, a flicker of spirituality—but it doesn't lure me—I don't really get religion. Still, something about the place slows my pulse and by the time we complete our circuit up the centre aisle, I'm calm.

Owen joins us and we emerge, squinting, into the sunshine. We stroll to the café, settle at an outside table and order drinks. Mollie and I sit in the shade and Owen moves his chair from under the parasol into the sun.

Our drinks arrive and Owen blows bubbles in his glass

through a straw to entertain Mollie, who tries to copy him. Orangina trickles down her chin and sets her giggling. She gets up and runs around the traffic-free square, flapping her arms to scare off pigeons.

A nearby clock strikes four.

"Do you think Dad's lost?" asks Mollie.

"Can we just go?"

Owen kicks his feet against the metal struts of the table and the repetitive clanging sparks a dull pain in my head.

"No, Owen. Besides, Dad's got the car keys."

"I'm bored."

"Here he is."

Although she's the smallest, Mollie is first to spot him. Shielding her eyes from the sun, she runs over and he swings her up into his arms.

"I thought you were sending that to Manifold?" I remark, as Paul drops a bulging envelope onto the metal table. "Didn't you find the post office?"

"I did. This is something else. Far more exciting."

He draws out a sheaf of papers and hands them to me.

There are pages of legal-looking documents in small print and more property bumph but the photograph on the top sheet is familiar: a long, low stone building in a grassy field, set back behind a cherry blossom tree.

"Isn't that. . . ?"

He nods. "Les Quatre Vents. And now it's ours."

A shaft of sunlight sneaks under the parasol and illuminates his slow smile.

"What!" I shout, scrambling to my feet.

"I've just been into the estate agent's and put down a deposit."

CHAPTER 3

EMMA

August 2015

Some holidays exist in a bubble—airy and transparent—happy families floating above the stresses of everyday life. Not mine. I've spent the fortnight refereeing fights between the children and cheering Paul up. And now this bombshell. I'm furious, even more so because I'll have to wait until the children are in bed before I let rip.

While I'm moping through the evening in silence, Paul transforms back into his normal cheerful self. He makes supper and neutralises the latest feud between the children by handing Owen his precious work laptop.

"Can I play Minecraft?" asks Owen.

"Sure." He doesn't even utter his usual warning about viruses and dodgy downloads.

I'm pouring my third glass of wine when Paul comes back downstairs after reading Mollie's bedtime story.

"Perhaps you'd like to explain yourself?"

"Come on, Emma!" He takes my hand, but I snatch it away. "It's an adventure."

"You always want more, don't you! More holidays, more stuff and, now, more houses. Why can't you be satisfied?"

His face tightens. "I did it for you. Because you love France."

"For me? How dare you say that!" I yell, no longer caring if the children hear. "And making such a huge decision without consulting me."

"I wanted to surprise you. I thought it might make up for missing out on your year in France and your degree. And it's an investment."

"And what about the renovation cost?"

He smiles. "See, I knew you'd worry but it's such a bargain."

He's not listening so I aim my blow lower.

"You should sort out your work problems before jumping into a new project."

He stiffens and the crease between his eyebrows deepens.

"And when my working life falls apart, then what? I need something else to focus on. Lighten up, Emma!"

I knew his excitement was a veneer—underneath, he was struggling—but that's no excuse for making a life-changing decision without consulting me.

"I'm going outside." Paul gets to his feet to follow me, but I stop him. "Leave me alone. I need to think."

I walk out onto the terrace, where it's still light, and sit beside the pool. The air is heavy with the scent of honeysuckle and the cicadas tune up their unique evening chorus. Paul's right—I do love France—and not completing my degree still rankles. I try to stay focused on this current dilemma, but my memory flips back eleven years. . .

I was a second year undergraduate when I found out I was pregnant. Zak, my boyfriend, was a post-graduate, ten years older than me, and already established in his career. The oil company he worked for was sponsoring him through a business degree.

Zak and I thought we were in love, so we decided to marry and make a home together before our child was born. To my surprise, my family accepted my decision. My mother found a dressmaker, who cunningly disguised my bump under an empire line so I resembled a bloated character from a Jane Austen novel. My dress was ivory silk to suit my redhead's complexion and, if it wasn't for my fiery hair, I'd be a ghostly blob in the wedding photos, standing beside my handsome, dark husband.

On the night before my wedding, my mother came into my room and perched on the narrow single bed where I'd dreamed all my teenage dreams and I waited for her to say, 'You've made your bed, now lie in it,' and other platitudes. But she took my hand and said, "Zak's a fine man, Emma. Your dad and I like him very much. We hope you'll have a happy life together."

"Thanks, Mum." I gulped.

"There's one thing you need to understand. I'm not ready to be a hands-on granny—I've just accepted promotion to deputy head. Don't expect me to drop everything and come running to help."

"Of course." Back then, I didn't know how hard it would be.

It turned out Zak was already married—to his career. He worked in some of the most dangerous countries in the world; if his company needed someone for Chad, Libya, Mali—Zak was their man. When he did come home, we had nothing to say to one another.

When I left Zak, my parents blamed me. Careless words were spoken and I took umbrage at my mother's moralistic tone. There was fault on both sides and I was too stubborn to admit I needed help, so Owen and I stumbled on alone and never saw my parents.

We slipped into a life of poverty. Sometimes I only had a tin of baked beans and a packet of rice to get us through the weekend, but I was cautious and we always managed—somehow. To save on heating bills, the library became our sanctuary. Owen mixed with other children, but when the storytelling sessions ended and the other mums headed off for coffee, I had to refuse. . .

I lift my eyes and see streaks of red bleed into the evening sky, as the sun drops low on the horizon. There's a hint of citronella on the air and Paul appears, carrying a candle.

"Thought you might need this to keep the mozzies away." He sets it down on the table. "Forgive me?"

"S'pose I'll have to." I stand up and slide an arm around his back and we watch the sun setting. "I do love France. You were right about that."

"I wish you'd let me spoil you more, Emma. I want this for you—for us. Work is hell. Your support means everything."

I think how Paul lifted us out of poverty and supported my son by another man. Whenever I could, I took casual work because I wanted to contribute. Paul understood I needed the dignity of work and, on many Friday and Saturday evenings, he looked after Owen while I went out waitressing for banqueting events.

It's not his powers of persuasion that have won me over. Sitting here, tuning into the cicadas' twilight din while the sun sets, has shuffled my thoughts into a new order.

The idea of owning Les Quatre Vents—having a foothold on French soil—has captured my imagination.

CHAPTER 4

EMMA

September 2015

Back in London, reality awaits us. Within days of returning to work at Manifold, where the accident investigation is dragging on, Paul's mood darkens.

"Perhaps you should see the doctor?" I suggest, as he sits at the supper table gazing into space.

"What for? I'm already on sleeping tablets."

Sleep eludes me, too. At five in the morning I wake drenched in sweat and slide my hand across the mattress to touch Paul's cool body, but he's not there. Yawning, I pull on my dressing gown and pad downstairs on bare feet, towards a faint light framing the kitchen door. When I ease it open, Paul is at the table working on his laptop.

"Paul?" He doesn't hear me. I stir a slight draught as I step inside.

He spins round. "Emma." He snaps his laptop shut and presses on the lid as if it were Pandora's box. Under the kitchen spotlights his skin looks chalky, his eyes bloodshot.

I pull up a chair next to him and take his hand. His fingers feel cold, but he doesn't pull away.

"What is it? Is it the case again?"

He shifts in his chair and nods. "It's doing my head in. No one's keeping me in the loop."

I gather my thoughts. "Is that a bad thing?"

"About as bad as it can get. The accident investigation could lead to charges related to Dorek's death. If it's gross negligence, I could go to prison; never work again."

I shiver. Paul frees his hand from mine. His restless fingers drum on the table.

"But you weren't even there when it happened."

"Doesn't matter. I'm the responsible director. Even if it's a lesser finding, I'll probably lose my job."

I try to swallow but my mouth is dry. I think about the plans we were making for Paul's renovation project—a symptom of his desperate state of mind.

I know all about surviving poverty, but I've always been terrified of debt. It's like a current that swells up to overwhelm and drag you under. When it was just me and Owen, I always knew that, if I was careful, I could pull us through every crisis because there wasn't far to fall.

I say the first thing that comes into my head. "That's it then. We'll have to economise. We can't buy Les Quatre Vents."

"What do you mean?" Paul's eyes narrow.

"I mean, if your job's at risk, it's too expensive."

A hint of colour returns to Paul's face and he speaks with real passion. "France is our future. All that's keeping me going."

My bare feet feel chilly on the hard floor.

"Come back to bed?" I suggest.

He picks up his laptop and tucks it under his arm, the power lead dangling like a slack tow rope.

"Not really worth it now." He yawns and shuffles out, his slippers slapping on the stairs.

I stand in the hall and watch him disappear into our room. Minutes later, the shower roars into life. My thoughts are too tangled for sleep so I potter about the kitchen, laying the table for the kids' breakfast. Not that anyone ever sits down to eat.

Mollie and I go to school together now. She's in reception and I've started my new job as a learning support assistant. As one of the younger pupils, Mollie will only attend in the mornings until Christmas, so my contract fits around her, but my salary's correspondingly low. I've been thinking how else I can boost our income to take some pressure off Paul and, during sleep-starved nights, I've hit on an idea of running an after-school French club for infants.

"Can you book me an appointment with Mrs Harker?" I ask the school secretary, putting my head round the door of her office.

"Five minutes enough?"

"Should be."

She smiles. "I'll squeeze you in."

At break, I'm still fuddled from lack of sleep, as I wait in the corridor outside the head's office. The door opens and a mum emerges, clutching a small girl by the hand. I recognise the child because she comes to school hungry and the teachers have been discreetly feeding her cereal and sandwiches. I feel for the mother and her child. Could that have been me? But, however hard up we were, surely I'd never have let Owen go hungry?

The woman scowls at me and tugs at her daughter's hand, dragging her along, her dirty trainers squeaking on the polished floor.

Mrs Harker appears at her office door. "Come in, Emma. Sit down." She swaps her bright smile for a rueful one and sighs. "Usual hectic start to the school year. Sorry I've not had a chance to ask how you're getting on."

"It's going well." I seem to be getting through to the six-year-old boy with complex needs that I'm supporting. It's not so long since Owen was his age.

Mrs Harker takes a sip from the mug sitting on her desk and wrinkles her mouth. "Ugh—that's cold." She puts it down and pushes it away. "How can I help?"

"You know I read French at university?"

She nods.

"I was wondering about starting up a French club after school for infants."

"Tell me more."

"Do you think parents will want to pay for classes? They'll get it free later on."

Mrs Harker tugs on the double string of pearls clinging to her fleshy throat, "In Wimbledon? Parents will pay for anything if they think it will benefit their children. Besides," she says with a smile. "When they come to learn a language, there's no guarantee it'll be French."

"Would you let me run it in one of the classrooms?"

"Don't see why not. We may need to make a small room hire charge. I'll raise it with the governors."

The fog in my brain disperses as I stroll along the corridor back to my classroom with a smile on my face. I begin to see a future where I'm useful again, not labelled as somebody's mum or wife.

*

Every evening Paul follows the same ritual. Dropping his bag in the hall, he sticks his head into the kitchen to greet me and Owen, then runs upstairs to read Mollie's bedtime story. Tonight, he's whistling a tune under his breath.

"You've cheered up since this morning," I call, but I don't detain him.

Story time is precious to both of them. When he works late, I'm his understudy, but Mollie tells me I don't do the voices as well as her dad.

I cook the couscous, stir the lamb and put a jug of water with lemon slices on the table.

"I have news," I say, as he enters the kitchen. "A plan to help with family finances."

"Good news?" His eyes crinkle into a smile.

I nod. "Mrs Harker has agreed I can run an after-school French club. You'll have to help me figure out how much to charge."

"What about Mollie?"

"She'll come to the club with me."

Paul opens the fridge and takes out a bottle of Chablis. "This calls for a celebration."

"I think that's the last of the whites we brought back from France." We've drunk them all in a month.

He pours out two large glasses, hands one to me and clinks his against mine. "To the linguist in the family."

I take a sip. "Can't wait to use my French again."

"And you'll use it in France."

I put the supper plates on the table. Paul loads up his fork with lamb and couscous and pauses with it in mid-air. "I've got some good news, too."

He keeps me in suspense while he chews his first mouthful. Could it be the report on the accident? Has he been exonerated?

"I've raised the rest of the money." He smiles.

"Money for what?"

"To buy Les Quatre Vents. I've organised the funds."

"Oh that." Now, I'm the one who isn't smiling. "What if you lose your job?"

With a wave of his fork, he dismisses my concerns. "It was easy. Just added a bit onto the mortgage on this house."

I lean across the table, take hold of his arm and squeeze. "Didn't you listen to what I said this morning? We can't afford it."

Shrugging off my grasp, Paul sets down his glass clumsily and clips the edge of his plate. "Damn."

The base of his glass shears away from the stalk with a splintering sound. He drains the last of his wine then dumps the broken glass in the bin.

"C'mon, Em. Don't worry about the money. It's under control."

"It's not just the money. What about everything going on at work?"

He grimaces. "Thanks for reminding me."

"I didn't mean—"

"There's not much to do. I'll transfer the money across and we'll need to swear an oath in front of a notary. I said we'd go over at October half term to complete the signing."

This takes me a while to process.

"Perhaps the kids can stay with your parents?" He says, his eyes sparkling. "How long is it since we had a break? Just the two of us."

I look down at my plate where the lamb is congealing into brown gunge and try to recapture the buzz I felt back in the summer when I agreed to go ahead with the purchase. Since then, Paul has been through hell at work and held onto his dream. It makes sense to focus on a plan for the future. If I support him, maybe these dark times will pass.

CHAPTER 5

PAUL

June 2015

One sparkling June day, I took Emma and the kids to the races at Goodwood for one of those family-friendly events. Manifold paid our annual bonuses every June, so I wanted to treat them to a meal in the restaurant, but Emma persuaded me a picnic would suit Mollie better. As she spread out a rug on the ground and started setting out lunch, Owen wandered off to kick a football around with kids from the family next to us and I took out my Nikon and snapped a few photos.

Emma was wearing a cotton dress patterned with tropical birds. The wind picked up and flattened the dress against her body, lifting the hem above her knees to show off her pale, shapely legs. When she noticed my camera, she smiled and smoothed down her skirt.

"I need a new family photo for my desk," I said. "Mollie's still a baby in my current one."

"Sure." Emma gathered Mollie onto her lap and they both smiled up at me.

I felt a lump forming in my throat.

"Come on, Owen. I want you in the photo, too." He'd

drifted back when he spotted food and was cramming a KitKat into his mouth, two fingers at a time.

"Nah," he spluttered, through a mouthful of chocolate.

"Please, Owen," said Emma, extending her hand.

He shook his head. "Give me the camera. I'll take one of you."

"Fair enough." I handed it to him and showed him how to focus, then I knelt down on the rug with my arms around Emma and Mollie.

Owen took a few shots and started checking them, flicking back through my camera roll.

"This one's crap. Mollie's shut her eyes again. . ."

Cold sweat dripped down my back. How far back through my gallery had he gone? I scrambled to my feet. "Give me the camera, Owen."

He shook his head. "Nah. Still looking."

"Listen," I said through tight lips. "Here's the race programme—you can choose some horses to back. I'll swap you for the camera."

"Cool. When's the first race? I've brought my own money." He opened his fist and showed me a crumpled tenner.

I smiled. "Put that away. Today's my treat. I'll place a few bets for all of us."

"Any horses you fancy?" I asked Emma, passing her the race card.

"How about Dream Team? And Puppy Love for Mollie."

"Okay but pick a few more. The racing goes on all afternoon."

She screwed up her eyes against the sun and shot me a warning look that I decoded as *'Don't spend too much money.'* Instead she said, "You choose for me."

I nodded and squeezed her hand. "Don't worry. Just a few quid. Today's not all about the racing—it's a family day. There'll be farrier demonstrations, a racecourse walk and storytelling, but it'll be more exciting for the kids to have a horse to back while they watch the races."

"Can I come with you?" pleaded Owen, leaping to his feet.

"Sure."

Emma protested. "I think it's best he stays with me. Those crowds. . ."

Owen aimed a surly kick at the cool box and I put a restraining hand on his shoulder. "Don't fret, Emma. He'll be fine. We'll be half an hour—tops."

We headed off before she could protest further.

"When I was your age, I never went on outings like this with my parents," I told Owen.

"Me neither. Not with both my mum and dad."

As we waited in line to place our bets, he showed me the back of his hand where he'd scribbled the names of the horses he'd chosen. It was rather a long list but, lately, Owen and I hadn't been getting along so well. Today was a chance to win him back to my team.

"That's fine," I assured him. Ahead of me in the queue I spotted a burly man in a blue jacket. From the back it looked like Jimmy Jonas, a client of my previous company. Not someone I'd have expected to see at a family day and definitely not someone I wanted to bump into just now.

I turned sideways, lowered my head and studied the race card. It would be good to make some dosh from our family day out. Could I risk an accumulator? But if just one of my horses lost, all bets would be off. I settled for a Yankee; at least that would give me eleven different potential winning combinations.

A raucous laugh, a hefty back slap that almost winded me and a voice boomed, "Paul! Long time no see!"

I turned around and found myself staring into Jimmy Jonas's sweaty face. He'd put on weight since I last saw him and his jowls spilled down from beneath his chin to join his thick neck. He slung a matey arm around me and tweaked me out of my place in the queue to introduce me to a man whose name I didn't quite catch: Tel—or Tez?

"Now, here's a chap you must meet," he said to his mate, waggling a pencil stub close to my face. "What this man doesn't know about the gee-gees isn't worth knowing."

"And who's this young man?" Jimmy asked, grinning down at Owen.

I stuck out one leg to try to hold onto our place in the queue, but it had already formed a meander around me and Owen, as if we were obstructing the flow of a river.

"Owen. My stepson."

Jimmy took Owen's hand and shook it in the mock avuncular way of men who've never spent time around children. He slid his other hand into his pocket, as if he was about to produce a bank note and gift it to Owen, but he drew out a handkerchief instead.

"Me and old Paul here," Jimmy continued, dabbing his sweaty brow. "We had some great times together. Remember Cheltenham that year? And Royal Ascot?" He winked at me as if we were conspirators, then roared with laughter.

My memory of those occasions is of Jimmy freeloading on my corporate hospitality and never putting any new business my way. I nodded, but my face felt tight with the effort of smiling.

"You still in that racehorse owners' syndicate?" Jim asked.

My heart started hammering.

"Oh—you know," I muttered, praying Owen wouldn't pick up on it.

My armpits felt damp and clammy. I'd been trying to get rid of my stake in the syndicate for months but no one wanted to take it on. Experience had taught me there was no upside in being part-owner of a racehorse in training. I couldn't really afford it when I was single but, since having a family, my debts had been spiralling and I'd been borrowing more against the house in Wimbledon.

Emma didn't know about the racehorse syndicate or the extra borrowing and, if she found out, I worried she'd lose respect for me, so I hid it from her.

I'd owned the house before our marriage, so the mortgage was in my sole name. Emma didn't need to see the statements. The monthly payments weighed me down and, after our family holiday, I planned to start the hunt for a new job—one that paid higher bonuses.

Jimmy planted his bulky frame so close I could smell sour beer on his breath.

"Where are you working now?" Tel/Tez asked, politely moving the conversation on.

I cleared my throat. "I'm at Manifold Developments. Operations Director."

"Good for you." Jimmy poked me in the ribs. "Onwards and upwards, eh? Have a good one." And turning to Owen: "You too, young man." They drifted away, leaving us to re-join the tail of the queue.

"Who was that man?" asked Owen. "Your friend?" His tone was accusatory and I bristled as I felt my judgement being called into question.

"Just an old business contact. Someone I knew in my last job before I moved to Manifold Developments. No need to mention him to your mum."

CHAPTER 6

PAUL

July 2015

On the evening of the day Dorek fell, Manifold's head office was in a state of siege. I was lurking in my office with the blinds drawn when our head of human resources, Genevieve, entered without knocking.

"It's mayhem out there," she remarked, placing a mug of black coffee on the desk in front of me. "Manning's brought in a media trouble-shooter from our PR company to handle all enquiries."

"Then he's doing everything arse about face, as usual!" I exclaimed, still smarting from the bollocking Manning had given me earlier.

"As in. . . ?"

"We've already issued a press statement!" The words echoed inside my head like an earworm:

The directors of Manifold Developments are profoundly saddened by the death of Dorek Nowak. Their thoughts and prayers are with the family of Mr Nowak, his friends and co-workers at this sad time.

Earlier on, when the directors gathered in the boardroom to

approve the statement, I'd suggested adding a line to say we'd be co-operating fully with the investigation and Manning had turned on me, his face red and blotchy, "Shut the fuck up, Paul. You've caused enough problems."

A rush of blood warmed my face. "But—"

"This is fucking serious, Paul. A man died, for God's sake."

I think that was when the force of the thing hit me. My legs turned to pulp. I've been shaking ever since.

During the evening Emma had phoned a few times—must have seen brief details of the accident on the news—but I couldn't face speaking to her.

"Talk to me, Paul," said Genevieve, pulling up a chair. "Let me help you."

She threw me a lifeline and I grasped it.

"The Spinney Towers contract terms included a bonus for early completion," I told her. "I brought in more men, most of them foreign workers. Some may not have had experience of working at height. But I knew the site was being poorly run because I recently found out the site manager was turning a blind eye when labourers went home on holiday and deputed mates to do the work in their absence."

"How did they do that?" she asked.

"Probably sorted out a private deal to pay their friend cash in hand. Meanwhile, we kept on paying wages into our original hire's bank account. Ultimately, we didn't have jack shit of an idea who was working on that site."

"That's appalling. How did you find out?"

"A whistle-blower came to me and spilled the beans. Of course, I went ballistic. The workers were fired; I disciplined the foreman on another matter—fiddling overtime records—and warned Jez Williams, the site manager, he'd be toast if it ever happened again."

"What did you do next?"

"I covered it up. What else could I do?"

If the scam had come to light, Manifold could have been in for huge fines. Breaches of immigration, employment law, health and safety, corruption, it could have driven Manifold under.

"I'm not even sure the new safety procedures were ever issued in the Spinney Towers site packs." I groaned.

Genevieve raised her hand, palm towards me. "Stop it Paul. You mustn't say anything that would incriminate Manifold or you."

I knew what she was saying but I needed to share this burden. I wasn't thinking straight or considering consequences.

"I doubt the site managers or foremen had up-to-date checklists. Probably didn't test the harnesses and safety gear."

Genevieve eyed me with concern as she twisted up her dark hair and pinned it into a bun, remodelling herself as an icon of calm efficiency.

"Say as little as possible. Leave this to me. I'm meeting with the site manager at eight tomorrow morning and I have a call with the lawyers at ten. After that we can plan. Don't worry."

She produced a slim silver hip flask and poured brandy into my coffee and I felt a small rush of relief. Genevieve had a genius for problem solving. Alongside her human resources role, she oversaw all the company's legal stuff with our external lawyers. She was paid a director's salary but refused to have the word 'director' in her job title.

Someone suggested she dodged a director's responsibility because she passed all official documents to the finance director for signature, or to Cyril Manning, the octogenarian dad of our CEO who held the official title of Company Secretary but, I doubt, had done any actual work since the last millennium. Cyril turned up for Board and Executive meetings but it was Genevieve who took the minutes; decided what to record and what to omit.

"I've heard that Dorek suffered from anxiety," said Genevieve slowly. "Seems he had a wife in Poland and a pregnant girlfriend in London."

"How do you know that?" I asked, pricking up my ears.

If Dorek's foreman and fellow workers suggested Dorek was neglectful of his own and others' safety on site it might help our case.

Genevieve gazed back at me, forcing me to meet her eyes. "We're going to work this out together Paul. Trust me."

CHAPTER 7

PAUL

December 2014

When Genevieve joined Manifold most of the guys were shit-scared of her.

"What do you think of her?" my deputy asked. "Reminds me of a piranha with her perfect sharp teeth. I get the feeling she's circling me."

"Nonsense. She's just challenging us. Professionally, I mean."

But I began watching her more closely and one day I noticed her giving me a look and I knew what that look meant.

Women who work in the construction industry are a special breed. Once they put on their hard hats and fluorescent jackets, they have a choice: become one of the boys or push off and retrain in hairdressing. Soon their language is blue, they kick arse, fire people and teach brickies new words Even in office roles, they wear their toughness like a second skin. Until I met Emma, those were the women I dated.

I'd always vowed never to get married. I'd watched my mother suffer in the shadow of my father's miserliness, even though he earned a good wage. Every day he weighed out a portion of blame and doled it out between us, but he kept his own emotions locked away. To me, family life was a prison viewed through a distorted lens made of opaque glass.

When I met Emma she had nothing: no resources, no support, no proper job, but her fierce love for her son, Owen, had forged him into a remarkable child—articulate, intelligent and self-possessed.

She'd faced down hardship and grown strong and independent. I vowed to lift the burden from her and spoil her, if only she'd let me. She didn't make it easy. Emma wasn't keen on fancy meals and smart restaurants—she'd rather stay home and have pizza with the kids.

"Do you want to come to the Manifold Christmas party?" I asked Emma.

It was an exclusive do for the senior team and head office staff in a private room in one of those swanky London hotels where Michelin-starred chef, Pietro Cassollini, was enjoying his fifteen minutes of fame before the caravan moved on.

She made a face. "Do you mind if I don't?"

I wasn't surprised. Other halves were always invited but, despite the glamour, few of them accepted.

As I entered the bar, I noticed Genevieve in a figure-hugging red dress. At work her clothes were androgynous and she'd wear a crisp white shirt, gold jewellery, black pants, sometimes with a bit of pinstripe going on.

She was standing by the bar, swirling a glass of champagne in one hand. She seemed to be watching me but before I could cross the room to speak to her, someone called my name.

"Paul, can I have a word?" It was Anna, my former personal assistant.

"Hey, Anna, you look great."

She'd changed her top for a floaty one, but her trousers

were creased. Must be the ones she'd been wearing all day at work. Her hair was escaping from a messy bun and, in her right hand, she was holding a batch of place cards and distributing them round the starched white tablecloths.

"What's up?" No doubt she was double-checking that the place cards had the secret codes that indicate vegetarian or gluten-free in waiter-speak.

When we worked together, Anna became rather too attached to me. I did nothing to encourage her, stayed faithful to Emma, but it wasn't healthy. So now she works for Genevieve. Organising the Christmas party is part of her role.

Turning her back to the other guests congregating at the bar, Anna showed me a copy of the seating plan. Her fingernails were immaculate, long, with sparkly gold polish. I remembered she used to bite them.

"We have three round tables seating eight," she said. "Nineteen men and five women: that's me and the other two personal assistants, plus Genevieve and Mrs Manning."

"You mean Ms Silver?" Our Chief Executive's wife insists on being called by her maiden name.

Anna blushed. "Yes. I got it right on her place card this year."

"So you need to share the women between the tables, but you're one short of an equal split. Is that it?"

Why was she telling me this?

Anna shook her head. "No. It's something else. I placed you on table three, as table host, next to Ms Silver."

"Fine with me."

It's traditional to have our three most senior directors—Bruce Manning; Ralph, our Finance Director, and me—hosting a table. None of the junior staff want to sit on Bruce or Ralph's table.

Last year, Anna told me people tried to bribe her to seat

them on my table: the one where work is never mentioned and festive fun is had.

She lowered her voice to a whisper, so I had to bend closer to hear. "Genevieve made me rearrange the seating plan. She said you and Ms Silver wouldn't have much to talk about, because she's an accountant, and it would be better to put her next to the Finance Director. So now you're on Mr Manning's table, sitting next to Genevieve, but you're not hosting a table anymore."

There was a glint in her eyes and I was touched she still cared enough to worry about a minor dent in my status. My hand brushed hers, ever so lightly and a flicker of electricity made a circuit between us. She felt it too. Her head jerked up, she stared at me with her soulful eyes and, for the briefest of instants, I wondered if she'd taken up the company's offer to book a room at the hotel for the night.

After a boozy work function, Manifold picks up the bill—as Manning always said, "It's company policy to take our employees' safety seriously."

I pushed the thought away.

"No problem," I assured her.

"You honestly don't mind?" Poor Anna. Her eyes reminded me of a young calf.

I took my place at the table alongside Genevieve, who returned my smile with a tight-lipped grimace, as she hitched the narrow strap of her dress back onto her shoulder.

The waiter appeared with a bottle of Sancerre; I waved him away and asked him to bring me a beer. While this was going on, Genevieve turned her back to me and started trading banter with Bruce Manning, seated on her right. I waited for her to lean back in her chair and signal me to join their conversation but, after five minutes of pretending to study the menu, I shrugged and turned to my other neighbour, Jack Brown, whose only topic of conversation was sport.

As our fish course was cleared away, I shuffled in my seat, twisted my stiffening neck to the right and found Genevieve looking at me. I dropped my gaze only to find I was staring at the curve of her rather magnificent breasts.

The evening dragged on until the staff, who'd declined the offer of a free overnight stay, slipped away to get taxis or catch their last trains. That left seven of us. Ms Silver made her excuses and went to her room. How I regretted not taking my cue from her.

Waiting for me upstairs was my own room—first chance of a decent night's sleep in months because Emma was always disturbing me by getting up to check on Mollie, even though she was three years old.

Once his wife had gone to bed, Manning needed an audience. He loosened his tie and frog-marched us across to the lounge of our private bar where the leather armchairs and low sofas seemed to be designed for a race of deformed giants.

Whisky in hand, I lowered myself onto one of the sofas and Genevieve sat down beside me. After ignoring me all evening, she'd left it till I was seriously tipsy to pay me attention.

The hotel bar staff, anxious to go home, dimmed the overhead lighting, so the chilly gloom of the grey-black lampshades was reflected onto our pallid faces. A more sensitive crowd would have settled up and departed, but not us.

"So, how's it been?" I asked Genevieve. "Your first few months at Manifold?"

"Oh, you know. Has its charms."

She threw back her drink like a slammer and breathed

fumes of pure alcohol into my face. I felt unsettled by her raven hair, her low voice, her height, her large hands, the too-delicate bracelet dangling from her wrist. She reminded me of. . . but no, she was definitely all woman and her skin was flawless, with a translucence that can't be bought over the makeup counter.

Manning called us all to attention. He talked business, the future, how Manifold would be moving up the rankings, challenging top players in our industry. It was a spiel I'd heard before in every company throughout my career. Why had I stuck with these small players like Manifold? Why didn't I move to a top company when I was in my twenties?

"Why have you stayed at Manifold, Paul?" Genevieve's mind-reading jolted me out of my inebriation.

I took a sip of my Scotch and muttered, "Interesting work, new challenges, chance to get involved with a range of projects, I s'pose."

"That's not it, is it?"

"How do you mean?"

Had she guessed my secret? That it's the status I crave. Here at Manifold I'm operations director but if I went to a bigger company I'd be two, maybe three, levels lower with no expense account to entertain clients at Royal Ascot.

She narrowed her eyes. "You're better than them, Paul. Think bigger, spread your wings. Believe me, I've worked for top firms in our industry. They need people like you."

"You really think so?"

"I know so." She underlined her words in a way that shifted my mood from boredom to elation. We both laughed.

The drinks waiter appeared with his silver tray and notebook, stifling a yawn as he asked for any more orders.

"Let me see what single malts you have," said Manning,

trailing the exhausted waiter to the bar and demanding a guided tour, by distillery, of the hotel's selection of sixty-plus malt whiskies.

Grey-faced colleagues sneakily texted overdue goodnights to sleeping wives. No one noticed Genevieve lean towards me, take my hand, as if in a goodnight handshake, and press a slip of paper into my clenched fingers. She stood up, adjusted her dress and strode to the bar to say goodnight to Manning.

As I watched, he encircled her waist with his arm and tried to pull her towards him but before his hand slid down to grope her, she pirouetted away, pausing in the doorway, to flutter her fingers in a goodnight wave, then vanished.

I peered at the scrap of paper, so tiny I could conceal it in my palm. On it was scribbled room number 542. I scrunched it in my fist, rammed it into my pocket and summoned up thoughts of Emma to fill every space in my mind and block out Genevieve.

As I stood up to say goodnight to my colleagues, I felt reckless from the after-effects of alcohol. I took the lift to the fifth floor and strolled along the corridor following the directional arrow towards rooms 530 to 550. As I drew level with 542, I saw Genevieve had propped the door open with the kettle from her tea tray.

CHAPTER 8

PAUL

January 2015

The Skylon cocktail bar shimmered like a temporary extension of the festive season, lights gleaming on curved shelves and the array of coloured bottles, while I sunk deeper into new year misery.

I shifted uneasily on my stool; my flaming orange cocktail made me feel queasy as I apologised to Genevieve and explained why our night together, two weeks' earlier, could never be repeated.

She took a sip of her gin and tonic.

"What's the problem Paul?" She leant in close and locked her eyes onto mine. "I'm a free agent. I can choose who I sleep with and I choose you."

"But I'm married." The miserable cliché sat bitter on my tongue, as I tried to catch the barman's eye to ask for the bill.

"Listen—we're equals at Manifold, right?"

I nodded, but in truth, I felt lower than vermin.

"So there's no power imbalance between us." She gestured with her left wrist so her cascade of bracelets jingled like far-away laughter. "Your wife will never find out. No one gets hurt."

Beneath the protective overhang of the bar, she stroked my

thigh, diluting my resolve. Emma was still preoccupied with the kids, pleading exhaustion and turning her back on me in bed. A brief fling, a mature relationship between grown-ups—where was the harm in that?

*

Our affair drifted on through the spring of 2015. When we met for drinks after work, Genevieve was sparkling and witty and, unlike Emma, had no qualms about dining in top London restaurants. Sometimes the bill came to several hundred pounds and, as equals, we'd take turns to pay, but my credit cards were beginning to buckle under the strain.

"Did you live in London as a child?" Genevieve asked one evening when I'd chosen a more modest restaurant and was taking my first mouthful of Malabar fish curry.

Her question caught me off balance. Usually, we talked business or food; wine or travel, because anything personal was trespass.

"I grew up in Finchley with my parents, but I lived in Sussex, with my grandparents."

"Intriguing, tell me more."

So I did. I told her about my bleak childhood; how I hated my father and feared for my mother's mental health.

"Every holiday, my mother drove me to Sussex and dropped me off to stay with her parents, but my father wouldn't let her spend even one night away and she was too terrified to cross him."

Why was I telling Genevieve this stuff? Memories I'd not even shared with Emma because it made me seem weak.

"I think my grandparents must have known how things were

at home but felt impotent to intervene. During the holidays, they took me to karate lessons, skating, surfing and riding and bought me everything I asked for; a skateboard, guitar, my first computer but I had to leave those treasures at their house so my father didn't see them."

Genevieve's eyes clouded and she covered my hand with hers. The electricity of sexual excitement between us was still strong but I felt we'd crossed some boundary and hated myself for it.

The realisation came to me slowly—Genevieve didn't want a mature fling between adults, she wanted entertainment, companionship, romance, the full works—and I'd been too blind to see it.

She had a way of ambushing me with her plans. One evening when I was clearing my desk for an early escape home, she appeared in my office all sparkly-eyed and waving a red cardboard wallet. "Tickets!"

I feigned innocence though my heart was sinking. Through my office window, a fireball of evening sun was dipping towards the Thames.

"What are you going to see?"

"Wrong pronoun. We are going to Covent Garden."

"When?"

"Tonight." She glanced at her watch. "Now, in fact. Our table for dinner is booked for six o'clock."

I closed down my computer and followed her through the reception lobby and out to the waiting cab like I was hypnotised.

"Why drop this on me?" I asked glumly, as I huddled on the taxi's bench seat, texting apologies to Emma for yet another forgotten evening 'work commitment.'

"The tickets only just became available. Anna booked them for Manning."

"I thought Manning didn't like opera!"

"It's not opera. It's ballet. He was due to entertain that new planning consultant. Red-haired woman, you know? She pulled out this afternoon."

"Didn't Manning's wife want to go to the ballet with him?" I asked miserably.

Genevieve yawned. "Far too busy."

"So, what are we going to see?"

"Swan Lake—Anthony Dowell's production. You'll love it."

If there's one thing I loathe more than opera, it's ballet.

Our dinner table wasn't in the restaurant but on the first-floor, pressed up against the glass balcony, where diners are in full view of the arriving audience. This must be how a caged animal feels in a zoo.

I hunched over my plate taking staccato bites of my salmon and twisting my neck to right and left to check if I'd been spotted.

"Lots of celebs here tonight," Genevieve remarked, pointing with her fork to that pink-shirted guy who's on a late night politics show and someone off *The Apprentice*.

I summoned a faint smile. With media personalities to ogle, no one was going to notice me. And then the back of my neck prickled as I spotted someone I recognised in the atrium bar below—Lucinda, wife of my best friend, Malcolm.

I turned my head away but, every few minutes, I snatched a glance down at the bar where Lucinda was chatting to a stick-thin friend with hair scraped back in a tight bun. By the time the performance began I was a quivering wreck.

In the interval I refused to go to the bar, in case I bumped into Lucinda, so Genevieve went on her own. By the final act, I was dying for a pee and closed my eyes to block out the swans prancing on stage. Genevieve poked me in the ribs to silence a looming snore.

"Stay at my place tonight?" she suggested, as we shuffled out of the auditorium with the crowd surging around us.

I shook my head. "Have to get home."

"Don't do this to me Paul," she held onto my arm, forcing me to stop in the aisle so a queue of people built up behind us.

Lucinda could have been anywhere in that crowd. I pulled away, strode on ahead and, when I emerged onto Bow Street, I'd lost sight of Genevieve.

Even our disastrous night at the ballet didn't deter her from planning future events.

"See what I've got for you," Genevieve said one evening, in the tone of voice she adopted when breaking news to Manifold's senior team, so they couldn't tell if the news was good or bad.

We were at her house in Chiswick and I was perched on the sofa, wondering if I dared risk heading home. I'd told Emma I was at a dinner in Manchester, but I could easily have changed my story and say I'd sneaked off early to catch a train. Genevieve handed me a bulging envelope.

"What's this?"

My heart thumped as I slit it open with my index finger and a small avalanche of glossy brochures and lanyards dropped into my lap. Speechless, I examined the details of a travel package that must have cost thousands.

A smile flickered on Genevieve's lips. "Sorry about the hotel. Metropole was the best available."

I gaped at her, my hands lifting of their own accord, to

clutch thin air. "But this is impossible, Genevieve. Monaco in May? There's no way."

"Of course you can. It's business, right?"

"Formula One Grand Prix? Manifold would never spend this sort of money on entertaining clients."

"But Emma doesn't know that."

The package she'd bought was non-refundable and I forced myself to smile and pretend I was thrilled we were going on the trip of a lifetime to the Monaco Grand Prix. Until then, I'd convinced myself our affair was harmless, but now she'd ramped it up. I knew I should refuse the trip and end the relationship, but I was scared of the havoc she could wreak on my career and marriage.

Motor racing's not normally my thing—I prefer the horses—but Monaco was hedonism disguised as sport and ticked all the boxes of self-gratification. I tried to imagine Emma with me but I couldn't: the waste, the luxury, the environmental impact would appal her.

Genevieve had booked the motor racing package and hotel, so it fell to me to pay for all the frills: meals, taxis and a Riviera tour in a chartered yacht with lunch and champagne. When I got home all my credit cards were maxed out.

I applied for new ones and argued hard to increase the paltry credit limits being offered. Until the first one arrived, I had to stand in line at Wimbledon station each morning to buy day return rail tickets because I couldn't afford a monthly season.

Around this time, life at home changed for the better. As Mollie became less clingy and learnt to sleep at night, Emma turned her sunflower face back towards me and the spark returned to our marriage. I came so close to dumping Genevieve. Then came Dorek's accident and the stakes were too high.

CHAPTER 9

EMMA

Late October 2015

As our half-term visit to France approaches, Paul's enthusiasm has become my own and we feel like a team, embarking on an exciting new venture, together.

We've booked a room at the only hotel in Sainte Violette but the foyer is gloomy and deserted when we enter. Paul rings the hand bell on the desk and Madame Cordier bustles out from behind a curtain to check us in.

I remember when we ate here, back in the summer, she wore a blue dress with a nipped-in waist and ensured her team of student waitresses tended promptly to diners' needs. Her image has slipped and now she's dressed in a slouchy cardigan over trousers.

"What time is dinner?" Paul asks, signing the register and handing over his credit card.

"Ah, *non*," Madame Cordier spreads her hands in front of her as she explains it's winter hours and she doesn't offer evening meals out of season. "*Désolé!*"

She doesn't sound sorry at all.

Our room is vast and smells of dust. The décor dates from a pre-vintage era with a tapestry bedspread, immense embroidered curtains and a carved bed with long bolster pillow. The wallpaper is black with huge pink flowers and the en-suite comprises a washbasin and a free-standing shower in a cubicle that resembles a telephone kiosk with frosted glass panes.

"Where are we going to eat?" asks Paul.

"She said to try the bar."

Paul sighs and kicks off his shoes. He lies on the bed, reading from his tablet, while I shower. The water has two settings: scalding or so icy it makes me gasp. I opt for being boiled alive and use my own shower gel because the complimentary bottle of Gardenia looks, and smells, as if it's been there since the 1950s, but the white fluffy towel is enormous and comforting. I wrap it around me and shuffle across to the bed.

Paul puts one arm around me and slips his free hand under the towel to stroke my breast. The towel slides from my shoulders as I lean over him, my wet hair dripping onto his face and we kiss.

"I'm sorry I've been neglecting you," I whisper. "I love you."

He pulls me closer. I shut my eyes and relax into his embrace as we rediscover the familiar curves and angles of each other's bodies.

The church clock strikes seven and Paul stirs. "What if the bar's not serving food either?" He props himself up on one elbow.

"Let's go and find out."

I put on the tailored jacket I've brought for the meeting with the *notaire* and we walk down the stairs and exit through the silent hotel lobby.

Paul drapes his arm around my shoulders and steers us along the dark street of tightly-shuttered homes and businesses. A thin drizzle settles on my hair. I feel it frizzing up and smooth it with my free hand. There's no illuminated sign outside the bar and the interior lighting is so dim we only notice it after we've walked past. We turn back, Paul gives the door a firm push and it opens.

The proprietor glances up from his newspaper and seems to flinch at the sight of customers.

"*Bonsoir.*" He walks round from behind the bar to introduce himself. "Anton Bonneau."

"Paul and Emma Willshire," Paul says and we all shake hands.

"You visited here in the summer." His voice has an accusatory tone, perhaps because we never came to his bar, but the village grapevine knows everything. "And you have come back to buy an 'ouse. What will you drink?"

"Um, white wine?" I ask.

Anton measures out a thimbleful of Muscadet.

Paul has a draught lager then takes a laminated snack menu from the bar. "Can we order some food?"

"Lilianne is not 'ere," he says. "But some things I can do."

We scan the menu.

"Hamburger and *frites?*" asks Paul.

"That I cannot do."

"Omelette?"

"No."

"Perhaps a *croque monsieur?*"

He nods and our choice is made for us. Anton disappears through a secret door and we carry our drinks to a table.

When we entered, the bar was empty except for a teenager who appears from the toilets and starts pummelling a pinball machine. He stinks of cigarettes.

From the kitchen wafts a smell of grilling cheese and wisps of smoke.

Paul tugs a napkin out of an aluminium holder, pulls out his pen and sketches a design.

"Bedrooms at this end and en-suite here. " He draws a cube. "Family bathroom there."

His ideas are grander than I expected, but he's only sketched two bedrooms.

"We can't expect Owen to share with Mollie for much longer."

Paul applies himself to the challenge. "If we can get planning permission to add a wing here." He sketches an L-shape extension off the original cube. "Bathroom would fit here—between these two bedrooms."

"Much better," I say. "But. . . it looks quite expensive."

He frowns. "Sure. Could be twice what we've paid for the property."

I choke on my wine. "I'll have to run the French conversation club for a hundred years to raise that sort of money."

"Stop worrying, Emma." He grins. "It'll be fine. No need to do everything at once. And I can easily borrow more against the house."

He's right. Property prices in Wimbledon have shot up.

Anton approaches carrying three plates. Along with the *croque monsieurs*, he presents a side of French fries: bland yellow food on white plates, ungarnished by a shred of lettuce or tomato.

"Is okay?" Anton calls to us from his stronghold behind the bar.

"*C'est bon*," I lie.

A single fisherman's lantern dangling above our heads casts a pool of concentrated light on our table and an electronic fly catcher contraption above the door emits a chill blue light.

The bar is gloomy but decent lighting and a coat of paint would freshen it up.

"How does he make money?" I ask Paul.

"Profit must be in lunches and summer visitors."

Paul has hardly touched his beer, but my thimbleful of wine is empty. Anton approaches, brandishing the Muscadet bottle in front of him like a weapon.

"*Encore du vin?*" I reach out to cover my glass with my hand, but he's already started to pour. "*Merci.*"

I wonder about the life of the village. It can't be much fun for Anton, waiting behind the bar for customers who never come.

*

The next morning, we're the only guests in the breakfast room. A young girl with dirt under her fingernails serves us stale croissants and huge bowls of coffee. We linger because our appointment at the *notaire's* office in Limoges is not until eleven.

A receptionist takes our names and waves us through a door into the waiting room where a man in a belted raincoat, with a 1970s walrus moustache, steps forward to greet us. He reminds me of Inspector Clouseau from those *Pink Panther* films my dad found so hilarious, but when he speaks, his accent is English.

"You must be the Willshires." He extends his hand. "Henri Wilson. I've been drafted in to do the translating."

I catch Paul's eye. Does he think I'm not up to it?

"All part of the service when the buyer's from abroad," Henri explains kindly.

The door opens and three women in sensible coats troop in. "Here come the opposition," he whispers in my ear.

Two men follow, one in a scuffed leather jacket, the other in a suit and tie. They traverse the room, shaking hands with us and murmuring, by way of introduction: *Monsieur, Madame*.

Paul is leafing through our file of paperwork, so Henri takes the seat next to me.

"Madame Durand had no children," he explains. "So her property is divided between distant relatives. They've waited ten years for their money. Everyone turns up to check they get their fair share."

The receptionist ushers us upstairs into a meeting room where thick carpets and reproduction Louis Quinze furniture contrast strongly with the austere waiting room below. We take our seats around a polished oval table. There aren't enough chairs so the receptionist, assisted by Henri, fetches two more from another room.

The *notaire* greets us and confirms our payment has arrived. He clears his throat and launches the meeting, reading aloud from impenetrable French legal documents, pausing for breath and nodding at Henri, who translates for us. I'm glad now not to be cast in the role of linguistic lead and smile my gratitude. Henri nods back.

Formalities move rapidly. When it comes to me, there's a short hiatus over my personal details. I use Paul's surname now; before that it was Zak's, but it turns out they want to go right back to my maiden name, so the name that gets recorded alongside Paul's on the property title is 'Jones.'

After that, the meeting gallops to a close. The receptionist hands Paul a pack of signed documents; the Durand relatives beam; the *notaire* unfreezes and we all head to the bar next door to celebrate over a drink. The Durands don't stay long and the *notaire* goes back to his office, leaving us with Henri.

Henri stirs his coffee, pausing with spoon poised. "Perhaps I can help you organise the renovations?"

"Are you a builder too?" Paul asks.

"No, but I gather there's no electricity supply at Les Quatre Vents, or water. The old lady used the well."

"So. . ."

"I could arrange that for you." Henri clears his throat. "That's what I do. Fix things for people, help them navigate the bureaucracy."

"How much will it cost?" Paul asks suspiciously.

"It depends. There are different types of electricity connection. How much voltage will you need?"

"I mean your fee?"

"Two hundred and fifty euros. That's for arranging both utilities and being on site when they install the meters," Henri says.

"Okay. Come over to Les Quatre Vents tomorrow. You know where it is?"

"I do. I live in the next hamlet, a few kilometres further on."

"Aren't you British?" Paul asks.

Henri smiles. "My father was, but my mother was French. I grew up in Bristol—never planned to live here but the French way of life is like a siren call to some Brits—once it grabs you, it won't let go."

*

The following morning, the hotel breakfast ritual improves. The *croissants* are fresh and flaky and there's a choice of *pain au chocolat* or *pain aux raisins*. The young waitress has painted her fingernails purple so I can't tell if they're still dirty underneath.

"You ready?" asks Paul and I nod, swallowing the last of my coffee.

Les Quatre Vents lies about a mile outside Sainte Violette, separated from the village by sodden fields of cattle, a mill, a river and a narrow bridge with stone parapets. From the pack the *notaire* gave him yesterday, Paul produces a massive key, resembling something a sixteenth century jailer might have used and unlocks the newly-rehung front door. It groans and swings outwards on its hinges.

"Doubt we'll ever get it locked again." Paul laughs. "Let me carry you over the threshold?"

"Don't be daft. I'll crack my head on the lintel."

As my eyes adjust to the dim interior, something tickles my face: a spider's web; I brush it away with my hand.

Since August, the part-dirt, part-concrete floor has cracked and insects have made homes in the spaces. Creepy-crawlies don't bother me but I'm glad to escape back outside and wander around looking for a task—any task. Autumn leaves snap beneath my wellington boots and I seize a rake. Soon I've gathered a large pile; the physical work lifts my spirits and brings me out in a sweat.

"We can burn this in the old fireplace," says Paul, who has been digging out old tree roots and stripping away ivy suckers from the front wall, his muscles tensing beneath his t-shirt as he works.

While he splits logs with an axe, I lug armfuls of kindling inside to burn the leaves in the old fireplace. The leaves are snap-dry and fire sparks from the first match. Soon it's spitting and flaring but the chimney breast wall is riddled with holes and fumes seep back inside the room. Coughing, spluttering and laughing, we scramble outside and watch grey smoke curling up into the sky.

A wine-red Renault 4 crunches through a gear change and stutters along our track.

"Thought they were extinct," I mutter to Paul, as the car rattles to a halt and Henri clambers out, zipping his leather jacket against the wind.

"So you've decided to burn down the ruin and start again?" he asks.

"Tried, but not yet succeeded," agrees Paul.

Smoky and sweating from all that raking, digging and fire-raising, I roll up my sleeves.

"Sorry we can't offer you a coffee, Henri."

"Because there's no electricity," he agrees. "And that's what I'm here to sort out." He draws Paul aside. "First decision—where to place the meters."

"Where would you recommend?"

"Perhaps further away from the building because you don't know how much you'll need to demolish."

They stroll along the drive and Henri points out options.

"You'll be able to turn off the water when you're away," says Henri. "No flooding."

The land is low lying and the river flowing under the old bridge is less than two hundred metres away from the end of our track.

"Does it flood around here?"

"Not since I've lived here. But, with climate change, who knows?"

Paul takes his outline design for the rebuild from his pocket and talks Henri through his thoughts.

"I'll introduce you to an architect. His name's Maxim and his practice is in Limoges. He can draw up the plans and apply for planning permission."

I've no idea how complicated our project is but I half-expected Paul would want to draw up the plans himself. I remember him telling me his ambition was to train as an architect, but he'd had to settle for becoming a surveyor. His training included designing simple structures and he once drove me and Owen to Hertfordshire to show us a warehouse he'd designed early in his career, pointing out design details as proudly as if it were a mansion.

"How did you make so many contacts?" Paul asks.

Henri grins and I realise he's younger than I thought, perhaps late-thirties. It's the ridiculous moustache and the broken capillaries on his face that make him look older. Signs of a life lived outdoors? Drugs, alcohol? Or a combination.

"When my mother died, I inherited her family's house. It's in a small hamlet of four houses, a few kilometres from here."

"Is there enough work for a business helping foreigners move into the area?"

"Sure. It's not just Brits. I have Dutch and German clients too. I do translating, organising gas and electricity, finding builders—I even help people set up their own businesses."

"It must be precarious."

He nods. "I own the house, so I get by. And I work with the *notaire* to publicise properties for sale."

I remember that in France it's not just estate agents who sell properties. *Notaires* do, too.

Henri leans inside his car, rifles through some papers and produces a grubby business card. Paul is scribbling his email address and phone number on an envelope so Henri hands his card to me.

"Don't hesitate to call me if you need any information or advice."

I can't think of what advice I might need but I thank him and stash the card in my purse.

"I'll forward you the water and electricity companies' contracts to sign," says Henri, taking our address details from Paul.

He gets into his car and drives off, winding down his window to wave.

"What d'you think?" Paul asks. "Can we trust him?"

I hesitate. "I think so. But there's something a little strange about him."

"Odd, d'you mean?"

"No. More like lonely."

Why do I recognise that in him? Is it because, until I met Paul, that was me—isolated, lonely and too proud to confess it.

*

"Looking forward to another *croque monsieur?*" I joke, as we traipse from the hotel to the bar.

"Where's everyone expected to eat?" grumbles Paul, as if it's my fault.

I'm not surprised his mood has slumped. He's spent the last hour in our hotel room hunched over his phone, returning calls from work, while I showered and read my book.

We push open the door. Anton folds up his newspaper and brings out the bottle of Muscadet, untouched since I last drank from it.

"Can we get something to eat?" Paul asks.

Anton's fake smile evaporates. Perhaps the *croque monsieur* banquet he cooked for us on Monday night was a stretch too far, but he takes pity on us. "I will call Lilianne."

His mobile is lying on the bar. He selects a number and gabbles in a thick regional accent. I get the impression that Lilianne's not happy.

Anton clicks off his phone. "All right. She will come. Please wait."

We sit on bar stools, uptight and silent, sipping our drinks in an atmosphere thick with embarrassment. Although I know Anton speaks good English, I compose some French small talk to lob into the vacuum, but Paul is ahead of me.

"Anton, how do you make a living from this bar?"

I wince but Anton shrugs, his face is shuttered, but his reply is frank. "Sometimes I do, sometimes not. Sunday I close. Other days Monday to Friday we do, how do you call it, *ouvriers* lunch."

"That's the set menu for workmen," I remind Paul.

I've always wondered how electricians, plumbers and skilled craftsmen focus on their afternoon's work after three courses and a quarter litre of wine.

"And I have Lilianne," continues Anton. "She comes each morning for the cooking. Ah, she is here."

Lilianne knows the knack of opening the stiff bar door without making it creak. She steps inside, her dark hair dishevelled from the wind. As the door clunks shut behind her, she takes a band from her pocket and pulls her hair up into a rough knot. Ignoring Anton, she inclines her head towards us.

"What do you want?"

"Omelette?" I ask, hopefully.

"Cheeseburger and *frites?*" Paul says.

Lilianne nods, slides her arms out of her coat and hangs it over the back of a chair. She strides around the bar and disappears through the mirrored door into the kitchen. The freezer lid groans open, a knife taps on a chopping board and olive oil sizzles in a pan. The bar fills with the aroma of melting butter but no smoke and no smell of burning.

Anton rouses from his gloom and asks us, "Where do you come from in England?"

"London," Paul replies.

Anton becomes animated, telling us of a journey by overnight coach to watch a rugby match at Twickenham. Paul and Anton swap Six Nations war stories until Lilianne appears with our food. She sets the plates on the bar, puts on her coat, nods to Anton and strides off into the dark street. She's been there barely ten minutes.

My omelette has a firm coat, melting cheese inside and a salad garnish. "Delicious."

"She is very good, yes," agrees Anton. "But, for me, this place is not working out."

"Why's that?" asks Paul between mouthfuls of his longed-for meat feast.

"People here have no money. Next month I will leave. Try my luck in the south."

Paul leans towards Anton, propping his elbow on the bar. "So, tell me—roughly how much rent do you pay for the bar?"

If we were in England, even Paul wouldn't ask such a direct question but, in France, politics, religion, race are freely debated, so why not money? Anton doesn't seem to find our interest intrusive and openly shares a few details of his income and outgoings while Paul listens, head on one side—a study in empathy, nodding in the right places. When Anton takes our empty plates to the kitchen, he turns to me and says, "He's paying a peppercorn rent— I don't get why he's struggling."

"Perhaps his gloomy personality keeps people away?" I suggest.

Paul sighs. "Sometimes I dream of jacking it all in to run a bar."

"Who hasn't had that fantasy!" I reply, although Paul has surprised me.

For years I've worked casual jobs in catering and often wondered how hard it would be to set up in business. Once I checked out the cost of mobile catering vans—four and a half grand on eBay—but running a bar is not an ambition I'd have associated with Paul.

CHAPTER 10

EMMA

End of October 2015

My estrangement from my parents lasted more than three years and it was Paul who engineered an end to that unhappy period. I'd confided in him how I'd boxed myself in, too proud to make the first move. Without telling me, Paul contacted my dad and they met up for a chat.

The following weekend, we were invited to visit them in Wales and, slowly, filled in the gaps of the missing years. Since then, I've made it a rule never to trespass on my parents' goodwill, so the morning after we arrive home from France, I drive down the M4 to collect Mollie from my dad at our usual handover point in Marlborough.

On the way home to London, I reflect on what Dad confided in me over lunch while Mollie had gone to get a new colouring-in sheet from the waiter.

"Mollie thinks you're planning a permanent move to France," he said. "She's been quite upset about it."

I guess it's Owen who's been drip feeding her this idea. He loves baiting her. I'll be having words with him when he comes back from his half-term visit to his dad.

Since Zak stopped working overseas and moved to a role in

London, their father-son bond is strengthening. I'm happy for them but there's a cost to our family unit because, gradually, Owen is turning away from Paul. The flare up during our summer holiday was a symptom of the growing rift between them.

Mollie shows no sign of being upset. She chats about her mini-break and the trips with my dad. Grandma, who now works as something senior in Ofsted, scarcely gets a mention.

When we get home, I call Paul's office number but it goes straight through to voicemail. I'm about to try his mobile when Mollie distracts me. I give her the job of weighing the pasta, but she soon tires of it and runs off to the sitting room, peering out of the window, waiting for Paul.

"Here he is!" she calls, racing me to the door. "Daddy!" She flings her arms around his knees. "I've missed you."

"And I missed you, too, darling."

He swings her up into his arms, her curls brushing against his cheek.

"I've made you a present," she announces.

Paul sets her down and she scampers off upstairs.

"She's probably going to give you the picture she said was for me." I grin at him.

His lips try—and fail—to curl into a smile.

"What's wrong?" I ask.

He touches my arm lightly. "Emma, we need to talk—later, when she's asleep." He keeps his voice low as Mollie's footsteps clatter back down the stairs.

"Something serious?" I feel the beginning of a headache and touch my fingers to my forehead, hoping it will abate.

"Something important." Paul bends down to accept Mollie's drawing.

"Do you like it, Daddy?"

"I love it."

Her small fingers fasten onto the hem of his jacket. "Come and read my story."

I linger in the hall until I hear the tap running in the bathroom where Paul is helping Mollie to clean her teeth, then go to the kitchen and boil water for our pasta. Steam rises from the pan turning the kitchen into a sauna. I open the window. Cold air rushes in.

"She was exhausted," says Paul coming into the kitchen. "She's fallen asleep already."

I lift my head and summon a wan smile.

"What's wrong?" Paul asks.

"Migraine." I grimace, realising I can't fight it any longer. I used to get them often. "Sorry. Look, dinner's ready." I get to my feet, point to the saucepan. "I can't eat. Think I'll go to bed."

"Sure." Paul kisses me gently on the cheek. "You go up. We'll talk in a bit."

Leaving him to his supper, I go upstairs to the bathroom and splash cold water on my face. I crawl into bed and screw my eyes shut but I can't relax, then I remember Paul had something to discuss with me. I must stay awake until he comes up. . .

*

A mobile beeps and sparks me into morning consciousness. Incoming texts usually signal toxic work messages on Paul's mobile, but this is definitely mine—it's a WhatsApp message from Owen asking me to fetch him from Zak's.

My drowsy head slumps back against the pillow as I reply:

> *R u sure? Thought u*
> *staying till Sun teatime?*

Owen: *Stuff to do.*

> *Homework?*

Owen: *Yeah.*

"Can't wait to see Owen," says Mollie, as we drive to Streatham where Zak's bought a house with a mainline railway running along behind his garden fence.

Every few minutes express trains rattle his windows. When we were married, Zak and I lived in rented flats and never owned a property. After we'd split up, he became a nomad with no fixed country of abode but, when he returned to London, house prices had rocketed. He blames me for that too and resents that I've landed on my feet in Wimbledon.

While I'm reversing into a tight parking space, Zak appears on his doorstep. I steel myself to confront him.

Zak's still a breath-catchingly handsome man but he has sad eyes and a wounded expression. He used to shave his head but his hair is longer now and flecked with grey.

He steps onto the pavement towards me, as if guarding his home from my malign presence, and greets me with barbed politeness, not meeting my eyes or saying, 'Hi'.

"Owen tells me you've bought a house in France."

I laugh. "You couldn't call it a house. It's some land with a tumbledown *longère* and a few outbuildings we're converting into a holiday home."

"Holiday home. That's not what Owen said." His voice has a steely edge.

I glance at Zak's neglected window boxes, stumps of geraniums, wizened and throttled by grass.

"Don't be melodramatic, Zak. It's a holiday home."

"That better be right, Emma. Like I told you when we split—my boy needed his mum when he was little. Now he's older, he needs his dad too."

Footsteps clatter along the uncarpeted hallway.

"Hey, Mum!" Owen appears in the doorway and thrusts a carrier bag full of dirty washing into my hands.

"Hi—we missed you." He ducks away from my kiss. "Where's your rucksack?"

"Here." He tries to dump that into my arms too.

"Hey, son. You carry that to the car yourself, okay."

"Yeah, Dad."

They fist-bump, exchanging identical grins.

"See you real soon, okay?"

"Okay," Owen calls over his shoulder.

Zak doesn't wait to wave goodbye and retreats inside, banging the door.

"Owen, Owen," Mollie sings as she's reunited with her big brother and he seems touchingly happy to see her.

"Good time?" I ask, crunching the gears, as I ram the car into reverse.

"All right."

"Anything you want to tell me?"

"Nothing."

As we drive away from Zak's animosity, skirting Tooting Bec Common and turning left at the underground station, pedestrians seem hell bent on stepping out in front of my car.

At Colliers Wood, Owen glances up from his iPad and announces, "Dad's got religion."

"Really?"

When we got married—admittedly in haste—I'd suggested a church wedding, thinking he'd prefer it, but Zak insisted on Cardiff Register Office.

"Last Sunday we spent, like, the whole day in some church. So boring."

"Which one?"

"How should I know. I don't friggin' live here."

"Language, Owen."

"And Dad's changed. He says God's called him. He's almost like a lay preacher now."

My grip tightens on the steering wheel. "I can't believe it."

"He made me go to Sunday school."

"I want to go to Sunday school," says Mollie, swinging her feet and kicking the back of my seat. "But I don't want to go to France."

CHAPTER 11

EMMA

End of October 2015

There's a rectangle of dry ground on the damp road outside our house—a clue that Paul has recently driven away. He didn't say he was going out and his breakfast dish is still on the table.

"Right, you two. Time for some chores."

"Homework!" says Owen, brandishing his folder as a get-out-of-jail free card and disappearing to his room.

Mollie and I go next door to collect Dylan, her rabbit, from our neighbour who's been looking after him. As soon as we get home, she lets him out of his cage and hugs him against her chest.

"He smells of cabbage, Mummy."

"Better clean out his hutch then."

"Ugh, no! You do it."

Around six-thirty, Paul appears, shaking rain from his anorak onto the kitchen floor, and dumps a soggy newspaper on the table. I raise one eyebrow—Paul and newsprint ceased contact years ago.

"Your tablet not working?" I ask.

"Didn't take it."

"Where did you go?"

"Football—Wimbledon. Over at their ground in Kingston."

"Really?" I raise an eyebrow.

Paul's a rugby man through and through. On International days when I'm belting out *Mae Hen Wlad Fy Nhadau* or *Delilah* and shaking my cuddly red dragon at the television screen, he plies me with cold statistics and brags about the England team's superiority over Wales. Paul only attends football matches if he's entertaining clients and Manifold's corporate allegiance is Chelsea.

"Can I come with you next time?" Owen asks over supper.

"Sure you can."

This small sign of Paul and Owen edging towards common ground fills me with hope.

"Don't you want to hear about our adventures in France?" I ask.

Both children turn blank eyes towards me, and I realise they've forgotten we went away. Les Quatre Vents is a blip on their radar. I tell them about Anton and the *croques monsieur* and invite Paul to comment on our brush with starvation but he's hunched over his plate, not listening.

"Staying to watch TV with us?" I ask Owen, after Mollie has gone to bed.

"Nah. Stuff to do." He flees upstairs to his boy-cave.

I make a pot of coffee and carry it through to the sitting room. The curtains are still open but the only light in the room comes from a table lamp. Paul is standing with his back to me, silhouetted against the window.

Outside, the grit-grey sky is incubating another storm. Headlights of passing cars glint on a plane tree that's breaking up the pavement outside our house. A violent swirl of wind catches our neighbour's wheelie bin and sends it clattering against their gate.

As I set down the tray and pour the coffee, Paul turns and attempts a smile, but it won't stick to his face. He sits down heavily on an armchair.

"What is it?" I ask, feeling his hand tremble as I pass him a mug.

"It's happened." He rocks forward and perches on the edge of his seat.

"What?"

"I'm going to be made redundant."

Shock sucks oxygen from my lungs. "What? They can't do that!"

He hangs his head.

"You must fight it. Take them to a tribunal."

"I wish it was that simple. Manning called me in for 'a chat' and asked me to sign a bloody compromise agreement."

I find a tissue stuffed in my cardigan sleeve, dab my face and crumple it in my fist.

"Say something, Emma."

I can't. I don't want a row. I know I ought to throw my arms around him and comfort him but I blurt out, "How much will you get?"

Before the words are out of my mouth I know I've said the wrong thing. Paul's chin jerks up, as if I've punched him.

"Not much. Only been there two years."

"But why now? Is it because of Dorek's accident?"

"Who can say? The report's still not out but everyone blames me. Perhaps it would have happened anyway."

"That's so unfair."

"Since the accident, Manifold's work's fallen off a cliff. They mismanaged the PR and new clients won't touch us."

White-faced, he bangs his mug down on the table and I

realise I'm the only one he can vent his wrath on; I'm the only one here.

"Plus, they're insisting I work part of my notice."

I grope for words to comfort him, but my head is tangled with worries about the children and their future.

"I thought they'd put me on gardening leave," Paul continues. "Give me space to look for another job but Manning refused."

"Why would he do that?"

"He says he's going to take over my work for a while. I'd say that's impossible but it's not my problem."

"I'm so sorry—" I begin but he cuts me off.

"I don't fucking give a damn."

I sit down heavily on the sofa and something sharp jabs my buttock. It's a knitting needle, attached to the Aran sweater I'm making for Mollie. I pick it up and stare at the complex pattern.

Paul watches me with sullen eyes. "What are you doing?"

"Nothing."

My ball of wool drops to the floor, rolls towards Paul's armchair. With a reflex movement of his foot, he taps it back towards me as if it were a football.

"There's worse," he says. "No way I can dress this up. We'll have to sell the house."

I stare at him. I can't swallow. "What the hell do you mean? We'd be mad to do that."

"If we don't sell the house, we'll lose it. I increased the mortgage and haven't kept up the payments. The outstanding loan might be more than the house is worth."

I gape at him. Rain hammers on the window pane. I stay silent.

"Say something, Emma!"

"How could you do that without telling me?"

This is like a soap opera. This doesn't happen in real life.

"It was when Mollie wasn't sleeping and you were exhausted. I didn't want to add to your worries."

"So instead, you put Mollie, and our whole family, at risk?"

"I'm sorry." His face is set hard and wrinkles mark his brow. He reaches out and tries to draw me to him. I sense he's trembling and I stiffen. "We have to face this together. My redundancy pay-off will help, but it isn't enough. If we don't sell quickly, the house will be repossessed."

"And where will we live?"

"We'll work something out."

We stumble across to the sofa and sit down, his hip bone pressing against mine. I close my eyes and memories of our years together crowd my mind. Years when Paul has been supporting me and my son, because Zak's child maintenance payments were erratic. *Could this have contributed to his financial problems?*

I remember how Paul mended the rift between me and my parents; how he took time off work to support me when Mollie wouldn't sleep and I was plagued with migraines. Isn't that what 'in sickness and in health' is all about? Now we're in the next phase 'for richer for poorer,' and it's my turn to stand by him.

I remind myself that the house and mortgage were Paul's territory from before we were married. Was that why I've never insisted he shared the details with me? Because it would have felt like trespass?

Paul stutters more apologies, "I shouldn't be putting you and the kids through this. It's all my fault."

Outside our window, rain hammers down, but the eye of the storm has moved on.

"I've had it with this life, Emma." Paul tilts his head up and meets my eyes. "The hours, the stress. I want a fresh start."

I understand now where this is leading. There's a pattern and everything is connected—I should have worked it out.

"You mean France, don't you? You never intended it to be just a holiday home."

"Things have changed. With my small pay-off and what's left after selling this house, we'll have enough cash to start the renovations."

"Well. . ."

"It would be a new life for us—as a family."

My eyes feel hot and gritty. "You really think that's best for us?"

He holds me so close, I feel his rapid heartbeat through his sweater. "I do."

I'm not as confident as Paul in thinking this is the right choice but as long as we're together, as a family, we can stay strong.

"I'll support you," I hear myself say.

Light rain whispers against the window pane and the tree's branches stand stiff and unruffled.

Paul kisses my cheek. "I love you, Emma. I'd never do anything to hurt you. You know that, don't you?"

CHAPTER 12

EMMA

Early November 2015

The estate agent pokes into every corner, takes photographs, laser-measures from bay window into the tiniest alcove and converts our warm, comfortable house into a list of cold statistics.

"We'll soon shift this," he tells me, with a smirk. "We have a list of waiting buyers."

Promising to confirm the price in writing, he departs, his jaunty footsteps retreating down the drive. I plump down on a kitchen chair and stare at the number I've jotted on the back of my hand.

The agent's figure sets my heart racing because I now know how much we need to raise from the house sale to pay off the mortgage. Paul has kept to his promise and given me access to his statements.

"There's a drawdown facility," he explained. "So I don't have to seek approval every time I need to raise funds."

"What's this?" I asked. The statement showed a series of missed monthly payments in the spring, a top up in early summer and a sizeable drawdown in September. "Is this the money for Les Quatre Vents?"

"Yes, this mortgage arrangement allows me to underpay or overpay. When I received my bonus in June, I caught up the missed payments and that gave me headroom to borrow for Les Quatre Vents."

I remember his blasé reassurances when I challenged him about buying it.

"Even though you'd let your monthly payments slip again?"

"Once I'm unemployed it will be hopeless."

"And is that all?" I question.

"It is."

"Now I know, I can help."

I ring Paul to report back on the agent's visit and, as I wait for him to answer, I gaze around our cosy family kitchen where Mollie took her first faltering steps. This house has been a happy place, our sanctuary. Leaving it will be a wrench.

Paul's office phone goes straight to voicemail so I try his mobile. When he answers, I hear a kettle coming to the boil. He must be in Manifold's staff kitchen.

When I tell him the suggested price, he gives a low whistle.

"Are you sure he said that much?"

"Quite sure. If we get that price, we should clear over thirty thousand—enough to make a start on the renovations in France."

Before the particulars of sale have been published, my phone starts ringing. From early evening, prospective purchasers trek to our door: young families upsizing from flats; smug couples, leap-frogging onto a higher rung of the property ladder, bringing a buzz of nervous activity into the house. It's painful to view our family home through the eyes of strangers.

After sitting out three guided tours, I offer to do the next one myself. The agent looks dubious but agrees to sit in the kitchen with his paperwork while I show a young couple, Will and Lucy, around. Twisting the woven friendship bracelet Mollie bought me, round and round my wrist, l long for them to see the house through my eyes before they start mentally demolishing walls.

Lucy's ecstatic about every room. "I love this colour scheme. Did you make those blinds yourself? "

While Mollie shows Lucy her bedroom, Will pulls me aside and explains that they can only afford the house because Lucy's parents recently died in an accident and left her everything.

"She's been distraught with grief. If we get this house it might give her back a purpose."

Picturing Will and Lucy living here brings brief solace. Offers trickle in. There's so much interest, the estate agent organises an open house, followed by an auction for prospective buyers to submit sealed bids.

On the day of the open house, there's practically a stampede. Paul can't face it. He takes Owen and Mollie swimming, but I lurk in the garden, driven outside by sharp-elbowed couples and buy-to-let investors picking over our home, exposing the entrails of our life.

When the agent calls us with the results of the sealed bids, I keep my fingers crossed, hoping Lucy and Will might get the house. They don't. It's sold to cash buyers and they want to move in before Christmas.

"You understand why we have to do this, Owen?" My voice sounds unnatural, as if I'm pleading with him.

He pushes past me, out through the back door and into

the garden. The kitchen wall vibrates as he kicks his football against it, time after time.

The following day I summon courage to phone Zak and ask, "Can I come and see you?"

There's a pause before he replies. "What about?"

"Owen, of course."

"When do you want to come?"

But I don't want to go to his house. It would be too personal, awkward.

"Let's meet halfway. How about The Windmill on Clapham Common? On Saturday?"

"Ah—neutral territory. Must be something incendiary."

The next day I hand in my notice and tell the school Mollie won't be coming back after Christmas. Mollie's class teacher is thrilled that we are moving to France—more thrilled than me—and designs a day of class activities around our move.

"What an adventure! She'll grow up bilingual."

I raise a bleak smile but the last thing I need is a jolly reminder of how our life is turning on its head.

On the celebration day, Mollie's classmates dress up in blue-and-white-striped t-shirts and bring *baguettes*.

I keep a low profile, arranging the picnic on a table and fending off the children, who hover like gannets, sticking their fingers into a box of *Camembert* and trying to tear scraps of crust off a *baguette*.

"Come and sit on the carpet," the teacher calls. "Mollie's mum is going to teach us a song in French."

Mollie jumps up and urges me forward, basking in her celebrity status, not understanding how her life is about to change. I take a seat next to the teacher and stretch my lips into the brightest smile I can muster as their eager faces stare back at me.

"Right. We're going to learn the words of *Frère Jacques.*"

*

Paul takes the stack of supper plates from me, rinses them and arranges them with engineering precision in the dishwasher.

"Sometimes, I dare to believe the investigation won't lead to prosecution," he says. "Maybe we'll get a lesser sanction, a fine for health and safety breaches."

Paul chooses times like this, when he has his back to me, to start important conversations. The dark nimbus of his work crisis still hovers above us. When he turns to face me, I trump his anxieties with one of my own.

"I'm meeting Zak on Saturday to talk about our move."

"This could be the best thing for Owen," Paul says.

"How so?"

"Living in rural France instead of London. While he's at a vulnerable age."

"What are you suggesting?" I raise my eyebrows at him.

"Gangs, knife crime. . ."

"Nonsense." But the thought, once planted, germinates.

On Saturday, I drive to Clapham Common. As I stride towards the pub, the wind ramps up and I turn back to fetch my quilted jacket from the car. I need to look confident; I can't let Zak see me shivering—but as I open the bar door, a fug of warm air engulfs me and brings me out in a sweat.

Zak is already there, leaning back in his chair, arms folded behind his head and eyes half-closed. Zen-like.

The pub echoes with laughter from the youthful Saturday lunchtime crowd. I'm not many years older than them but I feel like an ancient soul as I battle through the press of bodies.

Zak spots me and half-rises from his seat. "Drink?"

"Orange juice, thanks."

He's drinking Coke. Zak never was much of a drinker.

He returns from the bar, sets my drink on the table and waits for me to speak. I curl my hand around the cold glass and take a quick swallow before raising my eyes to look at him. Our break-up was my decision, but Zak didn't see it coming. His reaction was brutal, not in a physical sense, but in the way he scorned me, stamped me out of existence.

"What do you want to talk about?" he asks.

I remember how, as our divorce proceeded, he would only communicate through solicitors. I couldn't risk running up huge bills so I conceded everything he asked. He made modest financial provision for us, though his payments were erratic, but he locked in his parental rights over our son.

Over the intervening years, nothing has thawed between us. When we're forced to talk, it's always about visit arrangements or Owen's schooling. We never enquire after one another's health or extended family. Our exchanges are brusque as we toss clipped monosyllables at one another like shuttlecocks over a high net.

"We're moving," I say. Zak fixes his piercing brown eyes on me. "To France."

"When is this happening?"

"Soon. We've sold the house."

"And when were you planning on telling me?"

I mumble excuses, but he trumps my discomfort with a surprise of his own.

"I already know. Owen's been keeping me posted."

I lean forward in my chair. I've never asked Owen to keep secrets from his father; it's obvious he would talk to him about our plans.

"He's not signed on to your rural idyll, Emma. He's furious with you."

"He's fine about it," I insist. "I've shown him pictures of his school, told him he'll get extra coaching in French. . ."

But now thinking about it, Owen's only given the occasional nod or grunt and spends most of his time in his room. He hasn't said much at all.

The clatter of the bar forms a backdrop to my discomfort until a splintering sound ratchets up the decibels. I wince and look round. The barman has dropped a tray of glasses. Cheering spreads like a Mexican wave around the tables of drinkers. The flustered bartender kneels on the floor, collecting shards of glass with his fingers and placing them on the tray. A second barman appears with a broom and sweeps debris into a pile. I move my feet while he extends the brush under my stool.

Throughout this drama, Zak doesn't flinch. I mentally run through reasons Owen would thrive in the French education system but, before I've stuttered out my first point, Zak silences me.

"It's no good, Emma. It won't wash."

I feel blood rushing to my face and hope he doesn't notice. "What d'you mean?"

"Owen doesn't want to move to France. And I won't let him. He's coming to live with me."

My skin prickles. "You've been plotting against me!"

"I could say the same about you."

"That's so unfair." As if I had any choice in the direction our lives have taken.

Zak frowns and the hint of silver in his closely cropped hair, gives him gravitas beyond his years. He's the grown up, I'm still an unruly child but he looks more troubled than angry.

"Let's not fight over this, Emma. It's not about us, it's our son's future. We need to put our boy first."

"But if he lives with you, who'll be there for him when you're away working? You could be posted anywhere in the world."

Zak clears his throat and takes a sip of the Coke he's hardly touched since I arrived. He sets it down and looks at me.

"This has come at a good time. Part of my aim in moving to an office job in London was to spend more time with my son. He's at that age when he needs his dad."

I dig my fingernails into my palms. I want to tell him Owen has a great stepdad, but that would be provocative and it's no longer true. Owen loved Paul when he was younger but, as he's grown, his personality has developed on an alternative track, exposing the gulf between them. They don't get each other at all.

"But it's impossible for you to look after him."

Zak picks up a beer mat and taps it on the table. "Carlene's moving back from Washington. She'll be staying with me."

"But won't she be working?" I try to imagine Zak's high-powered lawyer sister pulling on an apron and standing in my place like a front-of-house mother substitute.

"Family," he replies, and I sense the bitterness in his tone. "That's what we do."

"Please, Zak—"

"Carlene's changing career into academia. She'll be working on her PhD at the London School of Economics. When Owen needs her around, she'll study at home."

I understand now—the bitterness Zak has felt towards me—the agony when someone rips your child away, rips out your heart.

When Owen was born, the love I felt for him was so all-encompassing I couldn't leave him in another room. That bond between us is still there, stretched and tangled with day-to-day grumbles, but never broken. Now Zak's trying to snatch my son away.

"I have custody," I remind him.

"No, you have a residence order. The contact arrangements allow for Owen to spend time with me. If you move abroad, you can't fulfil them. Remember Nigeria?"

I do. When Zak wanted to take Owen to Nigeria to meet his grandparents, I put my foot down, refused permission, because secretly I was terrified he'd keep him there and I'd never see my son again. But I should have known, as I've always known deep-down, that Zak is an honourable man.

"If you take Owen to France, you can't honour the contact arrangement. We'd need to go back to court."

Tears sting my eyes. In one swift move, Zak has bounced me from stalemate to checkmate. But this isn't a game. My strategy was limited, my tactics too weak, when I set up this meeting I'd not thought of any outcome, other than the one I'd plotted. In my tunnel vision the only certainty was that Owen would be coming to France with us.

I fight harder, grasping at the fears Paul trickled into my mind.

"Owen will soon be a teenager. He'll be safer in the Limousin than here in London." I don't need to mention gangs or drugs or knives, Zak understands my meaning perfectly.

"Owen won't be out roaming the streets, Emma. He'll be involved with the church; the youth choir. Carlene and I will take good care of him."

"I know. I know you will." But how will I live without my son?

I'm so fraught with tension and misery I almost miss Zak's next words. "There's something I've been meaning to tell you."

It sounds ominous. "What's that?"

"I've been earning good money. Saving up. Owen will be going to a decent school."

"He already goes to a good school, which he loves. Why cause him more disruption?" I argue.

"Don't you want him to have the best education? He could go to Emmanuel or Dulwich—give him a decent start in life."

"Oh. I've never thought. . ."

Everyone in my family went to state school, but Zak and his sister were privately educated and forged successful careers. I've always been against private schools, but if Zak and I had stayed together, we would have had this conversation.

I think back to how poverty defined Owen's early years. It wasn't just physical deprivation, but social isolation because I knew no one, couldn't afford mum and toddler drop-in sessions and I'd lost contact with my family. My close friends were just starting their careers; some were still at university. I still feel guilty for putting Owen through that.

Zak leans towards me; so close I can smell his leather jacket.

"Owen loves you, Emma. And he's fond of his little sister, but he doesn't want to move to France."

I nod, choking on a sob and trying to turn it into a cough. A girl at the next table is staring at me, making no secret she's been eavesdropping on our conversation.

"If we fight about this and go to court, Owen would choose me," says Zak. "Do you want to put him through that?"

Zak leans back on his chair with his arms crossed over his chest. He has a satisfied look on his face. He knows that he has won.

CHAPTER 13

OWEN

November 2015

Someone is knocking on my bedroom door. It must be Mum. I ignore her and turn my music up to full volume.

She taps again. "Can I come in?"

"Why?"

I know she's been to tell Dad about us moving to France and I'm not ready to listen. My fucking family is so messed up.

Mum doesn't force her way into my room like some of my mates' mums do. She waits for me to say it's okay.

"I'll come back later," she says quietly.

"No. Wait."

On the way to the door, I kick my dirty laundry under the bed. She's stopped collecting it from my room. I'm supposed to bring it downstairs but I don't. I open my door. She has her coat on but she's shivering.

"What?" I yell.

"I need to speak to you in private."

I stand aside to let her in. I've kept my blinds shut all day and it's grey and gloomy. Mum switches the light on and wrinkles her nose. There is a smell. I hadn't noticed until now but it's egg and orange peel.

She glances at the plate of egg sandwiches I left when I couldn't pick out all the pieces of eggshell and seems to guess I made them myself.

"Didn't Paul make lunch for you?"

"Didn't want fish fingers."

And I don't want Paul to do stuff for me either. I know I can be harsh on him. When I was little I thought he was cool but, back then, I didn't see much of Dad. Now it's just confusing.

Paul used to be all matey with me, buy me stuff, take me places, but lately he doesn't have the time. It's his fault our family is breaking up and my mum and Mollie are moving to another country. All because of some stupid cock up he made at work.

I kneel on the floor and fiddle with my laptop but I can feel her eyes watching me. After a while she sits on my bed and says, "I've been to see your dad."

"Uh huh."

When I look up, her eyes are all watery.

"Is it true what he told me, Owen? That you don't want to come with us to France?"

I slam my computer lid shut. "Yeah. Why would I?"

"You never said."

"You never asked! You just went on and on telling me it was going to happen."

Mum sniffs and dabs her eyes with a paper hanky.

"Stop making me feel bad!" I yell. "It's not my fault, you can't sort out your shit."

She doesn't tell me not to swear, doesn't say anything. She just keeps on staring at me in a mushy way so my own eyes feel hot and sore and I have to shake my head to make the feeling go away.

"Sorry."

"It's okay." She holds out her arms and I jump up from the floor and run to her. She hugs me tight and strokes my head. I don't like anyone touching my hair but I don't stop her.

"I can't leave my whole life and move to France," I say, easing my head away from her shoulder.

"I understand," she says, but I think it's a lie. "Have you thought how it'll be? Living with your dad?"

"And Carlene."

Dad's already told me his plans and promised I can finish this year at my school in Wimbledon. He or Carlene will drive me. That's what I like about Dad—he works everything out and he sticks to it. He doesn't hit me with surprises—like Mum and Paul.

"Do you remember how it was before I met Paul" she asks. "When it was just you and me?"

Why does she have to bring this up?

"I was only, like, four years old," I say. "Was it when we were in that flat that was always freezing?"

She nods. "I'm sorry I put you through that."

"I do remember it." The memory makes me shiver. "We had no friends. We were lonely."

Mum gives a kind of gasp. She hugs me again and her cheek is wet so I know she's crying.

"I love you, Owen. I'll miss you so much and you'll come to visit us in France, but I want what's best for you."

This is NOT my fault. Why must she make me feel bad?

CHAPTER 14

EMMA

December 2015

Our buyers are serious about moving in between Christmas and New Year. I thought it would be impossible, but not, it seems, for cash buyers, who also happen to be solicitors and can fast-track their own conveyancing.

"Shall I look for a house to rent in Sainte Violette?" I ask Paul, as he opens the front door to leave for work.

I've been thinking about this for some time but, while there was a shred of hope Owen might change his mind, I dallied.

"Don't look just yet," says Paul. "I've had an idea."

When I told Paul Owen's decision, he understood my anguish but spoke to Owen and reassured him we would respect his choice. He explained that, even living in different countries, we were still a family and Owen was free to come and live with us if he changed his mind in the future.

I stand on the front step and wave goodbye to Paul. A single robin sits shivering on our garden wall, as if waiting for a Christmas card photoshoot but I can't linger. Mollie and I will be spending the day offloading sacks of possessions at Oxfam and in the storage unit I've rented.

When we arrive home, Paul is waiting for us. And there's

something else—something huge, blocking the road in front of our house and overhanging our neighbour's drive.

"Isn't she smart, Emma? One careful owner. You wouldn't believe some of the others I've looked at. Stank of unwashed dogs and cigarette smoke."

"What the—"

Mollie claps her hands and bounds from the car. "Let me see inside, Daddy!"

Grinning, he unlocks the caravan and pulls down a step. Mollie disappears inside; oohing and aahing at each discovery; to her, it must seem like a giant play house.

My car keys slip from my fingers and jangle as they fall into the gutter, centimetres from a drain.

"Tell me this doesn't mean what I think it means," I say as I stoop to retrieve them.

"Only for a while, Emma. Until the renovations are done. Look inside—nice and cosy, a gas heater."

"It's December!"

"And soon it will be spring," Paul says cheerfully.

*

On Boxing Day, Owen moves to Zak's taking Dylan, the rabbit. Mollie cries herself to sleep and so do I. In three days' time we're due to leave for France.

I'm smugly ahead of schedule, when Paul comes home from work and announces, "My notice period at Manifold has been extended. They're insisting I work another six weeks before they'll pay my redundancy."

"Tell them to stick their job." My voice is frosty but inside I feel sick and empty.

"It's another few weeks of decent money, Emma."

He balances his mug of tea on the radiator and avoids my eyes.

"But you signed a bloody compromise agreement!"

"I haven't signed it. Not yet. Still negotiating."

Six weeks. That takes us to mid-February.

"And you expect me and Mollie to live in France on our own—in a bloody caravan?"

"I'll be there while we get the caravan set up. If there was any other way. " He reaches for my hand.

I shrug him off and push him back against the kitchen counter.

"We're not going. We'll stay here—wherever you're staying."

He flinches. "I'll be bunking up with Malcolm. He's only got a one bedroom flat."

On the floor is a box of crockery, individually rolled up in paper by my aching hands. I grab a mug—Mollie's gift to Paul saying 'Best Dad in the World'—and dash it to the floor where it shatters sending splinters around Paul's feet.

"How could you?" I yell. "This is your cock-up!"

"I'll make it up to you."

"Too late. I've lost Owen!"

I stamp upstairs and peer into Mollie's room, relieved she's fast asleep and hasn't heard raised voices and breaking crockery. I whisper a kiss onto her cheek and creep out.

I edge open the door of Owen's room, snap on the light and choke on emptiness. The bed is neatly made up, as if awaiting a guest. No randomly-scattered clothes, no guitar, no laptop, no half-constructed Airfix models. I stare at the dabs of Blu-Tack left behind when he ripped posters off the wall.

"I'll get new ones," was his parting shot as he crumpled

a poster of his Formula One hero, Lewis Hamilton, into the bin, wiping out all traces of himself.

Nothing to show that my son ever lived here.

I perch on Owen's bed, gathering the pillow that still smells of him into my arms and burying my face in it. *What will Mollie and I do in France on our own?* Paul's redundancy pay and any money left from selling the house is earmarked to renovate Les Quatre Vents. In six weeks' time Paul's salary will stop but we'll need income to live on.

Thoughts circle in my head as I fall into a fitful sleep. When I wake up, I have the answer.

CHAPTER 15

EMMA

December 2015

The front door slams. I check the time on my phone and guess Paul has left early to avoid another confrontation. Mollie's still sleeping but the time in France is one hour ahead so I can make my call, uninterrupted.

My empty kitchen shelves yawn, as if they've been plundered by a thief with a crockery fetish. I'm searching for supper plates when Paul arrives home, apologies spilling from his lips before he's through the door.

"Six weeks will pass quickly, Emma. I can't antagonise them before I get my redundancy pay. We'll still need an income. "

"I was thinking the same."

"You were?" His face brightens with surprise.

"So I'll need to find work," I say, remembering how Paul hated me doing temporary waitressing jobs.

"Perhaps you could do something part-time in Mollie's school?" suggests Paul.

He approved of my work as a learning support assistant and was delighted when I showed an entrepreneurial flair by running the after-school French club for a few weeks. I wonder how he'll react to my latest scheme.

Now is the time to tell him.

"I've had an idea," I begin. "Do you remember Anton telling us he was packing in the bar in Sainte Violette and moving south?"

"What's that got to do with us?"

"I've been discussing it with Henri, today. There's a small upfront payment for the lease but the rent's quite low. We could take it on."

"But Anton told us he wasn't making any money," says Paul.

"Yes but, don't you remember saying that you couldn't understand how it could fail with such low outgoings?" I pause to give him time to think back over our conversation with Anton.

"Anyway," I continue. "Henri told me Anton was drinking the profits. He'd lost the cigarette sales licence. We could get that back."

"But we don't know anything about running a bar."

"You don't, but I've done bar work and worked in catering. I even have a food safety certificate tucked away somewhere. I could employ Lilianne to help with the lunches."

"How will the locals feel about a foreigner running their bar?"

"Henri's put out feelers with the authorities," I reply, choosing my words carefully. "If the bar stays closed, it damages the whole village so there'd be no objections. Henri will help me set up the business and tax side. It's called something like *microenterprise* or *microentrepreneur*."

Paul stares at me. "You've surprised me, Emma, and I'm proud of you but—"

"But what?"

"How will we afford the lease?"

I take a deep breath— this is the question I was waiting for but it's complicated, so I say the first thing that comes into my head. "My parents."

Paul seems satisfied. "We must raise a glass to thank them."

From his bag, he produces a bottle, nestled in a silver cooler, and presents it to me. Sparkling Saumur—I'm guessing this must be his apology gift to me.

I laugh. "You won't find a glass here. They're all in storage."

"Then I will search the house," he says, heading for the stairs. "I'm sure there are tooth glasses in the bathroom."

Is it so unreasonable to have a small financial secret of my own? The amount I've set aside would never have filled the black hole in Paul's mortgage account, but it's enough for the lease on the bar.

When Zak stopped sending me child support for Owen, I assumed he was punishing me and learned to manage without it. Later, when I challenged him, Zak claimed he'd sent the payments and blamed the banking system in the remote countries where he was posted. Since returning to work in London, Zak has paid promptly and I've let the money build up in a separate account. I was saving it for Owen's future but with Zak paying for an expensive education, he won't need it now.

CHAPTER 16

EMMA

December 2015

Paul has renovated the caravan, examining every fixed and moving part, repairing loose beading and replacing a wonky tap. I cram winter clothes into the tiny wardrobe and roll up towels and stuff them in the overhead lockers.

Mollie becomes my shadow, permanently attached to my side, forcing me to stay cheerful because her future mustn't be clouded by uncertainty.

We take the ferry to Calais and head south on the Autoroute, Paul battling to stop the caravan snaking in the buffeting headwind. He soon masters the knack, the caravan submits and we drive on, racking up tolls and stopping to refuel on black coffee and Orangina.

We trundle through Sainte Violette, raising some stares. On the wall outside the bar is a large sign saying that the lease is available.

But not for much longer, I think, with a smile.

We take the winding country road out of the village and ahead of us, in all its sodden winter glory, lies Les Quatre Vents, our place for all seasons.

Paul yanks the steering wheel ready for the sharp right

turn. The car makes it, but the caravan gets wedged against the old gatepost. He slams the car into reverse, metal scrapes against wood.

"Shit."

The car rocks as the van settles. Paul gets out to view the damage. The caravan has swung out at an angle, blocking the road.

"Stay in the car, Mollie," I say as I prepare to help.

"I'll unhitch it. You hold the van steady."

Paul unhooks the tow bar and I struggle to support its weight.

"Hold the van up while I drive the car forward."

"Can't. It's too heavy," I groan.

How I wish Owen was here to help. Paul drives the car closer to the house and jogs back down the track. Between us we manhandle the caravan out of the road and closer to the house.

"Leave it here for now. I'll make some tea."

"But we need gas and water," I say.

"What d'you think that is?" Paul points out an electricity meter box and a green metal hatch cover, where our brand new water supply is buried. "Henri's organised everything."

We sip our tea, Mollie snuggling up next to me as Paul unpacks a flat box containing a television. He fiddles with it for ages but can't get it working. Dusk creeps up on us and Paul draws the curtains.

"I'm shattered. Let's leave the caravan here for the night. I'll move it round the back in the morning."

We'll be sleeping just a couple of metres away from prying eyes and passing traffic but I'm too tired to care.

We wake to a sound like a whispering tide. As I listen, the timbre changes to a rustling, rising in volume then falling away.

"What's that?"

"Pheasants. They raise them at the farm across the road," Paul says sleepily.

I lever myself up on one elbow, open the blind and peer out of the window. Opposite us is a huddle of farm buildings visible behind the naked trees. Strange that I didn't notice the farm when we were here in the autumn. I squint to read the painted sign, nailed to a tree: La Petite Ferme.

Paul notices where I'm looking. "The family's called Gaspard. According to Henri, they stay aloof from the rest of the village. Henri's invited us for an early supper tonight."

"Great. He should have some more news for me about the bar."

"And he's been liaising with Maxim, our architect. He sent me the first draft of the plans yesterday but I haven't looked at them yet. I'll show you when we go somewhere with WiFi."

Henri's house in the next hamlet is a short drive away and, when we arrive, he's in the yard scattering grain for a troupe of free-range hens. He looks different: smarter clothes, healthier complexion, less gaunt.

"Can I help?" begs Mollie, tugging at my sleeve.

"Of course." Henri hands her a rough woven bag, shows her how to take a pinch and walk around as she scatters it.

"Keep moving so the birds at the bottom of the pecking order don't miss out."

"What's pecking order?" Mollie asks, and Henri explains.

The hen house is hand-crafted in wood.

"Is this where they sleep?" I ask.

Henri nods. "I built it last winter. The stilts are to keep out the foxes."

Henri finishes feeding the hens and puts down the tin. "Come and see what's inside the barn."

Intrigued, Mollie and I follow, leaving Paul in the yard, taking a call on his mobile phone. Henri puts a finger to his lips as he lifts a scrap of frayed blanket and uncovers a hay bale. On the top, huddled in a sort of nest, are five new-born kittens. Gently, he scoops up a black and white one, small enough to nestle inside his palm, and shows Mollie how to cradle it against her chest. The kitten yawns and rubs its head on her jumper.

"Look, Mummy. He's sleeping," she declares, enraptured.

"He's still very tiny. His eyes aren't open yet."

"We must put him back now." Henri lays the kitten next to its brothers and sisters and replaces their covering.

"Can we have one?" begs Mollie.

"No, darling. Anyway, you have Dylan," I say, briefly forgetting her rabbit is hundreds of miles away at home with Owen.

She makes a sad face and I bite my lip, annoyed with myself that I had brought up the rabbit. We head out of the barn.

Henri's house is built of grey and honey-coloured stone, evolved over decades, if not centuries. The roof is red clay tiles and wood smoke curls from the chimney into the grey-blue sky. At the upstairs windows, white wooden shutters, with black metal fixings, flap open, and, on the ground floor, there are window boxes planted with thyme, mint and other herbs.

Entering the house is a step into a man's world—no curtains to soften the shutters, wooden furniture with no upholstered seats or cushions, and a bare flagstone floor. There are a few books but no pictures or photographs and empty beer bottles, in varying shapes and sizes, line one windowsill, passing for ornaments. The main room is warm with logs glowing behind the sooty window of a wood burning stove.

Henri extracts a bottle of Ricard from his bookshelf, where it's wedged between a bible and a road atlas of Europe, dated 1988. He pours out two measures, hands one to Paul and fetches water from the kitchen tap in a small crested jug.

"Emma? Sorry, did you want one?"

I shake my head. "Glass of wine, please."

I follow him out to the kitchen where shelves built from reclaimed wood are stacked with pans and chipped crockery. I run my hand over the rough door of a free-standing cupboard. It's painted pale grey and I wonder if Henri knows the colour he's picked is high fashion in London.

"Did you build the kitchen yourself?" I ask.

He looks up from pouring my wine. "I did. There's not much work around here in winter."

The kitchen wall is unpainted and the plaster is a patchwork of pale and darker shades of pink. Henri follows my gaze and pats the wall with the flat of his hand.

"Still waiting for it to dry out. These old walls act like a sponge and soak up years of damp."

He turns to stir a pan bubbling on the stove. I catch the scent of tarragon and keep my fingers crossed that Mollie will eat it. He carries on talking as he stirs.

"I'm still fixing the house up. It's a slow process. The bathroom's next." He wipes his forehead with the back of his hand. "It's downstairs, along the hallway if Mollie needs it. I was going to put a new one in upstairs but funds have been tight."

"What's the latest news on the bar?" I ask, but before Henri replies, Paul joins us in the kitchen and sets up his laptop on the scrubbed pine table.

"Can I use your WiFi to show Emma the architect's plans?"

"Be my guest."

At home in England, Paul has been developing his back-of-a-napkin ideas for remodelling Les Quatre Vents using a professional architectural design package. His grand scheme is strong, while I'm hooked on the small details, like the way he can supplement the design by bringing window boxes, trees and manicured blades of grass zooming onto the page to beautify our wasteland plot.

Paul sent his outline design and a long email explaining his ideas to Maxim, the architect Henri recommended. I peer at the screen as Paul loads the plan and see immediately that he's ignored Paul's proposals.

The architect has stretched the building, adding two ugly extensions, making it even longer. To the right of the front elevation he's inked-in an archway leading to the outbuildings we plan to convert into holiday homes to rent out but his schematic shows the old barn and dairy, modernised into soulless brick boxes.

Paul stiffens. "What the fuck is this?"

"Shush, Paul—Mollie's here."

"This isn't the L-shape I asked for."

Henri abandons the pot he's tending on the stove and studies the design.

"Your kind of long, low building is traditional," he explains. "We call it a *longère*. *Longères* were built with their backs to the wind and people and animals lived side by side in adjacent parts of the building. They stored winter feed for animals in the roof space to provide insulation."

"Why does that affect our design options?"

"The planning authorities might insist on keeping this original shape. No Ls, no Us. Just straight."

"I want to explore my proposals first."

"Sure. I'll go with you to talk to Maxim."

The smell from the pan on the hob caramelises but the men are engrossed. *Should I intervene to stop it burning?* I half-rise but Henri gets there first and pronounces it ready. He rolls up the sleeves of his dark denim shirt as he ladles chicken onto plates and I realise why he looks different. He's shaved off the offending moustache to reveal a younger, more attractive Henri underneath.

As we take our seats at the table, Paul begins another question about planning rules but his time is up. I cut across him.

"Enough about planning. Let's talk about the bar. What's our next step?"

CHAPTER 17

EMMA

January 2016

Mollie's new school, in an austere building with high walls and an iron gate, reminds me of a convent. I ring the bell and we stand in the biting wind until a woman arrives with a key and ushers us inside. In the echoing vestibule we sit on hard wooden benches and wait for Madame Moreau.

"I'm scared, Mummy."

So am I, but I can't tell Mollie. I've been in touch by email and phone and a place has been reserved for her, but this is the first time we've stepped inside the gates.

"No need, darling. Everyone will be friendly." I hope that's true.

Madame Moreau greets us in English and bends down to shake Mollie's hand.

"*Bonjour*, Madame," Mollie replies, and I swell with pride that she's mastered one of the few French phrases I've taught her.

Madame Moreau guides us along a corridor, pausing to let us peer through glass door panels into classrooms with an air of quiet orderliness. Sometimes a child spots us looking in and waves at Mollie. All the while, Madame is plying me with details of the learning process. Her information offload is vast, and I soon know everything children of Mollie's age must cover in the *école maternelle* to prepare themselves for the next stage.

"The small ones—they sleep for some time in the afternoon," explains Madame and her stern expression softens into a smile.

It's coming up to lunch time. A classroom door opens, and a boy pushes past Mollie, so she stumbles and clings to my hand. We walk back to the office and start the lengthy process of form filling.

"School day starts at eight-forty-five with a lunch break at twelve," explains Madame. "The afternoon runs until four. On Wednesdays, there's no school for the small ones. Do you work?" Behind her thick glasses, Madame Moreau's pupils appear pinpoint sharp and I wonder if she's judging me.

"I will have to," I admit, but it's too soon to tell her I'm destined to be a bar owner.

She nods. "We have a dining room for school lunch and there is a *garderie* until six, if you need. For this you must pay a small fee."

"Sounds perfect." Everything is falling into place fast. Mollie can start school the next day.

Next morning Paul and I go with her to the school gates, where one of the helpers steps in to look after her. She looks tiny and lost and my heart clenches as she battles to hold back tears but, when the children are called together to form a line, a girl about Mollie's height takes her hand to enter the building two by two. Mollie glances back at us and tosses her head, her smile no longer wan.

"See," says Paul. "She's fine."

We drive slowly back to the caravan. It's freezing inside so I put on the heater and Paul demonstrates for the third time how to reconnect the gas canister and shows me where he's stashed a spare one in the barn, though you're not supposed to store them. He lifts the new one onto a trolley so I can wheel it to the caravan. "I'm sure you won't need to change this until I'm back, but just in case."

His face is grey from lack of sleep and it's clear he doesn't want to leave me and Mollie. In France, the shadow of Dorek's tragic death recedes but it will be waiting on his return to England.

"We'll miss you. But at least I'll have space to stretch out in this damn bed."

The caravan bed is nowhere near long enough for Paul's six-foot-two frame but he laughs and pulls me down beside him. "Come here." Paul kisses me and reaches up to pull down the caravan blinds.

CHAPTER 18

EMMA

January 2016

January mists shroud Sainte Violette in melancholy. Each morning I drop Mollie at school, smile at the other mums and wait for one of them to smile back. They respond politely to my, *"Bonjour"* but they've yet to make up their minds about me.

I don't reveal how much French I understand so eavesdropping wrong-foots me. They gossip about us without bothering to lower their voices. *Why would a woman from London come to this isolated village?* I overhear the phrase *'gens du voyage.'* Apparently, they think we're travellers because we live in a caravan.

After this, I stop hanging around trying to fit in but dawdle home to the cheerless caravan. I write long emails to Owen, though he never replies.

With no WiFi in the caravan, Mollie and I take round trips to a distant McDonalds to catch up with Owen on Skype, but not Paul.

"I don't do Facetime or Skype, Emma, you know that. Ring me, okay? Or I'll call you."

"Mollie will want to see you," I protest.

Paul remains implacable. "We'll set a time for a phone call each day before she goes to bed."

Henri's handling negotiations for me to take over the bar. The building's neglected frontage fits perfectly with the morose high street. The shutters are drawn tightly across the windows and someone has fly-posted handbills for a concert in Limoges on the front door.

I'm planning a food shopping trip when my mobile rings. "Henri?"

"Good news. I've got hold of the keys to the bar. Fancy taking a look inside?"

"Fantastic. I'll meet you there."

I leave the car and fetch my bike from the barn, reversing it out between coils of chicken wire left over from some long-ago project. The rear tyre is flat. Pumping it up delays me briefly and when I reach the village, Henri is waiting for me, leaning against the outside wall of the bar. He's wearing his leather jacket, scarf wound twice around his neck and, in his hand, a vast bunch of keys.

"Prepare yourself. It may not be pretty."

He turns the key and gives the door a firm shove. I remember it sticking when we came here back in Anton's day. It creaks open but inside it's darker than a cave.

"Electricity's disconnected. Wait there."

Henri heads back out to his Renault, parked a few metres along the road and returns with a torch. I wait in the street squinting up at the sign board, so faded it's hard to make out the bar's name. Perhaps I'll christen it with a new one.

With a clanking sound, Henri unfastens the first set of shutters and shafts of daylight illuminate sections of the floor. I step into the closest light pool while Henri tackles more shutters.

My eyes are drawn to the empty shelves behind the bar where Anton kept bottles of spirits. The tarnished mirror glass forming the back wall of the bar reflects gloomy emptiness. Elsewhere are signs that Anton left in a hurry. Empty beer bottles squat beside unwashed glasses and a bottle of expensive Cognac has tipped over, dribbling its contents in a sticky puddle.

I tease it upright with my thumb and index finger and wipe it with a tissue.

"Looks like quite a leaving party."

"It lasted several days, so I heard," says Henri with a grimace.

"Weren't you invited?"

"I was." He shrugs. "But I left early. I heard Anton's brother had to carry him into the car next morning when he moved out."

I follow the beam of Henri's torch through a door into the sour-smelling cooking area where my shoes stick to the floor.

Henri opens the shutter and looks around. "Ugh."

Some surfaces look furry, where dust has settled on top of grease. Henri flips up the lid of the deep fat fryer. Congealed grease on the handle of the chip basket is turning black. The oil can't have been emptied for ages. I can't believe a woman would have let it get this bad.

"I thought Lilianne did the cooking?"

"No, for some weeks Anton didn't pay her. She left."

Around the walls are open shelves stacked with pans and plain white crockery. It's sticky to the touch but serviceable and there's plenty of it.

"Does all this come with the place?"

Henri consults a sheaf of papers and nods. "So it seems. Fixtures, fittings and contents are in the lease."

I wander round peering into cupboards. Beneath the sink, Anton has left cleaning products. Thankfully, the bin has been emptied and lined with a new plastic bag.

"Alcohol licence shouldn't be a problem," says Henri. "Neither of you has a criminal record in the UK, do you?"

I think of the possible charges facing Paul and shake my head. "No, I don't think so."

Henri smiles. "Don't look so worried. Parking fines don't count. But the alcohol licence is quite expensive. There are different levels of licence but, if you want to sell spirits, you'll need to go for the highest, which is level four."

I clear my throat because my next line is awkward to deliver. "Paul wants you to put the bar in my sole name."

He gives me an odd look but nods. I don't elaborate. There's no need for him to know that Paul fears being sent to prison in the UK.

We retrace our steps into the bar where tables have been pushed against the wall, some with chairs tilted up against them. A few chairs lie sideways on the floor like assault victims in a foetal position seeking protection from a kicking.

"This one's broken." Henri moves it aside and spreads out his folder of papers on a table near the window. He draws up two chairs. "Let's get started on the paperwork. Prepare for plenty of red tape—licences, declarations and security checks."

"Security checks?"

He nods. "It includes inspections by the fire services; food safety checks and so on. We must get the opening hours approved but, because you're taking over an existing business, it shouldn't take long. You'll soon have the place up and running."

Henri's encircling the project with ownership and driving it forward. *Is he joining my team or am I part of his?* At this precise moment, it feels good. Like I'm not alone. Paul will want me to open the bar soon and start bringing in some money.

"Let's crack on with the forms. What the heck."

"Good plan. See what happens."

When I finally straighten up from the paperwork, my wrist aches from signing. I glance round the room to rest my eyes and catch sight of a spiral staircase, winding up into the ceiling.

"What's upstairs?" Could there possibly be some accommodation? Somewhere for Mollie to sleep if I'm working in the bar in the evenings?

"Nothing is mentioned in the lease." Henri flips on his torch and goes ahead of me. "Take care. The handrail's loose."

His head and shoulders disappear into the loft space, but his feet are still halfway up the staircase. I'm itching to get past him.

"What's there? Can you see?"

"A skylight window covered by a blackout blind. Wait there while I raise the blind." He climbs into the loft and his feet clump across floorboards.

I mount the last few steps in time to hear him yell, "Ouch," as he bangs his head on a low slanting beam.

As light streams in, I see it has a boarded floor but has been used as a storeroom. Empty cardboard boxes are strewn everywhere. A stained mattress with a cover of black and white ticking stands against the wall. I touch it. It's damp. At each side of the loft, the ceiling slopes at a sharp angle, but I'm shorter than him and I can stand upright.

"It's freezing."

"And damp," adds Henri.

I sigh.

"What?"

"Nothing." I don't want to tell him I was hoping this could be a space for me and Mollie to live in, instead of the caravan. "I was thinking perhaps if I put a heater in and a camp bed, Mollie could sleep here while I'm bartending in the evening."

Henri shoots me a look as I cling to the wobbly handrail and make my way back down to the bar.

"I'm surprised at Paul. Expecting you and Mollie to spend winter in that caravan."

I spring to my husband's defence. "Back home, lots of people live in caravans while they're renovating properties."

That's not strictly true. It's not something I've noticed in London, but I once saw smoke pouring from the steel chimney of a mobile home on a building site in Wales.

"Anyway, it's much warmer here than at home."

"Not in January. It's been mild so far, but that could change." He reaches for the bottle of Cognac I righted on the counter, pours himself a glass and knocks it back with a grimace. "Didn't think this stuff would go off."

He offers to pour a glass for me, but I wave the bottle away.

"Let me have a think. See if I can come up with any ideas."

Just for a moment, I have the crazy idea he's about to invite us to move in with him. If he does, I'd be tempted to say yes. I wonder what Paul would think.

*

My confidence in the mildness of Limousin weather was misplaced. After an overnight freeze, I have to chisel the caravan door open with a carving knife. When it thaws, the sky darkens and rain pelts down for days. Overnight, a storm brews, shaking the tops of the barren trees and making eerie patterns on the caravan walls.

Mollie lies in her cramped bunk, clutching Benjy bear. "I want to go home," she sobs.

The midnight wind howls and buffets the flimsy walls. Windows rattle. My bed rocks; I wake from dreaming I'm adrift on a troubled sea. If I swing my legs out from beneath the duvet, grope my way to the door, plunge my feet into damp wellies and step outside, mud and water will suck at my ankles.

Mollie mumbles and turns over in her bunk. In my drowsy confusion I listen out for Owen's gentle breathing. Then I remember he's not here—I've lost him—and the agony of loss continues.

CHAPTER 19

PAUL

January 2016

Genevieve wants Emma out of my life, but she doesn't want to be dragged into anything as sordid as a divorce.

I've blundered into this situation. I didn't see the trap until it closed over my head but, since Dorek's accident, my future—even my freedom—is in her hands and it comes at a price.

"Crack on with building your place in France and let them settle there," she says.

"For fuck's sake, Genevieve!"

This is beyond a nightmare.

"Emma speaks French, doesn't she? They'll get used to it."

"I'm not having this conversation." I turn and walk out of her sitting room, slamming the door behind me.

Genevieve controls everything: communication with the investigators, witness statements, evidence, the company budget for legal advice.

Genevieve wants children—her own—she's thirty-eight and she thinks time is running out. Sometimes I think a prison sentence would be a doddle compared to a lifetime with Genevieve and the baby she wants to bring into the world: my baby—a punishment to last an eternity.

CHAPTER 20

PAUL

July 2015

In the immediate aftermath of Dorek's death, Genevieve and I used to meet at a coffee house some distance from the office to talk strategy. I queued for the drinks, deafened by the gurgling coffee-machine and slopped her skinny latte onto the tray as I wove my way through the obstacle course of tables.

"Sorry." I mopped the bottom of the mug with a napkin.

Genevieve must have noticed my hand shaking as she took it from me and hastened to reassure me.

"Don't worry, Paul. You know as well as I do that this process is routine in work-related deaths. The health and safety inspectors' findings will prove there's been no breaches or negligence. I'm assembling the evidence to prove that."

"I wish I had your confidence," I said. "What about their English? We're reliant on the foremen to do health and safety briefings but we don't have handouts in Polish and Slovakian."

She brushed my concerns aside. "Jez Williams and I have it covered. Don't worry. The outcome's almost as critical for him as for you."

"What about his role in the impersonation scam?"

"I've forgotten about that, Paul. It never happened and it's best if you forget it yourself."

That incident continued to haunt me after Dorek's accident and I had many bad days wondering if our deceased worker would turn out to be the real Dorek, or someone else.

"I keep thinking about our procedures," I confessed to Genevieve.

Previously procedures would have been the last thing on my mind, but if I've learnt only one thing from this sorry mess, it's that procedures are the only thing that matters. Forget recruiting good people, skills, experience, training and professional standards—procedures are the safety blanket you wrap around yourself and the company when it catches fire.

Throughout my interrogations by lawyers and investigators, I repeated the same mantra: *Yes, our procedures have been maintained, updated and issued; yes, we do regular internal procedure audits.* But in my heart, I knew we'd been too lax.

"Don't worry about that." Genevieve stilled my drumming fingers with a touch of her hand. "I've had all our site processes professionally reviewed, made a few updates. I've been through the site records with Jez Williams, checked all his paperwork going back two years. Everything's in order. Exemplary, in fact."

I felt my lower jaw sag. "You mean you've falsified records?"

"Did I say that?" She shuffled her feet under the table, catching my ankle with the point of her stiletto. "Anyway. Our detailed response with supporting documents is due to go to the inspectors next week."

CHAPTER 21

PAUL

September 2015

After we returned from holiday in France, I was suspended on full pay while Manifold launched its own internal investigation into the fatal accident. It was Genevieve's job to inform me and the irony of the situation wasn't lost on me.

"Suspension isn't a punishment, Paul," she told me in a brisk, impersonal tone. "It's routine. You had overall responsibility for health and safety so Manifold must make an independent assessment of what went wrong."

Anger was brimming inside me but I held my tongue and let her continue.

"While you're suspended you don't come into the office but your pay and all your employment rights continue. The company can stop you speaking to colleagues or clients."

She twisted her gold bracelet around on her wrist. A gift from me, chosen when we were in Monaco.

I cleared my desk, pausing to gaze at a photo of Emma and Mollie taken on our day at Goodwood. They both looked so happy and trusting and I'd let them down.

I resolved not to tell Emma about my suspension, to spare her this latest indignity but I still had to plan for a future where we might lose everything. I think that's when my thoughts turned to our place in France and I realised the ruin could become our sanctuary.

Time for thinking was the one thing I wasn't short of. Every day I left for work as usual but took up residence in a coffee shop, huddling over my laptop in my sad raincoat.

At first, I pretended to be waiting, for a colleague, a meeting. I glanced regularly at my watch, kept an eye on the door and eked out my Americanos with free water from a jug next to the packet sugars and napkins. Soon I discovered no one cared, no one noticed. There were plenty of other sad cases: writers, freelancers or homeless youngsters. I saw the same faces regularly and they didn't spend as much on coffee as me.

Most lunchtimes Genevieve came to join me. She didn't say in advance whether she was coming or not. She just turned up. We'd cross the road to a pub that still cradled the smell of cigarette smoke in its ancient blackened beams. A grizzly bearded man squatted outside, selling The Big Issue. Every day I had to remind him I'd already bought the current edition.

"Spritzer?" I asked, though Genevieve's lunchtime tipple never varied.

I ordered a pint of guest ale and we sipped our drinks moodily, keeping an eye on the door in case someone from the office came in. No one ever did. Why would anyone walk half a mile from the office, unless they were having an affair?

We stood at the bar and Genevieve kept her coat on and sneaked regular glances at her mobile phone. A twinge of lonely self-pity hit me. Perhaps she was getting bored with me. What would happen then?

Genevieve put away her phone, took something out of her

bag and passed it to me. With her diamond-hard smile, she said, "This is crazy, Paul. Here's the key to my house."

From then on, the coffee shop had to manage without me.

I continued taking my morning train from Wimbledon to Waterloo, crushed shoulder to spine against strangers and acquaintances who'd seen me make the same journey every day for years. I was on nodding terms with a few of the guys, but we never chatted. Everyone understood that our fifteen-minute commute was the airlock between home life and the world. We needed that space to decontaminate and adjust to whatever awaited us on the other side.

Every day I lingered by a coffee stand until anyone from my train who could recognise me disappeared into the underground or strode out to cross Hungerford Bridge. Then I caught the 7:52 to Chiswick. Skulking along the road from the station to Genevieve's cottage, I kept my head down like a tramp scouring the pavement for lost coins.

When I reached her cottage that first morning, I fumbled the key into the lock and scratched the dark red paintwork. I held my breath while the door swung open, sprinted to the control panel in the under stairs cupboard to disarm the burglar alarm before shutting the door.

Although I'd spent many hours and several nights in her house, this was the first time I'd been there alone. I stood with my back leaning against the closed front door, my heart pounding as if I was having a seizure. I imagined Genevieve coming home and finding my lifeless body slumped in the hallway. How would she explain my demise? To the ambulance crew? To Emma? Or would she find a way of bundling my corpse outside under cover of darkness and dumping it in the park?

CHAPTER 22

PAUL

January 2016

That was then. . .

Chiswick is where I live now. A half-life, a life on hold. The people I love, Emma and Mollie, are in France, and I have this brief interlude of waiting to learn if I'll go to prison and lose everything.

CHAPTER 23

EMMA

January 2016

Henri's voice on the phone is upbeat. The paperwork's completed, along with the small upfront payment for the lease and the bar is mine. Weekly takings will have to cover rent, wages and other costs but I'm ready to embrace that challenge. Having no one to celebrate with, I cross my arms over my chest and give myself an excited hug as I visualise our family's new life unfurling like a water lily.

"I thought French bureaucracy had a life of its own, rolling on forever?"

Henri laughs. "Not if you know the process and the right people."

This magic has been woven by Henri. "Thank you."

"Meet me at the bar later. I'll bring all the keys."

"About eleven?" Already my feet are inching across the floor towards my shoes, itching to get out of the caravan.

"Twelve-thirty," he replies. "There's someone else I need to see first."

The reminder that Henri has a life to lead, work to do, leaves me guilty and flat. I'm taking too much of his time but without him, I'd be floundering. Days when I don't see him, my only conversation is with random shopkeepers and Mollie.

Kicking my shoes back under the table, I tumble onto Mollie's unmade bunk. It creaks beneath my weight. My head is overflowing with plans as I reach into the drawer where I keep my phone and punch in Paul's number.

He answers on the second ring. I spill out our news in a rush.

"Fantastic! When are you opening?"

My heart sinks, knowing he won't be with me. Not until mid-February at the earliest. Why do I feel so helpless and frustrated? The business was my idea but he should be here supporting me, doing his bit. I revert to the practical—news giving.

"I've organised an industrial clean of the kitchen and Henri's helping me restock and set up the bar. You have arranged that credit, haven't you?"

"Henri," echoes Paul. "How much is he charging?"

"Shut up, Paul! You're not here. I can't do it all on my own."

He's right. Naively I'd assumed Henri was helping me out as a friend, but he needs to make a living just like everyone else.

"I'll ask him. If we can't afford it, I'll manage. My French is getting more fluent by the day."

"Okay. Let me know. I've put money in the French business account but go easy, right? Don't hold too many bottles of spirits in stock—buy one of each until you know the pattern of sales," Paul says.

Deflated and fidgety, I glance around the caravan to see what needs doing. It's so compact there's practically no clearing up to do. I fold away my double bed and recreate the seating area around the fixed table, where Mollie and I eat supper, read stories or play cards before bedtime. I don't really need the double bed. I could keep the table and seating area erected permanently and sleep on one of the bunks, but that would feel strange, as if my marriage was over.

At ten to twelve, I slip the padlock off my bike and cycle down to the bar, where I leave it propped up against the front wall. Who's going to nick a forty-year-old Raleigh with a transfer of a basket of fruit peeling off the cross bar? In England, people laughed when I cycled along the road. Here, my ancient bike with its child seat on the back fits right in.

Paul's given me custody of our Volvo, but to save on fuel, I only use it for longer trips to the supermarket.

Pausing on the pavement to catch my breath, the sharp wind sets me coughing. Brown and yellow leaves are barrelling along the road, catching in the gutters, clogging the drains. The pavement slopes away from the road towards the building. I wonder if a heavy storm will cause a flood.

Henri hears me coughing and opens the door for me. The temperature inside is a few degrees colder than outside and Henri has his coat on, spattered with mud around the hem.

I shiver. "First we must test the heaters."

He nods. "Tomorrow. It's all arranged."

Hugging my coat around me, I feel a shiver of excitement as I turn slowly through three hundred and sixty degrees to view the space from every angle.

A vast tilted mirror hanging on the wall opposite the bar is the best feature though the original backing has worn away leaving black and silver spotting. Collectors in London would pay good money for a replica, but this is the real deal. Deep grooves are scored into wooden tables and some chairs wobble on spindly legs. Something is missing. The place feels sterile, lacking warmth and colour.

"I'm going to paint it," I announce.

Henri raises an eyebrow. "On your own?"

"Why not? The white walls are chilly. It needs at least one feature wall—a strong colour to warm the place up."

"I'll help."

"Would you?" I lift my arms but the urge to hug him seems over-familiar. I squeeze his arm instead.

"Take care choosing the colour," he warns. "Winters here don't last as long as they do in England."

"You're right. Red walls wouldn't work. How about blue?"

"Like the summer sky?"

"Perhaps peacock blue, with a hint of turquoise."

I've always loved bright colours, and this is my chance to work with a strong palette.

"Right." Henri rolls up his sleeves. "Let's get to work. Clear some space."

We shift the tables into one area and line up chairs against the wall, upend them and mark the base of the ones needing mending with blue felt tip pen.

"I'll bring my toolkit tomorrow," Henri promises.

"Thank you." Now is the time to broach the subject of his fees but he changes the subject.

"I have more good news for you."

"Yes. You told me on the phone. Everything's gone through," I say.

He shakes his head. "No, it's something else. Remember I mentioned an elderly English lady, Mrs Browning, who lives opposite the church? She's decided to go back to England for the rest of the winter. I suggested you and Mollie move into her house."

"What!" A thrill of excitement shoots through me and I gape at him. "Impossible. No way we could afford the rent."

"There's no rent."

"I don't get it. Why?"

"You'd be house sitting. She doesn't want to leave the cottage empty. If it's not heated or ventilated over winter, damp seeps into the stone walls."

"Henri, that's amazing!" I can't believe it's coincidence. Henri must have talked her into it. "So, we'd be sort-of caretakers?"

He nods. "She's worried someone may break into the cottage if word gets around that it's empty."

I try to recall what Henri told me about Mrs Browning when he gave me a run down on the locals. She and her husband retired here twenty-five years ago; she speaks immaculate French and she's carried on living here alone since her husband died. She must be in her mid-eighties by now.

The kettle boils, I pour boiling water onto the coffee granules, hand a mug to Henri and sit with him at one of the small tables.

"Mrs Browning's scared of falling. That storm and the recent freeze convinced her to spend the rest of the winter in Somerset with her son and family. She won't be back before Easter."

"That's amazing." I stand up and glide across the room; step behind the bar and try on my new role for size. It fits!

A short time with Henri and my winter gloom subsides.

CHAPTER 24

EMMA

Mid-January 2016

Preparing to move into the cottage feels like emerging from hibernation. The bar has given me a purpose—my days are filled with decorating and meetings—and soon we'll have a home.

On the day before Mrs Browning leaves, we're invited for an early supper.

"It's open," she calls, in response to my rap on the door.

We squeeze into the tiny hallway and I take off Mollie's dripping anorak and look for somewhere I can hang it. She lingers, staying close to my side.

"Go and see what Milou is up to," I suggest.

At the mention of the dog, Mollie forgets her nerves and hurries into the sitting room. I linger in the hall, soaking up the scent of dried lavender and a hint of damp dog.

"What's happening to Milou?" I ask as I enter the kitchen. "Are you taking him to England?"

"Henri's having him. Such a kind man."

Yet again, Henri makes all the pieces fit together.

"I couldn't go to England if I didn't know Milou would be taken care of. Sit here with me for a moment, dear. Supper won't be long."

Mollie has been listening in. She sidles up beside my chair, leans over the arm and whispers. "Can't Milou stay with us, Mummy?"

I shake my head. "No, darling. Why don't you take him into the garden to play?"

It's stopped raining, but the evening sky is dark and grainy. Faint dots of pixelated street lighting flicker outside the church opposite.

"There's a light for the courtyard beside the back door." Mrs Browning produces a biscuit tin with a picture of the Queen Mother from a shelf under her table but the biscuits inside are for dogs. "Take a handful of these, Mollie." She turns to reassure me. "Courtyard's quite safe. Back gate's bolted. Too high for her to reach."

Mollie pushes past me, clutching a handful of dog treats, the Westie panting at her heels. I watch them through the kitchen window, Mollie holding up the treat, Milou leaping up to snatch it from her hand. Soon she has him performing tricks, walking backwards on his hind legs.

Leaving them to play I return to the sitting room. A small log burner built into the grate singes my legs. Pure bliss. It's the warmest I've been since we moved here.

"I can't thank you enough for letting us stay. Mollie and I will take great care of your home."

"I know you will, dear. Now tell me about your plans for the bar. Henri says you're opening in a week's time."

She glances at the gold carriage clock on her mantelpiece as if all time and dates are bound up in its dainty casing.

"I'm only opening at lunchtimes until the spring," I explain. "To fit in with Mollie's school hours and until Paul, my husband, joins me."

"And Lilianne Dubois is going to be working for you?"

"Yes, it's such a relief. She'll be cooking and serving the *ouvriers'* lunches. We're going to include a few British pub classics on the menu."

"Talking of food—supper's nearly ready."

I hand her the walking stick and offer to help her up from her chair, but she waves me away, counting one-two-three under her breath as she presses down on the arms of her chair and levers herself to standing. She walks ahead of me to the kitchen and I notice her delicate ornaments on the mantelpiece and open shelves.

"Would you mind if I packed away your treasures? Just in case."

She pats my arm. "Do exactly as you like, dear. It's your home."

In the kitchen, she bends awkwardly and takes a chicken pie out of the oven.

"Just a tiny portion for Mollie. She had lunch at school."

Mollie's impressive manners won't extend to eating food she doesn't like—especially meat or fish. Last time we ate supper at Henri's, Mollie wrapped up her prawns in a paper napkin and hid them in her pocket.

"I've left you a file with instructions for the appliances." Mrs Browning taps a clawed finger on a bundle of documents on the worktop.

"Thanks." I pick it up and flip through the pages.

"And phone numbers for the electrician and plumber. But Henri will sort that out for you. He does for me."

Does she pay him, I wonder? Or do his days expend in running errands for helpless British females? He's been driving me to wholesalers, stocking up, overseeing the industrial kitchen cleaners and doing minor repairs.

"And what about bills?" I ask. "Electricity, water?"

"We'll sort that out later. They're paid automatically from my account. And there's WiFi, too. I don't use it, but my son, Peter, insisted I had it."

"WiFi! That's wonderful."

I'll be able to Skype Owen every day if I can persuade him to answer our calls. The distance between us will shrink. Mrs Browning's generosity will transform our lives. Throughout supper my conscience nags. We'll be living here rent-free, but we don't seem to be offering much in return. Perhaps we could . . .

I open my mouth and blurt out. "Perhaps Milou could stay here in his home? Mollie and I could look after him."

"Yay, Mummy! Hooray!" Mollie jumps from her seat and rushes to embrace the Westie, who is slumbering in front of the fire.

"Well if you're sure, dear. It would be a weight off my mind."

"Looks like that's settled then."

From shivering in the caravan, Mollie and I will soon be moving into a comfortable house with a dog to look after. Almost a home, almost a family.

*

Henri perches on a wooden bar table, with his feet on a chair. "You should throw a small opening party."

I carry on polishing the furniture while he explains. "We'll invite local tradesmen, electricians, plumbers. . . people who'll come to the bar for lunch. And Roland, the mayor."

"Can we invite the Gaspards? My neighbours from the pheasant farm?"

"Of course. And the village shopkeepers."

We agree a date and I abandon my polishing to draft the invitations. Henri checks my French spelling and I type them up back at the cottage that evening while Mollie crouches in front of the log burner, baiting Milou with her teddy bear.

"I like this house, Mummy, but I miss Owen. When's he coming?"

"May half term. He'll be here for a whole week but we can Skype him."

From now on Mollie and I can contact Owen every day.

I ring Paul to update him about the party, but his phone goes to voicemail. Paul and his mobile are inseparable so I wait a few minutes and call again. This time he answers, sounding out of breath. In the background I hear a scrambling sound, followed by someone banging doors.

"What's that noise, Paul?"

"It's Malcolm. He's just . . .um, moving furniture around."

"Let me say hi and thank him for taking you in."

"Sorry, Emma. Malc can't talk just now. He's waiting for me to help. Sends his love."

Somewhere in Malcolm's flat, a door slams and I realise how little thought I've given to Paul's living arrangements. It can't be easy for either of them, going back to a flat share and Paul's told me that Malcolm's been severely depressed since his marriage to Lucinda broke down.

"Henri and I are planning a launch party at the bar."

"He's not inviting that bloody architect, is he?"

"Maxim? Don't think so."

What's that got to do with anything? And anyway, Paul liked Maxim's revised plans and the planning application for Les Quatre Vents has already been lodged.

"It's a marketing do for potential customers. We're inviting them to sample the *ouvriers*' menus."

"Good plan." His voice sounds thick and he coughs.

"Are you okay? Not coming down with flu?"

"Sorry, Em. I'm distracted. Inspector's report should be out soon."

I'm sick of hearing it. I drum my fingers on the polished surface of Mrs Browning's lamp table and think of those storm-blasted nights Mollie and I spent in the caravan while he's been warm and comfortable in Malcolm's flat. I click the red symbol. He calls me back; three times—I let it ring.

*

It's Henri, not Paul, who stands beside me to welcome guests to our opening party. As he introduces me to each new arrival, I file names in my memory and hope they'll stick.

Delicious aromas, just heavy enough to disguise the chemical smell of freshly-painted walls, waft from the kitchen, where Lilianne is producing miniature versions of the food we're planning for the workmen's menu. Mollie offers round bowls of peanuts and cheese straws, her golden curls bobbing, while I rehearse my barmaid role.

A tall, elegant woman of about forty-five arrives with her stouter husband, who is dressed in a French version of Harris tweed.

"You're honoured," Henri whispers in my ear. "The Gaspards rarely support village events."

Madame Gaspard slips off her coat and hands it to Henri, along with her husband's flat cap and gloves. Henri introduces them to me. Monsieur Gaspard's hand crushes mine, while his wife's handshake is light as the brush of a spider's web, and more fleeting. She has intelligent grey eyes in an unsmiling face and her first question is about our plans for extending Les Quatre Vents.

"Of course, from our house we do not see it."

I force a smile. Perhaps she was offended when we rocked up and started living in our caravan.

"I see now you have moved to an 'ouse in the village," says Madame Gaspard, bending to accept a cheese straw from Mollie. "That is good for the winter, no?"

"It is. We're so grateful to Mrs Browning."

My neighbour nods. "When your house is finished, you must come to us for an *apero*."

Roland, the mayor has arrived and the Gaspards move away from me to talk to him while Remy, the owner of the *boulangerie*, slots into the vacated space next to me.

"You and me, Madame Willshire. . ." he begins.

"Please call me Emma."

"You and me, Emma. Slowly we shall bring this village back to life."

He spreads his red, roughened hands and I picture his chunky fingers, dusted with flour, as he labours and sweats in his bakery before dawn each morning to keep the people of Sainte Violette supplied with fresh *baguettes* and *croissants*.

"When I came here," he continues. "The bar was closed, hotel was shut for the winter. What will you call the bar?"

"Bar les 4 Vents," I reply. "It links the business to our new home, but I'll use the numeral 4 instead of *quatre*."

His smile is warmer than freshly-baked *pain au chocolat*. "*Oui*. People will flock from far to support our village."

With thirty guests crammed shoulder to shoulder, chat and

laughter bounce off the turquoise walls and warm the space. Lilianne brings the first platters of buffet food and distributes them onto the candle-lit tables.

"Red or white?" I walk round with a carafe of wine in each hand. Red is the most popular and I make a mental note for my next trip to the wholesalers.

Lilianne joins me behind the bar. A couple of strands of dark hair are stuck to her forehead but she's otherwise unruffled by hours in the muggy kitchen.

"They enjoy the food, I think."

"I can't thank you enough, Lilianne."

The conversation volume drops as guests dig into their miniature portions of toad in the hole and *hachis parmentier*, scooping up sauces with chunks of Remy's *baguette*.

"I must thank you for the job," says Lilianne and her smile is tinged with wistfulness.

She glances towards a table where Henri is chatting with Martine, the hairdresser, and her husband. Henri—I wonder? Lilianne's single. It strikes me that she and Henri would be a perfect match.

The Berger brothers, Guy and Giles, arrive. Henri intercepts them at the door and steers them towards me. I notice Guy's hands are white with plaster dust.

"Any hot food left?" I whisper to Lilianne.

"I will see." She slips away through the secret mirrored door that leads to the kitchen.

Guy asks for draught beer; Giles has bottled. Guy is the younger brother but it's soon clear he's the boss. He drains his glass in a few swigs and pushes it towards me for a refill. Henri manoeuvres the conversation round to our renovation project and Henri insists on translating their responses for me.

"Guy wants to come for a site visit."

"*Oui*," agrees Guy between gulps of beer.

"They will get the quote to us next week. If you and Paul are happy with it, and the *permis de construire* is approved, they will start work during February."

"That's wonderful!"

As I prepare to hand Giles another bottle of beer, Guy neatly checkmates his brother by moving his empty glass directly into my eyeline.

"When is it good for them to come?" Henri asks me.

"Um—I can't do tomorrow. That's when the bar opens for business." I think of how my time will be sandwiched between dropping Mollie at school and collecting her from the *garderie*.

"Do you want me to do it?" asks Henri.

"Would you?"

"Of course." They agree a time to meet and shake hands.

Guy accepts a cheese straw from Mollie, inhales the flaky pastry and coughs. I pour him a glass of water and he wanders off to sample what's left of the food.

The Gaspards stand up and don their coats sparking an exodus. Guests queue to thank me. When everyone's gone in a fanfare of slamming car doors, Henri and I sit on bar stools and lift Mollie onto the rotating one between us.

"Spin me round! Spin me faster." She laughs.

We pick at the cold buffet leftovers.

"All the hot food went!" I say excitedly.

"Yes—they loved it. Especially the toad in the hole," Henri says.

"Really?" I wasn't sure but, it seems, people no longer think British food is disgusting.

From the kitchen comes the sound of pots clanking on the metal draining board.

"Lilianne don't do that now," I call. "Come and have a drink. Join us."

She appears in the doorway, wiping suds from her hands onto her apron. "Someone must do it. We open tomorrow."

She takes the stool next to me, furthest away from Henri, and accepts a small glass of red wine.

"*Santé!*" We laugh as we clink glasses.

Closeness has sprung up between us as we've worked to prepare the bar for opening. I've looked to them for guidance and they've worked unstintingly. And still I haven't paid Henri a single euro.

Mollie clambers across from her stool onto my lap and I wrap my arms around her. Soon Paul will return and I can't help but wonder, how will he fit in with our team?

CHAPTER 25

EMMA

Late January 2016

Each day when the clock on Sainte Violette church strikes eleven, I stand behind my bar and watch the door, alert for customers. According to Henri, lunchtime trade is exceeding expectations but each evening when I count the takings back at the cottage, I feel like a fortune teller reading tea leaves and waiting for a pattern to emerge.

"Stop worrying." Henri stamps his boots on the doormat as he enters the bar and yanks off the knitted hat that he wears pulled down over his ears. His cheeks are glowing. "I'm spreading the word through my clients."

He's sent one Dutch and two German couples to the bar but they live twenty kilometres away and spend their days ferreting out good value lunches.

"This bar needs locals, people closer to home."

"You have Claude," he reminds me.

His mention of my favourite regular's name brings a smile to my lips. Retired carpenter, Claude Armand, was so desperate for the bar to re-open that he ignored my hand-scrawled '*Fermé*' sign and stumbled in while Henri and I were painting the walls, tripping over Henri's open toolbox. Turquoise paint dripped from my roller onto the floor as he marched up to the bar and demanded, "*Un Ricard.*"

I gave him his first drink free of charge and let him perch on a bar stool watching me and Henri decorate. Since we opened, he's repaid me many times over, visiting the bar most days and bringing his cronies.

I finish washing up glasses from yesterday and fill the coffee machine with water.

"No Lilianne?" asks Henri.

I check my watch—this will be a test for me.

"I'll start on the lunches. Can you make sure Milou doesn't follow me into the kitchen?"

The dog cocks his ears, raises his head and flops back down at Henri's feet.

What did Lilianne say we should serve today? I check the freezer: several portions of a prepared chicken dish; hamburgers and steaks but I'm not yet confident about grilling a perfect steak *à point*. I rub the frost off the chicken and peer at the label to decipher Lilianne's spiky handwriting.

I test the deep fryer, prodding buttons, flicking knobs, pretending to be in control. From the fridge, I assemble salad leaves and cold meats ready to slice and lay out in the chilled cabinet for diners to help themselves. Lilianne has warned me to leave this task until the last minute so it stays fresh.

"Anything I can do?" Henri puts his head around the door, patting down his tousled hair.

The bar sounds ominously silent.

I flap my hands to usher him out. "Don't bring Milou in here. Just hold the fort for me."

As I finish chopping, I hear voices and stroll through to the bar.

"*Bonjour*, Madame!" Claude beams at me like a long-lost friend, though I saw him yesterday.

I nod and smile as I chalk up the day's menu on the blackboard. Italicising my handwriting takes concentration, I'm not wearing my contact lenses, so I lean close to the board and squint. Sensing someone standing behind me, I drop the chalk on the floor.

"You've spelt '*chasseur*' wrong." Henri picks up the chalk and hands it to me, reaching his arm around my back to point out my mistake.

As I turn towards him, laughing, a frosty draught blasts in through the open door and Lilianne pauses to shake rain from her umbrella.

"Lilianne, you've made it. Is everything okay?"

I shuffle out from behind the bar to greet her but she nods and strides past me, sweeping hair from her eyes and twisting it up into a bun.

In the kitchen doorway she pauses and glances at Henri but he's bending over the blackboard, proofreading my *menu du jour*. Her lips move soundlessly and I hold my breath, waiting for her to speak but she shrugs and disappears into the kitchen.

When Henri and Lilianne are together, there's a formality between them, more distant than is usual between colleagues. Yet sometimes I detect a shift in the atmosphere, as if there's more of a connection and things are being left unsaid. As an onlooker, I want to break down the barrier between them. It seems to me that Henri and Lilianne are made for one another. Only he doesn't seem to notice.

*

Another week passes and I fall into step with the rhythm of

each day. Claude arrives soon after opening time and sips a coffee before moving swiftly on to Ricard. Hubert Dupont watches me pour his Cognac. His budget is tight; he counts out coins to settle his tab and spaces out his drinks with water from the jug. Claude has his walking stick clenched between his knees, while Hubert's clawed left hand rests on the bar.

"When do you get the licence?" Claude asks in a wistful tone.

"Licence?"

"Tobacco, cigarettes." He pulls an empty pipe out of his jacket pocket and clutches it between nicotine-stained fingers.

Now I get it—the older villagers have waited impatiently, their lungs growing stronger with every day deprived of cigarettes and pipe tobacco. Sainte Violette has no *tabac* and their hopes are pinned on me getting a tobacco stand in the bar but the cost of the licence terrifies me, and stocking cigarettes might increase the risk of break-ins, so I'm disinclined to help them damage their health.

Hubert has other grumbles. He wants to buy a local newspaper. I bottle my annoyance. I can't do everything at once. Until I shouldered the burden, the bar was standing empty. Can't they be grateful for the spark of life I've breathed back into the village?

"The newspaper we can arrange and soon," promises Henri, stepping in to soothe the situation.

Hubert grunts and seeks out alternative reading matter: a few tourist leaflets from a rack on the bar. He sidles away from his lifelong friend, Claude, and carries his Cognac and his grumpiness to a table, where he sits studying leaflets of places he will never visit.

"Hubert makes a good point," says Henri. "We should have

Le Populaire on sale here. Later, you can offer other services—cigarettes, perhaps even *La Poste*."

"Hang on!" I laugh. "I'm still getting used to cooking and bartending. I can't run a post office, too. Perhaps I should do a customer survey!"

Feedback on how we're doing has been anecdotal. Sylvie, the first of the school gate mums to talk to me, said her husband had been in for his lunch.

"He said food was good," she told me. "And I am happy too, because he asked only a salad for his tea that night."

A young couple, sharing a Coke between them, are arguing at a window table; a passing mum drops in to ask if her son can use the toilet and I realise we've only served four lunches. My chest tightens as I think of the *hachis parmentier* portions I took out of the freezer and will have to chuck away.

Lilianne asks if she can finish early to visit her parents in Limoges. Henri escorts her to the door and they linger, conversing in low voices, while I brood and wonder if this business venture is another in the litany of failures comprising my life.

After Lilianne's gone, Henri props the door open, letting cold air rush in, while he lights a cigarette and blows smoke into the street. I rinse the few empty glasses and bang them down on the side of the sink.

"What's wrong, Emma?"

"It's nothing."

I slit open a box of tonics and start restocking the shelves.

"Are you worrying about your boy?"

Owen is in my thoughts from the moment I wake up. Our Skype calls are the highlight of my day but, in the bar, I'm forced to focus on the business. Why does Henri choose this moment to remind me?

"I'm his mother. I've worried about him—and loved him—from the moment he was born."

"My mother never worried about me." Henri unpacks a few cans of tonic from their box and builds a pyramid on the bar. "When I was ten, she left me and my father in England and returned to France. Every summer my father sent me here to stay with my mother. I hated it."

"Are you implying I've pushed off to France, abandoning my son with his father?"

I put my hands on my hips and scowl at him but my eyes are stinging and I fumble in my bag for my glasses to mask incipient tears. My face feels tight with the effort not to cry. I snatch cans from his stupid pyramid and stash them away on the shelves. As I turn, Henri touches my hand lightly.

"I didn't mean to suggest—"

My voice catches as I speak. "I'd have done anything to keep Owen with me."

"I know you didn't desert him. I'm not comparing you to my mother."

My glasses mist and I sniff. "Everything's such a mess. Paul was made redundant; we had debts—couldn't keep up payments on our house."

"I've heard—house prices in England are insane."

"We could never afford to start again. Not in London."

"You've made a difficult decision. It'll be good for Owen to have a strong relationship with his dad. Mine was amazing. It was much tougher for a single father back in those days."

"Why did your mother leave, then? If he was so great."

Henri shrugs. "She went to England as an au pair. Met my father and they married when she was only nineteen."

"Was she pregnant?" I wasn't much older than that when I married Zak.

"No. She was a God-fearing Catholic."

"So how did it work? Only seeing your mother in the summers."

He screws up his face. "To be frank. It was grim."

"As in?"

"My grandparents never accepted her marriage, but they didn't believe in divorce. When she returned home, they were furious. The worst insult of all was me. If my grandparents could have denied my existence, they would have done."

"You mean because of their faith?"

"Partly that. They resented that I spoke only English. All summer they jabbered away at me in French. I did understand a little, but I pretended not to. Grandfather told me I had the manners of a cur. Sometimes he made me sleep outside with the dog."

"What happened to your mother?"

Henri picks up an empty glass and twirls it in his hands. "She died. Thirty-six years old. Killed herself."

"I'm sorry." I fear my words sound clumsy, but it's a flash of insight into his solitary lifestyle. Perhaps it doesn't have to stay that way.

CHAPTER 26

EMMA

Early February 2016

February in the bar is bleak. Bleaker even than Henri foretold. We only open at lunchtimes and on Saturday evenings but there are days when I gaze out along the icy street and wonder if hell has frozen over. It's so cold that builders are forced to abandon work. The ground is too heavy even for mechanical diggers to break.

Claude and Hubert are propping up the bar when Lionel, the electrician, comes in rubbing his hands and stamping frosted mud across the floor and bragging, "Pah! In this weather, even plumbers cannot work, but we electricians have the power. Always we can work."

He orders toad in the hole. It's the only lunch we've sold today.

I join Lilianne in the kitchen, seize a cloth and pummel the metal surfaces until they gleam.

"We'll have to edit the menus. Restrict to two choices—one must be from the freezer."

"But you insist always on a vegetarian option!"

She's right to tease me. Demand for meat-free meals is low and I end up eating our veggie choices for my supper.

"There's something else." I force myself to meet Lilianne's eyes. It's good she's kept her coat on under her overall because my next words will chill her. "I think we'll have to close on Monday and Tuesday lunchtimes."

"I see." She fiddles with the strap of her bag.

"I'm sorry."

"No problem. I will find cleaning work."

She leaves her overall hanging over a chair, instead of folding it neatly away. Lilianne rents a tiny apartment with a balcony, where she grows geraniums and tomatoes in summer. If you stand in the centre of her kitchen, you can stretch your arms out and touch all four walls.

When I first met her, I assumed she was younger than her forty years. She has perfect bone structure and luminous skin, though her long dark hair is flecked with grey. She knots her scarf in that elegant way I've never mastered and gives a farewell flick of her hand.

As she reaches the door, Henri arrives, glancing back over his shoulder, perhaps checking his car, and canons into her.

"Sorry, Lilianne."

"Really, no problem." She rubs her arm, pulls her coat tighter and slips away.

"What's got into her?" asks Henri.

I grimace. "My fault. Had to give her bad news."

Henri raises an eyebrow. "Something I should know?"

"I've decided to close on Monday and Tuesday lunchtimes."

"Things that bad?"

I shrug and fiddle with my phone. "I'm not taking enough to cover costs. From Wednesday on, it's a little better."

"I'm sorry to hear that." He removes his gloves and stuffs them in a pocket. "I came to bring you some news."

"Good news? I could do with that."

He nods. "The Bergers can start work on Les Quatre Vents next week. If the big freeze lifts."

"That's brilliant!"

"They've asked for ten-thousand euros up front for equipment hire, materials and so on."

"Of course," I stutter.

"Have you thought about project management?"

I shudder. "I was hoping I wouldn't have to. Paul should be back in a couple of weeks."

"They'll need some direction to get started."

After the last customer leaves, Henri strolls behind the bar, lifts down a bottle of Scotch and pours himself a glass. He takes the exact change from his pocket and lays it on the counter, drains his Scotch and bangs the glass down.

"Come on. Let's take a drive up and check the lie of the land. Figure out what they need to do first."

I grab my coat and hang the *Fermé* sign on the door. Henri waits in his Renault, with the engine running, leaning across to open the passenger door for me. As I exhale, the windscreen mists over. He fiddles with the ventilation controls and unleashes air that smells of burning dust.

"Turn it off. I'd rather freeze!" I laugh, covering the vent with my palm to block the blast of hot air trained on my face.

Henri winds down the window, wipes the inside of the screen with a cloth and we wait for it to clear the old-fashioned way.

Les Quatre Vents looks blurred against a background of frosty fields; the oaks on the boundary are flecked silvery-white. As we bump along the rutted track, I take a picture with my phone.

"Here." Henri holds out his hand for my phone. "Let me take one of you to send to Owen."

I pose with one hand on the weather-beaten front door and smile. Something looks odd. "Where's the caravan?"

"Don't panic. Paul asked me to drag it inside the old barn to keep it weatherproof."

He leads me round to the rear courtyard, tugs the heavy barn door open and shows me the caravan, snug inside.

"Shouldn't we lock the barn?"

"Yes, but I'll give a key to the Bergers. They'll need somewhere to store equipment."

We traipse across to the main building, my feet skidding on icy patches. I need two hands to turn the key in its stiff lock. Inside it's dark, rotting shutters blot out exterior light. I edge across the floor and water slops over my shoes from a brackish puddle collected in the dirt.

"Oh no. The roof's leaking," I say but really, why am I surprised? At the far end of the building, the roof collapsed long ago.

"Doesn't matter. Roof will have to come off."

Henri shines his torch along a wall, blackened by damp and soot, and finds a window recess. He opens the shutter and makes a sawing motion with his hand on the adjacent wall made of rough stones, sandwiched together with dirt.

"The new bricks will start from here."

"Are the foundations strong enough to hold new bricks on top of old?" I ask.

"Yes, once the structure's reinforced. I've seen it done before."

My mind is waking up to the complexity of our project. This is no quick fix. It will take months to transform Les Quatre Vents into a home.

"You mentioned demolition?"

Henri nods. "That's first. Then site clearance before they can dig foundations for the extension. That's why they'll need guidance."

"But it's all in Maxim's plans."

"Sure but that's only an interpretation of what you're looking for."

I cast my eyes around the rough walls, the piles of debris and loose stones.

"I don't know anything about demolition." Or site clearance or digging foundations.

"Would you like me to be here?"

Would I! I snatch a breath. "Henri—we're broke. You've done so much for me already and I'll settle up with you for that, but we can't afford to pay you to do any more."

He switches off his torch. The light tumbling in through the open shutter is grit-grey. I can't see Henri's face and guess he can't see mine, so this is the moment to confess.

"Paul's still waiting for his redundancy pay-off. Until then we've barely enough for the Bergers' ten-thousand euro deposit."

I stumble outside and lean against the wall, shivering.

Henri follows me outside. "What's going on, Emma? Why isn't Paul here with you?"

"Nothing's going on!" I yell, clenching my hands. "We've been through a bad patch. I'm doing everything I can."

I stomp off towards his car, hesitate by the passenger door, and continue down our track to the road. As I reach the end of the drive I glance round and see Henri locking up. I set out along the road towards Sainte Violette.

Moments later, his Renault pulls alongside me. I hold my

head high, jut out my chin and stride on. He slows to a crawl, winds down the window.

"Emma, get in."

I shake my head and march on.

Henri's done nothing wrong. He's helped me in every possible way, but I can't handle my own humiliation. For a few hundred metres, he keeps pace with me, his car crawling along on the wrong side of the road and pulling onto the verge when oncoming drivers sound their horns or flash their lights.

"I'll be at Les Quatre Vents to meet the Bergers at eight on Monday morning," he calls through the window. "And there's no need to pay me."

He accelerates and I hobble on towards the village in my high-heeled shoes.

CHAPTER 27

EMMA

February 2016

The bar limps along on the tightest of margins. I scrutinise stocks, rotate dishes from the freezer and Mollie and I live off the leftovers. Our regulars grumble about the Monday and Tuesday closures but, on Wednesday mornings, Claude is waiting outside when I arrive.

"Did you miss me then?" I ask.

He screws his face into a grimace that softens when I hurry across to the bar and fire up the coffee machine, before switching on the heating or the lights.

"Merci, Madame."

Claude treats me to one of his rare smiles when I hand him his coffee and we're friends again. He's a man who rations cheerfulness and thrives on discussing the gloomier side of life and where better to do this than from a stool at our bar?

"What progress on the building?" he asks.

"Nothing," I reply.

His eyes light up and he wriggles his stiff buttocks on his stool but I'm not in the mood for sharing misfortunes.

After taking our ten-thousand euros, the Berger brothers

turned up at Les Quatre Vents on the appointed Monday morning. Henri and I were there to meet them. While Guy smoked, Giles stalked the site in his heavy boots, pausing every few metres to dig his shovel into the ground, scarcely breaking the surface. Before Guy had lit his second cigarette, Giles returned and pronounced the frozen conditions, "Impossible."

The three men leaned their heads together in a murmured discussion, impenetrable to me.

"What are they saying?" I asked Henri, struggling to catch his attention.

"One moment."

"Can't they at least start on the demolition?"

Slowly Henri broke away from the others and shook his head. "It's not worth starting because of the equipment. They need to minimise the hire period."

Giles climbed into the driver's seat of their van and started the engine. Guy clutched his unlit cigarette and shook my hand in farewell. My heart plummeted.

"What happens now!"

"Don't worry, they won't disappear with your money," Henri reassured me. "They'll bring forward a small indoor job and return when the weather improves."

Lilianne has found a cleaning job to plug the holes in her income but never once reproached me. We're groping towards a tentative friendship.

"Come round for a coffee after supper," I suggest and I'm surprised when she agrees, and in my excitement, I bake a fruitcake.

I wonder what she'll make of the cottage. I've cleared away Mrs Browning's fragile ornaments and put a few framed family photos on the mantelpiece. Living with impermanence, it seemed simpler not to lay down too many markers. I hope Lilianne's keen eye will see that the essence of our family is not in this cottage.

Lilianne cuts herself a crepe-thin slice of cake and we chat about the regulars and changes she's seen in the village.

"So many new homes," she exclaims, referring to the *lotissements*—small estates of twenty or so houses, spreading like arteries away from the heart of the village. "That was the finish of the village grocery."

I recall Remy telling me it closed five years ago. The post office and bank shut two years before that.

"But surely, more people living in the village means more customers?"

"No. They are young couples. For them it is the supermarket on their way home from work. They do not shop local."

"That's such a pity."

She nods. "For the bar, it will be different. Perhaps some younger people will come, and in summer many visitors pass through to visit Oradour."

"Is that the village where over six hundred people were massacred at the end of the War?"

She nods. "Tourists from all over the world come to visit, but I have never been."

"Maybe we'll go there. When Paul gets back."

"You must miss him?"

I nod, but I'd rather find out about her than talk about myself. "What about you? Have you ever been married."

Her eyebrows arch and faint lines appear on her forehead.

"Sorry—didn't mean to pry."

She flicks her wrist as if dismissing my question then changes her mind and sighs, "When I was young it didn't happen. There was someone once, but it ended. Now, I think it is too late."

I'd love to ask what she thinks of Henri. Each carries their solitude like a burden: Henri's is so habitual he doesn't seem to notice, while Lilianne's intensity of longing is painful to witness.

Half an hour later, she stands up, smooths down her skirt and collects her coat but the evening must have been a success because the following week we repeat it.

"I hear Lilianne has visited you," says Henri the following day. He could only have heard it from her.

He and I have finally agreed on an hourly rate for his bar work. Since then, the bar's been so quiet, I've hardly needed to call on him, but he drops in most days for a coffee or a beer.

"Why don't you join me and Lilianne one evening?" I suggest.

He smiles. "We could play cards."

That's not quite what I had in mind. My name isn't Emma for nothing, and I'm not above smoothing the path to love like my namesake in Jane Austen's novel. Though, I seem to remember, she messed up her matchmaking attempts quite spectacularly. Still, this could be an opportunity for Lilianne and Henri to spend time together outside of the public arena of the bar.

"Come next week."

When we gather for the evening, Henri brings rough red wine that I feel obliged to drink, while Lilianne sticks with coffee. Henri drinks too much and I have to remind him to keep his voice low, so as not to wake Mollie. He apologises and slides a pack of cards from his pocket.

"I thought you were joking!" My head aches from the red wine and I put my hand over my glass to stop him refilling it.

The pack of cards, still in its cellophane wrapper, lies abandoned on the table as our conversation flags but when Lilianne stands up to leave, earlier than usual, Henri fetches her coat and walks her home.

CHAPTER 28

PAUL

February 2016

Genevieve stands in her hallway, dressed in her work clothes: black trousers, ivory silk top, red shoes. She's dropped a shopping bag containing fillet steak and a bottle of Veuve Clicquot. Genevieve never cooks but I'm guessing, she's planned a celebration—a cosy dinner *à deux* to celebrate the publication of an advance summary of the accident inspector's findings.

The report that's held me trapped in this half-life, unable to move a foot forward, unable to flee, is out in the world and its findings have set me free.

"Bastard!" she screams. "You can't do this to me."

"I'm leaving," I confirm for the second or third time.

I've been waiting with my bag packed and a fight to Limoges booked for tomorrow morning. I'm catching a late train to Stansted and I'll kip on a bench. I can't stay here one more night.

She jerks her chin up; her eyes seek out mine and lock on. "I don't believe you."

I incline my head towards my travel bag. "I've booked a flight."

The hallway is airless and suffocating. Genevieve sways but

puts a hand against the wall to brace herself and leans towards me. Her face looming inches from mine, she repeats, "Bastard," and a fleck of spittle hits my cheek. She stalks past me to the sitting room. "Get me a gin and tonic," she commands, as if I'm still her slave and nothing's changed.

I didn't have to wait here to face her— could have checked out while she was at work and posted her keys through the letterbox. But I needed to draw a line to make her understand that this is it—it's over.

With the edge of my shoe, I shunt my holdall against the wall, stroll to the kitchen and pour a triple measure of Bombay Sapphire. I open a can of tonic, take ice from the freezer and slice a lime thinly. I carry Genevieve's drink into the sitting room. I don't fix one for myself.

Genevieve is sitting on the sofa, leaning back against two silk cushions, with her eyes half-closed and one hand pressed to her temple. She's kicked off her red shoes; they lie on their sides like splashes of blood against her cream carpet. She reaches up and snatches the drink from my hand.

"Sit down," she barks. "Have some decency."

I do as I'm bid, perching on a chair in the full glow of an uplighter, ready for my interrogation.

"I don't get it, Paul." Her voice falters.

Genevieve never pleads. She barks orders, emotes, wheedles. Her face looks blurry, seeming to dissolve in front of me. Perhaps I could have liked this more vulnerable Genevieve better.

At work, and in our personal life, we were always bumping up against one another, exchanging sharp remarks and bouncing away. But in the bedroom—blissful carnage. Genevieve was never too tired, never had a headache. I'm the one who was too stressed to perform but, even on my worst days, she could lure me back nibbling my shoulder, my chest, my abdomen—working her way down until I was ready to explode.

She peers at me over the rim of the tumbler, her eyes foggy, words muffled by the glass.

"All the lies I told, the witness accounts I set up—everything was for you."

I stare at my shoes. Was it my fault she got it into her mind that our relationship was the real deal? That we'd be together for ever? Without her support, I'd be ruined. I could be heading for a custodial sentence. As it is, I've lost my job, but not my reputation. I'll still be able to work in the construction industry—maybe on contract, certainly at a lower level but, in time, I could rebuild a career. But that's not what I want.

I move to sit beside her on the sofa, take her hand, find a tissue to wipe the single tear she's rationed herself. I stroke her hair, kiss her cheek.

"I'm so grateful to you. For everything."

She puts a hand on each side of my head, yanks me close, kisses me with trembling lips. I pull away.

"Stop! How can I make you see?" I choose my words carefully. "All those months teetering on a cliff edge; not sure if I was going to jump, fall or be pushed. I have to get back to normal."

Genevieve gazes at me, a tiny spark illuminating her blank eyes. "That's right. It's the stress. I get it now. But it's temporary, Paul. It's over with Emma. Admit it. She doesn't enjoy the same things as you, doesn't get you. You two have nothing in common."

"You're a wonderful woman. You'll find someone who deserves you."

She straightens her back and fixes me with misty eyes. "Give it a few months. France isn't the answer. You know what we had. You'll come back."

She follows me to the door and watches me walk away, her gaze scorching my back. I lengthen my pace, my footsteps pounding the pavement. As I turn the corner, I hitch my holdall over my shoulder, take a deep breath and break into a run.

CHAPTER 29

EMMA

February 2016

The day after Henri and Lilianne spent the evening with me at the cottage, they're both monosyllabic and grumpy; neither offers a word of thanks so I assume my hospitality wasn't to their taste. I can't wait to finish work and escape from them. If I hurry I might have just enough time to stop at home for a moment of calm with a cup of tea, before picking Mollie up from the *garderie*.

As I round the corner and approach the cottage, I notice something on my doorstep that looks like a sack of old clothes. I bump my bicycle's front wheel against the kerb and reach into the basket for my glasses. The sack moves and coalesces into the shape of a man and suddenly I'm laughing and running—hurtling towards him.

"Paul!" He's sitting hunched-up on his holdall, his collar turned up against the bite of the wind. "Why didn't you tell me?"

He leaps to his feet and gathers me into a hug, so tight, it forces air from my lungs. "I wanted to surprise you."

I cling to him, breathless. It's the longest we've ever been apart.

"You should have come to the bar."

He shakes his head. "I didn't want to share this moment with anyone else. It's over, Emma. I'm off the hook!"

The corners of his eyes crinkle but his smile is fleeting and there's a new leanness about his lower face. When you live with someone day to day you don't notice small organic changes but, after a separation, you can't help spotting new hollows and creases.

"Come in." I unlock the door. "What do you think of our new home?"

*

After dinner, Paul fills me in on the final act of the drama at Manifold.

"My legal adviser talked me through the inspector's findings," he explains. "They found a raft of health and safety failings at Manifold, but no direct link to Dorek's death. They concluded it was an accident. The report censured the company without holding directors responsible."

"So that's it?"

His face relaxes into a smile. "I'm off the hook. At last. Manifold can expect a substantial fine—my lawyer said it could be half a million. But my redundancy pay's in the bank so it's not my problem."

"We can put it behind us."

Mollie's thrilled to have her father back, and so am I, but his arrival rebalances my fragile friendship with Henri and Lilianne. Paul slots into Henri's occasional place behind the bar. To my surprise, he's garnered enough French vocabulary to chat with the regulars about sport, food—even politics.

"Paul Willshire, you're full of surprises. How did you polish your French so fast?"

"Long boring evenings at Malcolm's. Nothing else to do."

Our evenings in the cottage are anything but boring and I wallow in the luxury of family time. As winter retreats, Milou creeps away from his place in front of the log burner and settles at Paul's feet, transferring his affections away from me now Paul's the one who rises early and takes him out for his first walk of the day.

"You seem so much more relaxed," I remark as Paul rubs his hand across Milou's tightly coiled coat.

He nods. "Here I can breathe again. London felt like a sewer—full of shit and problems." He shifts in his chair; the dog slides off his feet and gives him a reproachful look. "I have news. The Berger brothers are starting work on Les Quatre Vents."

"How did you find out?"

I'm used to updates coming via Henri but since Paul's return, his visits to the bar have tailed off.

"Guy Berger stopped by at lunchtime. The hire company's dropping off the digger tomorrow. Time for me to change professions."

"Back to surveying?"

"No, dafty." He smiles and ruffles my hair. "Project managing up at the house. So I'm passing the bartending baton back to you."

"Do you think it will be ready by May?"

Already I'm having nightmares about moving back into the caravan when Mrs Browning returns.

"With me project managing? Of course."

He heads upstairs to read Mollie's bedtime story and the dog snuffles and trots across to me.

"Sorry, Milou. I have to make supper."

When Paul joins me at the kitchen table, he's carrying his tablet and seems distracted.

"Leftovers from the bar again," I announce, setting a plate of *boeuf bourguignon* in front of him.

He glances at the food and turns back to his tablet, sliding it across the table towards me. "Did you see this?"

"No, what?" I pause with my fork in mid-air.

"Cameron's announced the European Union Referendum date for the twenty-third of June."

I savour my first mouthful of beef, wishing I had Lilianne's culinary skills. Reluctantly, I glance at the headline.

"How will it affect us? Our business is up and running, we're registered for tax and we've bought a property."

Paul's brow creases. "It's hard to say. The Remain side is sure to win but it could be close."

I must have done something bad in a previous life to be condemned to teeter forever on the brink of uncertainty and loss. Every time I think I've caught hold of life and pinned it down, some new threat ripples the waters.

"We must register for postal votes." Paul's practical streak takes over and I'm reassured. I shove the worry to the edge of my mind.

*

"What do you think about Britain having a referendum on whether to stay in the EU?" I ask Lilianne the following day.

She threads a loose strand of hair back behind her ear. "I have never heard about it." She plunges a knife into a potato, boiling harmlessly in a pan. "We French have our problems with the EU but why would we change?"

I sit down heavily on a chair and sip a glass of water. "We'd be mad not to stand together. Britain will do the same. You'll see."

CHAPTER 30

EMMA

March 2016

March arrives and the Limousin countryside dusts off its winter drabness. Buds burst into tentative blossom, green shoots spread across soggy fields and Paul spends his days up at Les Quatre Vents.

"How did it go today?" I ask as he kicks off his muddy boots in the porch.

He's persuaded the Bergers to knock a couple of thousand euros off their estimate by taking on a labouring role. They were sceptical at first, but once they realised he had relevant skills, they agreed. Demolition of parts of the old building was completed in February and now they're digging foundations for the extension.

"It's taking shape."

He washes his hands, wiping them on a tea towel with a picture of Mont St Michel. It belongs to Mrs Browning like everything in the house except our clothes.

"How long?"

"Come up with me tomorrow and I'll show you."

In the morning, we approach the house, barren branches shake in the wind, but the cherry tree is heavy with buds, waiting to unfurl in the first serious sunshine. With no foliage to shield it, the building resembles a bomb site. The last vestiges of the roof have gone but now someone has taken a sledgehammer to the walls. Great perpendicular gashes have been cut at intervals along the walls for doors and windows.

"The original foundations couldn't support the weight," explains Paul. "The next job is to tie the building together. We'll insert reinforcing rods down to the ground and just below roof level. Then we'll link up special blocks, with a channel carved into them, all the way round the building. Once it's set in concrete, it will stay solid and stable."

"You're enjoying this, aren't you?"

The fine lines around his eyes deepen as he smiles.

"I love being hands on. Shaping something strong and secure is better than giving instructions to teams and watching them become slapdash."

"Why didn't you choose architecture?" I ask. "I don't think you ever told me."

"It takes seven years to become an architect and my father made it clear I'd be on my own, if that was my choice." He shrugs. "But he stopped supporting me after my first year at university, anyway. That taught me an important life lesson."

"What was that?" It can't have been how to manage money.

"To make my own decisions and not listen to anyone else."

We tramp around the perimeter and Paul points out the trench where the pipes and services will run. At one end of the house, the Bergers have dug foundations for the L-shaped extension and, abutting the back of the building, a shallower trench where concrete will be poured to form a patio.

"I've told them to deepen the patio foundations to give us a base if we need another extension in future."

"You've thought of everything."

He grins and strokes my hand. "It's my profession—but on a bijou scale."

Mrs Browning is due back sometime after Easter so we'll all have to squeeze back into the caravan before Owen's visit.

While cooking supper, I try to imagine how it will be waking up in the caravan on a building site, picturing electricians and plumbers arriving while I'm getting Mollie ready for school.

Paul's phone rings and he steps away from me to take the call.

"Who is this?" I hear him say followed by, "Don't ring me again." He shoves his phone back into his pocket.

"Why don't you tell those chaps from Manifold to stop hassling you?"

"I have—sort of." He shrugs "Doubt I'll hear from them again but I have to keep up with some industry contacts."

"Why? We live here now."

He puts his arm around me but, when he speaks his face is serious. "I'm starting to worry Britain might vote to leave the EU."

My heart beats faster. "What would that mean for us?"

"Well, nothing would change overnight, but longer term Britain wouldn't be part of the club. So we'd have to expect the French government to set new rules."

"You mean they could force us to leave France?" I shiver.

Up to now the referendum has seemed unreal. France has been my sanctuary: juggling the bar with Mollie's needs, breathing life back into our ruin. I'm more settled than in our old life in London. It's because I have a purpose. If only we weren't separated from Owen, I could imagine staying here forever.

"I don't think they'd force us out," Paul continues. "But we could become pawns in bargaining between Britain and the rest of the EU. Who can say if the bar and a small holiday *gîte* business would support us? And the remainder of my pay-off would plummet if the pound loses value."

"So change it into euros now."

"I'll think about it. We'll have to wait and see. It's all we can do."

*

While an uncertain future comes barrelling towards us, Paul throws himself into the renovations up at Les Quatre Vents, but manual work no longer calms him. He buzzes with nervous energy and his phone rings constantly, but he never says who's calling. Could it be creditors?

"You did pay off all your debts in London?" I ask.

"Of course. And there's enough left from the house sale and my redundancy pay to do the work on Les Quatre Vents."

"I know. I've been checking the account." But what if there are other debts he hasn't told me about? Like before.

"Stop worrying, Emma. Everything's under control."

One night while I'm in the bathroom with the door open, locked in mortal combat with a contact lens, I hear Paul take a call on his mobile. His words are too indistinct to catch but his voice has a note of anger. Not noticing my lens has already popped out, I spend ten minutes trying to prise out my left cornea while the lens floats away down the plughole. I squint at my red eye in the mirror. Trying to make monthly disposables last three months is false economy; tomorrow, I'm going back to glasses.

"Who was that on the phone, Paul?" I ask when I go back downstairs.

"Um—just Malcolm."

"It sounded like something was wrong."

"I feel sorry for him. He's still arguing with Lucinda over money. Honestly, some women are so vindictive ." He jumps to his feet and gathers me into a hug. "Not like you, Emma. I'm so lucky."

The next day we take Mollie with us to a DIY store to look at bathroom fittings. Paul takes my elbow and steers me away from the designer brands towards budget buys and discounted ends of ranges. Bathrooms are laid out as miniature room sets and Mollie plays house, waving to us through cut-out windows in fake partition walls.

Paul hurries me past the stylish baths and basins, saying, "I've already found a deal at the builder's merchant."

"What are we doing here, then?"

"Thought you'd want to choose the fitments—taps, tiles."

There are hundreds of tiles on display, but my eyes are drawn to handmade Moroccan tiles in shades of blue—duck egg, peacock, aquamarine.

"How about these?" I pick one up, run my hand over the uneven glaze, admiring the centuries of craftsmanship that have shaped its imperfections. I turn it over in my hands and gasp at the stickered-on price. "So expensive!"

"Maybe we should stick with white," says Paul, pointing towards another display. "If we get those large ones I can fit them myself."

I bite my lower lip. Every step on our journey reminds me

we're not fitting out a dream home and I'll have to get used to showering in a bathroom that looks like a municipal toilet block but these details aren't important. Without Owen, Les Quatre Vents will only ever be a house, never a home.

CHAPTER 31

EMMA

March 2016

As early season tourists trickle into the area, bar trade picks up. A grey-haired couple from Yorkshire question me about the salmon dish and, before I can escape back to the kitchen, the woman strikes up a conversation.

"This morning we visited Oradour-sur-Glane. It made quite an impression, didn't it, Roy?"

Roy scratches the bridge of his nose where his glasses have left a red mark. "Yes." He continues studying the menu, as if hoping more choices will appear.

"I haven't been there," I confess.

Normal family activities like day trips belong to a different life but perhaps, when Owen is here for May half term, Henri could cover the bar while we have a day off.

"Where are you from?" the woman asks.

"Originally Wales. Before moving here, we lived in Wimbledon."

"You must be worried about this EU Referendum coming up in June?"

"Not especially. Should we be?"

The woman's face has pale patches where her bronzing

166

moisturiser didn't take. "We love France and being part of Europe. We're worried about some of the views being expressed at home."

The conversation preys on me and I wonder if tectonic plates are shifting.

"Have you registered our postal votes yet?" I ask Paul when he drops in for a lunchtime beer.

He's wearing the blue jumpsuit overalls, loved by French tradesmen, and his boots leave a trail of grit and dried mud across the floor.

"Not yet. But I will, I promise."

He nods to Hubert and they chat about the village football team. We've offered to sponsor their kit for next season to reinforce links between the bar and the village. After Paul leaves, Hubert goes back to staring silently into his drink. Claude, a man he's known since childhood, is sitting next to him but I've noticed they ration their conversation: a few words at a time. Perhaps they worry they'll run out of things to say.

Lilianne once told me that Claude's wife of fifty years insists he's out of the house for at least five hours every day. What does she do in that time? I asked, a vision of the elderly Madame Armand having a romantic liaison with the postman making me giggle but Lilianne's reply made me laugh even harder. "She must clean the 'ouse, of course. Five hours every day!"

Mollie's exhausted when I pick her up from school and dozes off in front of the television. As I tiptoe to fetch a rug to cover her, I notice a light blinking on Mrs Browning's answerphone. Paul and I use our mobiles, with French sim cards, sparingly, so I wonder if the message can be for us. I jab my finger on the button and listen to a man's voice with a faint Somerset burr. The message is distorted; I play it again. It's Peter Browning, our landlady's son, ringing to tell us she's had a fall and is in hospital in England. She won't be returning to France for a while. I dial Peter Browning back on the number he left.

"Peter? It's Emma Willshire from France. So sorry to hear about your mother's accident."

It's more serious than expected. Mrs Browning has broken her hip and had an operation.

"She's recovering, but she seems confused," says Peter. "To be honest, I'm wondering if she'll ever be fit enough to return to France. I don't think she could manage on her own."

"I'm so sorry to hear that. What do you want us to do?"

"Carry on living in the house for the time being. You'd be doing her—and me—a favour."

"But what about rent? We've been caretaking over the winter."

"I see." From his sharp intake of breath, I discover Peter didn't know our arrangement. Silence broods between us as he ponders. "Well stay on for now. I'll see how she recuperates and have a rethink towards the end of June."

I note the hospital's address so I can send a card but Mrs Browning's misfortune is our good luck. We won't be back in the caravan for Owen's visit; we'll be in the house.

CHAPTER 32

EMMA

May 2016

As the date of Owen's visit approaches, I stay late in the bar preparing all his favourite meals and stashing them in the freezer. I can't cook them at home because Mrs Brownhill's fridge has only a tiny ice box and I don't want to waste a single moment of our time together.

Mollie and I set out insanely early to drive to the airport and arrive before Owen's plane has taken off from Stanstead. We perch on a wooden chair, fixed to others to make a rigid line and I try to distract her with a story, but she yawns, snatches the book from my hand, rifles through the pages to get to the end.

To pass the time we take a stroll and my eyes are drawn to a poster on the wall outside the cloakroom: faces of missing children. The poster's caption appeals for help to find them. One face sticks in my mind. A little boy called Habib Nedder, who disappeared from Toulouse in 2014 and has never been found. A roar of engines rips through the terminal building.

"Look Mollie—that must be Owen's plane!" We watch the passengers cross the tarmac. "There he is!"

He's weaving his way past the slower walkers to reach the

head of the queue. We wave but he can't see us. Owen is among the first through the gate and Mollie darts forward, calling his name.

"Hey, Titch." He grins, dodging her kiss and giving her a high-five.

He's grown taller and lankier but when I hug him, I can feel new muscles on his upper arms and discover the reason when I try to lift his bag.

"What have you got in there?" I ask.

"A couple of free weights." He grins. He's developing the upper body of a young man, and I'm missing the last years of his childhood.

"Dad says all the tutoring was worth it," Owen tells me in the car. "Looks like I've passed the entrance exams for Dulwich."

"Well, clever you. That's fantastic." Does he hear the slight catch in my voice? "I'm proud of you."

"And Dad says, if I have too much homework, I won't have to go to church every Sunday. And he's agreed I can play rugby and. . . I can't wait for September."

If Zak's determined to launch Owen into an expensive school, I hope he's put enough money aside, I think grimly, because there's no way Paul or I can help.

As I park the Volvo in front of Mrs Browning's cottage, Owen acts confused.

"Why've you stopped here? This isn't our house?"

With a pang, I realise how far my son's life has drifted away from mine. So many times I've told him we're caretaking this cottage; Skyped him from here most days; updated him on renovations up at Les Quatre Vents— but my words haven't coalesced into a picture in his mind. He's locked into his London life—to him, our world in Sainte Violette means nothing.

"No—our house is still being renovated. We'll go up and show you later."

"Cool."

"You're sleeping in my room." Mollie leads her brother up the steep stairs and the grinding of metal across floorboards tells me she's demonstrating the pull-out bed.

From upstairs, Owen lets out a whoop of delight. "When did we get a dog?"

Paul comes home early and, as we gather for supper, everyone is smiling. Owen has spent the afternoon teaching Milou new tricks but I don't tell him Milou will do anything for a dog treat. My family is together again. I want to seal this moment in my heart.

"Let's do something special tomorrow. A trip," I suggest. "I'll talk to Lilianne."

But she can't run the kitchen and bar on her own so perhaps Henri will be free to help. Since Paul's return we've rarely seen him, but he can only say no.

Over supper, my once-monosyllabic son, pours out his news. A line of nonsense poetry by Lewis Carroll spools in my head. *'The time has come, the walrus said to talk of many things, of shoes and ships and sealing wax, of cabbages and kings.'*

Usually, when I ask Owen about Zak he clams up, but today he wraps up his tales of sport and school and moves on to the cabbages and kings: his home life. It's odd hearing about Zak's obsession with church and about Carlene taking Owen to visit the London School of Economics, where she's studying for her doctorate.

Owen stops talking and forks up a few mouthfuls of casserole. "Have you got any hot sauce?" he asks.

I fetch it from the kitchen.

"Thanks. Dad's turned insanely strict. Way stricter than you guys."

"In what way?"

"He doesn't want me hanging out with mates. Like Saturdays—I have to go with Carlene to Brixton and carry her bag while she shops for yam or cassava."

"What's cassava?" Paul asks.

"How should I know! Carlene makes it into *garri* and serves it with soup."

"Never heard of it," says Paul.

"Do you like Carlene's food?" I ask.

When Zak and I were together, his favourite meal was sirloin steak and chips.

Owen shrugs. "It's okay. It's not always Carlene. Dad cooks, too, and guess what?"

"I don't know."

"Dad's got a new girlfriend."

"Oh." I feel an odd twinge—surely it can't be jealousy after all this time?

"Her name's Aurelia. She's training to be a doctor and she goes to our church."

"Is she um—Nigerian?"

"No. Her mum's from Liverpool and her dad's Jamaican. When we go out together, people think she's my mum."

I lay down my fork and clasp my hands in my lap. Paul reaches for my hand under the table and squeezes it.

"But I tell them that's ridiculous," continues Owen. "Because Aurelia's only, like, twenty-three years old, and my mum would have to be way older."

*

Paul must have memorised the Oradour-sur-Glane guidebook and on the short drive he tells us what to expect. "The village has been left standing as a memorial to 642 people massacred by Waffen-SS forces on the tenth of June 1944."

Owen's attention is wrapped up in his own technology but Mollie's listening and she's grasped the big words.

"Did they all die, Mummy?"

"Not quite all, sweetie. I think six survived to tell their story." I swivel round in my seat to check on her. "Are you sure this is suitable for Mollie?" I ask Paul.

"She'll be fine."

But, as we clamber out of the car, I recall the victims included 205 children and slip my hand into Mollie's and grip it tight. The morning is charged with sunshine but a shiver slides along my arm. I wish I'd brought a cardigan.

Our visit starts with an amble through an exhibition setting out the background in sombre detail. We learn the history of the village and its inhabitants and the horrific massacre that took place four days after the D-Day landings. Paul listens to the audio description, scans all the maps and pictures and soon falls behind; Owen out-paces us, giving scant attention to the displays.

"It's no good, Paul. It's too dense for them."

Ungluing his eyes from sepia photographs, he nods and we emerge, blinking, into sunshine. We climb a few steps and pause to read the sign at the entrance to the ruined village: *Souviens-toi.*

"It means 'remember,' " I tell Owen.

We drift on in silence. Even Mollie seems subdued. This was a mistake—we shouldn't have brought them here. The first field, with its collapsed walls and randomly-strewn stones, could be an archaeological excavation of a site from the Middle Ages or earlier.

Owen whips out the smartphone Zak has bought him to replace the cheap pay-as-you-go I gave him and snaps away, as we roam the haunted streets of burnt out buildings. I wonder if he's using it as a shield from the horror? I don't need pictures. This place grips me with a visceral force. I will certainly remember.

Each ruined building was once the home or workplace of an innocent villager. Mollie creates a game, peeking into each house and calling out an inventory of any household goods still recognisable.

"I see a bed, two cooking pots, another sewing machine."

Only metal goods have survived; small things that make up family life.

"I've counted fourteen!" says Owen, sliding his phone close to my face to show another picture of a sewing machine, its metal twisted in the furnace of flame that destroyed the village.

Every house seems to have one: a valued emblem of thrifty times—iconic in this setting as a memorial to families who lost their lives. When Owen was a baby, I used to sew—curtains and simple clothes. Perhaps I'll start again. Stitch things back together.

"What happened here, Mum? Really?"

Owen didn't listen to Paul in the car and he drifted through the exhibition, not taking anything in but now it's gripped him.

Imparting the brutal facts falls to me.

"The Waffen-SS separated the men from the women. They took women and children to the church and the men to six barns. First, they shot the men in the legs so they couldn't run, then they set fire to the barns. In the church, the troops set off an incendiary device. When the women and children tried to escape, the soldiers fired on them with machine guns and hurled more explosives in through the windows. Then they burnt the church. Afterwards they torched the village to hide their evil deeds."

"But why?"

Salty sweat collects on my forehead and dribbles into my eyes, making them sting. I move into the shade of a tree, pour water from my drinking bottle onto a tissue, take off my sunglasses and dab at my eyes.

"The commander claimed they were retaliating against freedom fighters, searching for hidden weapons and seeking revenge for the kidnap of a German officer. But I think. . ."

My words trail away—what do I think?

Images of terrorism, war and injustice flood my brain. Villages are still being destroyed and people driven from their homes.

"These people were living here peacefully in their community when everything changed. Sometimes in some places, evil flourishes. It still happens."

CHAPTER 33

EMMA

June 2016

Owen's visit flies by too quickly and when he leaves, Mollie won't sleep alone in her room. When I go upstairs, I find her in my bed, curled up under the duvet. I let her sleep and climb in beside her, leaving Paul to fend for himself in Mollie's room if he can find a way of folding his long limbs into her narrow single bed.

"How long is this going on for?" he grumbles.

"Until she stops missing Owen."

He's changed into the big brother she always wanted—interested in her concerns, no longer treating her like an annoying brat.

"He's been gone a week."

As if she—or I—ought to have snapped out of it by now.

"I missed you every single day when you were in London. How d'you think I feel about being separated from Owen?"

"I didn't mean—"

"Then don't ask dumb questions!" I snap before I turn on my heel and walk away.

Paul gives me space to calm down and, when he comes to find me, he holds me close and whispers an apology.

Opinion polls back at home swing in favour of Brexit and away again. Our postal votes arrive. We place our crosses with strategic care and send them off. Although the UK feels far away, it's hard to plan for the future with a question mark hanging over us.

The next time Roland, the mayor of Sainte Violette, drops into the bar to chat to the locals, I ask him what impact he thinks a vote to leave the EU would have on Brits who live in France.

He wrinkles his brow as if having difficulty understanding what I'm asking.

"Brexit?" I venture.

"Ah yes." That phrase he does know. "Do not worry, Madame, I am sure it will not happen."

"But if it does?"

He shrugs. "Then our countries must work it out."

Paul reassures me the house is taking shape but it's a while since I visited, so I clear away the lunches, leave Lilianne in charge of the bar and cycle up to Les Quatre Vents.

The sun beats down on my bare head and the bike's tyres whip dust into my eyes as I peddle. I wheel my bike up the track towards the ugly extension: grey blocks waiting to be rendered and a roof of red concrete tiles.

The original structure has been patched so the exposed concrete blocks sit on top of the original stones and it looks unbalanced like a Lego castle on a mound of pebbles. In several places, the wall bulges where old joins the new. Instead of windows or doors, there are gaps draped with plastic, flapping in the breeze.

"Emma!" Paul appears from behind the building wearing his dark blue overalls and welcomes me with a kiss.

"All on your own?" I ask.

"Yes."

"Bergers knocked off early?"

He shrugs. "They've not been here for a couple of weeks. Nothing for them to do at the moment."

"What about the doors and windows?" I ask.

We picked them out of a catalogue, ready-stained a muddy shade of brown. Awful, but cheap.

"I haven't ordered them yet."

I feel a twinge of unease. The site has a stagnant feel; a casual passer-by would be hard-pressed to say if it was being built up or knocked down.

"So, what have you been working on today?"

"Come and see." He leads me across to the barn and points inside at a pile of newly-chopped logs stacked along one wall. "For the wood burning stove."

I glance up at the uninterrupted blue of the sky, the fierce globe of the sun beating down on the parched earth and disguise the irritation in my voice.

"Isn't that premature?"

There's a chimney, jutting out of our roof but, as far as I'm aware, no hearth, no shiny pipe and no stove for logs to burn on. And anyway, what would be the point of installing an expensive wood burner in a house with no doors and windows?

Paul ignores my question, takes a pack of cigarettes from his pocket and strikes a match.

"You said you'd stopped!"

When I first met Paul, he didn't smoke but the stress around Dorek's accident drove him to it.

"Sorry. Just the odd one—with the Bergers." His match

flickers out. He cups his hands around the cigarette, tries again and this time it flares into life. "Do you know what day it is?"

"June the twenty-third."

"Referendum day in the UK."

"Tomorrow we'll know our fate."

I've followed the news but there's no hard information, only speculation. Although our business is registered, our right to stay is based on being citizens of the European Union; we've not been here long enough to apply for a permanent *carte de séjour*. If Britain votes to leave, there's no guarantee we'll have the right to stay in France.

I move my bike away from the side wall where I'd left it propped up and wheel it towards the drive.

"I must get back to the bar so Lilianne can go home."

We've moved onto summer hours and the bar stays open most evenings, picking up passing trade from tourists. Lilianne does an occasional evening shift but usually it's me or Paul.

"I'll come with you."

He drops his cigarette end and stamps on it.

"No, you collect Mollie and take her home."

*

After the last customer leaves, I lock the bar and arrive home just before ten. As I open the front door, I hear the chime of Big Ben and see Paul is settled in front of the television.

"Hush a moment," he calls, putting up his hand to silence me.

"That's a nice welcome."

"Sorry—the news is just starting."

I fetch myself a glass of tap water and settle next to him on the sagging sofa. I must stop Mollie using it as a trampoline.

Paul puts his arm around me, without shifting his eyes from the screen.

"I think it's going to be all right."

He's smiling and his eyes gleam as television cameras swivel between leaders of both the Remain and Leave campaigns, all of whom seem to be anticipating a vote to remain. The City of London has called it that way; around the world, stock markets are booming.

"Thank goodness!" Paul leaps up and fetches a bottle of sparkling wine from the fridge. "Celebration."

Knowing he'd prefer a Scotch, I smile my thanks as he pours out two glasses, holding his up to the light and watching the bubbles until they fizzle out. "Leaving the EU could be dire for the UK property industry."

"But that doesn't affect you. You've left."

But I can see that his love of the property world hasn't left him.

"Uncertainty's always bad for the economy. Home-based businesses wouldn't make plans; foreign companies wouldn't invest. Banks might decamp to Frankfurt or Paris. It would dampen demand for office blocks and luxury flats."

"Huh—maybe that's a good thing."

I hated watching London being concreted over; ugly priapic towers turning the city into a maze of wind tunnels and flats left empty by owners, who'd bought them as investments.

"Investing in real estate isn't like having your savings in a bank," Paul continues. "Big corporate investors—like pension funds—rely on income from rents on offices and shopping centres to pay pensions. If there's a downturn, investors want to pull their money out but you can't sell vast buildings just like that."

I stifle a yawn. I am a little bit interested, but it's getting late. We listen to pundits droning on and watch the first results come in from Gibraltar where ninety-six per cent of people voted to remain. I get to my feet. "I'm going up. You coming?"

"I'll stay and watch a bit longer."

I don't remember falling asleep but, when Paul comes into the room, I'm vaguely aware that he crosses to the window and lifts an edge of one curtain, peering out at the grey dawn. I hear the first birdsong, isolated chirps marking a new day, turn on my side and slip back into my dream.

Later, Paul wakes me with a cup of tea and Mollie's voice floats up from downstairs, singing a song in French.

"Is it that time already!"

I wriggle out from under the sheet, stretch and prop myself up on one elbow.

Paul sits down heavily on the edge of the bed, trapping my foot.

"It's happened." He stares down gloomily into his mug.

"What? What's happened?"

"The UK has voted to leave the EU."

I'm wide awake but I rub my eyes and feel the weight of Paul's backside pressing on my foot. It tingles with cramp.

"I was hoping this wouldn't happen— thought our savings might last till we finished the house."

"But you've set the money aside. I've been keeping a check on the account."

He looks at me, bleary-eyed, and reaches for my hand.

"I should have moved the money to France, Emma—like

you suggested. The pound's already nosedived. We could lose ten per cent—or more."

"You mean, we won't have enough?"

He nods. "It was tight, anyway. That's why I laid the Bergers off. . ."

Paul sets down his mug and turns to face me.

"I'm sorry, Emma. I didn't want to worry you but when you work on an old building you can't know what problems you'll find. The costs have been escalating. I thought I could save money by doing more of the work myself."

"Listen. It may not be so bad. Trade in the bar is picking up. Soon it will be the main holiday season—"

"But we can't live on that, Emma! It's not enough."

"Have you looked at the bar accounts recently? Since March the takings have been far better than you expected."

He tugs his hand away from mine and pulls his phone from his pocket, scrolling through screens with restless fingers.

"What are you doing?"

"I'll have to go back to London for a few months. I'll take short term contract work to earn us some money."

"What!" I'm finding it hard to breathe. "I don't believe this!" I jump out of bed and try to snatch the phone from his hand. "We need to talk about it."

The phone drops onto the bed between us. We both stare at it but neither of us picks it up. Paul's no longer using a smartphone; he's gone back to older technology. He rummages through his bedside drawer until he finds a wallet of business cards.

"Surely you're not going back to Manifold?" I ask as he flips it open.

"No, I'm steering clear of that place. Let's see who's still around from the old days."

*

Less than a week later, in the flat grey light of dawn, I drive Paul to Limoges airport. We arrive in time to take first spot in the carpark and he grumbles at me for setting off too early.

"What do you expect me to do?" I snap, thinking of the chores awaiting me.

Mollie is dozing on the backseat, still in her pyjamas, wrapped in a rug. She stirs and reaches for my hand, gripping it tight as she clambers out of the car.

Paul unloads his holdall from the boot and drops it on the gravel.

"It's only a short contract, Emma, but the money's good." He lays his hand on my shoulder as if passing some of his strength and energy into my safe-keeping. "I'll be frugal."

I swallow. "Say thanks to Malcolm for putting you up yet again."

I don't want this goodbye to end in tears or an argument, but I can't face milling about in that gloomy airport among ghost-pale dawn travellers.

"Do you mind if we don't wait?"

Paul's hand drops from my shoulder as if he's been stung. "Sure. You get going."

He crouches down and strokes Mollie's hair, whispering in her ear something about being good and helping me. My stomach clenches—this is Paul's doing, why ask Mollie to carry that burden? She nods and puts on a serious, grown up expression as he kisses her cheek.

Paul stands and straightens his back. With the briefest of goodbye pecks on my cheek, he pulls away, hitches his bag over his shoulder and strides towards the terminal without looking back.

"Just you and me again, Moll."

"I don't want Daddy to go." Her voice is small and tearful. "Why does everyone leave us?"

"Well, you've still got me. . . and I'm not leaving you ever."

CHAPTER 34

EMMA

August 2016

Summer slips by in a blur as I pound the treadmill of passing days. Holidaymakers flood into the area, the bar and restaurant are at full stretch but at night I'm too exhausted to sleep.

I'm counting the days until Owen's visit but what sort of a holiday will it be for him when I'm tethered to the bar? I've found a childminder for Mollie and the cost is crippling but, some days, Sylvie, the mother of one of her school friends, looks after her and refuses to let me pay, so I swap money worries for guilt.

"Can you get next week off?" I ask Paul over the phone, half-expecting him to refuse, but he promises to speak to his client and juggle the project schedule so he can come to France. With Paul running the bar and Lilianne in the kitchen, I make plans for seven precious days with my son.

"What time does his flight arrive in Limoges?" I ask Zak in an awkward phone call.

"Change of plan," he informs me, brusquely.

"What?" My chest constricts. "You can't cancel his visit."

"No. It's not that. He's coming by Eurotunnel with Carlene." Somehow, I can't imagine Carlene dropping in for a visit. She hasn't said a word to me since Zak and I split up and, if she happens to pick up the landline when I ring, she hands the phone straight to Owen or Zak.

"Carlene's coming to France to visit a friend from the States, who's over in La Rochelle on holiday. She'll ring you and arrange a place for you to pick up Owen."

"Fine. I'll drive over and collect him from La Rochelle. Bye."

"Emma. "

"Yes?"

"Don't push the boy. He's finding it hard with so much change in his life."

And I'm not, I want to snap back but I don't. I hold my tongue and politely say goodbye.

CHAPTER 35

OWEN

August 2016

While we're waiting for Mum outside the aquarium in La Rochelle, Aunt Carlene holds my hand too tight, as if I was a small kid about to run away. I don't run away because there's nowhere to go. This is France and it's still boring.

Her American friend, Brad can't stand still. He's pacing around, looking like he's counting the number of people in the queue for the aquarium. What does it matter to us? We're not going into the frigging aquarium. Aunt Carlene and I went yesterday when we arrived.

I can tell Brad wasn't pleased to see me. I think he's got a thing for Aunt Carlene and wants me gone so he can have sex with her or something.

"Here she is," says Aunt Carlene, pointing along the road, and that makes me mad because I wanted to see Mum first.

"Owen!"

Mum runs towards us and bends to hug and kiss me. I let her, but I don't kiss her back. Mollie wants to fist bump, like I do with Dad. I don't mind that.

Brad stops pacing and says, "Hi" to Mum and Mollie.

I notice his eyes watching Mum while they talk about

boring stuff, like when to meet up for Aunt Carlene to take me home. It's like Brad's admiring her, and I'm not surprised, because Aunt Carlene is five years older than my dad so she's well middle-aged and Mum is pretty.

"Shall we go into the aquarium?" Mum suggests, after the others have gone.

"I went yesterday," I say. "I want to see Milou. Can we just go?"

I can see Mollie is disappointed, she wanted to see the tropical fish, but I don't care.

"Okay," says Mum. "We'll have lunch here, then drive home to Sainte Violette."

I grind my teeth. Why must she call it home? It's not my home. I don't know where that is.

*

Paul is minding the bar when we get back to Sainte Violette and we stop there first.

"I thought you were in London?" I say.

Paul's been messaging me to arrange to meet up but I've been too busy.

"Kent," he says. "I'm working in Kent but I've taken this week off to look after the bar so Mum can spend all her time with you."

"Right. Are we going to that Oradour place again?" I want to go back and check if I counted the right number of sewing machines.

"Not this time," says Mum. "We'll find some other places to go."

I remember we were here last summer in a house with a

scummy swimming pool we couldn't even use. It's only been a year and my whole life has been trashed.

*

The holiday's not too bad. I teach Milou to stand on his hind legs and walk a couple of steps towards me. When he topples over, Mollie stretches out her arms to catch him. We do the same things as last year, except, this year, we sit around in the bar more and I get to play on the pinball machine. Mum's put it out the back in a small annexe room.

Paul says she wanted to get rid of it but it draws in a younger crowd. He's right—sometimes teenagers come in and, if I'm playing on it, they stare and wait for me to finish.

"You should get a snooker table," I say to Paul.

"I'd love to but there's not enough room."

We eat some of our meals in the bar and, other times, Mum brings bar food home and we have it for supper. On my last night she makes my favourite meal—pizza.

"Just you and me this evening, Owen," she says, putting my plate on the table. "Paul will be working late at the bar."

"Where's Mollie?"

"She's at her friend's house. She'll be back before eight."

Mum and I sit down to eat together and this is what I've been dreading. All week, she's been trying to have a proper talk with me and, so far, I've dodged it.

"I've been talking to your dad," she begins. "About visits."

"Uh huh?"

"These long periods of not seeing you." She looks like she has something in her eye and dabs it with a corner of the tea towel. "I want to get dates for your visits set up."

I cough.

"How about October half term?" she suggests. "You could come and stay and, when Paul finishes his contract in Kent, maybe I could fly over to London and visit you?"

"I have school," I say. "The new one."

"Yes, I understand. I wish I could be there to help you settle in. "

"Dad will do it and Aunt Carlene."

Mum looks down at her plate. I didn't mean to upset her.

"Are any of your Wimbledon friends going with you? To your new school?"

"No one."

"Oh."

"But you'll keep in touch with Ethan and Kyle, at least?"

"Dunno." I haven't seen them all summer, but I don't tell Mum. Dad's made me go to a summer camp at his church and enrolled me for extra Maths classes. My life totally sucks. "I don't want to come to France at half term."

"I see." Now she's really upset and I have to say something— but what?

"Remember when I came to visit you in May?"

"Yes. We had a great time, didn't we?"

I nod. "It was okay. But when I went back to London, I felt too messed up."

She covers my hand with hers and strokes it. Perhaps now she'll understand. I can't separate myself into so many places.

CHAPTER 36

EMMA

August 2016

The day after Owen leaves, Paul flies back to finish his contract in Kent and Henri returns to the bar as a customer. Our interaction is stilted at first, but we soon slip back into our old rhythm of easy friendship.

"How are you coping?" he asks me, as I sip iced water from a large glass after a hectic lunch session.

"Not so well."

"I can cover some evening shifts, if it helps, but I can't commit to days—my other work is picking up."

"Henri, that would be a lifesaver."

It means I can spend more time with Mollie.

I tell him how much I can afford to pay, we agree on a weekly retainer and Henri re-joins my payroll.

"Promise me you won't do more hours than that."

He laughs. "I'll try, but I enjoy playing barman. If I'm on the other side of the bar, I drink more."

The threatened return of Mrs Browning is shunted further into the future. In one of his infrequent calls, Peter tells me the Limousin weather would be too hot for her, which strikes me as odd, considering she's lived here for twenty-five years.

So Mollie and I cling on, wisteria-like, to our tenancy of the cottage.

Every week I cycle up to Les Quatre Vents, where rampant weeds have colonised the track and are threatening to creep inside the house. I visualise tumbleweed blowing in through the gap that marks the front door.

Since Paul departed, progress has remained at a standstill and Guy and Giles Berger have avoided the bar. One morning, I catch sight of Guy in the Sunday market while I'm paying for vegetables. I quickly toss some crumpled euro notes to the stallholder and push my way through the crowds to the place where I saw him, but he's disappeared.

CHAPTER 37

EMMA

September 2016

I sigh with relief as I equip Mollie with notebooks, pens and new shoes. Over the summer I've religiously banked the bar takings, but my bookkeeping has been lax.

My feet ache from long hours of standing, as I settle at the kitchen table to tot up our position. I plough through till rolls and invoices, type numbers into my spreadsheet and run the formulae. I know the bar has been doing well but the result surprises me. Rechecking the income column, I wonder if it's possible I've doubled up a total but no—everything's in order. Even with Henri's fifteen-hour retainer and Lilianne's salary, summer visitors have been pouring money into Les 4 Vents' tills!

I slick my fringe back out of my eyes, run my index finger across the income totals, month by month, and figure out a strategy for the next few months.

Perhaps we could extend our season? Over at the Sainte Violette hotel, the student waitresses and kitchen assistants are preparing to return to university and Madame Cordier will be itching to slam down the restaurant's shutters and switch to winter hours.

"I'd like to try out serving meals on some weekday evenings," I tell Lilianne and Henri. "Once the hotel restaurant closes, there'll be nowhere to eat in the evenings in Sainte Violette."

Lilianne watches Henri and waits for him to speak first. He's standing in his favourite spot, leaning his arms on the counter. The floor behind the bar is slightly raised so he exudes a proprietorial air and anyone entering would automatically assume he was the owner. I can understand why Paul didn't like that.

"I can't commit," says Henri, rolling down his shirt sleeves and rebuttoning the cuffs to signal he's finished work for the day.

I was relying on Henri to relieve me of evening bar duties so I could get home to Mollie. I taste the metallic saltiness of blood and realise I've bitten the inside of my lip.

"It's fine, don't worry."

"Sorry, Emma. I have too much work on."

"Oh." I've been so stressed over the summer, I haven't asked him what's happening with his other business activities.

"It's odd with the strengthening euro," he explains. "But overseas buyers are flocking to the area. Especially Brits."

"But why?" My arm itches and I scratch it. Whenever I'm reminded of Brexit, it prompts a nervous reaction.

"Maybe they're worried how the future might turn out in Britain."

"Huh," says Lilianne, her mouth tightening. "Last chance to fulfil their dream of a place in France? When we natives cannot afford to buy."

He nods. "Several of my clients have said they're looking for a bolthole inside the EU."

We've slipped from speaking French into English. Lilianne

frowns, slides down from her bar stool and stalks away to the kitchen, knotting and reknotting her scarf.

"If I get the chance, I'll bring my house hunting clients to the bar," says Henri. "It will help to boost your trade."

He's as good as his word. Over the next few days he brings in a Dutch couple, who return the following day for lunch, and a family from London with a daughter about the same age as Mollie.

"Are you thinking of making a permanent move?" I ask the mother, hopefully, while her husband and Henri are looking at maps. Mollie would love to have an English-speaking playmate.

"Sadly, no. Just a holiday home for now. I'd love to relocate but John has to be in his office most days."

*

After his afternoon viewing appointments, Henri returns to the bar.

"One of my client's has found a property," he tells me.

"What did they buy?"

"Small place, easy to maintain, no garden. It was that couple from Oxford. They'll be using it as a holiday home for now but hope to move here when they retire."

"Sounds ideal," I say, but I wonder if the EU rules will allow that in the longer term after Britain leaves.

I've spoken to customers from non-EU countries, who have holiday homes in this area and they are only allowed to stay in France for three months at a time.

"My latest client will be tricky," continues Henri. "She's a woman on her own—can't make up her mind what she wants."

"A widow?" I think of Mrs Browning spending years here alone after her husband died.

Henri scratches his chin. "She's probably a bit young for that. Wants to see everything—city apartments, cottages, even mansions!"

"Nice problem to have."

"I'm showing her a place nearby tomorrow. I'll bring her here for lunch."

*

The next morning, Mollie wakes feeling unwell. "My head hurts Mummy."

I take her temperature. It's a little above normal so I try a cold compress and a spoonful of Calpol. She dozes off and I ring the school and explain I'll have to keep her at home. I pace the kitchen looking at my watch and ring Lilianne.

"No problem, I will cope," she says, but we both know it's impossible to cook and serve lunches and run the bar.

At half past eleven Mollie stirs, clatters downstairs and startles me. "I'm better."

"What shall I do with you?" I laugh, placing my hand on her now-cool forehead. "School?"

She shakes her head. "Let me come to work with you, Mummy, I can help."

I sigh but perhaps it is best if she stays off school. Her fever could return.

"Just this once, okay?"

I collect a colouring book and crayons and we set off.

There are ten customers in the bar; seven sipping drinks but three waiting to be served in trance-like poses of abandoned hope. Lilianne must be in the kitchen. Lionel, the electrician, raises his hand and shouts his drink order across to me before I've closed the door.

"*Un moment.*"

With Mollie clinging to my hand, I hurry through to the kitchen where Lilianne is labouring on the lunch buffet. Beads of perspiration dot her forehead and, as she straightens her back to greet us, she wipes them away with the back of her hand. There's relief in her eyes but her first thought is for Mollie.

"She's much better," I promise. "Can I leave her with you while I go and serve drinks?"

"*Bien sûr.*"

She pulls out a chair and Mollie clambers onto it to watch Lilianne's speedy knife slicing a tomato into filigree pieces of eight.

I wash my hands and take up position behind the bar, wishing Henri was here. Our regulars' eyes light up as the natural order resumes. I pour beer, Ricard and Cognac and, once everyone has a drink in their hand, I take baskets of *baguette* and small carafes of wine across to the patient lunch customers.

Soon the clock rolls forward to twelve-thirty and more customers trickle in, waiting for me to pick up my notebook and serve them. When I carry the first orders through to Lilianne, Mollie is helping her arrange salad garnishes on a plate.

"Stop that, Mollie!"

My voice is sharp. I snatch up the plate and scrape the salad into the bin. Mollie jumps and Lilianne arches an eyebrow and gives me a strained look.

"Sorry. Her temperature was high this morning. Can't risk having her near food."

"I hate you—you're mean!"

Mollie kicks her feet back against the chair and scowls at me. I take her hand and lead her into the bar, settling her, with her colouring book, at a table where I can watch over her. She leans her head close to the page and curls her arm around her art work, keeping it private.

Customers' demands tug my attention and I forget my daughter until, without prompting, Lilianne brings her a plate of food. Soon Mollie is spearing asparagus, and other vegetables she'd never touch at home, and nibbling from her fork.

As the lunchtime crowd thins, Henri arrives. I take a beer from the chiller, open it and slide it across the bar to him.

"Thanks, Emma."

He takes a long swig and I notice he's not alone. Standing behind him is a tall woman, with shoulder length dark hair, wearing cream linen trousers and a gold silk top.

Henri ushers her forward, encircling her back with a protective arm but not actually touching her. He clears a space for his companion to stand at the bar.

"This is Emma," he tells her, then turns back to me. "Meet Eve. I've told her all about you."

I reach across the bar, extending my hand. Hers is cool with a firm grip. She has a light suntan and faint laughter lines at the corners of her eyes. She's older than me but so elegant I feel dowdy.

"Henri tells me this is your own business." She smiles and I notice her teeth are perfect, small and white. "How's it going?"

"It's our first year. Summer season was great but earlier—especially January to March was, well, tough. Can I get you a drink?"

"Coffee. Black, please."

Lilianne, who has finished clearing tables and is sitting with Mollie, overhears. "I will get it."

She slips behind the bar and places a cup on the coffee machine. When it's ready she sets it on the bar in front of Eve and appraises her with cool grey eyes, glancing sideways at Henri and waiting to be introduced. But he's looking around for a stool for Eve and, as soon as Claude vacates his, he slides it into position. Claude stares at the newcomer who smiles back politely; Lilianne wipes her hands on her apron and disappears back to the kitchen.

"What about you?" I ask Eve. "Are you thinking of relocating?"

She stirs her coffee, though she's added no milk or sugar, and takes a sip. "My mother was ill. I took a break from work to look after her, but she only lived two weeks."

"I'm sorry to hear that."

Eve twists the ruby and diamond ring she's wearing on the fourth finger of her right hand. "She left me some money so it seemed a good time to step away from the rat race and think what to do next."

"Such as moving to France?"

"Not sure. Depends on a few things."

She fixes her dark brown eyes on me. Disconcerted, I glance down and notice a red wine stain on my t-shirt.

Henri has wandered outside for a cigarette, leaving me to host his client but Eve and I seem to have run out of things to say. As she drains her coffee cup, I feel a small hand gripping my leg.

"Mollie!" She's crept round behind the bar. I laugh and pick her up, placing her on the stool I keep behind the bar but never have time to sit on.

"Is this your daughter?" There's a new warmth in Eve's tone.

Mollie's normally shy with strangers but she shows Eve her drawings. "I used blue for the sky, but I didn't have a green crayon. So, I coloured the grass pink."

"That's very—err—original," says Eve.

We all laugh and the ice melts.

"I've just checked with Lilianne. There's still time to eat." Henri points to the blackboard.

"We do a simple fixed menu," I explain. "Hors d'oeuvres and two choices of main. But if you prefer just a salad. . ."

She takes a brief look at the board and checks her watch.

"We have another place to see this afternoon."

Henri's lips tighten. I can tell he's hungry.

"I can fix you a sandwich?"

"Could you?"

"Sure. Chicken salad, okay?" I wander to the kitchen door and call the order through to Lilianne.

When I return, Henri has taken a sheaf of papers out of his bag and spread them on the bar, showing Eve details of more properties. Mollie and I retreat to the sink; I let her squirt in the washing up liquid and hand me the dirty cups and glasses. The red lipstick stain on Eve's coffee cup is stubborn. I scrub it hard with a cloth.

Lilianne brings Henri's sandwich on a plate with salad garnish.

"Time to go," warns Eve.

Henri sighs, leaves the salad and wraps the sandwich in a paper napkin. "How much?" he asks me, putting the impromptu lunch in his bag.

"On the house."

"Thanks." He gives me a grateful smile, gathers his papers and rams them, dog-eared, into his bag on top of his sandwich.

"See you again," Eve calls to me from the door. But Les 4 Vents doesn't strike me as her kind of place so I don't expect to.

Lilianne thinks the same. "Who was she?" Lilianne jabs her index finger at the stool Eve has just vacated.

"Her name's Eve. She's looking for a place to buy."

"Around here? What's she going to do here?"

"I was wondering the same."

There's something about Eve's confident manner and fashionable clothes that we don't see in this village. Ever.

"Mummy your handbag's shivering." Mollie carries it across to me. Inside, my mobile phone is vibrating.

"Hello?"

"Peter Browning here. I'm bringing Mother over this weekend. We're putting her house on the market."

CHAPTER 38

EMMA

September 2016

Peter Browning is portly with short arms, a squashy block on legs. To cram his bulk through the doorway, he turns sideways. They're staying in the Sainte Violette hotel. Peter says his mother couldn't manage the cottage stairs. She totters in, leaning on her stick. I'm shocked at how she's aged. Folds of skin dangle from her upper arms and a gash on her cheek is surrounded by purple bruising.

"I fell down the stairs at Pete's and hit my face on the banister." She grimaces. "Lucky not to break my other hip."

She hands Mollie a paper bag full of chocolate bars: brands whose existence I was hoping she'd forgotten.

"Can I eat this one now, Mummy?" Mollie brandishes a Yorkie.

"Just two pieces."

"You've kept the house spotless!" she exclaims.

I was up at five, scrubbing floors and cleaning windows. It does look nice; the wooden furniture glows and I've put vases of flowers on every windowsill to disguise the smell of dog.

"Milou!" Mrs Browning bends to let him lick her hand

but winces as she straightens her back. "I miss my dog and my lovely neighbours. But Pete's right. I can't live alone any longer."

"How long do you think it will take to sell?"

We're all huddling in the centre of the sitting room, yet it feels awkward to invite them to sit—it's her house, not mine.

"Market's weak just now but we'll price it to sell," says Peter. "White elephant. Need to get it off Mother's hands."

"A friend of mine works with the local *notaire* to introduce clients and show them properties for sale," I say.

Peter's creased forehead glistens with sweat. Does he suspect me of trying to con him? "Is that so? We visited two agents in Limoges on our way from the airport. They'll be out to measure up on Monday. What's your friend's name?"

"Henri Wilson."

"Do you have his card?"

I don't, but I scribble Henri's number on the back of a supermarket bill.

Behind Peter's broad back, Mrs Browning and I exchange glances. Her eyes brim with tears. I reach out and touch her hand.

"Sit down. I'll make some tea."

*

"I may have a new client for you," I tell Henri, updating him on the Brownings' decision to sell the cottage.

His eyes narrow. "But where will you live?"

I'm touched that his first thought is for me and Mollie, not his own business interests.

"Paul thinks we'll be able to restart work on the house next month. But it won't be ready to move into before winter."

He takes a cloth and polishes the glasses I rinsed earlier. "I can't see the Browning cottage selling in that timescale. Some properties are taking up to two years to sell."

"But you told me there were dozens of people looking."

"Well, yes. Dozens of buyers, but hundreds of houses for sale. Anyway—if they want me to work on their project, they'll have to register the property with Bernard, the *notaire*. I'm just the link man."

"D'you think it's the type of place Eve would be interested in?"

"Hard to say. I've shown her six properties already. She wants to see everything in her price range. Can't seem to whittle down her priorities."

"Nice for some." Then I remember the reason for her good fortune. "Shouldn't have said that when she's just lost her mother."

"She was quite taken with this village," says Henri, putting the last glass back on the shelf. "And she enjoyed meeting you. She's planning to come here for supper this evening."

It's Saturday but Lilianne is taking a night off. Henri's agreed to work and I've ruthlessly edited the menu so I can cope alone. The meals are from the freezer but they're home-cooked so I don't feel any shame at serving them.

The Sainte Violette hotel restaurant also opens on Saturday nights but doesn't seem to affect our trade. I glance at the reservation book.

"Gaspard—I don't remember them booking." I'm intrigued. My neighbours never come in and I rarely see them.

"That's Lilianne's writing."

By seven o' clock, the bar is busy. Two middle-aged couples, who don't know each other, strike up a stilted conversation and decide to stay and eat. I ring Remy to ask for extra *baguettes* and he brings them in person and loiters with a Cognac, joking with Henri and Hubert.

More customers trickle in; the atmosphere buzzes with chat and laughter. Early diners are tucking in to their starters when a silver Mercedes sports car draws up outside and stops with the engine idling.

"Eve?" I ask Henri and I'm not surprised when he nods.

I've noticed that tourists favour large estate cars and the locals are loyal to their Renaults and Peugeots. It's rare to see a Mercedes in this part of the world. Leaving Henri in charge of meeting and greeting, I retreat to the kitchen, bracing myself for food orders. Mollie's on a sleepover with a friend so I can give the bar my full attention.

Between the bar and the kitchen is a serving hatch. It's never used because the shelf on the bar side is stacked with bottles, but I keep it open to watch the goings-on in the bar, unobserved. On the far wall is a vast engraved mirror, its top edge leans forward at an angle giving me a full view of the bar. Reflected in this mirror, I observe Eve's entrance and feel the frisson as all eyes swivel to watch her cross the room.

"Henri—you didn't say you had a second job. I thought you were all mine." Other voices mumble but Eve's strident tone reaches the kitchen, crystal clear.

She's wearing a black pencil skirt, emerald green top and green leather shoes with three-inch heels. She wriggles up onto a bar stool, smoothing down her skirt, and Hubert wishes her good evening. She replies in fluent French, quizzing him about the village and his family.

"How many children?"

Proudly he admits to three sons and two daughters—all grown up and married.

"Wonderful. And you have your family around you?"

"Sadly no," he tells her. "Three are in the Paris region; one in Limoges. My youngest son works abroad."

I'm impressed. Eve's gleaned more about Hubert's family in five minutes than I have in a year.

Without letting her attention waver from Hubert, she orders a gin and tonic. He offers to pay but Eve won't hear of it. I hear the clink of the ice hitting glass as Henri slides the drink towards her.

As he strolls across to a table to take their food order, I panic. Action stations—this is it, Emma. You're on your own—chef and waitress. I hurry to the chest freezer and ferret inside, checking stocks of this evening's main courses, wondering what I'll do if they run out. Footsteps tip-tapping across the tiled kitchen floor startle me and I drop the freezer lid, moving my hand just in time to stop my fingers joining the batons of sliced carrot.

"There you are!" An English voice, clear and commanding.

I spin round. "Eve."

She's holding her gin and tonic in one hand and unleashes her dazzling smile. "Sorry to startle you. Just came to say hi."

My kitchen should be my sanctuary, safe from intruders, but she crowds towards me, landing an air kiss on both my cheeks. I keep my arms rigid at my sides and wipe my frosted fingers on a cloth.

"I can see you're busy."

I nod. "If you're hungry, order straight away. We've several bookings at eight o'clock."

She glances at the blackboard I'm chalking up. "What's the casserole of *fruits de mer*?"

"Cod, salmon, scallops and prawns with celery in a saffron sauce."

"Sounds delicious."

"Coming up."

I take a portion out of the freezer and prepare it for cooking. Eve sips her gin and tonic and makes no sign of moving back to the bar. My throat constricts. Is she planning to stand there all evening, watching me cook?

Henri appears at the kitchen door waving a bunch of orders. His handwriting tends towards indecipherable.

"Can you read them out to me?"

Eve raises her glass then slips past him, back to the bar.

As I bustle around preparing meals, I keep up with the unfolding drama in the bar where Eve is surrounded by a group of regulars, spellbound at some story she's telling. I move my food preparation surface closer to the hatch and listen.

It's a harmless story about the apartment she's renting in Limoges. Apparently, it looks immaculate on the outside but, every time she touches an appliance, it breaks in her hand. Before coming out this evening, the showerhead dropped off onto her foot. As she says the word '*pied*' Hubert and Claude collapse in laughter. I don't get why that's funny. Perhaps it's the contrast between her immaculate appearance and the chaos she's describing.

When I carry the next meals through, I walk into a wall of noise. The Gaspards, from the pheasant farm, have arrived with visiting relatives. I greet them and show them to their table, leaving Henri to take their drink and food orders. Adding the garnish to Eve's *fruits de mer* takes a while and, when I carry the plate through, Eve is no longer perched on her barstool. Was I too slow? Did she give up waiting and leave?

No. I see her now. She's sitting with the Gaspards' family party at their table, sharing their red wine and chatting in fluent French. I feel a rush of annoyance. The Gaspards are my neighbours—or will be if we ever get the house finished. How long has it taken her to get to know them? Ten minutes? Five?

She waves to me and I carry the plate across.

"Justine and Pierre didn't like to see me dining alone. They invited me to join them. How sweet is that?"

Very sweet, I agree. Eve is now on first name terms with my neighbours while I still call them *Madame* and *Monsieur*.

"Here you go." Henri puts a lime and soda in my hand as I return to the kitchen.

For the first time, I experience a Cinderella feeling—crazy because I'm the proud owner, customers compliment me on the food. What is it about Eve that makes me feel this way?

Time speeds up. All evening I rush between kitchen and bar, chasing my tail. I feel flat and invisible like a silent movie character being projected onto the wall. The atmosphere is electric as if a party's going on.

Around ten, the clamour subsides and flows out of the door with departing customers, voices muted by car doors slamming. I stack the dishwasher and pile pans in the sink. Only two or three people remain when I collapse into a chair and kick off my shoes.

"That was a tough shift. You did well." Henri smiles.

I notice Eve is still there too. She carries her drink across to my table and I think of the dark winding road back to Limoges and worry she's had too many but, when she puts her bottle down, I notice the red cap—Evian water.

She leans towards me. "Henri told me your cottage is for sale."

"Not mine. But yes, it is."

"I'd like to see it. Is tomorrow okay?"

CHAPTER 39

EMMA

September 2016

Sunday is the closest I get to a day off. We open the bar for about an hour to coincide with when the congregation pours out of mass. Women dawdle from the church to the square, chatting with friends and join the queue outside Remy's *boulangerie* to stock up on *tarte aux fraises* and *baguettes* for their family lunch. Their menfolk dart into the bar and gulp down a Ricard or Cognac, standing up.

Claude uses his deafness as camouflage, parking himself on a bar stool with his back to the door. When his wife turns up, he pretends not to hear her summoning him from the doorway so she strides across to the bar to claim him and lets him entice her to stay and drink a glass of sweet wine.

Today I've two sets of visitors to fit in before I can think about opening the bar. Peter and his mother arrive at nine to pack more of her possessions and Eve is due at eleven. Mrs Browning's bruise is healing but her face is parchment pale and her hands shake as she wraps cherished possessions in newspaper.

"What shall I do with these, Mother?" Peter barges through the doorway clutching an armful of porcelain ornaments.

She winces. "Put them down there, Pete."

He opens his arms and delicate figurines scatter across the table.

I turn away and make tea in a proper pot, instead of my usual teabag-in-a-mug.

"I hope you don't mind Eve coming to view the house?"

"Not at all, dear. It would be lovely if it went to someone nice. A friend of yours."

Gulping his tea, Peter remarks, "She'll have to go through the agent if she's interested."

"Or Henri and the *notaire*?"

"Okay," he concedes.

With zero tolerance for our personal space, Peter intrudes into Mollie's bedroom, stacking boxes against the walls. When he begins a new stack in the kitchen, I point out the proximity of the cooker and he moves them back under the stairs, where most of the stuff came from in the first place.

While he's busy, Mrs Browning leans towards me and whispers, "Emma, would you consider keeping Milou?"

"Milou!" I'd almost forgotten he wasn't part of our family. Mollie would be devastated if she had to say goodbye. "Won't you miss him?"

"With all my heart. But Pete has an Alsatian—very jealous—and I suspect it won't be long before he and Hilary suggest I move out of their house to a residential care home."

"If you're sure. We'd love to."

She places her wrinkled hand on top of mine and squeezes it. "Thank you."

"Will you wait to meet Eve at eleven?" I ask Peter.

He fumbles with the top button of his shirt, a fold of neck flesh getting in the way of his fingers.

"No. I'm taking Mother to her favourite restaurant. Pont Saint Etienne by the old bridge of the same name. They do superb beef."

I imagine Mrs Browning would struggle to eat a fillet of plaice, but Peter is determined and they depart in his hire car, missing Eve by ten minutes.

Eve has brought a gift for Mollie: a DVD of The Little Princess. I'm glad it's not sweets. With a graceful movement, she bobs down to hand it to her and I notice Eve's upper arms are toned and muscular. She must spend time working out in the gym.

Mollie does a kind of thank you curtsy and hugs the film to her chest.

"Can I watch it now, Mummy?"

"We'll watch it together later."

"Well can I show her my room?"

I force a smile. "Give us a minute, Mollie. Why don't you pop up and make sure it's nice and tidy?"

"I can't make it tidy. Mr Browning filled everywhere with boxes."

She flounces off up the narrow stairs as I explain to Eve about the Brownings' packing binge.

I sneak a look at my watch. "Coffee?"

"I'd love one."

I leave her looking around the sitting room, while I make a cafetière.

"It's a bit cramped but it's cosy," I say as I carry the coffee through on a tray. "Kitchen could do with modernising."

But selling this house isn't my responsibility and there's one key piece of information I don't know.

"How much are they asking?"

"Sorry—no idea. The estate agent's coming in the morning," I say.

"No worries." She takes the mug and strolls across to the front window, overlooking the street and the church opposite. "Do the church bells bother you?"

I shake my head and smile. "After a while you stop noticing."

Mugs in hand, we stroll to the kitchen. As her eyes flick over the out-dated units and appliances, I know immediately this place isn't for her. She slides back the lace curtain covering the glass panel in the back door.

"Mind if I take a look outside?"

"Sure."

I unlock it and Eve steps out into the patio garden. Three paces and she's face to face with next-door's white-washed wall. I've hammered in hooks for hanging baskets and offset the blankness with pots of geraniums, but they can only do so much.

"What's out there?" She points to the high back gate.

"The lane. We keep our bin out there but I'm thinking of moving it to the front. I hate dragging it through the house." I reach up, unbolt it.

"Don't you have a lock?"

"No. It only leads into the yard. We just reach over from outside and slide it back."

The lane's not looking its best: empty bottles and crushed cigarette ends suggest this was the spot chosen by Saint Violette's youth for their Saturday night gathering. If they were there when I returned from the bar, I didn't hear a thing.

"Where does the lane go?"

"It curves round behind the houses and joins up with the road opposite the church gate."

"The plants are pretty," she concedes, as I lock up. "Only thing is—I was hoping for a view."

"You won't get it here, I'm afraid. This house was cut into a hollow. In winter it feels almost subterranean."

Eve does another circuit of the ground floor, as I fold my arms and fret about the time. If I don't leave in the next ten minutes, I'll be too late to open the bar for the exodus of thirsty worshippers.

Eve pauses to examine a framed photo of Owen and Mollie. "Who's this?"

"My son, Owen." I blush. "He lives in London with his dad." I practice a fake smile, anticipating she'll ask how it feels to be apart from my son.

"Not your husband, then?" She picks up our wedding photo in its silver frame and puts her mug down on the mantelpiece in its place while glancing from the picture to me, as if checking whether the dowdy bar owner could possibly be that radiant bride. "This is your husband?" It's more statement than question.

I nod. "Yes—Paul."

"Where is he?"

"Working in London." What's it to do with viewing the house?

"I see."

I reach out my hand to take the picture from her but she's gripping it firmly; our eyes meet, she smiles—white teeth, red lipstick—and lets it go.

*

"Eve's decided the house isn't right for her," Henri tells me on Monday morning.

He's sitting at one of the outside tables when I arrive and drops his cigarette butt on the ground. I give him a look and he picks it up and deposits it in the ashtray I've installed by the door.

"I'm not surprised—about Eve, I mean."

"She says she's still hoping for something in this area. I'm meeting her here later. We have more places to look at." He doesn't sound enthusiastic.

He follows me inside, refusing a coffee and pours a glass of tap water.

"I think she may be a time waster," he confides. "She's been here three weeks and is no closer to making a decision. I'm wasting time and petrol money driving her around."

He seems glum, but I can't sit and chat. Lilianne's coming in late so I must start lunch preparations.

"Could you man the bar for me?"

Once again, Henri has taken himself off my payroll, but he never seems to mind stepping in to help.

At midday, Lilianne arrives and we all shuffle round like musical chairs: she takes over in the kitchen, I step behind the bar and Henri retreats to a table and spreads out a map to route-plan his afternoon viewings.

"Why don't you use a satnav?" I ask.

"You think a computer can do this better than me?" he grunts, checking his watch.

Eve breezes in, ignores Henri and walks up to the bar. She orders a gin and tonic and exchanges a few words with Claude. Henri folds up his map and joins her, slotting into the space between her and Claude.

"Henri—I've just driven past the most amazing property," she exclaims, showing him a picture on her smartphone. "Three storeys, blue shutters, iron gates. . . and look at that stunning red and green photinia hedge!"

"I don't know it." Henri raises his glass of water to his mouth, but Eve puts her phone down and places her hand on his arm.

"You must find out. I want to view it."

Henri tugs his arm away, splashing water on his sleeve. "You'll have to follow up with the selling agent. Note their number from the board."

"But my French isn't good enough. I need your help," she says in a sharp voice.

Henri shrugs but Claude visibly flinches and edges his stool further away.

"I don't sell every house in this district." Henri turns his back on Eve and talks to Claude.

He's drawing his line in the sand and I admire him for it. I imagine few men would stand up to Eve.

She leans towards me. "Sorry about your friend's cottage."

"Not at all. I could see it wasn't right for you."

I take a tray of drinks to a table of customers and, when I return, Eve is twiddling her empty glass.

"Fancy a shopping trip to Limoges this afternoon?"

I blink. "Shopping?" Apart from supermarkets and suppliers, I've forgotten what that is. I shake my head. "I can't leave the bar and I must pick Mollie up from the *garderie*."

She's won Henri's attention back now. He turns slowly back towards us, the thread veins in his cheeks fuse into patches of angry red. If Eve changes her plans, he'll have to cancel the viewing appointments he's made.

"Nonsense. Old Henri will run the bar for you. Won't you, Henri?"

I brace myself for his anger to spill over, but he looks straight past Eve at me.

"Good idea. Off you go, Emma."

"You're sure?" A whole afternoon away from the bar, away from the village. . .

"You deserve a break."

"Well, thanks. I'd love to."

I rinse my hands in the washing up sink and stand on tiptoe to peer in the mirror glass behind the row of bottles, wishing I'd put on some make up.

Eve's Mercedes is parked outside the door. The sky is murky with clouds and the wind has a savage bite, but she opens the sunroof and I feel a surge of excitement.

"It's ages since I rode in an open top."

"I didn't get much chance in London. I bought it just before I left but it's exhilarating. You'll see," she says.

Eve puts her foot down and speeds away from the village. The engine purrs but we have to shout to hear one another as the tyres grind on the rough road. We fling conversation at one another, random remarks, snatches of news and I stop fretting about the bar, the house and life's problems.

On the outskirts of Limoges, she draws into a layby and closes the roof. Eve doesn't have a hair out of place but mine is matted and tangled.

"How do you do it?" I ask as I tease the knots out with my fingers.

"Hairspray," she confides, and we both laugh.

She parks in an underground car park and leads me up some steps into Place de la Motte. The square is vaguely familiar, but she turns down a maze of side roads where every street has refurbishment in progress. Pipes are being laid, cobbles and pavements repaired: a pick and mix of holes and trip hazards.

Eve lengthens her stride and I struggle to keep pace with her, though she's wearing heels and I'm in flats. She pauses in front of a shop—Comptoir des Cotonniers.

"Let's pop in here. I feel this would be your kind of style."

One glance at the price tags convinces me she's mistaken. Nothing could be further from my budget but it's good to browse the winter season styles. The clothes are stylish, but casual, and in my preferred neutrals: black, taupe, denim.

As Eve scans the racks, I feel tentative in the face of such opulence.

"My son calls me a moth," I remark.

Faint vertical lines appear between her eyebrows.

"You don't strike me as timid. I'd say the opposite. Strong and bold."

"No," I mumble. "Owen meant I dress like an insect—because my clothes are beige and black."

"Then we must prove him wrong!" She laughs, rifling through tops in jewel-bright colours, picking out two and a pair of tailored trousers.

"This green would be perfect with your colouring." She holds the top and trousers up against me. With a brisk nod, she summons the customer adviser, who leads me to the changing room.

The green top is too revealing. It's the kind of thing Eve wears, but it doesn't suit me. I wriggle out of it and slip into the magenta one, expecting it to clash with my hair but, when I look in the mirror, I'm transformed. The colour reflects warmth into my face, counteracting my pale skin and tense expression. I try on the trousers, a perfect fit. How did she guess my size? Especially in France where everything is cut for slender women with perfect figures.

"How are you getting on in there?"

I slide back the curtain and show Eve the outfit.

"Turn around." She tugs down the front of the magenta top to reveal more cleavage. "Perfect. You must buy it. I knew this would be your shop."

I fiddle with the price ticket. "It is beautiful, but there's no way."

"Nonsense. Like Henri said—you deserve it."

Her searchlight eyes sweep over me. For one horrible moment, I wonder if she's offering to pay and I retreat inside the changing room, away from her overshadowing personality. Teetering on one leg, I take off the trousers and put them and the green top back on their hangers. I drape the magenta top over my arm.

"Perhaps just the top." I can't believe I said that.

My fingers tremble as I offer my card at the cash desk. A moment of elation, remembering how good the top looked, is replaced by feeling sick inside. The assistant is brisk and the transaction slides through in seconds. She wraps the top in tissue paper and places it into a paper carrier bag.

Eve is waiting in the street outside, lighting a cigarette. "Time for a coffee. My treat." She leads me down more winding streets to a tea shop that looks oddly English, displaying wedding cakes and pastries in the window. "Isn't this quaint? I come here sometimes when I'm missing home."

I order a mint tea and a small pastry filled with raisins and *crème anglais*. Eve has black coffee but no food.

"You seem to know your way around Limoges. How long is it? Four weeks?"

"More. I stayed in a hotel for a while but I couldn't wait to move out into a place of my own. Rents here are so cheap after London."

"What's your apartment like?"

She's fumbling inside her handbag, checking her phone so I ask again.

"Lovely. It's an old building with high ceilings, wooden shutters and a wrought iron Juliet balcony overlooking the street.

"Close to here?"

"Limoges is compact. Nowhere's very far. I did make one mistake, though."

"What was that?"

"It's on a busy road. Most of the streets in the city centre are quiet but mine's a thoroughfare. Cars bump along it all night."

"What road is it in?"

She raises her arm and gestures towards the direction we walked from. "Not far—over that way." She stirs her coffee. "Now, tell me about yourself."

I begin with what's uppermost in my mind—Owen and the misery of being separated from my son. As a woman, she will surely understand when I tell her about the agonising decision for Owen to live with his father but I get the feeling she's not listening. I swallow. The mint tea is making my mouth dry; a glass of water would be nice.

I gesture to the waitress, but she looks straight through me. Assuming I'm asking for the bill, Eve calls the waitress across and it's presented immediately.

"And the bar. How's that doing?" Eve prompts.

"The summer was great, but trade slackens off in winter. I'm hoping to stay open on some weekday evenings, but it's tricky. The hotel goes straight onto winter hours in September but there are still tourists in the area, looking for somewhere to eat."

Eve slips her change into her purse and seems in no hurry to leave. "I've certainly been glad your bar's been open."

I think back to when we came to France to sign the contract and Anton rustled up *croque monsieurs* for us. Though Paul complained, how much more annoying would it be if there was nowhere to eat in Sainte Violette?

"We've carried on serving early suppers but there's not much trade. And I'm paying a babysitter to look after Mollie."

Eve leans back in her chair and crosses her legs. With her right hand, she rakes her hair out of her eyes. "Perhaps I could help you."

"In the bar?" I try to imagine her chopping vegetables or serving drinks.

"No. I could help you look after Mollie."

"I couldn't possibly."

She shrugs, examining her fingers and grimacing when she spots a microscopic chip in her nail polish.

"Think about it. Until I find a place of my own, I don't have much to do."

I wonder if she's lonely? She doesn't seem like a joining-in kind of person. I can't picture her playing bridge or doing voluntary work.

"You'd be doing me a favour. I spend my evenings watching TV or eating alone in a restaurant. That's why I've enjoyed coming to your bar where everyone's so friendly."

"Why don't you go back to London? To your friends?"

The chipped nail varnish absorbs her attention. She buffs it with the edge of her linen napkin, smoothing the nail's surface.

"When my mother died," she says, looking up from her nails and gazing over my shoulder into the middle distance. "It made me reflect on my future. My mother wasn't old, but she let her life shrivel away. Even when she was dying, she seemed to be waiting for her life to start."

"I'm so sorry," I murmur.

She dismisses my sympathy with a wave of her wrist.

"My life in London was kind-of broken. I'm not ready to go back. Not until it's fixed."

CHAPTER 40

EMMA

September 2016

Eve drives me home in time to pick up Mollie from the after-school nursery. She refuses an invitation to supper but agrees to a drink. I don't have any chilled white wine so I pour her a glass of red, and orange juice for me and Mollie. As I carry the drinks into the sitting room, there's an acidic smell of pear drops in the air.

I overhear Eve saying to Mollie, "How would you like me to pick you up from school sometimes and look after you while Mummy's working?"

"Yes!" Mollie claps her hands.

I give a tight smile. "I'm thinking about it."

She's sprawling on the sofa next to Eve, who puts out a restraining hand. "Oops careful, babe."

I notice an open bottle of blue nail varnish on the coffee table and see Eve is painting Mollie's fingernails.

"Look, Mummy." She twirls her hand for me to see.

Eve dips the brush into the pot, takes Mollie's hand and applies a second coat. Mollie's nails sparkle and I wonder how I'll remove it before school tomorrow. So neglected is my own beauty routine, I don't have a bottle of nail varnish remover.

"Will you come every day?" Mollie asks Eve. "Can I stop going to the *garderie*? Can we talk in English?"

Mollie's final request spears my heart. Some school days must be like Babel to her, when she comes home, she deserves to unwind and speak her native language.

"I can't promise to come every day," says Eve. "I'm still looking for a house, remember. I'll plan the days with Mummy, okay?"

I give Eve a grateful smile. "I wish you'd let me pay you."

"Absolutely not." She lifts a hand and waves the idea away. "If I move here, I'll know more people—as well as Justine."

I'm not sure who she means but I wonder what the school gate mums, who were so wary of me, will make of Eve.

"We could call into school tomorrow and register your details," I suggest. "Have you got a small photo of yourself?"

Mollie's school is diligent about keeping a record of people authorised to collect pupils.

"Sure. Let's do it. It will take some pressure off you." Eve smiles enigmatically at me.

After she leaves, I remember—Justine is Madame Gaspard.

Pressure release is exactly what I need. My 'to do' list is procreating. Paul has topped up the bank account and the Berger brothers have restarted work on Les Quatre Vents. Now they've been paid, the Bergers are no longer boycotting the bar, but I've been too busy to go to the site and check up on their work.

On the day Eve arranges to pick up Mollie for the first time, I leave Lilianne to finish clearing up and make an impromptu site visit. As I drive up our track, I see the outside front walls have been rendered, concealing the ugly joins between new and old masonry. There are still yawning gaps where the windows and doors should be, but it can't be too long before our home is ready.

The Bergers are sitting in their van with the engine running and a bass beat pounds against the closed windows. Guy nods at me and stays put in the driving seat, but Giles jumps down and beckons me to follow him around the side of the building to the yard. He jabs his finger in the direction of the flower bed, churned up by the digger they hired for the ground works.

"The inspection is next week."

He strolls closer and kicks at a crumbling ridge of concrete poking up above the flattened earth.

"You mean the old *fosse septique?*"

He nods. "I think the authorities will order that you get a new one."

"But it's been there for decades!"

"*Exactement.*"

More expense! Henri once tried to explain to me what the latest septic tank technology involved. I followed what he said about new tanks being made of polyethylene and we'd need one with a capacity of three thousand litres but, once he started describing that three pits would have to be dug for the complex bio-cleansing process, I was lost.

Giles is anxious to get going so I don't ask him any more questions. I wave them off and turn to enter the building. As a reflex, I duck but it's no longer necessary—the lintel has been raised. The open plan space with its high ceiling sloping up into the apex of the roof is light and airy. Parts of the interior will be reformatted with plasterboard walls to make three bedrooms, but not the lounge, kitchen and diner and, after the cramped cottage, it feels vast and a bubble of excitement forms inside my chest.

I gaze out at the coarse meadow at the back. Inhaling deeply, I catch the smell of cattle on the wind but there are no cows in view in the adjacent fields. This landscape is rolling and rough, its dips and curves hiding the secrets of centuries.

When I arrive home, Mollie is curled up on Eve's lap, sipping hot chocolate and reading aloud from an illustrated book in simple French. She never reads to me—always expects me to read to her—but for Eve, anything is possible.

"Will you stay for supper?" I ask.

It would be good to have company. My tentative friendship with Lilianne fizzled out when Paul returned and Henri's going through one of his chilly phases. I can tell he's not keen on Eve, though he still ferries her around to view properties.

Mollie pipes up, "Tante Eve, please stay."

"Well, in that case—how can I refuse?"

I pour two glasses of wine and leave mine in the kitchen.

"Anything I can do to help?" asks Eve but having an audience while I cook throws me off balance even though dinner is food from the bar freezer that needs eating.

"No thanks, but Mollie can lay the table. Place mats are in the drawer."

During supper, Mollie entertains us with anecdotes about her friends. My mind drifts and I relax. Most evenings it's just the two of us and my mask of cheerful positivity stretches ever thinner.

As I fork the last piece of chicken into my mouth, Mollie's voice draws me back, "Every night I make a wish."

"What's that, sweetie?" Eve asks her.

"I don't care if I have no friends."

"I'm sure that's not true, Mollie." I jumped in too fast. My daughter flashes me a look I've not seen before. Something like anger.

Mollie flings down her fork and slides from her chair.

"I want my brother back. I want Owen, and you don't care!"

Her small finger points at the centre of my chest: my heart. I freeze. Mollie has never, ever mentioned that wish to me, yet every night, before sleep, I recite an identical mantra inside my head.

Eve stretches out an arm and reels Mollie towards her like a slippery fish. She lifts my daughter onto her lap, strokes her hair and soothes her until the moment passes.

"Wanna get down." Mollie wriggles free.

I rouse myself but I'm still rattled. "Go on then—play in your room. I'll be up to read your story soon."

"I want Tante Eve to read my story."

Eve flicks me a glance. "I've been testing her on the French words for family. She knew most of them already."

Mollie nods and recites, "Tante Eve, Maman Emma, Papa Paul, Maman Eve—"

"No, Mollie, you were right first time. Tante Eve."

I hold out my arms for a hug, but she dodges round me and kisses Eve, before sprinting up the narrow staircase. I draw the wine bottle towards me and cradle it between both hands.

"Oops, sorry. I've confused her." Eve puts a hand over her glass. "Got to drive back into Limoges."

I pour one for myself. How did I get into the habit of drinking every day?

"How's the house hunting?" I ask.

She leans back in her chair and sighs. "I'm still waiting for

Henri to come up with something. I can't take on a renovation project. I'm not resourceful like you."

"It's Paul who has the vision. To me, Les Quatre Vents looked like a wreck."

"He knows about property renovation?"

"He's a surveyor but his background's in construction. Offices and commercial buildings."

She puts her empty glass on the table and slides her plate away. "What's he doing now?"

"Working on a project in Kent. He's staying with a friend in London. "

"You must miss him."

I nod. She's caught me off guard. She waits, not settling for silence, so I say, "I wish he was here with us but I guess this is what the future holds. He may need to take short contracts from time to time. Renovation costs have outstripped our savings and we haven't yet started on the *gîtes*."

"Mummy—when are you coming to read my story?" Mollie calls from the landing.

At least she's asking for boring old me, not her exciting new *Tante*.

"Soon, sweetheart." I half-rise from my chair.

"What about the bar?" asks Eve.

"Cashflow is strong but Paul doesn't believe it will make enough to support us. That's the difference between us—he's used to a high income but I'm happy with a more modest family life." I walk towards the stairs but pause before going up to settle Mollie. "Let me make you a coffee."

Eve shakes her head and reaches for the wine bottle. Odd, I thought she said she wasn't having another drink.

"No, it's okay." She gives a tight smile and pours herself a glass of red.

I was hoping to relax this evening but it seems she's planning to stay a while longer.

CHAPTER 41

EMMA

October 2016

My new childcare arrangements must be raising a few eyebrows at the school gates when Eve rolls up in her Mercedes with the roof down. While Mollie's credit amongst her school friends is probably sky high, mums who helped out with childcare over the summer become cooler towards me. What can I do?

Eve is picking up all the slack in our routine. I'm indebted to her with no chance to repay. The imbalance in our friendship makes me uneasy. Eve knows so much about me but clams up when I ask about her family. Now her mother has died, she has no close relatives in England. She's told me she sacrificed social life and relationships to her career but I'm not even sure what she did. Perhaps something in the City? She's prickly on the topic of relationships and I wonder if she might be gay but doesn't feel she knows me well enough to discuss sexuality.

Henri has invited me and Eve to supper. It's a school night so I take Mollie's sleeping bag. The friction between Henri and Eve has dissolved and she roars with laughter at his jokes. Until now, he seemed impervious to her charms, but Henri's the only eligible bachelor under fifty years old in the village.

Surely Henri, with his rough edges, isn't her type? The state of his house would put most women off!

While Henri's in the kitchen putting final touches to the supper, Eve gets up to use his bathroom. I wonder whether to forewarn her about the brown stains around the unscrubbed toilet bowl and his shaving hairs clinging to a soapy tidemark in the wash basin.

"Need a wee, Mummy," calls Mollie before Eve has left the room.

"She won't be long, Moll. You'll have to wait till she comes back."

But Eve takes her time and returns smiling with combed hair and retouched lipstick. She takes a gulp of wine.

"Henri showed me a great property today," she remarks but Mollie cuts across her, tugging at my hand.

"Come with me, Mummy." She hurries towards the door, turning her head to make sure I'm following.

I get to my feet. "Excuse me a minute, Eve."

"Sure—I'm just popping outside for a ciggie."

She hoists her bag over her shoulder and heads for the front door. As I reach the bathroom door, I catch a synthetic smell of adhesives and fillers. At long last Henri has started work on his threatened bathroom makeover. The grimy old bath has been replaced with a new one. Inside it, on a folded dustsheet, is a set of rusty old taps and Henri's tool bag bulging open to display paint-spattered hammers and chisels. Knowing Henri as I do, I'm not surprised he isn't the neatest of workmen. When he's done a shift behind the bar, I often have to rewash glasses he's placed back on the shelves. Before I can review his progress on the other fitments, Mollie puts both her hands on me and pushes me towards the door.

"I can go by myself, Mummy."

"If you're sure?"

She nods vigorously.

"Well don't lock it, then."

She slams the door, but I hear the scrape of a bolt and Mollie's giggle. I hope she'll have the strength to slide it back but at least the bathroom is on the ground floor and the window is open.

I linger, humming a tune under my breath. She'll call if she needs me. I hear the flush and the sound of water running. Good—she's remembered to wash her hands. And then there's a sickening thud, a splintering sound like a heavy tray of crockery smashing and Mollie's voice screaming.

"Mummy!"

"Mollie. What is it?" I press down on the door handle. "Let me in."

I can't believe she's locked it! She never does at home.

"Aah!" She's sobbing pitifully. She must be in pain.

I rattle the door. "Unlock it, Mollie."

"I c-can't."

"Mollie, what's happened? Let me in!" I yell.

I put my shoulder to the door and shove as I've seen cops do in films. The door creaks but doesn't budge.

Henri comes running. "What's going on?"

"Mollie's locked herself in. I heard something smash. I think she's had an accident."

White-faced he pushes past me and pumps the handle.

"Stand away from the door, Mollie."

He raises his foot and aims a kick at the spot adjacent to the handle. The wood creaks but the lock holds. He kicks again, harder, until the lock gives and the door bursts open.

Inside Mollie is crouching on the floor, surrounded by shards of smashed porcelain. There are cuts on her leg like shrapnel wounds and she's rubbing the big toe of her right foot.

"Mummy," she sobs.

I drop to my knees and gather her into my arms; chips of porcelain from the smashed wash basin grind into my legs, I sweep an area of floor with my hand and grab a towel from the rail to kneel on.

"Show me where it hurts."

Her sobbing calms and she straightens her leg to show me her foot. The cuts are shallower than I thought but some are flecked with blood.

"Did the basin fall on it?" I ask.

She nods. "On that big one." I examine her toe gently with my fingers. "Ouch. Stop it, Mummy."

"What happened?" Henri asks but evidence is strewn all around us.

Mollie must have leant her full bodyweight on the new washbasin as she reached over to turn on the tap and somehow managed to drag it off its pedestal.

"She pulled the basin down on herself."

"But that's impossible," he mumbles. "It was rock solid. I installed it this afternoon."

He examines two small holes in the wall, then bends to sift through the wreckage on the floor with the precision of an archaeologist. He picks up a fitment and two screws, places them in his cupped palm and stares at them, frowning.

"What's going on?" Eve is standing in the doorway, holding a glass of wine and looking down at the three of us, kneeling amid the rubble. "I wondered where everyone had gone!"

She touches Mollie lightly on the shoulder and Mollie smiles up at her.

I can't respond to her question because I can't speak. My pulse has slowed to a post-crisis recovery mode and, if I tried to stand up too quickly, I might faint. But Mollie stages a remarkable recovery, clutches Eve's hand and, forgetting her injury, jumps up and stands on one leg to show off her poorly toe.

"Poor poppet," coos Eve and Mollie's tears evaporate. "Come away from this nasty mess and sit quietly with me."

She takes my daughter by the hand and leads her off to the sitting room. Still squatting on the floor, Henri and I exchange glances.

"Emma, I'm so sorry. I don't understand how that could have happened."

I glance around at the devastation of Henri's new bathroom and struggle to my feet, putting out a hand to lean on the side of the bath then withdrawing it as if that too might collapse.

I shrug. "It was an accident. Maybe the new plaster on the wall was too wet or something."

He stands up, too and presses his thumbs into the holes where the sink broke away from the wall.

"That's odd."

But I don't stay to listen to his excuses and I'm not interested in blame. From the sitting room, I hear Mollie and Eve's laughter and take a step along the hallway.

I hurry to the sitting room where Mollie is propped up on the sofa with cushions behind her back. Eve has found the sleeping bag I brought and tucked it round her, leaving her injured leg and foot exposed. As I enter, Eve appears with a basin of warm water and a clean towel.

"Thought I'd clean up her cuts."

I snatch the bowl from her, spilling some water.

"I'll do it."

"Of course." She strolls back to Henri, who is sweeping up the remains of his washbasin.

I lean close to Mollie, checking her wounds for splinters. She yelps while I bathe her leg.

"Ow, Mummy, that stings."

But the ouches morph into a tongue-clicking sound she used to make as a toddler when she wanted me to feed her.

"We must get your leg checked out at the hospital."

"No. Don't want to."

I study her face to gauge how much pain she's in, she's still making that sucking noise and brown saliva trickles from a corner of her mouth. Blood! As my heart thuds, Mollie grins and opens her mouth a fraction. She's sucking a sweet.

"Where did you get that toffee?"

She giggles and turns her head into the cushion as Eve enters.

"I gave her a few sweets to cheer her up."

Mollie draws her hand out from under the sleeping bag and I see she's holding a bag of pic 'n' mix.

"You can have one, Mummy."

I shake my head. For me and Mollie the evening is over.

"We're off, Henri," I call.

He hurries in, his forehead creased in a frown. "How is she?" He glances at Mollie's leg.

"I'm still debating whether we should go to the hospital to get her toe X-rayed."

Mollie chooses that moment to hop off the sofa and parade around the room, walking normally. My heart unclenches.

"I could drive you to the hospital."

"No, Henri. You've been drinking. One accident in an evening is enough."

I gather our things and Mollie stuffs another toffee in her mouth and skips away from me, knowing I won't tell her off.

Eve lifts her glass from the coffee table and follows us to the door. My conscience stirs. That's the third drink I've seen her finish this evening. She can't drive back to Limoges, but would she want to sleep on my sofa?

In the doorway, I turn and ask, "Would you like to stay with us at the cottage?"

She shakes her head and moves out of the porch light into shadow so I can't read her expression.

"Don't worry about me. Henri's offered his spare room."

Eve and Henri. Perhaps I was wrong. Perhaps Henri actually is her type.

CHAPTER 42

EMMA

October 2016

The Eve and Henri conundrum flits through my dreams, interspersed with nightmares about how the accident could have been so much worse.

In the morning Mollie is her bubbly self, running into my room to wake me.

"Let me see your leg."

She hops into bed beside me and shows off the cuts, neatly scabbed over, and a purple bruise that has bloomed beneath her big toenail.

"Does it still hurt?"

I press it gently and she shakes her head but, as I press harder, she winces and pushes my hand away.

"Show me your walking," I ask and obediently she hops off the bed and waltzes round the room. "Can you stand on tiptoe?"

Solemnly she performs the exercise, raising her hands in the air, her ankles shaking. "I'm wobbly."

"But your toe doesn't hurt?"

She shakes her head and giggles. "Mummy, I've got a surprise to show you."

Her change of tack confuses me. "Is it something for Daddy?"

"No—it's for me!"

She runs back into her bedroom and returns, holding a silk purse, embroidered in pink and purple. She unzips it and shows me a ten-euro note folded inside.

"Where did you get that, Mollie?"

"Tante Eve. She said it was a secret present. But I know I have to tell you."

I feel a spurt of anger. Eve should know it's wrong to encourage Mollie to keep secrets. I put it down to her inexperience with children but it's still on my mind when I ring Paul later that evening to tell him about Mollie's accident.

"What were you thinking of—accepting a supper invitation from Henri?"

I'd forgotten about their mutual antipathy. Is it possible Paul's jealous of Henri? That would be ridiculous.

"Come on, Paul. Eve was there, too."

"I don't know Eve. Who is this woman you're spending so much time with?"

"Hurry up and get back and you'll meet her."

He sighs deeply. "I miss you both so much, Emma. Not long now."

"Did you see Owen at the weekend?" I ask, desperate for news of my son.

After our talk during his visit in the summer holidays, I've eased off the pressure for him to make daily contact. It's painful for me but Owen needs space—to inhabit his own life and settle in his new school without constant reminders of the mother and sister who are missing him. Our Skype sessions are intermittent and I'm lucky to get an answer to a

WhatsApp message. Like his peers, he acts as if the phone was never invented for spoken conversation.

"I did. He wanted to go to Pizza Express. Sounds like mealtimes at Zak's are turning into a competitive cook-off—Carlene gives him jollof rice and, when the new girlfriend, Aurelia, comes round, it's Jamaican jerk chicken with rice and peas."

Paul's telling that story to amuse me but my heart contracts thinking of those two women feeding and caring for my son.

"He wanted to go back to Wimbledon," Paul adds. "Got me to drive him past our old house."

"How was it looking?"

"They've paved over the front garden to make two parking spaces."

I think of the clematis I trained to climb up the front wall. Everything I nurtured—my garden, my son—must go on without me.

"And his new school?"

"He says it's hard-going academically but he's found his niche in sport. He's hoping to make the rugby team soon."

"Owen's never played rugby. Always football."

"He's making subtle adjustments. Trying to fit in."

"And he's made friends?"

"Of course. He's never had a problem with that." The phone amplifies the distance between us. Paul clears his throat. "They've asked me to renew my contract for three more months. I was going to ask what you thought about it, but they pressed me. "

"Well, you've obviously made your decision." Anger strips my voice of tone and colour. How much longer must I put up with this?

"I have. I said no."

"Really?" I ask, surprised.

"I'll be back before the end of October," Paul says and I wish he could see my smile.

CHAPTER 43

PAUL

October 2016

The months I spent in England were beyond tedious. My client was new to the property development scene. He'd bought an old brewery in Kent with planning permission to convert it into luxury flats. Residential property wasn't my specialist area, but the EU Referendum sent ripples through the commercial property sector, so I had to take what I could find.

Bunking up with Malcolm kept my expenses down but the poor guy's been in a terrible state since his marriage ended and, seeing the slump he'd fallen into, made me even more grateful I'd escaped from Genevieve.

When I was in London, I kept looking over my shoulder as if she might appear from the shadows and drag me back. If Emma had found out she would never have forgiven me.

Malcolm was drinking nonstop and only left his poky flat to go to work. One night I took him out to a club where I sometimes entertained clients back in the old days—sad-eyed East European girls and champagne, so rough, it would embarrass the hell out of a Sainsbury's shelf-stocker but it was good to see him brighten up.

Malcolm was no schemer. He was pathetically naïve and had

probably never cheated on Lucinda before, but he'd humped the Aussie barmaid from his local boozer and taken her back to his house while his wife was in Suffolk visiting her parents. He would have got away with it but Lucinda came home a day early and walked in on Malcolm and Roxanne making out in her en-suite shower room.

Malcolm's depression, the converse of my own lucky escape, had dragged me down, but the moment I set foot back on French soil my shoulders lifted.

*

My first night at home with Emma and Mollie is pure magic. We delay supper until Mollie's gone to bed but, while we're eating, she appears on the stairs to check I'm really there and haven't disappeared in a puff of smoke.

"*Boeuf en croute*—my favourite!"

"You love everything Lilianne makes," Emma retorts, as she lights a candle and places it in the centre of the table.

"Isn't this cuisine a bit expensive for our humble bar?"

"Cheek!" Emma smiles. "This is left over from a fiftieth birthday celebration meal—twenty covers. We took a fortune in the bar that evening."

The *boeuf* is pink to perfection and I've no room for dessert so I help Emma clear up. As we stand side by side doing the washing up, I count the minutes until bedtime.

Mrs Browning's bed is barely a double, but the last thing I want is sleep and, for once, Emma seems to feel the same. If only she was like this all the time without the barrier of tiredness, headaches and worries.

"Come here," I whisper.

Emma turns to face me and wraps her legs around me. Our bodies mesh, my tongue is in her mouth.

"Wait." She pulls off her t-shirt and leans over me.

We make love, slowly, passionately and I'm the luckiest man alive.

Weak autumn light filters through the curtains and Emma is singing in the shower. Perhaps I'll join her but then I hear Mollie stirring in her bedroom next door, so I amble downstairs and grab an over-ripe banana from the fruit bowl. I sip a black coffee and wait for Mollie and Emma to appear before I head up to site.

Mollie pads downstairs, yawning, her hair tousled from sleep. "Daddy!"

Her small body lunges at me, as if she's forgotten I'm back.

"Steady on, darling." I loosen her arms from around my neck.

Emma appears, hair damp from the shower, a towel draped around her shoulders.

"I'm just off," I say.

"Stay and have a *croissant*."

She touches my arm and my skin tingles.

"I'd love to but I must get up to site and see how the work has progressed."

"I'll wrap one up for you to take."

I wait while she assembles a small feast.

"Stop!" I laugh. "That's plenty." I hold out my hand for the sandwich box. "Will you manage without the car?"

"Of course. I always use my bike." She fumbles in her bag and hands me the car keys. "See you in the bar at lunchtime?"

"Definitely."

The early sun has fled leaving the sky brooding. Heavy

dew lingers on the fields as I cross the old stone bridge and arrive at Les Quatre Vents. There's no sign of Guy and Giles Berger—good. I wanted to get here first to review their progress.

Only I can't, because the doors and windows have been fitted and I don't have a key. I circle the building like a prowler, I can't even peer in through the windows because the shutters are closed and locked. I can't fault the Bergers' approach to security, but I'm less than happy with their time-keeping. I light a cigarette and wait.

When their van putters up the track, I grind my cigarette under my heel and stride across the yard to meet them. Giles is the taciturn one; Guy never stops talking. He's already nattering as he clambers out of the van.

"*Bonjour*." Guy nods and beckons to me to follow him into the house.

Inside it's dark but Guy has a torch. He goes to the kitchen where a new fuse box has been installed and flips a switch. The interior space expands as light spreads into every corner. Glancing up I notice single light bulbs dangling in the centre of each room and groan. We never asked for central fixtures; we need a mix—track lighting, wall lights, recessed spots—I'm sure it was marked on the plans. Now I'll have to call the electrician back.

Channels have been drilled at chest height in the newly-plastered kitchen.

"For the under-unit lighting?" I ask Guy.

"*Oui*." He nods.

Giles shuffles over to join us and delivers more bad news in clipped French and a smattering of English. It seems the old septic tank failed its inspection.

"So we'll need to install a new one?"

"*Oui.*"

"How much?"

Giles doesn't know. "Shall I arrange the digger?"

I grunt. More expense. More delay. I'm guessing it will be another ten-thousand euros but we have no choice. Giles presents me with a checklist .

"This is finish, yes?" He points a pen at his clipboard wanting me to sign off on completed items.

How the hell am I supposed to know? I need to get down on my knees, peer along skirting boards, stick a spirit level on the walls and floor. I take the clipboard from his hand and tick off a couple of items.

"I'll check the rest later."

Guy unpacks his toolbag and begins sanding down a window sill. Why is he faffing about with paintwork preparation before the kitchen's installed?

"Next job is flooring," I announce, flipping open the catalogue to show the elm floorboards Emma and I have chosen.

Guy glances at the catalogue and turns away with a shrug.

"So are we all agreed—flooring goes down next week?"

"*Non,*" Guy says.

It seems we're not.

"First we fit the units," Giles insists.

"No, the flooring first. It makes more sense."

"*Non.*"

"I think you need to remember who's paying."

Guy folds his arms and I sidestep a full-blown dispute and learn something else—laying the wooden flooring is not, apparently, their role and isn't included in their quote. Unless I can find a tradesman, I'll have to do that job myself.

Fuming, I leave them measuring up the kitchen and drive

into Limoges. At the building materials superstore, I locate the flooring but there are colour variations between packs and nowhere near enough in stock. I take a sharp breath and enter the glass-sided cubicle to the service desk, gripping my dictionary of French building terms as if it's a bible and I'm in court and about to swear an oath.

"*Pardon?*" The young, spectacled assistant doesn't know the product so pretends not to understand my halting French.

She calls a supervisor, who speaks some English and I write down measurements and we both calculate the number of packs. The assistant prints out a sales invoice for me to check and I hand over my credit card, but their computer rejects it because it's an English one and their system needs a French postcode.

Other customers are milling round, awaiting attention, but their computer is at stalemate over my address query. I won't give way but my French isn't adequate for the task and my authority's not respected here the way it was in my old day job.

I ring Emma at the bar, explain the dilemma and hand my mobile to the supervisor. A brief exchange and the order goes through. Emma's calm fluency makes the problem dissolve. When I get home, I'll thank her properly and tell her how much I admire everything she's achieved.

He hands the phone back to me while he finalises the paperwork.

"Did you know there's a forty-euro delivery charge?" asks Emma. "And the earliest delivery date is a week next Thursday."

This is news to me, but I pretend I knew. I sign the paperwork with the phone wedged under my chin, pick up the yellow copy and leave. The girl in the spectacles turns, with relief, to her next customer. My mobile is still clamped to my ear as I stroll back to the car.

"When are you coming to the bar?"

I glance at my watch. "Won't it be a bit late for lunch?"

"Please come. I want you to meet Eve."

When I reach the village, all the parking spaces outside the bar are taken, so I drive around to the square and park beneath a row of knobbly trees, next to a silver Mercedes convertible. The GB number plate tells me it was brand new in September. I let out a low whistle.

Emma's made several improvements over the summer while I was in England. The dingy plastic tables she kept outside for smokers have been replaced with elegant metal ones. On the threshold of winter, Emma still puts cushions on the outside chairs and Claude is sitting there, puffing on his pipe. He raises his flat cap in greeting and I nod back. Perhaps I'll join him later for a smoke though I've hinted to Emma I've given up.

The tatty blackboard has been replaced by a new one, hand-painted with the name of the bar and, in Emma's beautiful italic script:

Menu du jour—13 euros
Entrée
Plat
Dessert
Vin compris.

I approve. Before, there were too many choices, too much cooking and faffing about. But thirteen euros including a half carafe of wine? How does she pay Lilianne and make a profit on such meagre takings? My answer comes wafting through the grille in the wall—delicious cooking smells underlining our reputation.

The twenty-eight covers, across fourteen tables, can be

arranged in different formations for larger parties and she told me last night about private bookings for christenings and family birthdays.

Through the frosted window into the kitchen, I make out the silhouettes of Emma and Lilianne so drippy Henri must be manning the bar. Irritation flickers—that's my role and I'll want it back. I can't deny he was a big help when we first moved out, but I can't warm to him. Emma's convinced he's got the hots for this new friend of hers—woman called Eva, or something—but, back in the summer, she was certain Lilianne was his dream woman.

I look at things with a man's eye, pick up signals she won't notice, and it's clear to me that it's Emma who fascinates him and I understand why, but I'm jealous. I'm as certain as any man could be she'd never cheat on me. Besides, she likes manly types—look at Zak, look at me. No, she'd never go for Henri even after he's shaved off his retro moustache.

Whistling, I push the still-stiff door and step inside. A few tradesmen are tucking into the *plat du jour* and Lionel, our electrician, welcomes me with a nodded *Bonjour*. I turn my eyes towards the bar. Sure enough, Henri is behind my bar, holding court, acting like he owns the place and chatting with a dark-haired woman, perched on a bar stool. She has her back to me and looks both familiar and unfamiliar. Probably one of the regulars.

I ram my fists into my pockets so I'm not tempted to punch Henri in the face. This is my bar, not his—but no one would ever guess. I'm three steps away, when Henri greets me and the woman sitting on the bar stool swivels round.

My head spins and blood drains from my face. Time stops, my lower jaw sags and I stare.

"Genev. . ."

Did I say her name aloud or inside my head? Did Henri hear?

Lifting one perfectly-groomed eyebrow, she slides off her stool and extends her ice-cold hand.

"I'm Eve. You must be Paul. Pleased to meet you."

The corners of her mouth twist in a semblance of a smile but her eyes are hard and expressionless. I swallow, turn and stare at the door, but there's nowhere to run.

CHAPTER 44

PAUL

October 2016

Emma appears from the kitchen, carrying two steaming plates, with no cloth or tea towel to protect her hands. Her face lights up as she passes me but she delivers the meals to her customers before returning to stand beside me.

I try to work out if she's smiling—or taking part in some sick joke at my expense. She takes my arm and swivels me back to face Genevieve.

"I see you two have introduced yourselves."

"We have." Genevieve nods, her tight-lipped smile is a red gash.

This is beyond a nightmare. What's she doing here? I force a smile but waves of panic bring me out in a cold sweat. Mentally, I scroll through everything Emma's told me about this woman she calls 'Eve' who's looking after Mollie, for fuck's sake!

Henri leans across the bar to hand me a beer and it's an effort to stop my hand shaking. He's remembered my preferred brand from before. I was planning to stick with a soft drink but, right now, even a beer is a poor compromise—I could do with a stiff one.

Emma positions herself between me and Genevieve and

straightens her spine. She's still a good five inches shorter, but she juts out her chin, as if daring me to dislike her new friend.

"Eve's been amazing. I don't know how I'd have managed without her."

The two women exchange a conspiratorial smile, locking me out. As I gulp my beer, acid reflux burns my throat, but I force myself to speak.

"So what are you doing here? I mean, in Sainte Violette?"

Emma answers for her. "She's looking for a property to buy. Henri's been helping her."

"That's right. But I'm very picky, aren't I, Henri? Very hard to satisfy."

She tosses her hair and laughs. Henri's mouth twitches but he doesn't seem to share her amusement.

"If only there was somewhere in the village!" Emma sighs. "The Brownings' house isn't right. Too small and no views."

I clear my throat. Take time to behave normally. My voice sounds unnaturally high-pitched. "Is that so? What sort of house did you have in mind?"

She flutters her hands and her laugh has a familiar throaty ring with echoes from a time I thought I'd consigned to history.

"Something rural but large and airy. Fully modernised. I can't take on a DIY project."

"A *maison secondaire*? Or are you planning to settle and work from here?"

"Oh, I don't work at the moment," she says.

Genevieve not working? Impossible. She climbs back on her high stool and addresses me as if I'm one of Shakespeare's groundlings and she's Lady Macbeth.

"I was having a bad time in London. I needed some space."

I cough. "I'm sorry to hear that."

Emma nods, her face taut with compassion. "Eve's mother died. All very sudden."

A customer calls for Emma's attention. "*L'addition, Madame.*"

Henri prints out the bill and Emma carries the credit card machine over to his table, but the man is counting out the cost of his lunch in small coins.

"I'm going outside for a ciggie break," says Genevieve. "Join me?"

I'm about to say, "I don't," but, of course, I do, so I take the squashed pack out of my pocket and follow her towards the door.

Emma catches my arm. "I thought you'd given up!"

I pat her hand. "Soon. I promise."

Claude has shuffled off home, leaving his empty tobacco wrapper in the ashtray. I swap it with the one from the adjacent table, buying a few more seconds before sitting down with Genevieve.

"Perhaps you'll tell me what you're doing here?"

The metal chair legs scrape across the pavement.

She leans in with her face close to mine, as I light her cigarette.

"And perhaps you'll tell me why you pissed off, changing your phone number and leaving no forwarding address?"

I drag on my own cigarette, twist my neck around and blow the smoke into the street. Instinct warns me to be cautious. She's gone to these lengths to track me down.

"I was straight with you. I told you it was over."

"I don't believe you."

The bar door creaks and I jolt from my seat but it's not Emma, only a departing customer.

I pitch my voice low. "We can't talk here."

"Then come to my apartment in Limoges."

"I can't. I'm working on the house."

But until the flooring is delivered in ten days' time there's nothing for me to do, except follow the Bergers around and get in their way.

I lean my elbow on the table, making a fist with my hand and rest my head on it. My knuckle presses into my cheekbone—a sharp, welcome pain. I force myself to meet her eyes.

"Okay. Tomorrow. Around twelve-thirty."

"Good."

She slides her hand into her bag and passes me a printed card: Rue Jean Jaures.

I grind out my half-smoked cigarette in the ashtray and slip the address into my pocket.

CHAPTER 45

PAUL

October 2016

It's Emma's fault. Why doesn't she order me to stay in Saint Violette; run the bar, collect Mollie, anything? I sketch an outline of my day for her. It's full of un-joined dots but she doesn't notice.

She laughs and hands me an unconditional freedom pass.

"No need to check in with me. It's such a relief you're back in charge of the site."

The prospect of returning to live in the caravan on the cusp of winter nags at both of us. It's down to me to make Les Quatre Vents habitable, but the ten-day wait for flooring shunts yet another milestone off course.

Yesterday evening a young French couple came to view the Brownings' house and Emma frets, not knowing if they've made an offer. But how will we know? We're not in the loop.

Henri's daily running commentary on the buoyant property market adds to our gloom.

"My list of British clients is growing," he tells me. "Brexit seems to have spurred them on to claim a corner of a foreign field to be forever England." He glances at Emma, as if remembering her heritage, and adds, "or Wales—not so many clients from Scotland or Northern Ireland."

My morning task is re-measuring the floor area and drawing up plans for fitting the floorboards while the Bergers work to their own list, dodging around me as I pace, measure and mutter. Pausing to pour a coffee from his flask, Giles Berger consults me about fitting the kitchen.

"I want the units to stand on top of the new flooring," I tell him.

Why cut the expensive elm boards to fit around these cheap units? We might want to upgrade.

His facial muscles tauten as he warns me they'll have to down tools until I finish laying the floors.

"Can't you and Guy work on the exterior?"

Giles shuffles his feet. "It's the wrong time of year."

"Because?" I struggle to control my irritation when he says paint won't dry or something.

The fact is he thinks kitchen floors should be tiled and his shrug tells me he reserves special contempt for people like me, who lay wooden floors in a kitchen.

I leave the Bergers filling in cracks in indoor woodwork and drive to Limoges. The lunchtime traffic is insane. I'm late but why should I care? My professional career is already trashed—Genevieve's actions shielded me from criminal responsibility but I'll never claw my way back to director level after the scandal of Dorek's accident. But none of that matters, compared to the harm she can do if she tells Emma about our affair.

Hunting for a parking place delays me. I dawdle along the street, spinning out time and distance to our confrontation. Should I take something? A bottle? Flowers? No, a gift would give the wrong signal. When I reach Rue Jean Jaures, I have to search for the entrance to Genevieve's apartment block and find it in a side street.

The main door is immense and has a mirrored finish overlaid with black iron latticework and decorative scrolls. Genevieve's real name is on one of the buttons. I jab it with my finger, seeing my reflection in the tainted mirror glass, framed in pistachio green reflected from the shopfront of the chocolatier opposite.

A buzzer sounds. I push the door, step inside and climb the stairs ahead of me. As I reach the half landing between floors one and two, I glance up the stairwell and see Genevieve leaning over a bannister, a couple of floors higher—watching me. I grit my teeth and press on.

"You've come." Her voice is breathy.

She's wearing a pink cashmere sweater, black trousers and ballet pumps. Her earrings sparkle like chandeliers.

She clasps my hand and draws me inside her flat towards an open door leading to a sitting room. On the threshold, I pull my hand free and appraise the room, the architect inside me enlivened by lofty ceilings, original mouldings and black and white floor tiles.

"Cool, isn't it?"

I nod and admire the floor-to-ceiling windows, slatted shutters and a glimpse of the Juliet balcony beyond. The room smells of fresh paint and varnished floorboards. The décor is masculine, with soft edges.

"You did this yourself?" I ask.

The room is sparsely furnished like a stage set. In the centre is a high-backed sofa, upholstered in velvet, and a hard-edged ebony coffee table. The walls are hung with original artwork but there are no books, so the overall impact is sterile. A fake door has been installed in an alcove—probably to conceal a television and sound system—and an imitation log fire burns in the grate.

"I thought this was a rental?"

She shrugs. "It is, but I couldn't live with dark green paint and a stained carpet."

I stroll round the room's perimeter, viewing the paintings but they make little impression; semi-abstraction isn't my thing.

"Sit down, Paul." Genevieve's voice is flinty as she gestures towards the sofa.

I perch on the edge, keeping my back straight but the large, slippery cushions unbalance me and threaten to swallow me up.

"Drink?"

A bottle of something sparkling is sitting in an ice bucket on the ebony table and Genevieve's champagne flute stands on the mantelpiece, half empty. I open my mouth to ask for a glass of water, but she marches out of the room and returns, a few minutes later, with a Scotch.

"How did you track me down?" I ask, as she sets the tumbler down in front of me.

She rakes her fingers through her hair, lifting it up, then letting it fall and drape around her shoulders.

"Did you think, if you left no digital footprint, you could disappear?" I lower my gaze. "Finding you was easy."

I take a quick swig of the Scotch and stand up to face her. Her flat shoes have handed me back a four-inch height advantage. I step closer.

"Tell me."

"Think about it. What did you tell me about your little French project?"

My tongue burns from the Scotch. I'm sure I told her

nothing. I might have mentioned we were in the Limoges area, but never the name of the village and we're not listed in any phone books.

"Remember those long phone calls you made to your Mr Fixit when you were staying in my house?"

"Henri?"

She nods. "And you told me about his sideline—working with a local *notaire* to sell houses to British buyers."

"So you tracked down Henri and he led you to Emma?"

"Easiest thing in the world. I rang round all the *notaires* to ask about property for sale and made it clear I could only consider escorted viewings with the lovely Henri Wilson."

I slump back down on the sofa and run the back of my hand across my eyes. Genevieve picks up her glass but her drink has lost its sparkle, she grimaces and sits beside me on the sofa.

"How long are you staying?"

"That depends. My mother died. She wasn't even old."

"I'm sorry."

She shrugs. "Her death—so quick, so sudden—sent me a little crazy. But I learnt from it."

"What was that?"

"Seize the day."

I squirm as the springy sofa slides her hip against mine. Suddenly the room feels sweltering. Genevieve feels it too, because she pulls the sweater over her head. Underneath she's wearing a white t-shirt, low-cut and clingy. She's lost weight: her waist is more-defined; her boobs smaller, her nipples are outlined beneath the silky top.

I turn my head away and stare moodily out of the window at the balcony. The only sound in the room is her breathing, rapid and shallow. Tension mounts and I'm the first to break.

I turn to face her. "What is it you want from me?"

I can't meet the weight of her gaze.

She grabs both my upper arms, peers at me through dark eyelashes thickened with mascara.

"What do you think I want?" She strengthens her grip on my arms and tries to shake me. It takes all my strength to resist. "I love you but you walked out on me."

A cerise satin cushion tumbles from the arm of the sofa into my lap. I clasp it to my chest, folding my arms across it.

"I told you it was over, Genevieve. That's all."

"I don't believe you."

Her pale face looms, her nose is shiny and a mascara smudge is visible beneath one eye. And then she throws herself at me, smothering my mouth with kisses. I taste the bitter sweetness of champagne and cigarettes. She strokes my hair, nuzzles my face, my heart races.

I pull away from her, steel in my voice.

"You're stalking me. This feels like blackmail."

Genevieve draws back her hand and slaps my face. It stings.

"Blackmail, hey?" She holds up a hand and counts on her fingers. "And how exactly? Number one— I could tell Manifold I covered up for you? That's history—I left them; you left them—they wouldn't want to reopen that shit. Two—I could contact the authorities—say we both lied? Then that's trouble for both of us. "

She looks directly at me. "Oh, yes, there is one other small thing. "

My breathing quickens. I know what's coming next.

"I could tell Emma you've been cheating on her with her new bestie."

"You bitch! Stay away from Emma and my family."

Behind my anger, I'm drained and weak.

"Bit late for that, lover boy."

"Emma will believe me—not you." I bow my head and groan.

Genevieve grasps my hand, presses it to her lips. "I'm sorry, Paul. Didn't mean it. I'd never do that."

I don't believe her, though her eyes glisten with unshed tears as she leans towards me, hair tumbling forward.

"Just let me see you, Paul. Sometimes." She caresses me, strokes my hand, nibbles my neck. "I've missed you so."

She kisses me again on the mouth and now she tastes of fresh champagne and excitement and, before I know it, I'm kissing her back. She presses her body up against mine and I'm lost. My face stings with heat and pain, patterned on the grid of her slap, but I ignore it as a different kind of warmth infuses my body. Genevieve takes my hand and leads me through the door to her bedroom.

CHAPTER 46

PAUL

October 2016

And so it begins again. Genevieve promises not to say a word to Emma but her silence has a price tag. In her warped view of reality, she believes she can win me back and she seems to know no boundaries: falsifying documents, lying to the inspectors and now tracking me down in France and stalking Emma. She opens her assault by ordering me to visit her in Limoges.

"We'll take it slowly. Remember what we had."

She's rewritten our history by pinning my defection on the investigation into Dorek's death and how it affected me.

"You were under so much stress. I see it now. I was implicated in those bad times—you looked to Emma for security."

Does she honestly believe that I'd ever leave my wife and child for her? She's mocking, she's dangerous—and she's irresistible.

Some days Genevieve drops into the bar without warning, knowing I'll be there. We play a dangerous game: not speaking—ratcheting up the sexual tension. I sense Henri watching me.

One lunchtime, I make a fruitless drive into Limoges and Genevieve's not at home. I drive back, hot and grumpy, and stop in at the bar. There she is, perched on her favourite bar stool, chatting with Emma.

"I'll fetch Mollie today," she's saying, lifting her eyes to meet mine with a mocking smile. "I haven't seen her for a while."

Since my return, Genevieve's role in picking Mollie up from school has become redundant so I'm surprised when Emma nods in agreement.

"Mollie will be delighted. She's been asking when she'll see you."

It's a stomach-churning moment. I feel bad about betraying Emma—truly, I do, but Genevieve has brought danger back into my life which was, frankly, turning rather middle-aged. I thought I was inoculated against her, but she's rekindled the thrill, the adrenaline charge. I'm hooked.

The Bergers have suspended work while I fit the flooring so my solo schedule at Les Quatre Vents becomes my alibi. Emma's sick of the building site and busy with the bar and with Mollie. She's unlikely to turn up and surprise me. Besides I have the car and she makes do with her pushbike.

As my footsteps pound the Limoges pavements towards Rue Jean Jaures I wrestle with a conundrum: cheating on Emma makes me feel sleazy, grubby; but when I leave Genevieve's apartment sated, I'm cleansed. We fall into a routine and she gives me a key.

The next day, I arrive early, thinking to catch her still sleeping. I fantasise about slipping under the warm sheets beside her, ready to fuck her as she wakes up. But I'd forgotten those early starts back in London. How she taunted me to join her for a six-a.m. run. As my key scrapes in the lock, she yanks open the door wearing a white cotton wrap over a black silk nightdress. Demure on the outside but, peel away the layers, and uncover the vamp beneath.

"Darling!" She smothers me with a kiss. "Join me in the shower?"

She pads across the hall and I hear the hiss and fizz of water from the bathroom. I showered before dropping Mollie at school, but I strip off and scatter my clothes on the floor. The glass door of the shower cubicle is misted over but she opens it, laughing, as water splashes onto the tiled floor. She grasps my hand and pulls me inside. With her dark hair slicked back, her forehead is sleek as a seal. Our bodies lock together beneath a tropical gush from the shower and she rubs almond-scented gel all over my body. I suck her nipples, push her against the tiled wall and listen to her soft moans.

Afterwards she towel-dries her hair and leaves it snaking down her back in loose, damp tangles.

"Breakfast?"

I follow her into the kitchen. She flicks back a cloth to reveal a plate of fresh croissants—so she was up and out at the *boulangerie* before I arrived. My fantasy of finding her in bed, waiting for me, is intact until another day. I despise myself, but I can't resist her.

CHAPTER 47

PAUL

November 2016

As Genevieve's visits to the bar tail off, Emma is disappointed but stoic. She really thought 'Eve' was her friend.

"I suppose she has other things to do. Helping me with Mollie must have delayed her house hunting."

"I've emailed her details of a few new properties but not heard back," Henri says.

"Perhaps she's gone back to England?" I venture, wondering if I can make her disappear and slowly dissolve from their memories.

I'm the only one who knows that she's waiting at home for me. I've warned her I can't commit to visit every day. I have to build my alibi, work on the house, be around for the school run and drop into the bar.

The hired mechanical digger arrives and the Bergers return to dig three pits for the new septic tank and then sign off, leaving me on my own to fit the flooring.

The day the materials are delivered, I'm up at Les Quatre Vents to greet the delivery driver and, together, we unload and stack the heavy packs in the barn. The kitchen units arrived weeks ago and are still in their flat-pack boxes, gathering dust. After the driver has left, I carry two packs across to the main house, slit one open with a Stanley knife, and then lay out ten planks across the open expanse of floor. The elm boards warm the space and, when the sun falls on them, the stark light alters to a mellow glow. With my mobile phone, I take some pictures to show Emma.

I consult my hand-drawn plan, smoothing it out on the floor in front of me and lay more boards. Time zips by and when my phone rings, I jump. It's Genevieve and she's angry.

"Where are you? I've been waiting in all day."

My watch says it's three o'clock.

"Sorry. I'm at the house. Flooring's been delivered."

"I made lunch," she hisses. "Langoustines. Fresh from the market."

"Sorry," I repeat. "But I can't make it today."

"What did you say?" Her voice bristles with anger.

"I've work to do here and I'm collecting Mollie from school."

"Don't do this to me, Paul. I've warned you. If I don't see you by noon tomorrow, you know what will happen."

She's twisting the knife. Feeling sick and trapped, I down tools and set off for Limoges.

*

In France, the prelude to Christmas is more muted and starts later but gathers pace. We've heard nothing from the Brownings about the house sale and I try to reassure Emma it won't happen until next year.

Smoking blunts my anxiety, but Emma gives me a hard

look when I sneak outside. I've noticed she's bitten her fingernails down to the quick—perhaps smoking would calm her nerves.

Every day I juggle, harder and harder, faster and faster—setting off early to Les Quatre Vents, cutting floorboards to size, scraping my hands, nicking my fingers with the Stanley knife. At around eleven, I drive into Limoges: lunch, drinks and steamy sex with Genevieve and race back in time to pick up Mollie.

"What happened to that English woman?" People often ask us in the bar. Genevieve seems to have got to know many of the regulars and her French was fluent, on a par with Emma's.

"I didn't know she was invited for supper at the Gaspards, did you?" Emma asks Henri when Pierre, our neighbour from the pheasant farm, drops into the bar to enquire after Eve. When he learns we've not seen her, he slouches off without even buying a drink.

"How does he expect us to know? She wasn't living in our pockets, was she?" Emma remarks when he's gone.

I can't tell if she's cross because she's missing her friend or because 'Eve' was on first name terms with the Gaspards.

Henri nods sagely. "She had a full social calendar—joined a film club in Limoges and she asked me if there was a bridge club."

Genevieve playing bridge? So many things I don't know about her.

"Eve chatted to everyone," says Emma. "She probably made loads of friends. I was too busy working to notice."

I slide my glass towards her for a refill, but she shakes her head and sets down a glass of water in front of me.

"I've thought about ringing her," she confides, drying her

hands on the cloth we use to wipe the bar. "But the odd thing is—she never gave me her number."

"I have her mobile number," says Henri. "But she never picks up or returns my calls."

Emma's eyes light up. "Do you know where she lives?"

I hold my breath, imagining Emma turning up at the apartment and finding me there—that would be the end of me and of our marriage.

Henri takes out his mobile and scrolls through his contacts, with Emma looking on. The silence in the room thickens.

"I thought I had her address, but I don't," he says, laying his phone down on the bar. I exhale. "Of course, I never met her in Limoges. She always drove out to me in that Merc of hers." He takes a gulp of beer and wipes his mouth with the back of his hand. "I can let you have her mobile number, Emma, if you want to call her."

"No, thanks." Emma gives a tight smile and slips away to help Lilianne in the kitchen.

"She was a time waster," Henri confides to me once Emma is out of earshot.

"What makes you say that?"

He shrugs. "You get them all the time in this business. They come out here on a whim, have a little dabble. After a while they get fed up. Wouldn't be surprised if she's packed up and left for England."

He swigs the rest of his beer and reaches for his jacket, hanging on the back of a chair.

"She had me driving all over the countryside to show her properties, but she never liked travelling in my car. Probably worried the seat was dirty and might stain her Chanel trousers."

Thinking of the condition of his thirty-year-old Renault 4,

I'm not surprised. Those cars became extinct in Britain years ago.

"Perhaps she was worried it might break down."

Henri gives a lop-sided grin. "And she'd find herself stranded up some rutted farm track with a dodgy bloke like me."

This view of Genevieve, through the lens of another man, is enlightening. He has a pulse and an eye for a good-looking woman but something about her leaves him cold.

Since my recent no-show and Genevieve's veiled threats during our phone tiff, I've been treading cautiously. When I visit her, half of my brain stays on high alert, one eye on the door plotting my escape route. Genevieve works harder and harder to reel me in. She couldn't be more charming. She embraces hedonism, pushes the boundaries of sexual adventure and indulges my fantasies.

*

A shaft of afternoon sunlight filters through the slatted shutters and makes a pattern of monochrome stripes on Genevieve's white bedcover—like a prison window. The bedroom walls are painted soft grey. Genevieve tells me it's called Elephant's Breath and very fashionable, but it plays tricks with my brain. Is it day or night? Is it fine or murky outside?

I prop two pillows behind me to protect my back from the struts of her iron bedstead and lie back, sated. Genevieve stretches out beside me. I reach under the sheet and stroke her breast. She wriggles in contentment and gazes at me, eyes luminous in the condensed daylight. She yawns. Perhaps she'll fall asleep and I can sneak away but she rouses herself and rolls across the vast bed to take something out of her bedside drawer.

With a slow smile, she uncurls her fingers and shows me. I recoil. "Where did you get that?"

Some things I am seriously not into.

She giggles. "Come on try some. It'll give you energy. You can lay me all afternoon then run home and lay your blasted floorboards all evening."

Genevieve saps my resolve, dilutes my free will. I go along with her. I tried cocaine once in my early twenties and I'd forgotten the rush of blood to the head, the explosion in my brain. Suddenly Genevieve is more luscious, more desirable. Sex is scorching, searing pleasure and pain. Afterwards I lie back stunned. She kisses my face, nuzzles my neck, nibbles, bites, sucks, pulls.

"Ouch. What the?" I rub my neck.

The drug masks the pain but there'll be a hell of a bruise. How am I going to explain?

Genevieve finds it amusing. "My mark is on you now, Paul. You're mine."

As I drive away from Limoges, dusk falls and the oncoming headlights swim towards me. Traffic lights loom brighter, silent ropes of Christmas lights swing from lamp posts and trees beckon me to stop and dance in the street. My reactions are muddled; my breathing heavy. I should slow down, but I drive faster.

Reaching Sainte Violette, I speed along the main street, passing the bar under camouflage of darkness, and drive on to Les Quatre Vents. As the Volvo jolts to a halt, nausea hits me—wave upon wave. I slump forward over the steering wheel, close my eyes and wait for it to pass. In the side pocket of the car I find a blister pack of paracetamol and swallow two tablets with a gulp of bottled water.

I stagger from the car and unlock the barn. Using my phone as a torch, I fumble my way through eerie packages towards the stacked bathroom fitments and the item I'm seeking. It resembles a framed picture. With urgent fingers, I tear the bubble wrap off the mirror and peer at my neck. The phone light flickers but it's too weak so I stow the mirror under my arm and carry it across to the house, propping it on a windowsill. I switch on the lights.

Instinctively I squeeze my eyes shut but, when I open them, I reel. The bruise has bloomed to the diameter of an egg cup and its brownish-purple tint is decorated by visible teeth marks. Panicking, I scan the empty space and find the solution in front of me—my floor laying tools.

I grit my teeth, pick up a hammer and grasp the handle in both hands. With the claw end pointing towards me, I heft it, swing it back and smash it against my neck.

Pain shoots through my neck and spears my skull. Head throbbing, I sink to my knees and lay my cheek against the cold concrete floor. How have I been reduced to this? I allow my eyes to close.

After a while, I stumble to my feet and check in the mirror again. My aim was on target. Fresh blood oozes beneath the skin, tinting the purple mark red. The claw end of the hammer has left scratches and cuts, obliterating Genevieve's teeth marks.

So, what's my story? Head swimming, I concoct an explanation—my aim ricocheted, my poor DIY skills led to my industrial injury—and pray that Emma believes me.

CHAPTER 48

PAUL

November 2016

"Look at this." Emma's voice falters as she comes into the bedroom, mobile in one hand, a mug of tea in the other.

She hands me the drink. Still groggy from my injury, I spill some on the duvet, but Emma doesn't notice. Her hair is damp as if she's run through a rain shower. She insisted I stay in bed while she took Mollie to school but I'm expecting her to reopen last night's conversation about my neck injury and urge me to go to hospital to have the wound checked.

I wriggle into a sitting position and she hands me her phone. "Screensaver's come up."

"Oh." She takes the phone back, sits down heavily on the bed and enters her passcode.

"What am I looking at?"

She taps the Message icon with her thumb. "This text I've just received."

My conscience is leaden after yesterday's chaos—it can only be from Genevieve. My heart thuds but I force my eyes to focus as I read. The text is three words long.

British go home.

I look at her, bemused. "Is that it?"

She's shivering so hard I can see the tremor running along her arm to her fingers.

"Who would send a message like that?"

Slowly, I shake my head and check the phone's settings. "Unknown number. Not someone in your Contacts."

She pushes herself up from the bed to a standing position and glares down at me as if I'm to blame.

"Did you get one?"

"Haven't checked."

I switch my mobile off at night to muffle the incessant vibration when Genevieve's messages flood my inbox. I constantly fret Emma will intercept one of her texts.

I gather my wayward thoughts. Could it be from some sad local reacting to the continuing publicity around the UK's vote to leave the EU?

Emma hasn't been back to England since the Referendum. She rarely watches British TV and only reads French newspapers—it's part of her strategy to immerse herself in life in France. She won't know about the surge in racist incidents, trolling and abusive messages in the UK after the Leave vote.

Now isn't the time for rambling explanations, or to upset her, so I say, "Just delete it and forget about it."

She shrugs. "I suppose you're right."

She takes the phone back from me and presses delete but I can tell she's still upset.

I swing my legs out of bed but they feel unsteady as I make my way to the bathroom. Emma's face is etched with worry.

"We need to get you to hospital."

"No. Really. I'm much better today."

As I say this, pain needles my skull. I wonder if this is what a migraine feels like and wish I'd been more sympathetic to Emma when she was suffering.

"Stay home and rest."

"I should press on with laying the floors."

She clucks her tongue as if I were a recalcitrant child.

"Absolutely not. I insist. And don't lock the bathroom door. What if you faint?"

I leave the door open while I turn on the shower, but my limbs feel too heavy to step over the side of the bath. I splash cold water on my face and glance back into the bedroom, where Emma is combing tangles out of her damp hair. In the mirror I see my reflection as it must appear to her—with the swollen purple neck of a vampire's victim. I forget about showering and turn up the collar of my bathrobe.

Coffee revives me—and the prospect of the cigarette I'll smoke as soon as Emma has left for the bar. I wait on the front doorstep as she un-padlocks her bike and rams her helmet on top of her hair, still frizzy from its earlier soaking. The rain has eased but the road is slick and greasy with soggy brown leaves clogging the gutters.

"Take the car," I call, digging in my pocket for the keys.

She lifts her arm and waves. "It's okay. I'm used to cycling." Her backpack drags on her slight frame and she wobbles as she sets off.

"Be careful, it's slippery," I call after her.

I watch until she rounds the corner and disappears from view.

Retreating to the warm fug of the kitchen, I light my cigarette, something I never do indoors when Emma and Mollie are at home. A half-cup of coffee remains in the cafetière. I pour it out and stir in a spoonful of sugar. I don't take sugar but whatever Genevieve gave me yesterday has wiped my brain. Perhaps nicotine and sugar will fill the vacant space. My neck throbs. I swallow a couple more paracetamol and do some serious thinking.

The dalliance with Genevieve has gone too far. I must end it and face the consequences. Can I risk telling Emma my version of the truth and beg her forgiveness? Perhaps, if I play up the blackmail angle—link my conduct to the stress of Dorek's accident, when I wasn't myself.

One thing in my favour is Genevieve's behaviour—turning up in France, cosying up to my family, stalking me—does that sound like the action of a sane person?

Groggy with exhaustion, I turn on the TV and find a UK channel. I fall asleep in front of rolling UK news. When I wake up it's past lunchtime and I ring Emma at the bar.

"I'll collect Mollie this afternoon," I say.

In the background, I hear the rise and fall of customers' chat, the clink of glasses. She's abrupt with me.

"No, I'll fetch her. You need to lie low for a while."

"What do you mean?"

She pauses. "I don't think people will want to see your neck injury. It's grotesque!"

I groan and tramp upstairs to peer into the bathroom mirror, shining a spotlight on my neck. Genevieve's teeth marks are faint—but only visible if you know what to look for. The sick feeling stays in my stomach as I take a scarf from the wardrobe and knot it round my neck.

The next morning, I wake early and tune in to Emma's soft breathing. When her alarm unleashes a cacophony of noise, she reaches out to cancel it and turns to me with a smile, stroking the bruise on my neck.

"Does it still hurt?"

"No," I lie. "Stay there, I'll make tea."

I clatter downstairs and as the kettle comes to the boil, Emma calls my name, her voice sharp and crackling with urgency.

"What is it? Is Mollie okay?" I call, running back up the stairs.

The rosy tint of sleep has drained from her cheeks. "Look."

She tosses her phone towards me. It lands harmlessly on the bedcover and I scoop it up before the screensaver kicks in. Today's text reads:

Trouble comes of your family.

I repeat the words aloud but reading them doesn't dignify them with meaning.

"There's another one."

She crawls across the duvet towards me, threads her arm through mine and presses her body against my side.

Brit leave EU. Now you leave France.

She sniffs and rubs the back of her hand under her nose but tears slide, unchecked, down her cheeks. I put my arm around her, nuzzle her neck and whisper soothing words. Her eyes flash angrily.

"We can't ignore it. It's harassment! We have to tell the police."

"I suppose we could report it," I say slowly. "But I doubt they'd take it seriously."

At the back of my mind nags a crazy idea that Genevieve

is behind these hate texts. It's not her style, but the way she's behaving anything is possible. Emma gives me a frosty look.

I rationalise. "The police have their hands full—what with terrorist attacks—"

"Are you saying hate mail's not important?"

"Well, in the scheme of things. . . look." I take Emma's phone from her and show her how to block the caller, even though the number is showing up as unknown. "There. They won't bother you again."

She sucks on her lower lip and asks, "Can you work with me in the bar today? I think Henri's coming in later, but I can't face customers—what if it's one of them sending these horrible messages?"

"Of course. And I promise I'll wear a scarf. All day."

"Idiot."

She kisses me and when she goes to wake Mollie, she's still smiling.

When we arrive, Emma hides away in the kitchen but I'm more than happy to man the bar. Polishing glasses has a soothing rhythm as I set up for the lunchtime rush. Compared to laying floorboards and rushing into Limoges, bar work is therapy.

"We won't need your help today," I tell Henri when he arrives.

I stroll to the sink and fill the jug of water to go with Claude's Ricard. He nods and hovers as if mulling over his next move, but he doesn't order a drink. I continue my chat with Claude and don't open a gap for Henri to enter our conversation. As the bar fills up, he pulls his phone out of his pocket, deals with a few messages, then turns to leave.

"Call me when you need me."

He's halfway to the door when Emma sprints out of the kitchen, wisps of hair escaping from her bun.

"Henri. Wait!"

He turns and his eyes crinkle as he smiles. Together they stroll outside and my heart bumps in my chest. Is she planning to confide in him about the texts?

Customers are queuing and soon I'm occupied with pouring beers and measuring *rosé* into 250 centilitre carafes, included in the *menu du jour*. With Lilianne tending meat on the grill, it falls to me to take lunch orders.

I call to Lilianne and she hurries through to collect the chits, drawing the back of her hand across her shiny forehead.

If I crane my neck I can see through the window to where Emma and Henri are sitting at a smoker's table. He's leaning towards her, elbows on the table, while she's gesticulating with raised palms. She has her back to me so I can't read her expression but their body language underlines how relaxed they are together. Henri lights a cigarette, turning his head to blow the smoke away from Emma. When she stands up, Henri hands something to her—presumably her phone. She slips it into her apron pocket.

Emma comes back inside, heading straight for the kitchen. Can't she see I'm run off my feet? I nod towards a table of new arrivals. "Orders?"

She hesitates, pleating her apron into folds with her fingers, then reluctantly picks up a spare order pad. I overhear them asking for the *rosé* so I measure out a carafe.

"Did you tell Henri about the texts?" I ask when she comes to collect it from me.

She nods. "He thought it could be youths."

"Youths?" I echo. It doesn't sound likely to me.

"Henri told me a couple of holiday houses owned by Brits were broken into last week. Apparently, they pick an English-sounding name from the phone book and ring the numbers over a couple of weeks to check if the house is empty."

"I hadn't heard that." How would I? I miss out on all the bar gossip. I'm either working on my own up at Les Quatre Vents or in Limoges at Genevieve's.

"One of the houses they trashed was that *gîte* we rented last summer. Imagine!"

"I see."

Henri's done me a favour—calming Emma by planting the idea she's not being personally targeted. Even if Genevieve did pull a trick like that, what would she achieve? She must know if she unsettles Emma and drives her away from France, I'd go with her.

CHAPTER 49

PAUL

November 2016

My bruised neck throbs. I dose myself with painkillers, put my key in the ignition and focus on the task ahead. The slow crawl through Limoges traffic gives me space to compose my thoughts. I'll say my piece and it will be over.

For two days, I've been ignoring Genevieve's texts and calls, keeping my phone switched off. I don't tell her I'm on my way. If she's out, I'll let myself into her apartment and wait but, after parking the car, my resolve falters.

I hole up in a coffee shop and sip an espresso. I order a ham *baguette* but without salad or cheese it's cardboard-dry. I abandon it on the plate, pay in cash and wander out into the street.

I stroll along Rue Jean Jaures but, when I reach her mansion block, I keep walking. At the next junction, I turn and retrace my steps. My breathing calms and I'm as ready as I'll ever be. My fingers play with the knot of my scarf, wrapped tightly around my neck. I enter the lobby and tackle the stairs.

Cautiously I slide my key into Genevieve's lock and edge the door open. The scent from a vase of white lilies cloys the entrance hall. Their over-ripeness reminds me of death. From the sitting room floats the sound of faint music: some female vocalist—Adele?

The music unbalances me. I glance over my shoulder to turn back, but the sitting room door opens and it's too late.

"You!" Genevieve looks unnaturally pale without her trademark red lipstick. There are dark circles under her eyes and her hair is matted as if she's just woken from sleep.

She raises her head and scans my face, grabbing the ends of my scarf and unwinding it to reveal the swollen mess of bruises.

"Oh my . . . did I?" Her hand flies up to cover her mouth. She peers more closely and says, accusingly. "You did that yourself, didn't you?"

I shrug. Words catch in my throat.

"What an awful mess. Come with me."

Meekly I follow her into the kitchen. She takes a tray of ice cubes from her fridge, wraps it in a clean tea towel and hands it to me. It's too little, too late but I press the icepack against the swelling and turn away from the intensity of her stare. She pours me a drink.

"I don't want that."

"Suit yourself. Come and sit down."

Carrying the tumbler, I follow her into the sitting room where Adele is singing her heart out. I take a small sip of Scotch and feel warmth spreading through my body. I take another and ask, "Have you been sending hate mail to Emma?"

"What are you on about?" She frowns. "No I haven't."

I slump down on the sofa, forgetting how it likes to swallow me in its folds. Genevieve tames it by sitting sideways with her back against the armrest and stretching out her legs towards me, trying to rest them on my lap. I stay rigid and balanced with my feet planted on the floor as the sofa fights back. It's four o' clock. I'd love a cup of tea. I pick up my Scotch again with a sigh.

"I didn't think poison pen would be your style."

"What do the letters say?" She picks up a remote control from the coffee table and points it, silencing Adele.

"It's texts. Go home Brits hate stuff. Must be a local. Any ideas?"

"Poor Emma." She fiddles with her tangled hair, smoothing it back behind her ears. "I can see she'd be upset. But no."

Emma's name on Genevieve's lips infuriates me.

"Genevieve, we need to talk."

Does she sense what I'm about to say? She won't sit. She fidgets, agitated, breathing heavily. Time is on my side. Sooner or later she'll have to hear me out.

"Not in here, Paul," she announces, seizing my hand and tugging me to my feet.

Her perfume triggers a reaction in my throbbing head where pain congeals and intensifies. To block it out, I close my eyes but my legs are leaden and I sway. She catches me and holds me so close I feel her heartbeat pulsing through her thin sweater.

"You're exhausted. You need to lie down. Come with me."

"Do you have a painkiller?" I mumble.

"In the bedroom."

I follow her and sit on the edge of the bed. She bends down and removes my shoes, lifts my legs.

"Lie down. I'll fetch the tablets."

She covers me with a quilt. It's a relief to stretch out. I wait for her to bring the painkillers and a glass of water.

"Here." She hands me it and I gulp it down in one go. "Close your eyes and rest."

I sigh and close my eyes, allowing my mind to drift...

"How's your head?" she asks, leaning over me, when I wake up so her hair tickles my face.

"It's better—much better." No doubt her painkillers are prescription strength.

"Good. I have a surprise for you."

It's inky black in the bedroom. She must have closed the shutters while I was sleeping. She leans across me and switches on a lamp and I see she's changed out of the sweater and jeans into her white cotton robe. The belt is loosely tied and falls open, exposing the curve of her breast. In her hand, she clutches some velvety material and strokes it against my cheek.

"Soft?" she laughs.

"Very. What is it?"

She runs her fingers up over my injured neck and through my hair, kneading the base of my skull and sending tingles of pleasure down my spine. She strokes my hair forward from the crown to my brow, rolling the velvety cap down over my eyes and tightening an elastic string behind my ears. It doesn't cover my nose or interfere with my breathing but it's tight and uncomfortable. I slide my fingers beneath the strap and ease it away from my right eye socket.

"I don't need a sleep mask," I grumble. "I'm awake."

Genevieve grips my hand and kisses my fingertips into submission.

"Relax, you'll love this."

I struggle to prop myself up, but she pushes me back against the pillow and straddles me, pressing her nipple against my mouth. I remind myself this is the last time. For old time's sake, I go along with her, squeeze my eyes shut beneath the mask and hold my breath while she unbuttons my shirt, removes my belt, unzips my jeans. Not seeing where her next touch will land is explosively erotic. My body stirs and tenses.

She lifts and caresses my right arm. I let it go limp in her hand. There's a tinkling sound: metal striking her iron bedstead and some kind of bracelet clamps shut on my wrist. I tug my arm away. The metal clinks but it won't budge and my arm is angled uncomfortably above my head.

"What the fuck's going on?"

"Patience," she whispers in my ear. "And you'll see."

Her mouth is all over my body. Her flesh against mine. My body strains for release. I give myself up to the sensation, to orgasm, and, finally, sleep.

When I come round, I'm shivering and clammy; eyes still masked with the ridiculous hood; right hand shackled. The bedroom echoes with tomb-deep silence while sporadic traffic noise: brakes and gears grinding, cars navigating the calming humps, filters in from the street.

"Genevieve," I call.

Silence. I roll onto my side and listen. From far away, lilting strains of a female vocalist.

My right arm is cricked and aching; my wrist sore. I tug on the restraint, it rattles. I pull harder and the iron headboard flexes and clangs against the wall. With my free left hand, I fumble with the straps and yank the ridiculous mask off my eyes.

"Genevieve, you bitch. Get in here."

No one comes. Panic sets my heart thudding against my ribcage. My throat is parched. I touch the roof of my mouth with my tongue, but my saliva ducts seem to have packed up and I can't swallow.

What time is it? I'm not wearing a watch, but it was almost

dark when I arrived—hours ago. I'm on the brink of despair when she comes. She stands in the doorway, not switching on the light, a faint glow from the hallway picks out a halo around her hair.

"Were you calling?"

"Bitch. Take this fucking thing off my wrist."

"You were exhausted, darling. I let you sleep." She stands a pace away from the bed, out of reach of the arc of my free arm. "Stay with me tonight."

"What time is it?"

"Not so late. Not midnight yet, I'm sure."

"Midnight!" Straining every sinew, I drag myself upright and tug on the handcuff. "I'm warning you, Genevieve." She steps close and I grab her with my free left arm, pinion her wrist to the mattress. "Let me out of here."

She screams, her voice shrill. I grab for her throat but, as I release my hold on her arm, she darts out of reach.

"Why should I let you go?" She puts her hands on her hips. "I spend my whole life waiting around for you. Now it's on my terms. You're staying."

She turns, as if to leave the room. Desperation claws at me. What will I tell Emma? Think back—hostage movies, Stockholm syndrome. Box clever. I extend my tongue and run it over my cracked lips.

"Can I have some water?"

"Of course, darling." She brings a glass, holds it out and watches me drink.

"I'm cold."

She passes me my boxers, watches me struggle into them, hoisting my body up on my free arm and twisting like a gymnast on a pommel horse.

"Please, Genevieve. I need to pee." Through thick, dry lips, I force out the word, "Darling."

She snaps on the bedside lamp and scans my face. I raise my left hand to shield my eyes against the sudden brightness.

"It was good for you? You enjoyed it?" She's pawing at me with her hand.

"Yes, yes," I splutter. "It was good for me."

Isn't there supposed to be some sort of safe word couples use when they embark on these sexual adventures? But Genevieve never sought my consent.

She folds her arms and gives a half-smile. "Next time it'll be your turn. You can put the restraints on me. I love you. I'd trust you with my life."

Still she won't release me. We act out a sick reversal of strip poker as she hands me my clothes, one garment at a time, and watches me dress. Last comes my shirt. With my right wrist still fettered, I insert my left arm and raise it so the shirt dangles like a limp flag. Perhaps this pathetic image stirs her because she fetches the key, inserts it into the lock of the handcuffs and it springs open.

I'm free to rub my wrist and hobble to the bathroom. I check my phone. Five missed calls from Emma. It's half past midnight.

"Stay and have a nightcap." Genevieve's fingers scrabble at my sleeve.

I'm firm. "I have to go."

I show her my mobile with the list of missed calls from Emma.

"Then stop being a coward. Go home and tell Emma you're leaving her!"

CHAPTER 50

PAUL

November 2016: later the same night

Emma is waiting just inside the door, wearing her dressing gown and slippers, phone clasped in one hand. Her face is white and drawn.

"Where were you, Paul? I've been frantic. About to call the hospitals, the police!"

"Car broke down on the Limoges road."

"Why didn't you ring me?"

"My phone battery died. I walked miles before I could get hold of emergency services."

"I don't get it. You said you were working late on the house. So why were you on the Limoges road?"

Shit! Did I tell her I was driving back from Limoges? It must have slipped out.

"Give me a minute." I hold up a hand, as if nature's call is urgent, and dash to the bathroom.

I unbutton my shirt and splash water on my torso and under my armpits, but I can't seem to rinse away the musky smell of Genevieve's perfume. It's in my hair. I lather soap, wash my face and slick my hair back with my damp hands. When my heartbeat slows, I unlock the door and clatter back down the stairs.

Emma is leaning back in an armchair, with her eyes closed, a half-finished coffee beside her.

"When you didn't answer your phone, I left Mollie sleeping and cycled up to the house." She opens her eyes and glares at me. "I felt so guilty leaving her alone. How could you put me in that position?"

I kneel beside her chair. "Sorry," I say, over and over. "I didn't mean to worry you. Everything happened so fast."

"What's going on, Paul? You've been acting weird lately. Have you been drinking?"

Emma's always worried I'll have a couple of drinks and get behind the wheel.

"No, honestly. I've only had the one Scotch and that was hours ago."

Her eyes fall on my neck and I realise I must have left my scarf behind at Genevieve's. She reaches out her hand and touches my bruise.

"I. Don't. Believe. You! You must have been drinking on that day when you tried to chop off your head with the claw hammer."

She walks away from me, breaking into a jog as she mounts the stairs. I hear a flumping sound and look round. She's thrown down a spare duvet. I groan, grab a couple of cushions and try to sleep on the sofa.

The next morning, we rush through breakfast, focusing attention on Mollie. If I catch Emma's eye, she glares at me so I push back my chair and stand up.

"I'm off."

"Pick me up from school, Daddy."

Mollie stretches up her arms for a hug.

"I have lots of work to do, baby." I'm so far behind with

the flooring, Emma will soon get suspicious. "Maybe later in the week."

I run outside and jump into the Volvo before Emma can interrogate me further about yesterday's breakdown. The rain lashes down and the wipers struggle to keep the windscreen clear as I drive to Les Quatre Vents. I don't have a mac or an umbrella so I wait in the car for the downpour to slacken, gazing gloomily at the rain pouring off the roof and cascading down the walls.

Why didn't I insist the Bergers installed the gutters before they downed tools? This is the first storm since the outside was rendered so I run inside and check the walls for traces of damp.

Satisfied that the house is watertight, I kneel on the floor and press on with the flooring. My body feels like it's been in a car crash. The bruising on my neck is slowly reducing, but my right wrist is puffy, with a red weal.

Around mid-morning my phone rings.

"Emma." Hearing her voice soothes me. Maybe she's forgiven me?

"I've had another of those texts." The quiver in her voice is audible.

"What does it say?"

"Never mind what it says. I thought you blocked the number."

"I have." Someone sending hate texts is going to take precautions. "It's probably a disposable sim card."

"You'll have to come to the bar. Lilianne's late and I can't cope with all this."

I glance at the tools strewn across the floor. The floorboards are cut to size and ready to fit. "Well, it's difficult."

"Paul can you do this one small thing for me?" Her voice breaks into an anguished sob.

"I'll be there in ten minutes."

I grab the new scarf I pulled from the coat rack this morning, knot it round my neck and hurry to the car.

The bar is deserted apart from Emma, who is staring into space, one hand resting on the blackboard with its half-chalked up *menu du jour*. Her phone is on the table in front of her, next to an empty coffee cup. She lifts her eyes in a blank stare.

"Show me the text."

She keys in the passcode and hands me her phone. This message is even nastier than before:

Leave now or danger comes to your daughter.

I flinch. The mention of Mollie gives the text a visceral sting. I imagine Emma feeling the words as a physical blow.

"Okay," I say. "Don't delete that one. We'll show the police. Give it to me—I'll block the number anyway."

"How do they know my mobile number? I've hardly given it to anyone."

"That's easy." I point to the hand-painted details at the foot of the menu blackboard. "It's here."

We have no fixed phone in the bar so the number shown for table reservations is Emma's mobile.

She flushes. "Of course. I'm being foolish. I worried it might be someone close to me."

The door opens and Emma relaxes as Hubert wanders in, removing his flat cap and shaking rain off his jacket.

"Could you serve?" she asks me. "I'm so behind with the food preparations."

"Where's Lilianne?"

"Her mother's sick again. She's not coming in."

Before Hubert's ponderous footsteps have crossed the floor, I'm in position behind the bar ready to serve.

"What can I get you, Hubert?"

I guess, correctly, that he'll opt for a Cognac but I always ask.

Emma chalks '*coq au vin*' on the blackboard and passes it to me to display.

"Can you cope with that?"

She nods and vanishes into the kitchen and I hear the freezer lid groan as she opens it. Perhaps I shouldn't have been so down on old Henri. It would be handy to have him on standby for bar duty at times like these.

Hubert gives me his grim weather predictions for the winter.

"There's a harsh one coming," he says, rubbing his hands with pessimistic delight. "Birds have eaten all the berries off the holly."

I smile, grudgingly, but my good humour vanishes as my phone beeps and Genevieve's name appears. I scan the first line of her text—something cryptic about last night. As I skim the message, my hand is shaking. *Unforgettable,* she calls it, *a memory we'll treasure forever.*

And then she tells me why our night will never be forgotten. It isn't just a memory. She's captured the whole thing on film.

CHAPTER 51

EMMA

December 2016

Lilianne's mother's illness lingers for days and Paul steps in to cover the lunchtime bar shift, while I prepare the food. He frets about the time he's losing on laying the floors and by mid-afternoon he's heading back to site, where he works on into the evening. We're both exhausted and relieved when Lilianne returns.

"How's your mum coping?" I ask her.

"Crisis is over. Until the next one." She raises her hands in a dismissive gesture. "Perhaps they will move into a *maison de retraite*."

Lilianne will be free to get on with her own life but it may not be the life she'd choose. She exudes wistfulness like a perfume. How I wish she and Henri could overcome their mutual myopia and see a joint destiny.

After our lunchtime customers have left, I leave Lilianne in charge and cycle up to surprise Paul at Les Quatre Vents. There's something I need to discuss with him.

When I arrive, flushed and breathless from the bike ride, he's standing outside, smoking. His clothes smell of tobacco with a lingering whiff of paint or varnish. I'm not happy about the smoking but at least he's stopped smothering himself in that musky after shave. He drops his cigarette and stamps it out before greeting me with a hug.

"Can't wait to see inside."

I prop my bike against the wall and follow him into the house. The elm flooring has worked its magic, lifting an otherwise-cold open plan space and transforming the bones of a once-derelict building into a comfortable home.

"What do you think?" Paul asks.

"Stunning but . ."

"But what?"

I stretch out a hand and wave at the exposed concrete floor of the kitchen area.

"Come on, say it. Don't you like it?"

"It's just . . . I thought you'd be a bit further on, that's all."

Paul grimaces. "My fault. Took me a while to get into practice. Made a few false starts." He steps nimbly across an open pack of boards and indicates a scuffed area of floor with the toe of his shoe. "I wasted a whole pack here. I cut planks to fit, then realised I was laying the boards in the wrong direction."

"You mean from side to side of the room?"

"Yeah. Didn't look right so I pulled it all up and re-laid it on the horizontal so it runs in a continuous line through the house."

"It certainly has a wow factor," I agree but my spirits slump at this lack of progress. What if the Brownings find a buyer? He takes my arm. "Come and look out the back."

Together, we stroll around to the rear of the building.

"Oh my!"

The digger the Bergers hired to dig the trenches is still parked on the grass, looming over three deep pits. Beside it is a vast black plastic tank, almost as tall as me, waiting to be installed.

"Watch your footing. That pit's two metres deep. If you stumble in there I'm not sure how I'd get you out."

We circumnavigate the first trench, squeezing through the narrow gap beside the digger and Paul knocks on the hollow polyethylene tank.

"The waste from the house collects in here and solids sink to the bottom as sludge."

"Gross." I wrinkle my nose.

"Yeah, but it slows down the process so bacteria can break it all down. Gradually new waste water flushes it through into these next pits where we'll have perforated pipes buried in gravel, way below the surface, to complete the treatment. That's called a drain field."

"Enough," I protest, but still he hasn't finished.

"By the time the effluent comes out the other end, the water should be pure enough to drink!"

I shudder. Now's my chance to ask him. I take a deep breath. "Paul—I want to go to London to see Owen for a few days. Could you cover for me at the bar?"

I read my answer from the spark of alarm in his eyes. He rearranges his expression and waves his arm towards the digger.

"Of course you must go but right now it's impossible. The guys will be installing the new septic tank in the next couple of weeks. I'll have to be on site to oversee the work."

"How long's it going to take? Can't Giles Berger manage it for you?"

He sighs. "We've had too many false starts. It's hard enough getting the Bergers to take responsibility for their own work."

I press him. "What about Henri?"

"He doesn't have the experience."

"So you're saying I can't go and visit my son?"

"He's coming here for Christmas, isn't he? If I press on now, there's a good chance we'll be in the house by then."

"Well, get on with it!" I yell, turning my back on him.

I fetch my bike and ride back to the bar.

*

Lilianne has finished clearing up. Her hands are red from the washing up—she's been neglecting herself, forgetting her routine of applying hand cream.

"I missed you," I tell her. "And I'm sorry but I used up most of the freezer stocks while you were away."

"Then I will stay late today and cook," she says. "What do we have? *Poulet? Legumes? Cabillaud?*"

I check my stock list. "We have chicken and vegetables, but not cod."

She fidgets, but makes no move towards the kitchen to get started. Her face is pinched and her skin looks sallow. After a week of nursing her mother, day and night, she must be exhausted.

"Emma, there is something I must tell you. Something not nice."

She must be planning to hand in her notice!

"Lilianne," I stutter. "I don't want to lose you."

"Ah—you think I am leaving the bar? Well, perhaps I am. That is for you to tell me."

Lilianne lowers her head and studies her hands. "It's about the notes."

"Notes?" I rack my brains.

Has money gone missing from the till? But Lilianne rarely deals with the takings. That task is down to me and Henri.

She raises her head and allows her eyes to meet mine. "Texts."

"Texts?" The word is hollow and meaningless. And then I remember. "Those poisonous messages?"

"They were from me."

I stare at her. "What!"

"I sent them."

"I don't believe you. Why would you do such a thing?"

Lilianne is talking in riddles. She's not her calm, elegant self. Her face is blotchy and her left eye inflamed; she rubs it with the back of her hand and it turns pinker.

"I went a little crazy. Looking after my parents while my life rotted away but I think it was because of Henri."

"Henri?" Now I'm really confused. Is she trying to tell me Henri was involved in sending those messages? "He'd never be so cruel!"

She flinches and continues in a flat voice, barely above a whisper. "Last year Henri and I were having a relationship. I thought there was a future for us. But it ended—soon after you arrived."

So there was a connection between Lilianne and Henri! Yet they always behaved so coolly to one another. More like strangers than work colleagues but that doesn't explain why Lilianne targeted me with hate texts. Was she lonely after breaking up with Henri?

"What happened?" I ask. "With Henri."

"Henri ended it. I think he could only see you."

"What?" I'm beyond stunned.

I remember Paul once hinted that Henri was smitten with

me, but it seemed unbelievable so I took it as a sign of Paul's jealousy at me spending so much time with another man. Henri and I were business colleagues. Nothing else.

I think back over the past year, remembering occasions when Henri stood close beside me, or took my hand and held it for a little too long and remember Lilianne sometimes walking in on us. But those were times when we were exchanging confidences—him telling me about his childhood; me explaining about Owen—and Zak.

"There's nothing between Henri and me," I tell her, shuffling my feet. "Never has been." Never will be.

"What I did was wrong, Emma. I wish I could change it. I will carry on and do the cooking now, but I think you will ask me to leave my job."

"I can't discuss this now, I have to collect Mollie. I'll think about it over night and we'll talk again tomorrow."

"Okay," Lilianne says quietly.

When Mollie and I arrive home from school, a light is flashing on the answerphone. Calls to our landline are rare so I'm convinced this message will be from Peter Browning ringing to tell me the cottage is sold and we have to move out. After Lilianne's confession and the disappointment of not being able to go and see Owen, today is tainted with bad karma. I can't take any more bad news. I leave the answerphone to blink itself into a stupor.

Mollie's asleep in bed and I'm dozing in an armchair, when I hear Paul scraping his boots on the metal doormat. Reluctant to talk, I keep my eyes closed and feign sleep. Paul tiptoes around me on his way to the kitchen and returns with a beer but his next action cuts through my torpor.

He jabs his finger on the answerphone play button and

a voice I've not heard for a while—friendly, breathy and commanding—addresses me by name.

'Hi Emma—and lovely Mollie—Tante Eve here. It's been a while—sorry. I've missed you Mollie. I'm coming to see you soon, I promise, and I'll take you out for a treat after school. Okay, sweetie? Love and kisses.'

I open my eyes and sit upright, straining to listen. There's a click as Paul presses one of the answerphone buttons.

"Can you play that again, Paul? I didn't quite catch that."

He turns to me, with a strained expression. "I've deleted it."

"Why?"

"She's messed you about Emma—and Mollie. You're well shot of her."

I agree with him. It doesn't matter to me, but Mollie was fond of the woman she called Tante Eve and quite upset when she seemed to lose interest. But I wish I could hear it again to remember word for word what she said in her message.

CHAPTER 52

EMMA

December 2016

The day after Lilianne's confession, the atmosphere between us is strained because I still haven't decided what to say to her. Paul told me to fire her immediately but I didn't tell him the whole story—I left out the part about Henri and invented a different motivation for Lilianne's actions. I told him she'd gone a little crazy under the stress of looking after her elderly parents and it had stirred irrational resentment against me.

"You've been nothing but generous to her!" he exclaimed.

"She's spoken to her doctor," I replied, easily summoning up a white lie. "She's on medication. She's said sorry—it won't happen again."

"All the same—"

"I'll handle it. The bar is my business, after all."

I've built it from scratch, run it without his help for almost a year. The final decision will be mine.

All night I think about what Lilianne told me but, in the morning, I still haven't reached a decision.

Throughout the morning, we keep to our separate territories: Lilianne in the kitchen; me in the bar, until the quiet lunchtime shift is ambushed by a minibus of tourists, returning to Limoges from Oradour and we have to work as a team.

The tourists have a professional driver so they linger in the bar all afternoon, ordering extra drinks. When they finally leave, I glance at my watch and take a sharp in-breath. I'm running late to collect Mollie.

"Mollie's teacher will be mad at me." I grab my bag, take out my compact and dab powder on my shiny nose. "Could you keep an eye on things?"

"Of course."

And there's something more awkward I need to mention.

"Henri will be here in fifteen minutes to do the late shift. Tell him I'll be back later to lock up."

Lilianne blushes. Now I'm seriously late but my head reels with thoughts of Lilianne's anonymous texts and her relationship with Henri. She's apologised, explained, but how can I keep her on? And how will I manage if I let her go?

The church clock strikes and I break into a run. When I reach the school, the yard is silent and deserted. Poor Mollie must be stuck in her classroom, waiting for me.

Expecting the main door to be locked, my finger hovers over the bell but I give it an experimental push and it swings open. My footsteps echo on the cold floor tiles and there's a smell I remember from my own school days: stale lunch mixed with chalk dust. Mollie's infant school in England smelt different: a chemical smell of varnished wood and marker pens. I cast my mind back to when I was a learning support assistant but it seems to belong to another life. Now I'm a businesswoman and I'm proud of what I've achieved, mostly on my own.

Madame Moreau is bending over her desk, sifting through a pile of exercise books. She doesn't notice me at first and my eyes wander to the children's artwork displayed on the wall behind her desk and wonder which of the paintings is Mollie's. She looks up, startled, and peers at me over her rimless spectacles.

"What can I do for you, Madame Willshire?" she asks in a sharp tone.

When she talks to the children her voice is as soft as gentle waves breaking on the shore.

"I'm sorry for being late. I've come to collect Mollie."

I glance around the room. Tiny chairs are neatly stacked on top of tables, ready for the cleaners to sweep the floor but there's no sign of any children.

"Is she in the cloakroom?"

Madame Moreau gets to her feet, her desk forms a barrier between us. She leans towards me. "She has left."

"Left?" I echo.

Madame nods and speaks slowly as if my understanding is faulty. "For her dentist appointment in Limoges. Your friend, Miss Laurenson, picked her up. Over half an hour ago."

Half an hour ago? Dental appointment? I feel my jaw sag. "What?"

Madame opens her desk drawer and rifles through it, producing a signed form with a photograph stapled to one corner— the form we filled in when we registered Eve as a responsible adult, with permission to pick up Mollie.

Madame Moreau's eyes meet mine and I detect a flicker of alarm, reflecting my own unease. As I gaze at the face of my one-time friend, it wakens a memory: the message Eve left on the answerphone yesterday but I was so confused by Lilianne's confession I didn't fully process what she was saying. Something about how she was missing Mollie, and that she'd be stopping by to take her out after school for an overdue treat. Did she mention a date? Paul had deleted the message before I had a chance to listen to it again.

I back out of the room.

"My mistake. I—err—mixed up the days. Sorry."

I try to laugh but it sounds empty. I haven't seen Eve for—what—three weeks? If she wanted to take Mollie for a treat, why whisk her off to a mythical dental appointment?

I half-run, half-stumble back towards the bar.

Eve and Mollie must be playing a joke on me. They'll be waiting in the bar, ready to jump out at me and chorus, "Surprise!"

Breathing heavily, I shove the door open and look around. Lilianne is standing next to the bar with her coat on, deep in conversation with Henri. There's no one else. No customers. I utter a small cry of distress. Henri swivels his seat round to look at me.

"Where's Mollie?"

"Sorry?"

"Mollie and Eve—are they here?" I have a stitch from running and press my hand over my side as I drag oxygen into my lungs.

Lilianne's eyes widen and Henri lifts an eyebrow.

"What is it, Emma?"

"Not here, then?" Although my feet are rooted to the floor, my legs feel too heavy to put one in front of the other.

Henri guides me to a chair. "What's happened? Tell me."

My ragged breathing turns to hiccups and Lilianne pours a glass of water and brings it to me. I take a sip and gasp out my story.

"Last night Eve left a message on our answerphone, saying she wanted to take Mollie out for a treat. I never rang her back to agree a date but, when I arrived at school just now, Madame Moreau said Eve had collected her early and said she was taking her to a dental appointment in Limoges."

Henri coughs and exchanges a glance with Lilianne, who asks, "Did she have a dental appointment?"

I shake my head.

"Have you phoned her?"

"No," I sniff, blotting tears with the back of my hand. "I don't have her number."

"Let me call her." Henri whips out his phone, selects a number and waits.

I lean forward in the chair, bracing my feet on the ground but the phone rings out. He tries again, shakes his head, infuriated.

"She's not taking my calls. Hasn't done for weeks.

"Give me her number." I grab his phone and tap the digits into my own mobile. "Perhaps she'll pick up if I call her."

The phone rings once, twice, ten times. No answer. The message kicks in but it's the default voice. What possessed me to let someone whose number I don't even have, pick up my child from school? But Eve was always around, wasn't she? Every day she came into the bar. I never needed to ring her.

I press redial and let the number ring again. Meanwhile Henri composes a text. My second call fails. I send a text too. The two of us fire off messages into a void. Where are they? How could she enter our lives, vanish into thin air and rematerialise to snatch my daughter? I cover my eyes with my hands.

"How can I find her?"

"We must call the police." Henri's voice is firm.

"Yes, yes—I'll do it."

Instinct tells me we're all over-reacting; there must be a simple explanation for this. Perhaps her message said she was coming today. *Why* did Paul have to delete it?

"It's bound to be a misunderstanding about dates," I say. "Let me talk to Paul. He might remember exactly what she said in her voice message."

I think of the poster I saw in Limoges airport showing missing children, the face of little Habib Nedder. Was Eve desperate for a child of her own? Did she earmark Mollie? No—that's impossible.

"If only we knew her address."

It's Henri's turn to hesitate. He twiddles his phone and presses the contacts icon with his index finger. "Actually, I have it here."

"But you said you didn't know it."

His face clouds. "Eve made me promise not to give it to you. I had to go along with it—client confidentiality. I thought she just wanted privacy."

I grab his phone and read the address. Rue Jean Jaures—one of the major streets in Limoges, close to the cathedral quarter and the old town. That fits with what she told me on our shopping day in Limoges, when I thought she was my friend. Even then she was evasive, refusing to answer questions about where she was living.

I key the address into my phone. "I'm going there."

"Don't be foolish, Emma. Who knows what she's up to?"

I can't let him block me. "I'm sure there's a simple explanation for this. After all she did leave a message on our answerphone yesterday about taking Mollie out. " My voice is firm. "I'll resolve it with her. Paul will come with me."

I call Paul's mobile. No reply. I leave a message on his

voicemail and grope inside my bag for the car keys but my hand slides out empty. I uncurl my fingers and stare at them.

"What is it?"

"Paul has the car. What can I do?"

I turn pleading eyes towards Henri, who seems lost for words. Lilianne has hovered in the background, shocked and silent, but now she rummages in her handbag and pulls out a set of car keys.

"Take mine."

"Are you sure?"

We exchange glances, raising a flag of truce over her confession and our discussion. My hands curl round the keys. I'm desperate to get to Mollie. I know in my heart Eve won't hurt her. It's a misunderstanding. A bad one, for sure, but I'll sort it out.

"I'll drive you." Henri collects his jacket, strides to the door and twiddles the sign to read 'closed'.

I turn it back. "Thanks, Henri. I'm truly grateful but no. It would help me if you stay and man the bar. I'll keep ringing Paul. He can meet me there."

Lilianne has followed me and Henri to the door. She rests her hand lightly on Henri's arm, as if restraining him.

"Emma's right. This is something for her and Paul to do."

I nod. "If Paul turns up here before I've spoken to him, tell him where to find me. He doesn't know Eve as well as we do."

CHAPTER 53

EMMA

December 2016

The road into Limoges is clogged with farm vehicles. Grit and mud shower down on following cars that dare to get too close. When the road ahead clears, Lilianne's elderly Peugeot zips along but I rein it in, cautiously skirting ruts and puddles from last night's storm. My mind hops. Stay calm, avoid prangs. Get to Mollie.

A voice inside my head nags at me. *This is your fault. You're an unfit mother—you left your son behind. Now you've lost Mollie.*

I struggle to slow my hammering heart as I see the traffic building ahead. I rarely drive into the centre of Limoges. The streets are narrow and I thread my way through a maze of road works and blocked junctions that tangle my sense of direction. Signs beckon me one way, then send me in a circle back to where I started.

My phone lies silent on the passenger seat. I join a slow-moving traffic queue and snatch my phone up. No messages. I curse, ring Paul's number again, dictate what has happened onto his voicemail and spell out Eve's address.

A horn alerts me that the queue is moving. Accelerate. Brake. Creep forward. Repeat.

Alongside the river, I pass the old bridge leading to the Pont Saint Etienne restaurant where Peter Browning took his mother. I pull over to consult the map on my phone, get my bearings and work my way to Rue Jean Jaures.

I remember Eve saying she lived on a two-way street and her apartment block was above a bank. I spot a Credit Mutuel—is that a bank or an insurance company?

Then I see it. Diagonally opposite, a branch of Credit Agricole with a grand mansion block above. The flats have Juliet balconies overlooking the street.

I've been dawdling and the driver behind me thumps his horn. I accelerate, resigned to making another circuit of the block but an Audi is pulling out of a parking space ahead of me. I signal and stamp on the brakes, the car behind screeches to a halt but I hold my ground until the Audi moves on and I slip into the vacant space.

With thudding heart, I switch off the engine and briefly rest my head on the steering wheel. I glance up at Eve's building across the road, the heavy classical apartments seem to crush the bank beneath. Where's the entrance?

The bank is shut and there's no sign of a door on Rue Jean Jaures but I find it, tucked away in a side street. The entrance door is embellished with swirls of black metal on mirrored glass, so grand and vast it seems to rear up in front of me. I scan the names on the bells and find Laurenson but the initial isn't E for Eve. It's G. I shiver. Is someone else living here with Eve? A husband? And what are they doing with my daughter?

I stab my index finger on the bell and hold it there. A voice—distorted but recognisably Eve's—floats from the speaker.

"Is that you? Use your key."

She's at home! So Mollie must be here. But who is Eve

expecting? I open my mouth to say my name, but something holds me back. I stay mute, press the bell again—and wait.

"Forgot it, did you?" her voice has an edge to it. "Come on then, you bastard. Come up."

The door buzzes. I push. It opens easily. My legs feel heavy. Leaning on the banister, I stump up the stairs. On the first-floor landing, every door is firmly shut. On and up, I climb. On the second landing, I pause for breath and a door opens. An elderly couple emerge from their apartment; the woman, dressed all in black, with steel grey hair in a bun, gives me a neighbourhood-watch type stare.

Clinging to my blueprint for a harmless outcome, I crane my neck expecting to see Eve and Mollie waving and calling out, "Surprise!"

I reach the third floor. The landing is empty, but a single door stands ajar and I can see inside to a dimly lit hall with panelled doors leading off it. On a console table, lilies in a vase bow their dying heads and drop saffron pollen on the floor. My heart thuds.

"Eve," I yell. "Mollie, where are you?"

Silence.

Directly ahead of me is a closed door. I push it open: a cloakroom, windowless, empty. As I close it some mechanism kicks in and a fan rumbles into action.

From the far end of the hallway, a door slams and I turn to face the approaching footsteps.

"You!" Eve halts a metre away from me.

The hall is gloomy and windowless, and a time switch has killed off the light from the main stairwell. A thin bar of light glows from beneath the closed door of a room at the end of the hall.

"Where's Mollie?" I step towards her, keeping my voice level.

She looks straight through me, craning her neck to peer over my shoulder and out through the front door I left open behind me.

"Eve—why did you pick Mollie up from school without discussing it with me?"

I reach out my hand. She brushes past me and out to the shared landing, to peer down the stairwell. A motion sensor triggers the lighting and, as she turns, I see the elegant woman, who mesmerised my bar customers, has uncombed hair and bloodshot eyes, with dilated pupils.

"Is Paul with you?" she demands, leaving the outer door open and returning inside. Her voice sounds thick, as if she's recovering from a chest cold.

I grab her upper arm and tug it.

"Why are you asking about Paul? Where's Mollie?"

Her eyes flick over me without interest, towering above me even in her bare feet. She stares as if hypnotised.

"Eve!" I tug her arm and shake her. "Where's Mollie? Why did you invent a dentist appointment and collect her from school?"

Still that blank stare—should I slap her to bring her round? There's no smell of alcohol on her breath but it's obvious she's taken pills—or something else. Did she drive Mollie while she was in this state? Getting through to her is hopeless. I let her arm drop and turn down the hallway.

"Mollie, where are you?" I shout, opening the next door.

It's a kitchen. No Mollie. I yank the handle of the door beside the console table, brushing against the lilies, their pollen staining my sleeve. A bedroom. Shutters closed, a table lamp, a vast bed with ornate metal headboard. Lilies, darkened rooms, echoing silence—this place is like a mausoleum. I slide back the doors of a wardrobe and peer inside. Mollie's obsessed with hide and seek, perhaps she's hiding from me. The air in the room alters: a sweet, sickly smell that drives out oxygen. It's not the lilies but a musky perfume.

I turn to see Eve, holding an atomiser, spraying perfume, not just onto her wrists, but all around the room. My eyes sting and smart.

"What are you doing?" I splutter, rubbing my watering eyes and wishing I was wearing my glasses, not contact lenses.

"I could ask the same of you." She puts the atomiser down on a bedside table.

"For God's sake, Eve. This is crazy. Where's Mollie?"

I edge towards the door but she's there first, closing it and leaning against it.

She meets my eyes and the expression in hers is bitter.

"Mollie's here. She's safe. Sleeping."

"WHERE IS SHE?" I shout. "MOLLIE!" I gather all my strength and rush at Eve, forcing my arm into the space between her back and the closed door and trying to prise her upper body away. "Let me out!"

Eve leans back hard, trapping my arm and the door stays firmly shut.

"No." Her voice resonates.

Pins and needles shoot through my arm as I twist to free it. Finally, she moves away and, while I'm rubbing my arm, she opens a drawer in a bedside cabinet and rummages inside.

I yank on the door handle. Too late. She kicks it closed and wedges it with her foot. And then I see what she's holding in her right hand: a serious knife, with a double-blade, not your average kitchen implement.

She brandishes it tentatively, then points it in my direction.

"What the . . . help!" I shriek, fixing my eyes on the gleaming blade. "*Aidez-moi!*"

"Shut up." She slashes the air with her knife. "Don't make a sound or—"

"Or what? Are you planning to harm me? Or my daughter?"

Her face contorts. I cower away from her, my calves pressing against her bed, while she guards the door. Is this a game? Is she keeping me in or keeping someone else out? She opens the door and peers out into the hall.

"Eve," I beg. "I don't know what this is about. Just let me see Mollie."

Her eyes flash at me. "Mollie's staying here—and you. Until he comes."

"Until who comes?" A tear trickles down my cheek. I scrub it away with the back of my hand. "Please explain. What's going on?"

She glares at me. What could I have done to infuriate her? I've never been one to make enemies, I always disengage and walk away.

Minutes pass. In the street below, a car whooshes past. I hold my head still and use my eyes to scan every nook of the gloomy bedroom for something to use as a weapon. A free-standing dressing table mirror catches my eye. Could I reach it and heft it, and would I have the strength to smash it over Eve's head? The difference in our heights puts me at a disadvantage but she seems unsteady on her feet.

Eve's voice breaks the silence. "Stop acting the innocent. I know he's told you."

"Who? Told me what?"

"Paul. He's leaving you. He's in love with me."

The sickly aroma of the perfume she sprayed around the room thickens and I recognise it. Musk—just like Paul's aftershave. I put out my hand but the wall is too far to reach so I sink down onto the edge of the bed and close my eyes.

When I open them, she's watching me with a mirthless smile and I say the only thing I can think of, "But you've only known each other a few weeks."

My sub-conscious mind reaches for pieces of a jigsaw. Odd incidents that barely scratched the surface of my mind. I remember what she said when I was downstairs ringing her doorbell. "Use your key."

Inside my ribcage, something twists and clamps shut. It can't be my heart—I can feel my pulse racing. I reach for words, but they won't come and it doesn't matter because Eve isn't listening to me. Her moody silence is over. She wants to talk. Her eyes gleam as she spins her tale, pitching it as a love story. All those weeks when she was pretending to be my friend. How she must have longed to tell it. Now I'm a captive audience and must listen as she describes how she and Paul worked together at Manifold and became lovers.

"After the fatality," she continues. "I put my career and reputation on the line to save Paul's neck. It was me who coached witnesses through their statements, put processes in place to cover his back."

I can't bear to look at her. I turn my head away and stare at the metal bedframe and spot something familiar—Paul's scarf, twisted and knotted around one strut of the headboard like a trophy. I feel sick.

All that time Mollie and I were battling winter storms in the caravan in France, Paul was shacked up with her in a Chiswick love nest. And when I naively thought Paul was labouring to finish our home, he was here in Limoges with his own key, for god's sake. Screwing her.

All I can think about is Mollie and how to get her out of the clutches of this woman. Eve's poisonous monologue drones on: how deeply in love she is, how much Paul cares for her. That's my cue. I'll negotiate. What's the thing she wants the most? The thing she perceives I have. My husband. A stranger, it seems, I never knew. I don't entirely believe her story—she could be obsessed, a stalker—but if Paul's what she wants, I have no choice.

I run my tongue over my dry lips.

"Paul and I have been having some problems," I say, cautiously.

She nods. Her dull eyes light up. "Yes, yes. I knew he'd get sick of your joyless approach to life."

I lower my head. "Now I understand the reason." Towards Paul and my marriage, I feel only numbness, but I'm terrified for my daughter. "It's obvious now. He's in love with you."

A smile plays on her lips. "That's right. He's been planning to leave, but you and that blasted child keep dragging him back."

I wince. "I won't stop him," I promise, my voice over-eager. I'll say anything. Anything to save my daughter. "Let me go to Mollie. I'll take her away. You and Paul can be together. He need never see us again."

She squints at me, displeased. I know my acting was over the top. "Rubbish." She pats the flat of the blade against her thigh. "If I let you leave, you'll run sobbing to him and turn him against me."

"I won't. I promise." And I'm not just saying it—it's true. It comes to me in a rush. Paul's lies, his betrayal, putting our daughter at risk. I will never forgive him.

"Forget it. You're not leaving. And neither is she. Not until he gets here."

Even after everything she's told me I feel a glimmer of hope. He may have fallen out of love with me, but he adores Mollie. "Paul is on his way? Have you phoned him?"

She takes her smartphone from her pocket and glances at the screen. Her mouth twists, revealing a pattern of fine lines. In a business environment this expression would signal contempt. I can see she's used to getting her own way.

"Seems he hasn't picked up my calls."

Was she bluffing when she told me Paul knew Mollie was here? Perhaps I'm one step ahead if he's picked up my voicemail or spoken to Henri.

"Why not let me try?" I suggest. Subterfuge comes easy—I'm learning from experts. "If I call him from my mobile, perhaps he'll pick up."

She hesitates, twisting a gold bracelet round and round on her wrist and lifting her arm to show me.

"Paul bought me this. When we were in Monaco together."

I don't need this. I slip my wedding ring off my finger and ram it into my jeans pocket. I take out my mobile and enter his number.

"Give me that." I hand over my phone.

She checks the screen and clamps it to her ear, so I can't hear the ring tone. It seems to go on forever. I count the seconds silently inside my head.

Silence is magnified. Eve glares at the screen, shakes it and flings it back at me. I dodge, and it lands on her white pillow. I reach for the phone and gather it—and the pillow. Holding the pillow in front of me like a shield, I dash towards the door. I almost make it. My hand is on the knob as she grabs me and hooks one arm around my neck. A brief choking sensation is followed by pain—radiating through my arm above the elbow.

"Ow!"

The blade cuts through my coat and sweater and a few drops of my blood land on her virgin-white pillowcase. I slip my arm out of my coat and roll up the sleeve of my sweater. The wound's not deep but I clamp the pillow against it and press hard.

"Stupid cow," she says. "See what you've done!"

Hysteria bubbles in my throat as Eve walks back towards the bed, performing a few practice slashes in the air with her knife.

I cringe away from her towards the pillow end of the bed. My breathing rasps and my eyes feel dry, but my head has cleared. The only pain that can touch me is harm to my children. Where is Mollie? Is she frightened? And then I see it.

My left knee is pressed up against a bedside cabinet. Keeping my body braced upright, I slide my hand towards an object standing on top of it. Eve seems to have forgotten me. Her eyes are fixed on the door. When I'm certain she's not watching me, not even out of a corner of her eye, the fingers of my left hand encircle the perfume atomiser. I hold my breath as I slide it off the cabinet and onto the bed, edging it close against my hip so I can work the cap off with the fingers of my left hand.

Time is not on my side. The cap flumps onto the bed, I whisk the bottle round in front of me and when Eve turns back towards me, I leap to my feet, point it at her face and spray perfume into her eyes and nose.

She shrieks but I don't stop. Her hands thrash around, the knife slides from her lap onto the floor. I dive for it and grab the handle but I keep on spraying. She screeches and clamps one hand over her streaming eyes, trying to lash out at me with the other, but her blow is feeble and off target.

Tears slide down her face and I know the pain is like acid rain. I keep on spraying, though inhaling the scented fumes—even from a distance—makes my own eyes smart. Arms flailing, she flees into the hall and I hear a door slam.

"Where's Mollie?" I shout, following her into the hall. No answer. From behind a closed door, water gushes from a tap. I hold the knife in front of me and work my way along the corridor, opening doors, calling Mollie's name.

At the far end is one final door. Dry-mouthed, I pause gathering strength for the worst scenario I can imagine—an empty room. There may be worse, but my mind is in protective mode and won't let me go there. Behind me is the sound of keys jingling. I spin round to see Eve dashing out of the front door and slamming it behind her. I let her go.

The door in front of me opens onto a large, comfortable sitting room. There's a low burble of sound—a children's programme playing on a widescreen television. A high-backed sofa stands in my path. I walk round it and there, curled up fast asleep, thumb in mouth, is my daughter.

"Mollie!"

She doesn't stir. I say her name louder as I bend to place my hand on her forehead. Hot, but dry. Gently I ease back the fur rug covering her and lean in close, repeating over and over.

"It's all right, baby, Mummy's here."

I drop the knife on the coffee table and lay my face next to hers on the cushion, her curls brush my cheek and I feel a flicker of a movement. On the table beside her are sweet wrappers, a can of fizzy drink and a congealing hamburger with one bite out of it.

As I sink to my knees beside the couch to raise her head, something digs into my leg. A blister pack of tablets, a French brand name I don't recognise—two pills are missing.

"Mollie!" I sob as I gather her in my arms. "Wake up."

She twists her head; her eyelids flicker open and she looks at me with bleary eyes. "Mummy!"

"You're all right now, baby. Quite safe."

The drowsy, faraway look fades. "Of course I'm all right!"

She struggles to loosen my embrace, I leave her to find a comfortable position and she levers herself up on one arm and pulls the rug back up to her chin. She opens her mouth, as if to tell me something, and I hold back, not prompting, not putting words into her mouth.

She pops one small hand out from under the furry rug and covers one side of her mouth and whispers her confession, "Tante Eve bought me McDonalds."

Tears spring to my eyes as she shares her guilty secret.

"But you don't like McDonalds!"

"I didn't say—in case she was upset."

I hold up the blister pack of tablets. "Mollie, did you swallow any of these?"

"I don't know." Her lip trembles. "I ate lots of sweeties. Don't be cross."

"Of course, I'm not cross." I slip the pack into my pocket. "Come on, Mollie, we're leaving."

"Can I say goodbye to Tante Eve?" She jumps from the sofa, the rug slides from her shoulders and settles around her feet.

"No!" I shout.

She recoils from my angry voice then notices my arm, "Mummy, you're bleeding."

I glance down. "So I am."

I scoop Mollie up, feeling her weight drag on my injured arm and I'm grateful when she says, "I'm not a baby. I can walk."

Gripping her hand, we totter down the stairs. "We're going straight to the hospital," I tell her. "I've borrowed Lilianne's car."

I strap her in and swaddle her in a picnic rug Lilianne left on her back seat, casting anxious glances across the road at Eve's apartment. Where is she? Has she gone back to her flat? What happened to the knife? I was holding it when I left the bedroom but I must have put it down in her sitting room before I picked up Mollie. I shudder.

We must get away from here. I start the engine and drive a few blocks to find a parking place where I can stop and use my phone. I dictate yet another message to Paul's voicemail and sign off with the hospital's address.

"If you want to see Mollie—meet us at *Les Urgences*—the emergency department."

And then I call the police.

CHAPTER 54

EMMA

December 2016: the same evening

The police call handler takes my name and I give her our address in Sainte Violette.

"I want to report a child being taken," I begin. "My daughter."

There's a flurry in the background, as she snaps into action, repeating the details I've given to establish my identity and taking my contact details. Her voice hums with efficiency and purpose as she records brief details of how Mollie was taken from school.

"You said by her childminder?"

"Former childminder. And without my permission." I give her Eve's name and the address in Rue Jean Jaures. "She is dangerous—armed with a knife—and I think she gave my daughter sleeping pills."

"Are you still at this apartment in Rue Jean Jaures?"

I confirm we're safe and heading to the hospital to get Mollie checked over.

"Will you send someone to find Madame Laurenson?"

What if Eve's gone back to her apartment and fetched the knife? The thought of her roaming the streets of Limoges in her unbalanced state gives me the creeps.

*

The lighting in the emergency department is harsh. I rub my burning eyes. It feels late. Very late. But it's only eight o' clock. Every moment in Eve's apartment stretched to eternity but the whole ordeal lasted barely one hour.

We don't have to wait long to see the doctor. She's young and intelligent, with eyes shielded behind unfashionable narrow glasses, and speaks good English. We duel briefly in one another's languages, but she backs down first and we continue in French. She listens to my account of what happened and I show her the blister pack with the missing pills.

"I'm not sure if she took these or how many."

The doctor examines the packet and gives me a stern look and I realise she's misunderstood. She thinks it was an accident at the childminder's. I explain everything again.

"We must report it."

"Yes, yes. I understand. I have already contacted the police and made a report but Mollie—is she okay?" I ask the doctor.

Mollie clings to me, heavy on my lap and keeps her face hidden against my chest. I have to peel her arms from around my neck, so the doctor can examine her. She checks her temperature, pulse and eyes with calm efficiency. Mollie's smile returns.

"When you found her, was she breathing normally?"

"Yes."

"Sleepy, confused?"

Mollie butts in before I can reply. "I'm not sleepy."

The doctor smiles and I stroke Mollie's hand.

"She was asleep at first, but soon bounced back."

"Any allergies?"

"No."

"Does she suffer from asthma?"

"No, thank goodness."

"We'll admit her and keep her under observation overnight." She registers my panicked expression. "It's just a precaution."

"I'm staying with her."

The doctor's pager beeps, summoning her to a new emergency. She gets to her feet. "It's possible, yes. Speak to the nurse."

The nurse is from the leave-us-to-get-on-with-our-job mindset and informs me they don't have facilities for parents to stay overnight. "You should return in the morning, after seven."

I beg, I plead until, grudgingly, she permits me a chair at Mollie's bedside. Loving the attention, Mollie chatters for a while, unfazed by the strange surroundings, but soon her eyelids droop as exhaustion, or dregs of the sedative, have a hypnotic effect. Still holding my hand, she turns her back to me and I lean across the bed, staying connected to her until her grip slackens.

I ease my arm out of my sleeve and rub my forefinger gently over the rust-brown stain. A fit of shivering grips me but I pull myself together and drape my coat over my own injury to hide the wound from the nursing team. I can deal with it myself.

Mollie's breathing is steady so I wander along the corridor to find the toilets. My arm throbs as I peel away my sleeve. The cut is about ten centimetres long but it's superficial because my arm was protected by two layers of clothing. I swab the wound with lukewarm water. It starts to bleed again, I press it with a paper towel just as the main toilet door opens and two nurses enter, deep in conversation. I dart into a cubicle and wait for them to leave.

I splash water on my skin and comb my hair. The mirror

reflects the face I didn't expect to see for another twenty years. Blotchy and haggard. As I step out into the corridor, I canon into a man striding past.

"Paul!"

"Emma!" He's more surprised than me. His face is grave. He holds out his arms but when I shrink away, he drops them to his sides. "I saw Henri—got your messages—where's Mollie?"

Something inside me shatters.

"I suppose you got the messages from HER too."

"I. . ." he begins, then his shoulders slump and he falls silent.

I jab my finger along the corridor towards the closed door of Mollie's ward and splutter, "You bastard. Thanks to you and your crazy bitch mistress, your daughter's lying in that ward with a stomach full of poison."

"Poison?" he echoes, his lower jaw sagging.

"Fucking sleeping pills! It wasn't enough for her to kidnap our daughter. What was it, Paul? Did she take Mollie hostage to get to you? Is that it?" His mouth is still hanging open in silent shock. Good. I want him to suffer. "I hate you."

"I must see Mollie."

He's holding a scrap of paper with the ward number scribbled on it. I try to bar his way, but he skirts round me and breaks into a jog.

"Stop." I chase him along the corridor. Two hospital staff stop in their tracks to stare at us. I catch up with him at the door of the ward and grab his jacket. "You can't just push your way in. You'll antagonise the staff."

His face hardens. He pulls away from me and shoulders the door open.

"Come back!" I lunge at him, he fights me off and suddenly we're brawling in the doorway in full view of everyone.

The heavy door swings back with a creak. A child wakes, crying. A second child joins in. Rubber-soled shoes squeak on the hard floor, as a nurse bustles to soothe them. In her bed near the door, Mollie slumbers on. Paul's shadow falls across her face as he bends to kiss her.

More footsteps. The senior nurse leaves her workstation and strides towards us.

"Come!" She grabs Paul's arm. "We will not have this behaviour. These children are sick."

Startled, he turns and frowns at her. She glares at this intruder who has forced his way into her kingdom of calm efficiency and gestures to both of us to follow her.

Paul protests, "My daughter!"

"Get out, Paul!" I scream.

Grim-faced, the nurse turns on me. "We cannot have this noise, this disruption."

She holds the door open and ushers us out into the corridor, shutting it behind us.

Her next words are punitive. "I told you, Madame—we do not have the facilities. You must leave. Both of you."

"But I need to be with Mollie," I plead, fighting back tears. I haven't deserved this. "He's leaving. Now." I push Paul away.

"No, I'm not. I'm staying here with my daughter." Paul's voice rises to a shout and his face and neck redden.

The nurse must think he's drunk or unstable.

"Paul—just go!" I hiss, trying to keep my voice low.

The nurse is fiddling with something in her pocket—a pager. "I have called Security to expel you from the hospital."

"Please." I stretch out my hands, palms raised like a supplicant. "Let me stay."

I had so few chips to bargain with and Paul has squandered

them. He can't be trusted so neither of us are welcome. I sense my case is hopeless. My shoulders sag as I turn towards the nurse.

"We will take good care of her," she says.

"You said I could come back at seven?" My voice is cracking with the strain.

"Not before eight." She disappears into the ward, shutting us on the outside, as a uniformed guard strides along the corridor towards us.

"Monsieur."

I walk over to him but he speaks French with a heavy North African accent and pretends not to understand me. One message is clear: we can't stay. The security guard escorts us along the hospital corridors to the main entrance and orders us out into the night.

CHAPTER 55

EMMA

December 2016: later that evening

Paul keeps pace with me as I stomp towards the car park. Soft lighting from the hospital's windows winks its reproach at me for abandoning my daughter.

"How could you create such a scene?" I yell, a sob strangling my voice. "The damage you've caused. Mollie needs me with her."

"Emma, I'm. . ." His words tail off and he grabs my arm.

I shove him away. "Leave me alone. What part of go away don't you understand?"

I break into a run through the silent car park, along rows of cars, trying to remember what Lilianne's car looked like and where I left it.

I glance behind me. Paul is still following, at a distance, and my urge to out run him wavers because I need answers, and only he can give them.

Lilianne's car is parked on the end of the next row. I lean against it and wait for Paul to catch up.

"Are you going to sit in the car all night?" he asks.

Exhaustion has seeped into my bones and I shake my head.

"I might as well head home. Meet me there—I need you to explain what this craziness is all about. And then you can leave."

In the fragile sanctuary of Lilianne's car, I fumble the unfamiliar key into the ignition, start the engine and take the road out of Limoges to Sainte Violette. When I reach the village centre, the houses are shuttered in sleep under the wintry glow of the street lights. I draw up outside Lilianne's flat and get out of the car. It's not yet eleven o'clock but the silence is palpable: no music, no television, no voices—too late to ring Lilianne's doorbell.

I scribble on the back of a supermarket bill, that Mollie was at Eve's. I use the metal prong of her car key to punch a hole in the note, so I can thread it onto the key ring and drop it in her mail box.

I walk home through the deserted streets, clutching my phone and scrolling through a long list of missed calls from Paul and Henri—and the Limoges police.

Paul is waiting outside the house in the parked Volvo, his head bowed over the steering wheel. As I approach he opens the car door.

"You took so long. I was worried. "

More hollow words. I shrug and head indoors. I need a drink. Scotch isn't my usual tipple, but it's the first bottle I see, so I pour myself a stiff measure to chase the chill from my veins. Paul has followed me inside and the dim light from the table lamp casts a shadow across his face.

"Will you let me say sorry?"

"Don't bother," I snap.

When I look at Paul, I see a stranger—the man who claimed to love and care for me and our daughter was a weak, dishonest cheat. Inside I feel only emptiness.

"I've heard her story—that crazy bitch who stole our daughter. Now tell me yours."

"Genevieve was blackmailing me," he begins. "It started after Dorek's accident. She took control of the company side of the investigation and helped me find a way through. She even falsified documents and statements to the accident investigators."

"Why would she do that?"

"I was vulnerable, not thinking straight. She invited me for a drink at her house. I drank too much, poured out my worries. I confess—I slept with her. I was so ashamed." He lowers his gaze.

My stomach tenses. I thought I'd moved beyond feeling but muscle memory remains. It's easier to hypnotise your mind than fool your body.

Paul takes a gulp of water and wipes his mouth with the heel of his hand. "She became fixated with me. I couldn't see a way out. I was in too deep."

"Why didn't you confide in me?"

He groans. "I felt so helpless. Guilty for the trouble I was bringing on you and the children. My financial problems were stacking up and I was facing a possible prison sentence."

His excuses are pathetic but his story has more resonance than hers. Whatever Genevieve believed, I doubt he ever intended to leave us, but I'm equally sure he was happy to have sex with her—in London or in France. I've seen for myself how hard she is to resist. That expensive maroon top from Comptoir des Cotoniers is still hanging in my wardrobe. Unworn.

"That doesn't explain why she snatched Mollie and attacked me with a knife." I roll up my sleeve to show him the rust-brown stain on my arm. The cut looks angry but has stopped weeping. "What do you say about this?"

He blanches, lifts my arm gently and examines the cut, his eyes widening.

"She did that to you? She'll be sorry for this."

"For fuck's sake, Paul. This is a matter for the police. I've already made a report and given them her address."

Then I remember the list of missed calls from the police. I should have waited at the hospital for an officer to make contact.

"They won't find her at her apartment," says Paul.

"Why not? Where the hell is she? Are you saying we're still not safe?" I have a nightmare vision of Eve stalking the hospital corridors.

"It's not Mollie she's looking for. It's me."

"So tell me where she is and I'll report it," I say, through gritted teeth.

Paul gets to his feet. "She's ordered me to meet her, but I had to speak to you first."

"Forget it. We're finished." I grab his wrists. "Where is she?"

He frees his wrists from my grip, pulls me to him and kisses my cheek.

"Emma, I love you."

I shove him away. "Too late."

"That woman's destroyed my life." His hands clench into fists. "I'll kill her."

"Don't be ridiculous," I snap. "I don't care what you do, but she's dangerous. Dealing with her—that's for the police."

I walk to the house phone and place my hand on the receiver.

"Go ahead. Call them."

"Stop it, Paul. Just tell me where she is!"

"She's waiting for me. Up at Les Quatre Vents."

CHAPTER 56

PAUL

December 2016: later the same night

Emma follows me to the front door.

"Don't do this, Paul. Think of Mollie."

Will those be the last words she ever says to me?

"I have to. It's me she's waiting for. I have to stop her craziness." I look at my watch. How much longer will Genevieve wait? "Here."

I dump my house keys in a glass bowl on the windowsill.

Emma's auburn hair is matted, her skin pale—when her freckles return next summer we won't be together. I fix her beautiful face in my mind.

She's still clutching the house phone, her fingers opening and closing around it as I hoist my backpack over one shoulder. It's one we bought for Owen and the stitching on the seams is unravelling. I think of the many ways I've wronged Emma—separating her from her son, dragging her off to live in France.

I point my key at the Volvo, then change my mind.

"What now?" Anger flashes in her eyes.

"Here." I hand her the car keys. "Keep the car. I'll take your bike."

The rain has stopped but the narrow country lanes are slick

and damp as I peddle towards Les Quatre Vents. My chest feels tight and the dank chill in the air makes it hard to breathe. I alternate my hands: one on the handlebars, the other rammed in my pocket to defrost.

As I cross the old bridge, I glance down at the suck and swirl of the brown water, swollen by days of persistent rain. I dismount and wheel the bicycle the last two hundred metres then I notice Genevieve's Mercedes is parked at a slanted angle in front of the house, a shimmer of silver against the heavy night sky.

I wedge the bike into a straggling winter hedge and continue on foot. Any minute now, Genevieve will spot me and pick me out in the beam of her headlights. I edge forward along the rutted track. As I get closer, I realise the car is empty. Where can she be? It's more than an hour since she summoned me and the temperature's dipping below freezing, but I know she'll be here somewhere, waiting. Because, this time, I didn't block her message. I replied:

I'm on my way.

"Ouch!"

Without warning, my left foot slides into an invisible pothole and, as I pull it free, my ankle twists. I flex my foot, and glance around. Where is she? The house is locked and shutters bar the windows. Could she have found a way to get inside? I dig my hand into my pocket, find the key and hobble towards the front door.

Inside it's darker than pitch. Leaving the front door open, I grope my way to the fuse box in the kitchen and flip the master switch. A single bulb glows, weak at first, and then strengthening. I glance round. The windows are closed, the shutters locked and bolted. I check the bedrooms, one by one, and the bathroom.

Where the heck is Genevieve?

I unfasten one of the rear shutters and stare out across the yard to the churned up ground, earth moving equipment and the two-metre-deep pit dug for the septic tank with its tributary trenches for the sand and gravel drainage system. As I ease the shutters closed, I hear a cough.

My clumsy fingers scrabble to secure the metal bar but it drops down with a clang. I turn away from the window as the air fills with a familiar scent of musk.

Genevieve is hovering just inside the front door. She scans my face, as if waiting to be invited in. I stay by the window, gripping hold of the sill. She looks odd. Her eyes are blank with mauve smudges underneath and her hair is dishevelled. She dredges up a smile—too broad, too fake—and spreads her arms wide as she advances towards me.

"Darling." Her scent chokes me.

"What the fuck?" I intercept the ambush of her embrace, clamp my hands on her shoulders and hold her at a distance. "My daughter!"

Her eyes brim with reproach. "Mollie's fine. Emma collected her."

I tighten my grip and shake her roughly so her head judders.

"Stop it, Paul!" She smacks my arms and ducks away. "What's got into you?" Her eyes narrow as if an animal instinct is signalling alarm.

My hands shake as I fumble for a cigarette. I can't find my lighter in my pocket, but I remember seeing a box of matches on the windowsill, probably left by the Bergers. Reluctant to turn my back on her, I reach behind me and feel along the sill until I find them.

"Everything's fixed," she says, sidling up to me as I strike a match. "I've done your dirty work for you."

My match flares and dies. In the pocket of my jeans, my phone vibrates.

"What do you mean?"

"I've told Emma," says Genevieve. "About us. That you're leaving her. I knew you'd be too cowardly."

"Us?" I yell. "There is no us, you bitch!" My self-control is slipping. I ram my balled fist hard against my hip and hold it there. "Was that before, or after, you dosed Mollie with sleeping pills and slashed Emma with a knife."

She drops her gaze and blanches. "That's not true. She's lying."

"So it's not true that Mollie's spending the night in a hospital bed?"

"Oh—I didn't know." Her eyes dart around nervously. "I only gave her a couple of pills. I sent you so many messages to tell you she was with me. That we were both waiting for you. Why didn't you come?"

"You're not getting away with this, Genevieve."

"Hah!" She throws back her head and laughs; her voice is shrill and her ghastly red lipstick distorts her mouth. "I'm not getting away with what? What did you get away with? You're pathetic! I risked everything, waited for you."

The fury inside me ignites as if my spent match has flared into life. As her laughter turns to a shriek; my head pounds. Her face blurs, becomes misshapen. It's as if she's no longer human, but decomposing. On and on she screams. I have to get her voice out of my head. My hands—no longer frozen numb—rise of their own accord, encircle her throat and press.

Her complexion reddens, the tendons in her neck tense, her eyes bulge in a freeze-frame of shock. She's strong. She clamps her chin down hard against my interlocked thumbs. I squeeze tighter, my hands controlled by a force beyond my conscious mind. I'm shaking with panic, but I can't release my grip.

Excruciating pain shoots through me as Genevieve knees my groin. The intensity hits my stomach and triggers a wave of nausea. As my fingers loosen, Genevieve ducks away, wheezing, and scrambles towards the door.

I inhale, count to twenty to control my nausea, and follow her outside. The front door slams shut behind me. The charcoal sky creates tangled shadows along the hedgerows but the darkness disorientates me. Her car is still there. Empty. There wasn't time for her to reach the road but the only other exit is across the field behind the house and through the line of oaks marking our boundary.

My groin aches and my injured ankle throbs as I hobble around the side of the building. Even in daylight our yard is an obstacle course with earth-moving equipment standing sentinel over the churned-up field. In the darkness, anyone who doesn't know the terrain would trip and fall. I drag out my phone to use the built-in torch and two messages pop up on the screen—both from Emma. One says she's contacted the police; the other: *Don't do anything rash.*

What did it cost her to send that message? After the anguish she's been through today. Despite the sub-zero chill, I start to sweat. I run my hand through my damp hair. I tried to strangle Genevieve. What possessed me? Perhaps she's collapsed and is lying out here somewhere seriously injured.

I shine my torch in a wide arc and call out, "Genevieve, where are you? I'm sorry."

No reply.

"I didn't mean to harm you. I was angry."

I pick my way across the yard. If she ran this way, she'd have to scramble past the digger, avoiding the mounds of earth, gravel and sand for the septic tank drainage system. As I step onto grass, pain stabs my ankle. I pause, clinging on to the digger and balance on one foot to massage it.

Something hard and metallic crashes down on the back of my skull. I cry out, then tumble forward, face down—into the pit, into blackness.

CHAPTER 57

EMMA

December 2016: early hours of the following day

In the hours since I learned Mollie was missing from school, everything familiar about my life has been shredded.

It's half past one when I dial the number left by the police contact, who has been leaving messages on my phone. When I explain that Mollie is in hospital and I'm now at home in Sainte Violette, he sets a time to meet with me in the morning at the hospital.

"There must be an inquiry into this matter. You said your daughter is safe in hospital in Limoges?"

"Yes. She'll be there overnight."

"That is good, because we must take a doctor's report on her state of health and tomorrow morning we will take your statement."

I find a gap in his stream of words to explain I've discovered that Genevieve Laurenson—the woman who took my daughter—might be at our house, Les Quatre Vents, outside the village of Sainte Violette.

"One moment." The line goes silent and muffled conversations continue in the background. It seems there's an issue about which force is responsible. In Limoges, I've been dealing with the Police National but the countryside and villages come under the remit of the local *gendarmerie*.

"She's dangerous," I plead. "She has a knife. Someone must go there."

Finally I have my answer. A patrol will come.

As I end the call, I feel deflated. They took me seriously but how quickly will they act? A voice inside my head nags, *it's not over.* I shudder.

I was so intent on fending off Paul's pathetic pleas for forgiveness, I overlooked his threats against Eve. Why did he race off to meet her at Les Quatre Vents? Why not wait for the police? Unless he meant to do her some harm.

I ring Paul's mobile. It goes to voicemail. I tap out a couple of texts and wait—five minutes, ten. Try his number again.

There's nothing I can do but wait. I slump in the armchair and close my eyes. And then I realise there is something I can do. I ring Henri.

He answers on the third ring, his voice heavy with sleep. "Emma? Thank goodness. Is Mollie okay?"

"Yes. It's a long story."

He yawns. "Paul came into the bar. Once I knew he was on his way to join you, I stopped worrying. "

"What time was that?"

"It was quite a while after you'd set off. Seems he didn't get your messages—his mobile was locked in the boot of the car, or something. I told him about Mollie and about Eve and gave him her address. He looked a bit sick but set off at once."

"Oh Henri!" The tears I've been choking back for hours, spill over. "It's not okay. I'm not okay. Paul has been having an affair with Eve—or Genevieve or whatever her real name was.

Her turning up in Sainte Violette was no coincidence. They weren't strangers—they worked together in London. Everything's such a mess."

"I can't believe it."

"It's true."

Henri's voice soothes me, but his sympathy makes me weep. I ball up my sodden tissue and chuck it in the bin. I tell him everything—starting from the moment I arrived at Eve's flat. Even as I recount the horror, it sounds unreal, yet I lived through it.

He listens, interrupting only once to ask about Mollie.

"She's recovering in the hospital."

"Couldn't you stay with her?"

"Paul turned up and made a scene so we were both forced to leave. We were thrown out by hospital security." The way Paul behaved at the hospital was wild. What else might he do while he's in that state? "I'm worried, Henri. About what Paul might do. He wasn't himself when he left here. He said Eve was waiting for him at Les Quatre Vents."

"You think they are going away together?"

"Perhaps that's it." But I don't believe it. I know there'll be no fairy-tale ending to their story, whatever Eve may imagine. "He seemed so angry with her—because of what she did to Mollie and to me."

"Have you reported this to the police?"

"Yes, and they're sending a patrol, but what if Paul does something rash? It would make things worse."

My heart is hammering and I feel the kind of anxiety that only ends by taking action. I won't rest until I know how it ends.

"Paul's not answering his phone. I have to go up there."

"For goodness sake, Emma. Haven't you been through enough?"

But I can't shake the image of Paul with a lifeless Genevieve.

"I'm going to Les Quatre Vents. Now."

"Emma, no—wait! I'll come with—"

I hang up and grab the car keys. I streak down the path to the waiting Volvo and drive.

*

The December sky is inky, starless. I hammer on the locked door and wait.

Silence.

The torch in my phone flickers like a guttering candle as I tramp across the uneven ground to the rear of the building. A sliver of light seeps through a gap between two shutters but dissipates without illuminating the ground.

Sliding one foot in front of the other, I inch across the yard, churning up loose grit with each step until I reach grass and mud. My eyes adjust.

A shadowy bulk takes shape, black against the patina of the sky—the hired digger, its metal bucket suspended at a rakish angle. Close beside it, mounds of soil, banks of sand and gravel, and three freshly-dug rectangular pits. I tread warily, remembering the first one is deeper than a grown man's height.

My phone emits a feeble beep, the battery signals its death throes. Heart pounding, I snatch a breath and train my flickering beam down into the trench.

Motionless, face down. Paul.

Shock forces air from my body but I don't scream. I call his name, over and over, as my weak light flickers over his inert shape. If I jump down, I might crush him and I'll never be able to lift him out. Where are the police? I press redial and wait for Henri to answer.

"I'm on my way. I'll be there in five minutes!" he shouts, above the labouring of the Renault 4's engine.

"Hurry, please," I beg. "Paul's fallen into the septic tank pit. I think he's badly hurt."

"What?" The engine cuts out. He must have pulled over to answer his phone.

"Paul's fallen into the trench. He's hurt."

"Right. You said the police are already on their way? I'll call the *sapeurs*—the emergency services."

Frost has hardened the muddy earth but at the bottom of the pit is a puddle of water from the recent storm. I sink to my knees in the mud, turn and extend first one leg, then the other, over the side of the trench, digging out toeholds in the frozen earth and lower myself down.

My feet slide the last half metre and splash into a shallow puddle. Paul doesn't move. I crouch beside him and slide my hand under his neck, feeling for a pulse. His face is in the damp dirt. Is it safe to move him? I ease his head gently to one side to clear his nostrils and mouth.

The inky sky mocks me. The walls of the pit block ambient light and seem to be closing in. Working by touch, I clear Paul's airways, but I can't tell if he's breathing.

Help me, I mutter under my breath. Where are the police? And then I hear the miracle sound of Henri's Renault and a car door slamming.

I listen for Henri's footsteps and shout, "We're here. Beside the digger!"

In seconds, a beam of serious torchlight settles on Paul's head and I see his hair is matted with blood.

"He's hit his head, Henri! And I can't hear if he's breathing."

Henri wastes no time on replying. I stand up and flatten my back against the wall to give him space to clamber into the hole. He crouches beside Paul in my place.

"I think there's a pulse. But it's weak," he says.

Don't let him die, I pray to the God I don't believe in.

"He's breathing—I don't think he stopped."

I'm too choked to speak. Henri takes my hand and guides it to the place on Paul's neck where a pulse beats.

"Feel that?"

"Th-think so."

"Listen, Emma—you need to climb out. Fetch a rug. There's one in my car."

"I can't leave him."

"I'll stay with him. Bring the rug then wait by the road to direct the police and paramedics."

He crouches down and flattens his back for me to use as a step. I clamber on and he slowly raises himself, and me, until I can stretch my arms over the side of the hole and haul my body back to the surface. As I grasp the cold metal of the digger to pull myself to my feet, I vomit into the mud.

The wail of a siren rips through the silence.

"Hurry, Emma!" Henri yells.

Earth and stones drop from my hair and clothes and shower down onto the ground as I scramble to my feet and run.

CHAPTER 58

EMMA

December 2016: before dawn

The paramedics rig up a stretcher and, with assistance from two *gendarmes*, lift Paul out of the trench. They all seem sceptical when I tell them that I think my husband has been attacked.

"Accident?" one suggests, unable to believe a sane person would amble around an unlit building site at night.

They examine Paul's head wound by torch light. He stirs and his eyelids flicker. One of the *sapeurs* tries to coax a few words from him before he lapses back into semi-consciousness. Questions hang heavy in the air.

While the paramedics work on Paul, Henri shields me from the police officers' questioning. I'm convinced Eve was waiting for Paul but why would she attack him if she still hoped to entice him back to her? It's too confusing.

"It is good you found him," a paramedic tells me. "By morning, he would have had hypothermia."

As they lift Paul into their vehicle, Henri returns to my side. We watch the tail lights of the ambulance bump along our rutted track and disappear into the damp mist and I feel empty and numb.

"Could he have hit his head in the fall, rolled onto his front and blacked out?" I ask Henri.

"I don't think it was an accident," he replies.

One of the officers has been photographing the septic tank pit and its surroundings, holding up a makeshift light. He's kept us at a distance and is taking infinite care, but if there were any footprints, they would have been trampled during our efforts to revive Paul.

"The officers want a statement from you," says Henri. "I mentioned you have an interview set up with the police in Limoges at ten but they need a brief report from everyone at the scene."

I nod and glance to the east where the sky is lightening. I'm anxious to get to the hospital—not for Paul, for Mollie.

"I'll speak with them. I hope it won't take too long."

A shout goes up from the second officer and I twist round to see he's holding an implement in a gloved hand. Henri and I edge forward for a closer look. It's a shovel. As the officer turns it over in his hands, even my short-sighted eyes can see those dark smears and stains aren't mud.

*

I can't let Mollie see me in these mud-spattered clothes and, if I turned up at the hospital looking like I've been sleeping rough in a field, I'd probably be permanently barred. I make a brief diversion home to shower.

Poor Milou races to the door, barking a greeting.

"Sorry, boy." I bend to stroke him, hastily refill his food and water bowls and give him a five minute run in the courtyard.

On the drive into Limoges, I try to silence my chattering

brain. I know reaction to shock follows a cycle—denial, anger, depression, acceptance, but yesterday's rapid string of events has catapulted me forward to acceptance, tinged with anger.

The ties of love that bound me to Paul have been severed. Brutally. Despite his injury, my concern for him is for his role as Mollie's much-loved father—or so I tell myself. In the realm of officialdom our formal connection persists, and will do for some time. I'm still his wife and next of kin.

When I reach the hospital, it's not yet seven o' clock so I head to the emergency department to track down Paul in the critical care unit. He's in a single room, watched over by a male nurse. I peer through the glass door panel and see he's wired up to a bank of machines and a drip. There's no mask on his face so he must be breathing normally. Spotting me, the nurse strolls over to the door.

"Madame Willshire?"

"Yes. How is he?"

"Come in—see for yourself."

Propped up against a slope of white pillows, Paul stirs. One eyelid flickers open, then closes again without focusing.

"You see," says the nurse. "He is doing well. Just now he was talking."

He fetches a chair and I sit at the bedside and study Paul's face, once so familiar to me. I stroke his arm, taking care to avoid the infusion cannulas taped to his skin.

The room is a soundscape of whooshes, punctuated by an occasional high-pitched beep. Wordlessly, the nurse meanders between his patient and the machines, giving equal attention to both, checking and recording readings. Occasionally, when he completes a reading, he nods and smiles encouragement at me.

Outside the window, morning traffic builds to a crescendo

and permeates the double-glazed cocoon. I glance at the wall clock and get to my feet. It's time to go to Mollie.

My lower back aches from the strain of the night and I stop in the doorway to massage it. The nurse calls my name and, as I turn, I see that Paul is awake and lifting his arm to beckon me back.

"He is recovering, I think," says the nurse.

I troop back to the bed. Paul smiles and moves his lips but the effort of forming words seems to defeat him.

"I'm going to Mollie," I tell him. While he was sleeping, I was able to stroke his arm and hold his hand, but now he's conscious, my fingers recoil. "We'll come back later. Both of us."

The hospital corridors bustle with the optimism of a new day. At Mollie's ward there's no sign of the nurse, who evicted me and Paul the night before but, when I give my name, the smile of the woman who greets me falters and I guess we featured in despatches when she was given her handover briefing.

"Mummy!" Mollie, pink-cheeked and boisterous, launches into my arms almost knocking over her cup of milk.

The nurse's frown softens. I perch on the bed and gather her wriggling body onto my lap; her sleep-matted hair smells of ripe summer fruit and some of her vitality transmits to my heavy limbs.

"She's fine, then?" I ask the nurse, as I stroke Mollie's hair.

"The doctor will come soon but, I think—yes."

I postpone telling Mollie her dad's in the hospital. My eye falls on a box of children's books.

"Let's read," I suggest, as we wait for the doctor, and she chooses one about animals and laughs at my pronunciation of the word for dog.

"No, Mummy—you said chin. It's *chien!*"

I let my mind wander from the surreal situation we're in and think of Milou, all alone in the house, waiting for us.

As the time of my police interview approaches, my throat feels dry and my reading falters. The doctor arrives, carries out a few rapid checks on Mollie and confirms she can be discharged.

"Home!" Mollie demands.

I explain she'll have to wait a while longer in the ward with the lovely nurses while I go to a meeting. The words 'with the police' are on the tip of my tongue but I hold back. So far, Mollie's come through this ordeal unaware of any threat to her safety—or mine. In her eyes the trip out of school with Eve was a prank—some kind of special treat. What would be the point of infecting her with my own fear?

"You're mean. I hate you. I want Daddy."

When I bend to kiss her, she places her palms against my stomach to push me away.

The hospital's network of corridors no longer mimics a maze; signs direct me to the meeting room and I knock on the door. Two police officers—one male, one female—are sitting at a grand polished table, on incongruous plastic chairs. As I enter, they get to their feet and shake my hand.

"Madame Willshire, please sit."

The younger, female officer pours water into a plastic cup and slides it across the table to me. She tells me their names and I immediately forget them.

"This morning we have had a report of another incident," she begins. "From the *gendarmerie* near to Sainte Violette."

She refers to some handwritten notes so I guess the details have been phoned through.

"That's right," I squirm on the red plastic chair, the seat is too low for the table and my back aches from a night without sleep. "The officers at the scene took a report from me."

It seems the officers weren't told I was British and it takes a while to convince them I don't need an interpreter.

"I studied French at university and I've been living and working in Sainte Violette for a year," I tell them.

They confer in low voices. Once they're satisfied, we begin at the beginning—perhaps before the beginning—because who knows when this nightmare began. The female officer explains the process. First, they will deal with my report of the taking of Mollie without consent. As a minimum they will need a report from me and from her father and a medical report from the hospital. They double-check my personal details and run through the initial report I gave to the call handler. Then they ask me to tell them about Genevieve Laurenson.

"I knew her as Eve," I say. "I think she arrived in Limoges in early September. She said she was house hunting. Henri Wilson, a friend, who sometimes works for me in my bar—Les 4 Vents in Sainte Violette—was showing her properties for sale. She began visiting the bar."

"She was your friend?"

"I thought so but it turned out she wasn't who she said she was. She was a former work colleague of my husband's and she'd been having an affair with him. When he broke it off, she traced him to France and followed him."

The female officer tops up my water glass and I realise her male colleague hasn't addressed a single word to me. Under the unblinking overhead light, his bald head gleams, as if smeared with a thin layer of grease. He concentrates on note-taking but when he glances at me, his lips curl into a smirk.

I explain about Eve offering to help me look after Mollie.

"But she was your husband's lover, no? What did he say about this?"

"He didn't know. He was in England at that time, working," I stutter. "But then he came back and their affair continued."

I stumble over my account of discovering Mollie missing from school. When I get to the part about what awaited me in Eve's apartment, my brain fogs.

"She attacked me," I tell them, rolling up my sleeve to reveal my wound.

I've covered it with a gauze dressing from our first aid kit; I peel away the tape and the dressing flaps open. It's no longer weeping and is beginning to scab over.

They both bend forward to examine it.

"Do you have the medical report?"

"No. I didn't get it looked at. I'll ask the doctor."

"What happened next?"

I tell them about picking up the perfume atomiser, finding Mollie, barely conscious, in the sitting room with the murmuring television and those pills. What were they called? I should have made notes.

"I'm sorry. I need a break."

Acid pools in my stomach. I could be sick at any moment—like last night.

I hurry to the women's toilets, but I've not eaten for twenty-four hours so I dry-retch into the toilet bowl. I dawdle back to the meeting room and open the door quietly. The officers are standing close together and some kind of argument seems to be going on between them. Seeing me, they fall silent and step apart.

The female officer has fetched coffee from the machine.

"Espresso?" she offers.

I nod, grateful for this small kindness, and gulp it down. The bitter liquid scalds my raw throat and burns my stomach.

A hospital official knocks on the door and comes in to say the room will be needed again in thirty minutes.

When she's gone, my interview restarts and the pace of questioning speeds up, from crawl to canter, forcing me to focus. My head clears and I answer their questions with a new fluency. The male police officer leans back in his chair and observes me from beneath hooded eyelids, as I tell them about bringing Mollie to *Les Urgences*. I miss out the part about Paul creating a scene and getting us evicted from the hospital.

"My husband has confessed to his affair with Eve—I mean, Genevieve Laurenson. He confirmed everything she'd told me."

"And what did you say to him?"

"That I couldn't forgive. I mean, he'd put our daughter in danger. I told him our marriage was over."

The female officer pauses, she glances at her colleague, who shrugs off his act of distracted boredom and leans forward in his seat. His eyes, no longer cloaked, drill into me. I lower my gaze.

"Please continue, Madame. What happened next?"

I mumble an explanation about Paul racing off into the night to meet Eve at Les Quatre Vents and how, when I couldn't contact him, I went there myself. "With our friend, Henri Wilson."

"Could you repeat, please?"

"I don't know what happened last night." How could they expect me to know? "Only that she—Eve—had demanded my husband meet her at the property we've been renovating. I can't tell you if she was there when he arrived or not."

"So why did you go there?"

How can I explain? My skin feels hot and itchy. With effort, I suppress the urge to scratch and grip the edge of the table.

"I was afraid he'd do something rash and make things worse than they already were, because of what she'd done to our daughter. He was so angry—he seemed to be out of control." I shake my head. "It's too hard to explain."

"Madame Willshire," the male police officer takes over the interview and there's an edge to his voice. "Your husband was unfaithful. You found out. I wonder—why did you go to his mistress's home?"

My jaw drops and I gape at him.

"Have you ever given your daughter sleeping tablets?"

I shake my head. "No. Never!"

"You knew he was going to meet Madame Laurenson at Les Quatre Vents late at night. Why did you follow him?"

CHAPTER 59

EMMA

December 2016: morning of the same day

I stumble from the meeting room, hyperventilating and blanking the last ten minutes of the interview from my mind. In the corridor, I lean against the wall to catch my breath and try to make sense of what's occurred.

The female officer explained they would be speaking to Paul, as soon as the doctor confirmed he was conscious and coherent. She assured me they had Eve's address, that my report would be sent to the *juge d'instruction*, the examining magistrate who carries out pre-trial investigations into allegations of crime. They'd liaise with the hospital to confirm details of Mollie's admission and obtain a medical report.

As if to pile on more grief and stress, they warned me they would need Mollie's own account of events and special arrangements would be made to support her.

I struggled to read through my statement, combing the words for double meanings, but the report simply recorded the facts I'd given. Did I come across as unhinged? A perpetrator of yesterday's events? A mother who might harm her own child in a sick plot to take revenge on her husband's mistress?

When I reach the ward, Mollie has forgotten our earlier spat and I'm briefly buoyed by her affection.

"Right, let's go home," I say, stroking her hair.

"Yay!" She skips around saying goodbye to everyone.

The staff wave us off with smiles and good wishes—so different from the night before.

"Now we'll go and visit Daddy," I tell her, as we navigate the corridors towards Paul's room. "He had a fall. Up at our new house. He banged his head."

"Hospital is making him better?"

"That's right."

I worry about Mollie seeing her father wired up to a bank of machines, but Paul's room is empty and there's no sign of the male nurse who was caring for him earlier. My stomach knots with panic and I run down the corridor looking for someone to ask.

"Where is he?" I ask the first uniformed staff member I meet, pointing to his empty room.

"He's been taken for a scan," she says.

"Is he recovering?"

This new nurse doesn't know. "You can wait." She glances at Mollie, who's clinging to my hand. "But it may be a long time."

"We'll come back later. This evening or tomorrow."

All the way home to Sainte Violette, rain drums on the windscreen and my wipers struggle to catch up. The house is bone-chillingly cold. Even Mollie, with her store of inner vitality, shivers as she bends to hug Milou.

"My teeth are ch-chattering, Mummy."

"I'll get the stove going, darling."

I haul logs in from the woodpile in the yard but driving rain has seeped under their cover leaving them sodden.

"Damn!"

"You said a bad word!"

"Sorry." I yawn. "I'll make us a hot drink."

I boil the kettle twice, make hot chocolate for Mollie and fill a hot water bottle, while Milou nuzzles my ankles. Dizzy from lack of sleep, my bed is beckoning but first, there are calls to make.

I ring Mollie's school to explain she won't be in. And then I call Henri.

"Emma, I've been so worried. How's Paul? And Mollie?"

"Mollie's fine. She's home with me and Paul's in hospital. He's conscious but having more scans and tests."

"And you?"

"About to keel over if I don't sleep soon." And then I remember. "The bar!"

"Don't fret, Emma. Lilianne and I will manage."

Tears well up in my eyes. "How can I ever thank you?"

"Not necessary," he assures me. "But what about Eve—I mean Genevieve—has she come forward?"

An ugly recurring image forms in my mind: dying lilies, a knife slashing my arm.

"The police are keeping a watch on her apartment but she seems to have disappeared."

"Surely they'll find her soon?"

I shudder. "My police interview was tough. It felt as if they didn't believe what I told them."

Henri reassures me. "Investigations work differently in France. We have an inquisitorial system under an examining magistrate but it will move on fast after a *juge d'instruction* takes control."

"What have you said to people in the bar?"

"Nothing. Just a word to Lilianne. I think the postman spotted the police tape at Les Quatre Vents and mentioned it to Claude."

I groan. "What did he say?"

"He assumed there'd been a break-in."

My yawn must be audible because Henri says, "Get some sleep. We'll speak later."

Mollie lags behind me, protesting, when I suggest we both have a nap.

"I'm not sleepy!" But before I've taken off my coat, she hops onto the bed and crawls under the duvet on Paul's side.

"I thought you weren't tired?"

She giggles. "I'm sleeping in Daddy's bed!"

"Mollie, I need to talk to you about something important." I try to weave words that won't scare her. "When Tante Eve fetched you from school yesterday, she didn't tell me first. So Mummy was worried."

"Didn't you know where I was, Mummy?"

"I didn't, darling." I stroke her hair. "So I want you to promise me, if you see her—at school or in her car—you won't go with her. Stay with Madame Moreau or run to me."

"I promise. Don't be scared, Mummy. I'll look after you."

"And I'll look after you," I say, kissing her forehead. "I'll be right back."

I go to the bathroom to check my wound. It's scabbing over with no sign of infection. I leave it uncovered for the air to heal it and head back to bed.

"Shove over, Mollie."

She doesn't budge; her chest rises and falls in a pattern of sleep and I slide in, next to her warm body, and lie on my side in the narrow space she's gifted me.

I try to doze but my head wants to rerun yesterday's terrors and pick apart my police interview from this morning. False memory plays tricks. Could it be possible? Not giving Mollie pills—I'd never do that—but could I have followed my cheating husband to Les Quatre Vents, lain in wait and attacked him? Did I stage an accident, knowing I could call on Henri to be my alibi?

I dig my fingertips into the edge of the mattress and cling on, afraid I'll fall.

CHAPTER 60

EMMA

December 2016

The hospital's main door yawns a welcome, so different from the other night. I've kept in touch by phone and learnt Paul's lapses into unconsciousness have stopped. He's back inhabiting his battered body; lucid and talking.

We detour to the shop, so Mollie can choose a gift. She lingers over the cuddly toys, stroking their soft fur.

"Daddy would love this bear," she exclaims. "So silky!"

"Perhaps some sweets or chocolate?" I suggest and, while she's choosing, I buy the silky bear for her and pop it into my handbag.

The hospital corridors bustle with life—people staring down at their mobile phones, staff pushing trolleys, the squeak and whine of floor polishing equipment, but Paul's room is silent with the blinds still drawn. The beeping monitor is disconnected and the machine shunted against the wall, leaving his body tethered only to the umbilical cord of a drip.

His head jerks up from the pillow as we enter and Mollie races across to his bed.

"Daddy, I've missed you." She thrusts a box of her favourite chocolates into his hands. "Shall I open these for you?"

"Go ahead."

A grimace replaces his smile as she leans on his fractured shoulder while kissing his cheek. Above her head, his eyes summon my attention.

"The police came to see me earlier. We need to talk."

I nod towards Mollie. "Not just now."

"What's this tube for?" She examines it with a forensic eye.

Paul explains. "But don't waggle it, okay?"

I step away and stare out of the window at people weaving between deep puddles in the car park below.

Paul settles back against his pillow and Mollie produces a book from her small backpack. "Read me a story, Daddy."

"I'll do my best. Bit short of puff."

"Silly, Daddy. I'll read to you."

Leaving them to read and chat, I pace the room. It feels hot and oppressive and is cramped as a cage. While I'm in the same room as Paul it's hard not to think about the future. I must get away.

"I'll get you a drink, Mollie," I slope away and wander the corridors until I find a vending machine.

When I return, Paul is dozing.

"He's sleeping."

Mollie puts on a bored expression, but I settle her on a chair in a corner of the room, with her Orangina and her book, and give her the silky teddy bear that I secretly purchased in the hospital shop. Then I take her place at Paul's bedside.

He stirs and his eyelids flicker open.

"Emma."

He touches my wrist and I flinch.

"Shush!" I put a finger to my lips.

Mollie glances at us, slurps her drink and turns the pages of her book.

"The police were here earlier to take my statement. I told them everything," he whispers.

"The whole truth?" I ask.

He nods. "About Genevieve and me. What she did to Mollie—and you."

"And about going up to Les Quatre Vents to meet her?"

"Yes. Genevieve was there." He touches the back of his head and winces, as if discovering his injury for the first time. "She was in total denial about what she did to you and Mollie. She acted as if nothing had happened. It was ugly." He drops his voice so I have no choice but to lean closer to hear him. "I lost it, Emma— tried to strangle her but she ran off."

"What happened? The police found a blood-covered spade."

"Something hit my head before I fell into the trench."

"And you're sure it was her? That there wasn't anyone else there?"

He looks at me, puzzled. "It must have been her. Her car was parked out the front. There'll be tracks."

I take a deep breath and exhale slowly. "Did the police tell you if they've found her? I keep calling but there's no news."

"They're watching her flat but no one seems to know where she's got to."

CHAPTER 61

EMMA

December 2016

Two more days pass and Mollie nags me to let her return to school.

I walk her to the school gates and her friends open a space in their ranks and draw her in. I've arranged to speak to Madame Moreau before classes begin and she tells me the police have visited the school to take her account of events.

"I am sorry, Madame Willshire," she says.

"You were not to blame," I assure her. "But from now on, only I will collect Mollie from school."

"And your husband?"

It's not a question I'm ready to answer.

"He's in hospital," I reply.

I head for the bar, thinking I'll be early but Lilianne is already there. Seeing me, she reddens and drops her gaze.

"You are here now. I will be in the kitchen."

She pivots on her heel and walks off. I can't leave the issue between us unfinished. So much has happened since she told me about sending those texts, but she's loaned me her car and, even though she expects to lose her job, has carried on

357

working in my absence. I could hold a grudge or behave like a compassionate friend.

Lilianne is standing at the sink with her back to me, peeling potatoes and dropping them into two vast pans. She doesn't hear me approach and spins round, frowning. I take the potato peeler from her hand, lay it on the draining board and pass her a towel and her tube of hand cream. She looks at me, puzzled.

"That thing you told me about before Mollie went missing. Can we get past it?"

She clutches the towel and whispers, "I don't know. I didn't expect you would forgive me."

"I do. Please stay." I hug her, clumsily, and she doesn't pull away. When I step back, I detect a glint of a tear in her eye. "That's settled then?"

She nods.

Through the hatch dividing the kitchen from the bar, Claude calls to me. "Madame, come here and read this."

"Drat—I meant to take over the potato peeling from you," I say.

"Never mind. You go."

Claude is seated on his usual stool, sipping a drink, a well-thumbed copy of *Le Populaire* spread out on the bar in front of him.

"She was your friend," he announces, rejoicing vicariously in the misfortune of others.

As he slides his newspaper towards me, I grit my teeth and scan the headline:

Incident à Sainte Violette

Underneath is a picture of Eve, sunglasses perched on top of her head, hair blowing in the breeze, against a background of azure sea. A brief paragraph says that police want to talk to *'une Anglaise de 39 ans'* in connection with two recent incidents, one at Sainte Violette; another in Limoges. There are no further details. The article names her as Genevieve Laurenson. Our locals knew her as Eve but hardly need to turn sleuth to make the connection.

I nod but have nothing to say. Henri's arrival spares me. He strolls across to the alcove and flicks a switch so lights glimmer on an artificial Christmas tree. The lights seem to be winking—or laughing at me. Henri puts on a CD of cheesy Christmas songs.

His eye falls on Claude's newspaper. He picks it up, skims the article and takes me to one side so Claude can't hear.

"You can't work with this hanging over you. That woman could be anywhere."

"Stop it, Henri. Working will help me."

I open the reservations book.

"Six bookings!" I run my eye down the list of unfamiliar names. Tradesmen don't make a reservation. They just walk in. "This one is a table for ten!"

"Office workers. From the business park."

Lilianne overhears. "This week is the special menu, you know?"

"Oh no!" How could I have forgotten?

Lilianne nods. "British Christmas dinner: turkey, roast potatoes. How you say it—all the trimmings?"

I advertised it, but I wasn't here to help her. She's performed this huge catering challenge single-handed for two days.

With so many bookings, the lunchtime session is hectic but it's good to be working as a team with Lilianne and Henri.

"Do you have a dinner for me?" asks Claude.

I suspect his wife will be waiting for him at home with lunch on the table but I rustle up a meal and give it to him free of charge.

"Christmas present," I say, placing it down in front of him and earning one of his rare smiles.

When the office party leaves, Henri hands me a lime and soda. "Or would you prefer wine?"

"No, this is perfect, thanks."

I perch on a stool and watch Claude scrape the last morsel of Christmas pudding from his bowl.

"*Delicieux!*" he exclaims.

A draught from the door alerts me to new arrivals and I look up as Pierre Gaspard enters, brandishing a copy of *Le Populaire*. His wife, Justine tags a few paces behind. She seems to be dabbing her eyes with a lace-edged handkerchief.

Pierre fumbles his newspaper into my hand and shows me the picture of Eve.

"Is it true? She is in trouble?"

I nod and my stare hardens. "She's not just in trouble—she's dangerous."

Justine sinks down onto a chair and blows her nose.

"Justine is very upset," says Pierre in a low voice, taking my arm and leading me towards the door. "Eve is her good friend."

Eve's friendship! The idea of it brings a sour taste to my mouth but I keep my reply terse.

"No one seems to know where she is."

"But she has been staying with us! And now she is outside in my car. Waiting for me to bring her news."

"Where?" I gasp, feeling my stomach tense.

"Look." He opens the door and points along the road

towards a Land Rover, parked two hundred metres away on the opposite side of the street.

I pull my glasses out of my apron pocket and squint at the vehicle, trying to detect if there's someone inside.

"Are you sure?"

"Of course." He drops his gaze, startled by my tone.

"Then I'm phoning the police."

I cross the room to grab my phone from the bar. Justine gets to her feet and paws at my wrist.

"Please wait." Her red-rimmed eyes implore me. "She agrees to talk to the police, but first—"

"No."

I brush her hand away and click on the number. Claude gapes at me from his bar stool, as I bark out the police case number I know by heart and report the current whereabouts of Genevieve Laurenson, the woman they want to interview.

Pierre and Justine press close to me and I fend them off while I finish making the report.

"A police patrol is in the area and on its way," I tell them as I end the call. "So, it's up to you to stop her walking away."

"She gave us her word," replies Pierre. "After we read *Le Populaire*, she said she would talk to the police, but first she wanted to come here, to know—" He picks up a beer mat and twiddles it between his fingers. "That Monsieur Willshire is recovering from his. . . um. . . accident."

He has just enough tact to lower his eyes as he says my husband's name and I realise he knows. She's confided in them about her relationship with Paul. I feel sick and numb. The Gaspards wait for me to speak but words fail me and I shake my head. Justine develops a nervous tic to fill the silence.

"We are so fond of her," she begins, forcing me to listen to how Eve visited them, often spending whole days up at La Petite Ferme and, for the past three nights, has been staying with them as their guest—hidden in plain sight. Did Eve cultivate the Gaspards, our neighbours, as another way of getting to Paul?

"And she is a natural shot," says Pierre, scratching an angry shaving cut on his chin. "She has joined us to drive away rabbits and vermin from our land."

I think of Eve roaming the nearby fields—with a gun—and shudder.

"And Pierre taught her to skin a rabbit," Justine rambles, barely coherent. "I was teaching her to cook dishes from our tradition. Recipes from my grandmother. She brought us so many gifts."

Pierre nods. "I gave her a present, too. A special knife for skinning rabbits."

"A knife!" Instinctively I rub the scab on my arm.

"Please," says Justine. "I must tell her news of Monsieur Willshire—how is he?"

Why should I give Eve, the woman who wrecked my family, a moment's peace? Justine's only the messenger but I spit my anger at her.

"Tell her, he's seriously ill. I doubt he'll ever recover. His life will be changed forever." All of that could be true.

Colour drains from Justine's face and her fingers clutch a small crucifix at her throat.

"I see. I must tell her."

She heads for the door. I step down from the stool and follow her onto the street, watching as she turns towards their car and picks up her pace until she's practically running—towards Eve.

A faint wail of sirens echoes from along the Limoges road.

Is that the police patrol? Why on earth would they broadcast their approach? It makes no sense. Perhaps they realise it too, because the siren stutters and falls silent. From the doorway, I watch as Justine opens the Land Rover's door and leans into the car.

Seconds later, the passenger door swings open and Eve leaps out. That's it—we've lost her, I reflect dismally. She must have heard the sirens so she'll race off, fetch her own car and disappear. I'm right. Eve does start running along the opposite pavement, but she's dashing towards the bar. Not away from it.

As she draws level, she spots me in the doorway and lifts an arm, as if to summon me.

"Emma!"

I fold my arms and stare back at her; I don't move.

It happens so quickly. With her eyes fixed on me, Eve steps off the kerb and into the road, without looking to left or right, just as the police patrol car rounds the corner travelling at speed. She's halfway across the road before she senses the car, so close I can see the horror frozen on her face. The patrol car brakes and she steps backwards to avoid it—straight into the path of an oncoming van.

The bang is hollow and loud as a thunderclap. Its echo reverberates off the ancient stone buildings. In slow motion, Eve rolls across the van's bonnet, shattering its windscreen, and bounces off onto the road. The driver struggles to control his vehicle, swerves and brakes as Eve's head hits the ground. The vehicle lurches on, crushing her legs beneath its wheels.

In the centre of the road, all on its own, lies a red slingback sandal. I can't take my eyes off that shoe.

CHAPTER 62

PAUL

January 2017

News of Genevieve's death was brought to my hospital bed by the same police officer, who'd been sent a few days earlier to ask if I had a photograph of Genevieve. I'd deleted all her pictures from my camera, after Owen so nearly stumbled on them, but I found one on my phone: Genevieve in Monaco, out-sparkling the Mediterranean. I gave them that one.

The young officer spoke little English and gabbled out his message crammed with vocabulary I'd yet to internalise.

"Accident?" I repeated. "Genevieve Laurenson?"

I remembered how she used to drive her Mercedes too fast for the winding country roads.

The young officer nodded vigorously, preparing to back out of the room.

"*Attendez-vous!*"

I raised my hand to detain him and signalled to my nurse, who spoke fluent English, to help with translation and so I learned Genevieve was dead.

I shrunk from their condolences on the death of a woman who was so alive, yet so lethal, it was hard to disguise my relief.

Some might say Genevieve didn't deserve what happened, that everything was my fault, and I accept that's true. But when I think of what she did to Mollie and Emma, there's no space in my heart for pity. I still believe I would have killed her up at Les Quatre Vents that night if she hadn't fled and turned her anger against me. Genevieve was irresistible, unstoppable—her obsession could only lead to ruin and destruction.

Emma had made it clear I wouldn't be moving back into the Brownings' cottage and would have to camp out up at Les Quatre Vents but, as there was no functioning bathroom or toilet, the hospital kept me in longer.

I've settled in at Les Quatre Vents now. I have the chemical loo from the caravan and water from the original well. I remember being told that old Madame Durand used the well all her life, but soon I'll have plumbing and drainage because the Bergers have installed the septic tank in the pit where I so nearly breathed my last.

My doctor told me, if I hadn't been found, I might not have lasted the night. I have Emma to thank for finding me and raising the alarm. From the moment we met, I knew Emma was a remarkable woman with strong principles, while I was still measuring my worth against empty values: money, prestige and career success. If I'd taken a lead from her, our lives would be so different now.

Emma knows all my flaws and weaknesses, except one—she never found out about the racehorse syndicate, which haemorrhaged funds from my secret bank account. Now she won't have to, because, shortly before I returned to France in October, I received an offer to buy out my share—from Jimmy Jonas!

As my strength returns, I've started work on the final phase of renovations. Mollie visits me regularly and, so far, she doesn't seem too scarred by what has happened. Les Quatre Vents will make a wonderful family home, but not for us, because Emma will never forgive me. I'll keep wondering, hoping and dreaming—but that's me. I have no one to blame but myself.

CHAPTER 63

EMMA

January 2017

Over the weeks that follow, I come to accept that Eve's death is closure. Paul and I are finished, but for Mollie's sake I'm civilised and I'll never stop him from seeing her. No one understands better than me, the desperation of being separated from your child.

When Paul leaves hospital, he moves into Les Quatre Vents, camping out with some makeshift furniture and a chemical toilet. I don't ask him how he copes. Once he finishes the renovations, maybe we'll sell it. Or Paul can stay on there himself and figure out a way to pay me off.

I'm keeping an eye on the Brexit developments and what this will mean for people like us, who are living and working in France, but haven't been here long enough to apply for the permanent *carte de sejour* that would give us the right to remain after the UK leaves the European Union. We still don't know what the French government will decide.

Perhaps Mollie and I will stay in France, perhaps we'll return to England, but whatever happens it will be my choice.

Le Bar les 4 Vents is in my sole name—Paul insisted on it when he feared he might be made bankrupt or sent to prison, so I can make my plans without consulting him or anyone else.

Lilianne and Henri still work for me in Bar les 4 Vents and I've detected a slight thaw in their mutual awkwardness. I won't be speculating on a rekindled relationship. I'm finished with matchmaking.

Paul kept on perpetuating the myth that the bar wouldn't support us as a family, and that he would have to keep returning to England to take short term contracts, at least until the holiday *gîtes* were renovated and bringing in income—but he was wrong.

The bar has been doing rather well. It easily covers our living expenses and I'm banking a substantial profit. If Mollie and I stay on in France, I can afford to rent a house or maybe, with help, we could renovate the attic flat above the bar.

Some people might wonder how I could face staying on here, on the site of the fatal accident that occurred on my doorstep. Perhaps the bar is jinxed, says local gossip: Anton couldn't make it pay, and now this—but Eve's death has attracted even more customers to the bar. People drive out from Limoges specially to see the spot where *L'Anglaise* died, depicted in *Le Populaire* by a photograph of a single red shoe lying in the centre of the road.

For forty-eight hours, no one picked up the shoe.

Or maybe we'll go back to London. Now I have the experience and confidence, I could take on a pub. I love the work, the buzz of getting to know my regulars—even the cooking. And there's another dream I've been nurturing—if we found somewhere close to Zak, maybe Owen could live with me for part of the week. I haven't shared this idea with anyone but it's something I should thank Paul for.

If he'd been with me in France from the beginning, I'd still be hovering in his shadow and would never have found the confidence to make my own decisions. From now on, no one will choose my future. Only me.

ABOUT the AUTHOR

Helen Matthews is the author of suspense thriller *After Leaving the Village*, which won first prize at Winchester Writers' Festival, and *Lies Behind the Ruin*, published by Hashtag Press. Born in Cardiff, she read English at the University of Liverpool. She has worked in international development, consultancy, human resources and pensions management but fled corporate life to pursue her dream of becoming a writer. She holds an MA in Creative Writing from Oxford Brookes University.

As a freelancer, she writes content for websites and business magazines and has, in the past, had columns published in The Guardian and broadcast on BBC radio. Helen's stories and flash fiction have been published or shortlisted in Reflex Fiction, 1000k Story, Artificium, Scribble and Love Sunday.

She is an Ambassador for the charity, Unseen, which works towards a world without slavery.

Find out more at:
https://www.helenmatthewswriter.com
Follow her on Twitter: @HelenMK7
Instagram @helen.matthews7
Facebook.com/HelenMK7Writer

ALSO BY HELEN MATTHEWS

AFTER LEAVING THE VILLAGE

PRAISE for AFTER LEAVING THE VILLAGE

I really wouldn't have known this was a debut novel. It's so well-written and has obviously been researched in detail. . . It's insightful, intense, interesting and really quite thrilling.
Nicola Smith, Book Blogger, Short Book and Scribes. Top 1000 Reviewer Vine Voice

One of the most important books I've been involved in launching in twenty years as a bookseller.
Peter Snell, Bookseller, Bartons Bookshop, Leatherhead

Recommended reading for getting up close and personal to the problem of modern slavery. Two women you can relate to—one on the inside; one on the outside. What would you do in their place? Totally absorbing.
Maria Donovan, Author of The Chicken Soup Murder

A captivating and accurate portrayal of trafficking and exploitation. Whilst it may not be comfortable reading, it brings to our consciousness the realities and experiences of this atrocity in an accessible and realistic way.
Kate Garbers, Founder and Director of Unseen

I found this an engrossing read; a real page turner. . . The book's main subject—sexual trafficking—is indeed dark but there is hope at the end of the book. This is a subject not often tackled in fiction and it should be. We may want to look away but I think Helen Matthews has looked at the issue sensitively and thoughtfully. Recommended.
Bronwen Griffiths, Author of Here Casts No Shadow

A well-plotted well-written international thriller. I am naturally drawn to international thrillers but I had to stay up to 4:10am on two occasions to finish reading this book as it was very tense and interesting.
Ivy Ngeow, prize-winning author of Cry of the Flying Rhino and Heart of Glass

This is a deeply engrossing read—and one which focuses on important issues of our lives today. The novel confidently explores the lives of its two female protagonists and I found the tautly-plotted story a compelling read. Their lives may be very different to each other's, but this novel explores a shared sense of vulnerability, our need for a community around us, and it also looks at the impact that the internet has had on the way we live today. It is a powerful novel and it opens up a largely invisible aspect of modern society. Highly recommended.
Emma Moyle, Book Blogger, Books and Winegums